I0714099

MAN MADE

GOD 003

By Brandon Varnell

Art by Lonwa

DEDICATION

This page is made in dedication to my amazing patrons. Without them, my characters would never get lewded by so many wonderful artists:

Aaron Harris; Adam; Alarinnise; Alexander Rodriguez; Armando Pastrana; Benjamin Collins; Benjamin Morgan; Brendan Smiley; Bruce Johnson; Bryce McClay; C.L. Holgrahm; Caxey G. May; Catcrazy9; Chase Corso; Charles Dorfeuille; Christopher Gross; Cody Woodard; CosmicOrange; Dane Smith; Daniel Glasson; Dhivael; Edward Grindle; Edward Lamar Stephenson; Edward P Warmouth; Emery Moore; Feitochan; Forrest Hansen; Forrest Hansen; Ine Airlcana; IronKing; Jacob Flores; Jacob Wojno; Jeremy Schultz; Jesus; John Patton; LarC85; Lucid Fayt; Mark Frabotta; Matthew Wallace; Max A Kramer; Michael Erwin; Michael Moneymaker; NA; Nathan S; Omegapudding; Philip Hedgepeth; Rfael Eriksen; Raymond T; Red Phoenix; Red Viking; Reent Dopychai; Repooc Ilahsram; Richard Garret; Rob McDagg; Roy Cales; Samuel Donaldson; Sean Gray; Seismic Wolf; Shotgunr12; Slim; Smudi Corp; Starwarscout Jon; Thomas; Thomas Jackson; Tim Nielsen; ToraLinkley; Travis Cox; Victor Patrick Bauer; William Crew; XY172; Yuriy Snyadanko; Zach Miller; Zach Strickland; Zenn Barger

Man Made God 003
Copyright © 2020 Brandon Varnell & Kitsune Incorporated
Illustration Copyright © 2020 Lonwa
All rights reserved.

To see Brandon Varnell's other works, or to ask for permission to use his works, visit him at www.varnell-brandon.com, facebook at www.facebook.com/AmericanKitsune, twitter at www.twitter.com/BrandonbVarnell, Patreon at https://www.patreon.com/BrandonVarnell, and instagram at www.instagram.com/brandonbvarnell.

If you'd like to know when I'm releasing a new book, you can sign up for my mailing list at https://www.varnell-brandon.com/mailing-list.

ISBN: 978-1-951904-18-0

CONTENT

TITANIA

A mysterious fairy who Adam meets in a dungeon. Guardien of the spear. She hates it when people talk about her height.

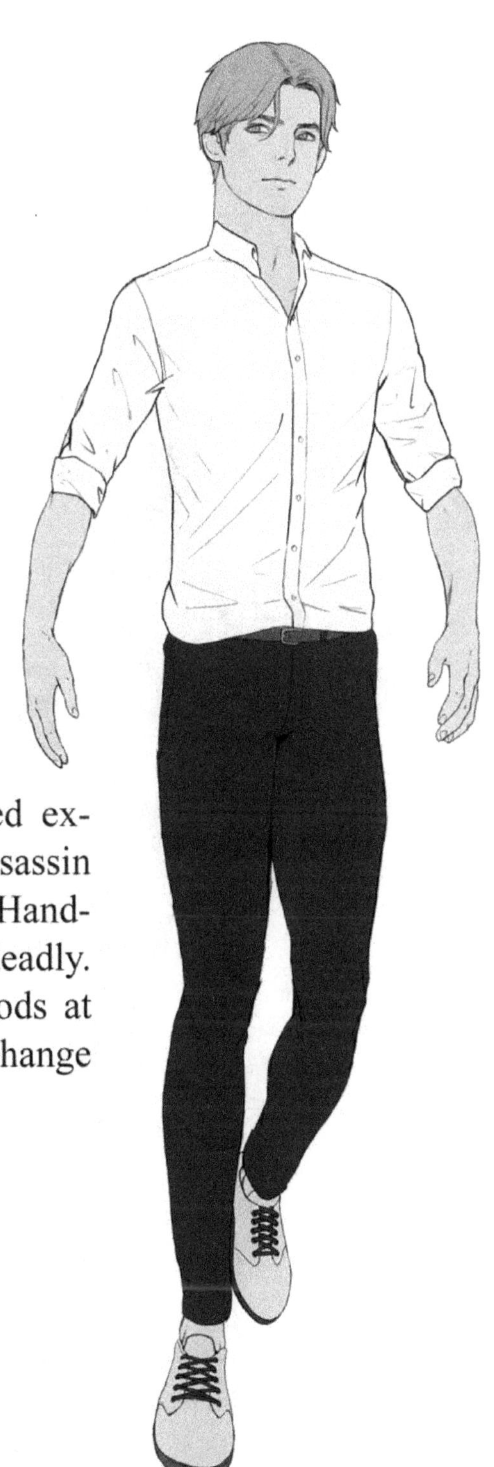

ADAM

A young man trained extensively as an assassin since childhood. Handsome, confident, deadly. He enters Age of Gods at Fayte's behest in exchange for her curing Aris.

SUSAN

Fayte's best and only friend. Genius hacker. Incredibly shy. Has trouble telling people no.

FAYTE

Daughter of the Dairing Family. Fayte is intelligent and determined to fight against her fate. She is the one who pulls Adam into Age of Gods.

LILITH

Adam's most loyal suborddinate. She is a highly skilled and quiet assassin who will do anything Adam asks without question.

ARIS

Adam's lover. She used to be rambunctious and wild, but she became a cripple after contracting mortems disease. Currently in stasis.

SURPRISES ON THE HORI-ZON

Because the area surrounding Suncrest Mountain contained level 30 and 40 monsters, Adam decided it was the perfect place to grind his level.

Adam glared at the current enemy he was fighting against. It walked on two triple-jointed legs. The large claws on its feet dug into the ground with every step. Leathery skin covered every inch of its muscular body, which reminded him of pictures he'd once seen of a dinosaur when he was young. This creature had large yellow eyes, a reptilian muzzle, and frills around its neck. It was also about two times taller than him.

Titania had already cast [scan] to show him its stats.

Name: Crestodon
Description: This reptilian creature is a monster that has survived since before the creation of the races of light. It's incredibly durable and exceedingly violent. Approach with caution.
Class: None
Lvl: 32
Health: 150,000/150,000
MP: 1,200/1,200
Physical Attack: +800
Constitution: +700
Dexterity: +500
Intelligence: +10
Speed: +50

Skills:
Claw: Crestodons have sharp claws that can rend through flesh, muscle, and bone
Deals Physical Attack + 5% chance of causing the bleed status effect
MP Cost: 50
Cooldown time: 0 seconds

Head Bash: When the Crestodon lowers its body, it will charge forward and slam headfirst into its enemies
Deals Physical Attack + Stun
MP Cost: 120
Cooldown time: 5 seconds

This enemy had some pretty impressive stats, and since its level was so much higher than his, he would gain a lot of experience points from defeating it. He would gain even more than normal since he was grinding on his own once again.

The [crestodon] scraped its left foot against the ground. Adam spun the spear around in his hands, eyes narrowed as he shifted from one foot to the other, moving as though he had eight legs instead of two. Anyone watching him would have probably said he looked like a spider. This made his movements more erratic and unpredictable, which would be useful for dodging. His enemy was fast, but that was only when it moved linearly. He'd discovered early on that its ability to turn around was limited.

He had already activated [Blood Sacrifice]. In the background, Titania was singing [Song of Vigor] to increase his attack power. Kureha was also waiting right next to her, prepared to fire off an attack as needed.

With a roar, the [crestodon] raced over with thunderous stomps that left deep imprints in the ground. Adam timed his dodge and moved out of the way, thrusting out his spear at the same time, impaling the passing enemy deep in its left flank. He activated [thrust] twice in quick succession. Thanks to [Blood Sacrifice], he did not have to worry about the skill's cooldown time.

-36,432; -36,432!

Two large numbers floated over the [crestodon's] head. His current Physical Attack power right now was +2,530, but that was tripled when he used [Blood Sacrifice], which was then tripled again and stacked when Titania sang [Song of Vigor]. His unique skill and Titania's buffing magic stacked on top of each other to deal truly massive damage.

"Yip!"

The moment the [crestodon] moved past Adam, Kureha raised her second tail, which sparked with electricity and released a blue bolt of lightning. This was [Thunder Bolt]. It slammed into the [crestodon] like a real bolt of lightning and lit the enemy up. If this was a cartoon, Adam was certain he would have been able to see the enemy's skeleton.

-7,920!

The moment Kureha finished attacking, Adam rushed in and swung at the creature with one of his newer skills. It was called [Energy Thrust]. It was an attack that ignored an enemy's defense to deal critical damage, which right now meant dealing 150% of the damage he normally did.

-34,155!

The [crestodon] still had some health left, so Adam spun around and swung his spear once more. [Slash] activated as he tore into the creature's side. His muscles strained with the very real sensation of tearing through flesh, though no blood emerged, and then it was over. His spear emerged from the monster's hide and a large number floated over its head.

-36,432!

With one more [thrust] for good measure, the amount of damage Adam dealt exceeded the amount of health the [crestodon] possessed. The enemy released a final croak like a whimper, then stumbled forward and slammed into the ground, tumbling across it for several meters.

Ding!

[Congratulations! You have defeated a [crestodon]! [Crestodon] has dropped the items [Durability Ring], [Monster Bone], and 40,000 gold coins! +300,000 experience points!]

Ding!

[Congratulations! You have leveled up! You are now at level 16! +1,125 HP! +20 MP! +5 SP!]

Ding!

[Congratulations! Titania has leveled up! She is now at level 15! +200 HP! +3,900 MP! +10 SP!]

Ding!

[Congratulations! Kureha has leveled up! She is now at level 15! +200 HP! +2,000 MP! +10 SP!]

"Finally," Adam murmured as he reached into his pouch and downed a [medium-grade magic potion]. His MP had dropped a lot from all the skills he used. "I feel like I've been grinding for hours to reach the next level."

"You've only been grinding for maybe an hour—two at most," Titania muttered as she landed on his shoulder. "Though I will admit it is very difficult to level up, you still have no right to complain. No one else I know can take on enemies more than 15 levels above them and come out on top. Thanks to that, you've leveled up much more quickly than even some of the most powerful—oh?"

"What? What is it?" asked Adam.

"It looks like your spear is evolving." Titania pointed at the weapon in his hand.

Adam looked down at his spear to see glowing motes of light surrounding it. The motes became more numerous before they were sucked into the spear like it was a black hole, then the spear began changing. The rust disappeared, the blade grew longer and gained a more prominent shape, and the shaft became a shade of deep red instead of a dull brown. It now looked like something that could actually be used in combat instead of something that belonged in the bargain bin at Spears-R-Us.

Since it looked like his spear had gained a new level, Adam checked out his equipment along with his new level. He also allocated his new status points.

Name: Adam
Class: Seven Forms Spearman
Lvl: 16
SP: 0
AP: 1,700
Experience: 632/4,915,200
Reputation: 132,000
Strength: +500
Constitution: +225
Dexterity: +5
MP: +5
Speed: +10
Physical Attack: +2,600
Health: 4,475/4,475
Hit-rate: 50%
MP: 160/160
Movement: +50
Comprehension: +1
Defense: +4,500
Magic Defense: +1,125
Dodge-Rate: ???
Magic Attack: +25

Resistances:
Fire: 50%
Water: 50%
Earth: 50%
Wind: 50%
Darkness: 50%
Slashing: 50%

Skill List:
Skill name: Slash
skill where the player swings his or her sword and attacks the enemy!
Current lvl: 5 MAXED
Ability: Causes 150% damage to enemy if it hits
MP Cost: 1
Cooldown time: 0 seconds

Skill name: Thrust
Description: A basic skill where the player thrusts his or her sword at the enemy!
Current lvl: 5 MAXED
Ability: Causes 160% damage with a 5% chance at getting a critical hit
MP Cost: 5
Cooldown time: 1 second

Skill name: Blood Sacrifice
Description: By sacrificing 50% of your blood (HP), you have gained the ability to increase the damage you do
Current lvl: 5 MAXED
Ability: Causes x3 attack power increase for 60 seconds
Disregards skill cooldown times, allowing the user to attack with every skill
MP Cost: 20

Special limit: Drops HP by half
Cooldown time: 30 seconds

Skill name: Dance of Sakura Blossoms
Description: A skill only Adam can use
Attacks with numerous spear thrusts that eventually forms the shape of a sakura blossom
Current lvl: 8
AP needed to reach lvl 8: 128,000
Ability: Release a constant stream of attacks, does x3 damage increase for every hit, and resets when Adam misses an attack.
Hit-Rate: 80%
MP Cost: 100
Cooldown time: 15 seconds

Skill name: Energy Sweep
Description: The wielder of Seven Forms Spearman infuses his energy into a sweeping attack that releases a powerful attack that extends past his natural range.
Current level: 3
AP needed to reach level 4: 8,000
Ability: Attacks every enemy within five yards of the user. Does 140% damage
MP Cost: 50
Cooldown Time: 10 Seconds

Skill Name: Energy Thrust
Description: The wielder of the Seven Forms Spearman infuses his energy into a thrust that can ignore all defenses and armor.
Current level: 2
AP needed to reach level 3: 4,000
Ability: Ignores enemy's defense and armor to deal critical damage. 170% damage dealt
MP Cost: 50
Cooldown Time: 10 Seconds

Equipment:
Item Name: Goddess of Creation Spear
Lvl: 10
Experience points needed to level up: 900,732/2,560,000
Item type: Spear
Grade: 5-Star
Use requirements: Can only be equipped by Adam. Cannot be thrown away, cannot be given away, and cannot be unequipped.
Description: The Goddess of Creation Spear was created eons ago by the Goddess of Creation and recently discovered by Adam. It has recognized Adam as its master and cannot be used by anyone else.
Abilities: Physical Attack+100; Strength+100
Special ability: Sentient Growth

Item Name: Dragon Bone Cuirass
Item Type: Armor
Grade: 2-Star
Use requirements: Can be equipped by Warriors level 10 and above.
Description: This chest plate was made from the bones of a powerful dragon. Not only does it look stylish, but it offers solid defensive abilities and some special stats.
Abilities: Defense+200; Constitution+100; 25% resistance to slashing, fire, earth, wind, and darkness damage

Ite4m Name: Dragon Bone Gauntlets
Item Type: Armor
Grade: 2-Star
Use requirements: Can be equipped by Warriors level 10 and above.
Description: These gauntlets are made from the bones of a powerful dragon. Not only are they stylish, but they offer solid

defensive abilities and resistance to elemental damage.
Abilities: Defense+50; Constitution+10; 10% resistance to
slashing, fire, earth, wind, and darkness damage

Item Name: Dragon Bone Greaves
Item Type: Armor
Grade: 2-Star
Use requirements: Can be equipped by Warriors level 10 and
above.
Description: Greaves made from the bones of a powerful dragon.
They are not only stylish; they also offer solid defense and
resistance against elemental damage.
Abilities: Defense+75; Constitution+25; 15% resistance to
slashing, fire, earth, wind, and darkness damage.

His Strength and Physical Attack stats had received a fairly significant boost. He also noticed that his spear's name had changed from [Rusted Spear] to [Goddess of Creation Spear] and its class was listed as 5-Star instead of "???" now. He wondered what that meant. Did the increase in level cause it to change, or did it change because he now knew of the spear's origins?

With a shake of his head, Adam dispelled those thoughts, opened his [Item Pouch], and looked at the new items he had gained.

Item Pouch:
Item Name: Durability Ring
Item Type: Accessory
Grade: 1-Star
Use Requirements: Can be equipped by anyone.
Description: An enchanted ring that adds to a person's Defense
and Magical Defense.
Abilities: Magic Defense+10; Defense+10

**Item Name: Monster Bone
Item Type: Material
Grade: 2-Star
Use requirements: Can only be used by the Craftsmen and
Blacksmith class.
Description: This item can be turned into a weapon or armor at
the hands of a skilled blacksmith or crafter.
Abilities: Defense+50; Magic Defense+50**

The [durability ring] wasn't a very good item, so he would sell that. While the [monster bone] would be useful to a Blacksmith or Craftsman, Adam was neither of those, so of course, he'd be selling that too. He sighed. It looked like while his level was increasing nicely, he still wasn't getting any good item drops. He wished he had the Luck stat like Susan.

"Now that we have leveled up, what should we do? Stay here and keep grinding or travel back to Solum?" asked Titania.

Adam knelt to pick up Kureha, holding the happy fox yokai in his arms as he looked at the fairy sitting on his shoulder. He considered staying here. He really wanted to raise his level even more. However, after thinking about it, he shook his head.

"It's almost time for Fayte, Susan, and Lilith to meet up with us. We should head back to Solum."

"Very well," Titania agreed easily enough.

Adam mounted the horse he had used to reach the valley near the Sunset Mountain Range and cracked the reigns to get it moving. Riding in Age of Gods was a lot like riding in the real world, but much easier. The horse obeyed all of his commands without question. That didn't always happen in the real world, especially for people who had no experience with horseback riding. The only anomaly was the first horse he rode, but Titania took care of that problematic mare for him.

Two days had passed since Lilith gained her new hidden class and snuck into his bedroom; three weeks had passed since the game was first released. He wouldn't say anything had changed. In fact, on the outside, nothing seemed to have changed. Lilith didn't treat him any differently now than she always had. In public, she pretended she didn't know him, but whenever they were alone, she still called him "Master," a title he had never been comfortable with. She hadn't appeared before him again like she had that night. He felt like she was waiting for him to make the first move.

While Lilith hadn't changed—at least, on the outside—Adam felt like the entire dynamic of their relationship was different, or maybe it was just him. Maybe *he* had changed. He wouldn't deny that he found himself watching Lilith more than he used to. It reminded him of... back then, back when he was still the leader of Lucifer's assassins.

Sometimes when he was lying in bed, he would remember what happened between him and Lilith when he was younger, the times when he lost himself to lust. He couldn't recall how many times he had explored her body. She was the first—and so far, the only—person he had ever slept with.

Back then, Adam was only using Lilith to satisfy his lust and to keep himself from going insane in a world that threatened to tear his sanity asunder. After they escaped, he had dropped her and everyone else to find Lexi, only to discover that she had gone missing. Then, when Adam was about to give up on everything, concluding that Lexi was dead, Aris had discovered him and given him salvation, which only further separated him from Lilith.

He believed part of the reason he stayed away from Lilith for so long was that he felt guilty. Lilith had completely given herself to him, but he had not treated her right, had not given any of himself back. The guilt he felt after realizing this was what made him tell her that he was no longer her master and that she was free to live however she saw fit.

And now she was telling him that she wanted was to give herself to him? How could he respond to that when he had already given himself to another?

To distract himself from these thoughts, Adam opened Kureha's stats and checked them over. He added the SP she gained to her Intelligence stat. Everything looked pretty good. As a magic-using class, she had a lot of useful skills. He was particularly interested in her AOE skills, which would be of great help during large-scale PvP battles. If he'd had Kureha back when those idiots from the Rising Phoenix Alliance attacked him, they would have been killed within a few seconds flat.

Just as Adam was about halfway to Solum, he heard ringing from his player chat function. His friend's list had increased from one to three, so he needed to check to see who was calling him.

It was Fayte.

"Fayte? What's up? Are the others here yet?" he asked.

"Never mind that, Adam! You need to log off right now!" Fayte shouted at him. There was an urgency in her voice that he couldn't ignore. It set off warning bells in his mind.

He furrowed his brow. "Why? What's wrong?"

"It's Aris. She's woken up," Fayte announced, leaving him stunned.

****

Adam did not even make it to Solum before logging out of Age of Gods. He shot off the bed like a bullet, ran out of his room, and raced down the hall. The stupid lock that needed a retina scan couldn't work fast enough. He tapped his foot impatiently, waiting for the soft "beep" that let him know the door was unlocked. It slid open and he rushed inside.

He looked at the cryobed.

He froze.

He couldn't breathe.

The cryobed that Aris had been sleeping in was open, and Aris was sitting up, wide awake and smiling weakly at him. Fayte was sitting by her side, but at this moment, he only had eyes for the girl inside the cryobed.

Skin like freshly fallen snow. Doe-like brown eyes that were warm and innocent. Brown hair that fell and surrounded her face, which contained a youthful innocent that left him breathless. She had a small, cute nose, and her pink lips were so kissable that it sometimes took all of Adam's self-control to resist claiming them.

Words like "pretty" and "beautiful" failed to do Aris any real justice. In Adam's eyes, she was the most enchanting woman in the entire world.

She was also currently naked.

"Aris…"

"Adam." Aris's eyes glistened with tears that she refused to shed as she stared into his already watering eyes. "Are you just going to stand there all day, or are you going to come over here and give me a kiss?"

Those words made whatever restraints had been holding him back shatter. A tearing sound echoed within his mind as he surged over to the table. Fayte pushed her chair back in surprise as he moved past her and pulled Aris into a tight hug. He sought her lips with his own and kissed her with all the emotions his body contained, emotions he couldn't possibly hold in without exploding.

He'd never felt this relieved. He felt like he might start crying.

Her lips were cold from being stuck in stasis for so long, but he didn't care. This was perfect. He could warm those lips right up.

Aris released a startled gasp from the intensity of his kiss. She seemed unable to keep up as he kissed her like a man possessed. Yet she didn't let that stop her from trying. Arms wove around his neck, weak and shaking, but still something he could sense, an action that had presence. Those delicate arms lightly rested on his shoulders like she didn't quite have the strength to fully hug him.

Only after Adam had kissed Aris until she was breathless did he release her lips and hold her close, letting her head rest against his chest as he engulfed her in his arms. She seemed so small and fragile right now. She had been like that ever since contracting Mortems Disease, but he felt like she was even smaller now than she had been before. Was this the result of being in stasis for so long, or had it just been such a long time that hugging her seemed unfamiliar to him?

"I'm so glad you woke up," Adam whispered. "I've missed you so much."

"Me too." Aris sighed and took several deep breaths, snuggling deeper into his embrace. "It only seemed like a second to me, but I'm still glad I woke up. I can't stand the thought of leaving your side for so long."

A soft noise alerted Adam to Fayte getting up from her chair and leaving the room. He felt a burst of gratitude toward her. She was easily one of the most thoughtful people he had ever met. Adam wanted to find some way to thank her, which was why he made a promise to himself.

He would help her win the bet she made against Levon no matter the cost. He wouldn't stop until he had thoroughly crushed every obstacle in her way.

"I have so much to tell you," Adam said.

"Hee-hee. I'll bet. What kind of things happened while I was asleep?"

Adam lifted Aris out of the cryobed and sat down on the chair that Fayte had vacated. He placed her on his lap. She was naked. At the moment, however, Adam was so relieved by her awakening that he couldn't even feel aroused. He relished in the feeling of holding this woman in his arms. It was a feeling he had missed for an entire month.

While they sat together completely embracing each other, Adam told Aris everything he could think of. He told her about how he began playing Age of Gods, what happened in the Village of Beginnings, his meeting with the Spider Queen, and how he had formed a party with Fayte, Susan, Lilith, Titania, and Kureha. He didn't know how long he talked for. It felt like he'd been talking for hours. By the time he finished, his throat was sore.

"It sounds like you've been through a lot." Aris paused. He couldn't see her face because she was pressed against his chest, but he could well imagine the way it was adorably scrunched up like she was pouting. "I wish I could have been with you when all this happened."

"It's fine. You're with me now. That's what matters."

"Hee-hee. That's true. Now that I'm awake, I can enter Age of Gods and play with you and everyone else."

Adam began stroking Aris's hair as he spoke to her. "I think you're going to like everyone. Fayte is an incredible woman. She's very kind and compassionate, but she has a will of steel. You won't find anyone more determined than her. Susan is shy and quiet, but she's a wonderful girl. You'll definitely like her. Once you leave the Village of Beginnings and join up with us, I can also introduce you to Titania and Kureha. I know for a fact that you'll like Kureha. She's the most adorable fox you've ever seen."

"She does sound very cute." Aris paused for a moment. "What about Lilith?"

Aris's question made Adam freeze. It wasn't that he didn't want to answer her, but that thinking about Lilith made him remember both the times he had used her to satiate his own lust and that moment in his bedroom just last week.

"Adam?"

"Lilith is… she's very quiet," he began in a soft voice. "She never talks much and it's sometimes hard to tell what she is thinking. Her quiet demeanor makes her seem cold, but she's actually very kind and strong. She's always watching out for the people around her and putting their needs before her own."

Adam wondered if maybe he was saying too much. The words were spilling from his mouth before he could close it. He wanted to stop, but the more he tried to keep his mouth shut, the more he found himself extolling Lilith's virtues.

"She's an incredible fighter and perhaps one of the most capable people I know. She's beautiful enough to make a man's blood boil, but she can also freeze your blood with just a look. Her ice-cold eyes are enough to scare the pants off regular men."

"They all sound like wonderful people." If Aris recognized the tone he used when he spoke of Lilith, she didn't say anything. Lifting her head from his chest, she looked into his eyes, her gaze warm, soft, and so loving he thought he'd melt. "I would very much like to meet them."

Adam calmed his racing heart and smiled back as he stroked her cheek. "You will. From now on, you'll be able to spend time with me and everyone else. You'll be able to make more friends and do more things. You can enjoy life." He paused. "Once we get you checked at the hospital. While I trust what Fayte said about this machine, I still want to have you examined by Dr. Sofocor. Is it okay if I schedule an appointment for tomorrow?"

Aris nodded once. "Of course. I would like to have confirmation that my Mortems Disease is gone too."

Now that Adam had run dry of topics to discuss, he stood up with Aris still in his arms and carried her outside. She was still weak. Even if the Mortems Disease was gone, her body had atrophied badly thanks to it, and she could no longer move under her own power. Adam was already planning a rehabilitation program to get her walking again.

Because she was naked, the first thing Adam did after leaving the room was dress her in a set of pajamas—cute yellow shorts and a spaghetti strap shirt. The light yellow color, like sunflowers, complimented her snow-white skin. After Aris complained about her feet feeling cold, Adam also slid some wool socks up her beautiful legs to cover her small feet. The smile on her face as she wiggled her toes told him he made the right choice.

When he emerged from the hallway and into the living room, he saw Fayte wearing her usual jeans and turtleneck shirt, sitting on the couch and watching television. It wasn't the news. She appeared to be watching old cartoons from the early 2000s. This particular cartoon was one that originated from Japan. There were a few channels that still played them like the Nostalgia Network.

She smiled when they entered. "I'm happy you woke up, Aris. I don't think I've ever seen Adam look this happy when he's around me."

There was something about the way she spoke that sounded off to Adam, but he couldn't quite put his finger on it. Then again, he was so happy that Aris was awake again that he couldn't think of much else. His heart felt like it was floating on a cloud.

"I'm sure that's not true," Aris said with a gentle look at Fayte. "When Adam was telling me about what he's been doing since I was put to sleep, more than half of what he said was about you and what a great person you are. He talked for at least an hour about how you two played old-school console games and the loser had to make dinner. Hee-hee. I don't know what you did, but you must be really incredible to have made such a strong impression on him."

"Th-thank you very much…"

It wasn't much as far as compliments went, but Fayte's cheeks still turned a light shade of red. The fetching color enhanced her pure white skin and beautiful golden hair.

As someone born from the aristocracy, Fayte Dairing was a woman whose beauty was as obvious as two plus two equals four. Her blonde hair, reminiscent of threads of gold, haloed a regal face with high cheekbones, a small nose, and full, red lips. The turtleneck sweater and jeans that she wore conformed perfectly to her well-proportioned figure. While Aris was very petite, Fayte had a body that put bikini models to shame.

Adam glanced at the clock and saw that it was already 10:30 AM, which meant more than two hours had passed since Aris woke up. He'd been speaking nonstop for two whole hours. He didn't think he had ever talked that much in a single sitting.

"I just have a great deal of respect for Fayte is all," Adam said as he sat down on the couch next to Fayte. Of course, he had not let Aris go. She was right on his lap, and she'd probably remain there until it was time for him to make lunch.

"Is that really all it is?" asked Fayte with a winning smile. "You haven't fallen for my charms?"

"I have always believed you were a very charming woman," Adam admitted honestly. "But I have Aris."

"I suppose that is true," Fayte said, and once again there was that odd tone in her voice that Adam felt he should recognize but couldn't quite place. She also had a strange look in her eyes that didn't match her smile. "I thought this the first time I saw you two together, but you really do look like the ideal couple."

"Hee-hee. Thank you." Aris wore the happiest smile he'd seen from her in a very long time, though said smile quickly turned sly. "But I think you might actually look better next to Adam than me."

"You're too kind," Fayte said diplomatically. "By the way, I let Susan and Lilith know that Aris woke up. I told them you probably won't enter Age of Gods for the rest of today and maybe even tomorrow."

Adam's lips trembled a little as he stared at Fayte with gratitude suffusing his heart. Perhaps she sensed his feelings because Fayte looked away, unable to maintain eye contact. She looked embarrassed. Even the tips of her ears were red now, which he thought was adorable. The contrast between her mature figure and innocent expression created a contradiction that he found appealing.

"Thank you," Adam said softly.

"You're welcome," Fayte replied just as softly.

Aris did not say anything, but the thoughtful look on her face made Adam aware that he should probably not stare at Fayte so intently. He didn't want his lover getting jealous or feeling left out.

Because Adam wanted to spend the entire day with Aris, he did not log on to Age of Gods even once. He spent most of that time sitting on the couch and talking to Aris and Fayte. He did leave the two women for a moment to make them lunch, but then he came right back. The three of them also spent a lot of time playing console games. Aris was the worst among the three of them and always lost, but she didn't seem to care at all. Her smile was infectious and her laughter was the most soul-soothing sound Adam had ever heard.

Later that night, after Adam had bathed Aris, combed her hair, and dressed her in pajamas, the two of them lay in bed, cuddling under the blankets. Aris was resting her head on his chest as he stroked her arm. Her modest breasts were pressing into him. Maybe it was because of how long he had been without her, but Adam found that even though he was impossibly content, it was harder for him to control his base instincts.

He wanted to devour her.

Aris was able to pick up on this. "Adam? When do you plan on taking my virginity like you promised?"

Her words caused the heat in his loins to flare up. She had to know what she was doing to him. Aris had always been aware ever since she promised to marry him that he wanted her. Perhaps she had known about his feelings even before then.

"When you have gotten better," he said after mastering his hormones. "First, we need to do the checkup with Dr. Sofocor to make sure your Mortems Disease is really gone. Then we need to begin your rehabilitation. Right now, your muscles have atrophied a lot. I've done what I can to keep them from degrading too much, but that's not enough."

"Then... when do you think I will be well enough for it?" asked Aris.

Adam scratched his head. He tried to estimate how long it would take Aris to heal, but he didn't know. There was no precedent for this. No one else had ever survived having Mortems Disease, much less been cured of it.

"I can't give you an estimated time, but I'll sleep with you once you can walk for an entire hour without exhausting yourself and straining your muscles."

"In that case, I'll work really hard to get better as fast as I can so you can keep your promise to me," Aris said in a determined voice. Adam wasn't sure what he could say to that, so he said nothing, allowing Aris to continue. "Adam?"

"Yeah?"

"I'm not tired right now. Can we keep kissing?"

Those words caused him to smile. "We most certainly can."

Adam spent the next several hours lying on the bed, kissing Aris until they both eventually fell asleep.

CURED

Because the population had declined by nearly a third thanks to World War III and Mortems Disease, the population of large cities had also declined. Cities like New York City, which used to boast a population of 33.5 million people, now only had a population of about 13.1 million. Larger cities were hit much harder than smaller cities.

With the decreased population, there had been a need to downsize large cities like New York City, which now had a population of less than half of what it was originally. However, that was easier said than done. Mortems Disease did not care if you were a blue-collared worker or a government official with a high position. Everyone's lives were equally claimed once they contracted it.

New York City had been hit especially hard thanks to the large amount of cars, pollution from factories and gas emissions, and unclean subway stations.

Many of the buildings in New York City were still abandoned even thirty years after World War III. Some of these buildings had been torn down and replaced with newer buildings, but a lot of them, like Fayte's apartment complex, still existed.

This usually meant the building in question would be taken over by a corporation or a powerful family like the Pleonexia Family, who owned more than thirty percent of New York City and had business holdings spread across the American Federation. They were not the only ones who owned property in New York City. There were many families and powerful companies that owned various businesses and real estate.

Of course, even these families didn't own every property in the city. Fayte's apartment was privately owned by a small family that operated under the radar. They weren't operating illegally, but they weren't large enough to own more than that single apartment complex. Consequently, this was also why her complex was not as well-maintained as similar complexes elsewhere.

The New York City Hospital was a six-story building made out of glass and red and white bricks. It was longer than it was wide, shaped like a rectangle with inverted corners, and possessed a flat roof surrounded by a large fence. Located in the busiest area of New York City, it was easily the most populated hospital anywhere in the American Federation. The reason this hospital was so popular wasn't just because of its location, however.

The New York City Hospital was one of the only known hospitals that willingly treated Mortems Disease. They had specialized equipment meant to quarantine and treat victims, not only helping people who had contracted the world's most fatal illness, but also keeping the disease from spreading.

Adam pulled his car into the parking lot on the other side of the street. He needed to pay a fee to park. After finding a secure parking spot, he stepped out of the car, unloaded Aris's wheelchair from the trunk, then lifted Aris from the passenger's seat and onto the wheelchair.

"How do you feel? Any discomfort?" asked Adam.

"I feel fine." Aris gave Adam that beaming smile he loved so much. It was much brighter than he remembered. "I actually feel great. Hee-hee. I think my body has become a lot more durable now that my Mortems Disease is gone."

Adam felt his heart soften as he looked at the girl sitting on the wheelchair. Aris was wearing a light blue dress that covered her knees but left her calves exposed. It was still cold, so black yoga pants were covering her legs and a red scarf was tied around her neck. The scarf was something Adam had hand-knit for her two years ago. Her hair was tied into a side ponytail.

"That's good. Do you need the blanket?"

Because of how weak her body was, Adam worked hard to keep her warm whenever they went out. Mortems Disease could be affected by body temperature. The lower the temperature, the greater the chances of it accelerating.

Aris shook her head. "I'm not that cold. Actually, this cool temperature feels really nice on my skin."

Since Aris said she didn't need it, Adam stowed the blanket in a small compartment underneath her seat. After locking the car, he grabbed the wheelchair by its handles and pushed her toward the elevator.

They were on the second floor, so they needed to travel down one floor, and then Adam went to the street light and waited until he could walk across it. The hospital was right in front of them.

"It's too bad Fayte couldn't come with us," Aris said.

"Fayte had something she needed to take care of today." Adam shrugged. "Also, I'm not sure going out with her is a good idea right now."

"Why is that?"

Adam wondered what he should tell Aris. He was certain that Levon Pleonexia was doing his best to monitor Fayte's movements. He had learned that Susan was interrupting Levon's attempts to track her (which he thought was incredible), but she couldn't monitor his activities all the time. She also couldn't monitor all the people working for him. There was no telling when he would find out about what she'd been up to and where she lived, and when that happened, there was also a good chance he'd find out about them.

If at all possible, Adam would like to avoid being associated with Fayte until he could properly guarantee Aris's safety.

"Let's just say that Fayte is in a dangerous position right now," he said, a diplomatic response if there ever was one.

"Is it because of that bet she has with that Levon guy?" asked Aris.

There was a soft creak as his grip on the handles tightened, but he didn't reveal anything on his face as he said, "Yes."

As they passed through the sliding doors, Adam studied the hospital's waiting room. There were a lot of seats. Some were full and some weren't. Adam saw a man nursing his leg, blood leaking from his thigh. It looked like a knife wound. There was also a mother and her daughter. The daughter kept coughing into her hand, had a red face, and bags under her eyes. He recognized the symptoms of a particularly bad cold.

Adam pushed Aris's wheelchair up to the front desk, where an older woman with grayish-red hair, blue eyes, and a kind smile sat. She looked like a kindly grandmother. The amusing thought that this was why she manned the front desk instead of someone else crossed Adam's mind, though he dismissed it seconds later.

"Hello, we're here to see Dr. Sofocor," Adam said. "We have an appointment."

The woman's eyes drifted briefly to Aris. Sympathy appeared within them. However, she was nothing if not professional and went back to looking at Adam.

"What are your names, dear?" asked the woman.

"Adam Lancer and Aris Purety."

"Adam… Lancer… Aris… Purety… ah. Here you two are." After typing on her console, the woman looked back up. "It says here that your appointment is set for 10:00 AM. You're a little early, and Dr. Sofocor is currently with another patient. Could you please wait for a little while? I will let her know you're here."

"Thank you," Adam said.

"Thanks!" added Aris.

He pushed the wheelchair over to one of the seats, then was about to sit down himself—until Aris held her hands out for him. The slight smile on her face and expectant look in her eyes made her desire obvious.

Adam slipped an arm around her shoulder and another around her legs. He lifted her off the wheelchair and sat down with her on his lap. It took a moment of shifting around to get comfortable. Aris's soft butt was pressed firmly against his crotch, which was distracting, but he was soon able to ignore it as she began playing with his hair. Her soft fingers threaded through his blond locks and gently rubbed his scalp.

"Do you think this will be the last time we see Dr. Sofocor?" she asked.

"Probably," Adam said. "Dr. Sofocor only accepts patients who have Mortems Disease. Since you're cured, there's no reason for you to see her after this."

"That's a little sad to think about." Aris twirled a strand of his hair between her fingers. It tickled. "I really like her."

"That's because she's sweet on you," Adam said dryly.

"Hee-hee. True."

Aris was the kind of girl most people couldn't help but like. Not only did she have a unique and innocent beauty, but her sweet demeanor and lovely smile could make a person's heart stop beating. Or make it speed up. Gamers knew she made Adam's heart accelerate whenever she smiled at him.

They continued to converse in hushed voices, not wanting to disturb the people sitting with them, but that was impossible considering the intimate position they were in. Several of the other patients stared at them with looks of either jealousy or pity, depending on who was looking. Adam wondered if he was weird for not caring about those looks at all. Aris was with him. Why did it matter if these people were staring?

A door leading further into the hallway suddenly slid open. Out walked a middle-aged woman in a knee-length black skirt, long-sleeve black shirt, and white lab coat. There was a security tag attached to the lab coat. Her brown hair swayed behind her, tied tightly into a ponytail. Only a few bangs framed her tanned face and hazel eyes.

"Adam. Aris," she called out.

Adam stood up with Aris in his arms. She pouted when he set her back in the wheelchair, but he just smiled before pushing her over to the woman.

"Dr. Julia Sofocor," Adam greeted.

Julia Sofocor was a renowned doctor who had dedicated her life to the study and treatment of Mortems Disease. She was in fairly decent shape and had an attractive face, though he wouldn't have called her super pretty. Her looks were average. Her husband was one of the first victims of Mortems Disease. That was why she had become a doctor who specifically worked with patients who had it.

"I see you two are as lovey-dovey as ever." Dr. Sofocor frowned at him. "The way you indulge Aris borders on insane."

"I'll take that as a compliment," Adam said. "And you have no room to speak."

"Hmph."

"Does it really bother you?" asked Aris, tilting her head curiously.

"Of course it does!" Julia snapped as a fire was ignited under her bottom. She raised a hand to her face and clenched it into a fist. "Do you know how much I want to be lovey-dovey with you?! But I can't because Adam won't let me!"

"You are a doctor. You need to maintain a sense of professionalism." Adam paused, then smiled. "And Aris is mine."

"Hee-hee. Adam called me his. He's so possessive." Aris placed her hands on her cheeks, which had turned red. The smile she wore was so wide and satisfied it reminded him of a cat with an entire bowl of cream.

"Grrrr…"

Emitting a soft growl from the back of her throat, Dr. Sofocor turned around and marched back the way she had come. Adam and Aris followed her.

Dr. Sofocor worked on the sixth floor, which was dedicated solely to patients who had Mortems Disease. The hallways were not as wide on this floor as they were on the bottom floors. The rooms were also bigger, but they appeared smaller because of all the equipment inside. Containing, studying, and treating Mortems Disease required a lot of advanced equipment.

Of course, even with the most advanced medical practices, Mortems Disease could only be halted—at least, that was what everyone believed.

The room Dr. Sofocor directed them to was one such room. The bed was more than just a bed. It had an advanced scanner around it that looked like a half-donut. Several large machines hummed and beeped with life, cabinets containing a variety of medicines, and a desk.

"Can you tell me why you asked for this appointment? You sounded pretty excited over the phone." Dr. Sofocor picked up a tablet from the desk and began inputting data into it. He knew she was accessing Aris's personal information.

"I want you to run a scan on Aris to check for Mortems Disease," Adam said.

Dr. Sofocor stopped typing into the tablet and stared at him, blinking several times as a stupid look crossed her face.

"I'm sorry. You want me to what now?"

"I want you to check Aris for Mortems Disease," Adam repeated.

The doctor did not say anything as she stared at him, then shifted her gaze to Aris. The seventeen-year-old woman didn't flinch under the doctor's intense scrutiny. She wore the same bright smile she had been wearing since yesterday. After looking at Aris for a moment longer, her gaze went back to Adam.

"There has been a change in her condition?"

Adam's smile widened. "We'll know for sure if you run that scan."

"Fine. Let's operate the scanner."

With Dr. Sofocor now onboard, Adam helped lay Aris on the bed, which was about a foot longer than she was tall. Dr. Sofocor went over to a computer connected to the half-donut shaped scanner.

She typed in a command code and set the scanner to run. Several lights on the scanner flashed before it began moving across the bed.

Adam came up behind the doctor and watched as the scanner mapped out Aris's body. It didn't just scan one aspect of her physique but all of them: muscles, skeleton, organs, veins, everything. Mortems Disease infected every part of the body. That was part of what made it so deadly. Scanners like this individually scanned each part of the human body to make sure it didn't miss anything.

The scanner moved back and forth across Aris's body several times, then stopped. When it did, Dr. Sofocor said nothing for the longest time. She stared at the information revealed by the scanner, her expression stunned, mouth open and eyes wide. Several seconds passed before she looked at Adam as he was helping Aris sit up.

"How?"

"Are you asking me how Aris no longer has Mortems Disease?" asked Adam with a wide smile. Dr. Sofocor nodded. She couldn't even form a proper sentence. "I can't reveal that right now."

The doctor's expression became dark. "Why not? Don't you know how many people have Mortems Disease? At least fifty thousand people die from it every year. Think of all the lives you could save!"

"Do you really think most people could afford this cure?" asked Adam, his words bringing the woman up short. "The method to cure Aris, from what I understand, cost over three hundred billion dollars to make. How many people do you think can afford such a cure?" Dr. Sofocor remained silent. Adam sighed. "Of course, I'm not saying I won't tell yo. Right now just isn't a good time. Even if you had the cure, there's nothing you can do with it. Also, the method we used to cure Aris isn't mine. I'll have to ask the person who saved Aris for permission to tell you about it."

Adam already planned on asking Fayte if she'd be willing to let Dr. Sofocor study the device that had cured Aris. If she could learn how it worked and replicate it using cheaper methods, it could become a viable cure. What's more, if Fayte brokered a deal with Dr. Sofocor or the group that owned this hospital, she could potentially earn trillions of dollars. There'd be no end to the lines of people willing to pay for a cure.

The only issue was that creating an affordable cure would take several years. Lucifer's machine was far more advanced than anything this hospital had. It was probably twenty or even thirty years ahead of current medical technology, and he didn't believe there was a person out there who could understand the inner workings of something made by that madman.

In other words, it would be impossible to use this cure to help Fayte win her bet, which was now the most important objective Adam had.

"I understand that, but—"

"Doctor," Adam said, and for the first time, his tone had grown cold. When Dr. Sofocor shivered, it had nothing to do with the temperature. "You are pushing it. I *will* tell you how Aris was cured. However, it will be on *my* time, not *yours*. Let me ask my benefactor for permission first. I'll contact you when I have her approval."

"Fine…" Dr. Sofocor sighed, shoulders slumping. "I understand what you're saying, but you had better keep your word and promise to speak with whoever gave you the method to cure Aris."

"I promise," Adam said.

"Bye, Dr. Sofocor." Aris waved as Adam pushed her wheelchair out of the room. "Thank you for everything you have done for us."

With nothing left to keep them at the hospital, Adam and Aris went across the street and entered the car.

"Adam?" Aris began as he started the engine.

The car thrummed with life, though it was soft and unobtrusive. This car didn't rely on gas. Cars no longer relied on gas but more environmentally friendly forms of energy, like solar, kinetic, and electric. His car was a hybrid that used all three forms of energy, making it one of the most efficient cars available on the current market.

"Yes?"

"Can we… stay out for a little while longer? Now that I don't have Mortems Disease anymore, I would like to spend more time doing things outside with you."

"Of course. Where do you want to go?"

"The movie theater!"

"All right. Let's go see a movie."

Adam pulled out of the parking lot and began driving down the road, their destination the nearest movie theater.

Movie theaters had fallen out of favor with the general populace. Ever since virtual reality took center stage in the entertainment industry, movies and theaters had begun shutting down, unable to afford to remain in business. The once-famous Hollywood was now nothing more than a few die-hard directors and actors who refused to give up on a dying industry.

But just because movies were no longer as popular as they used to be didn't mean they were non-existent. So long as there were still people who enjoyed watching movies, there would be movie theaters and people who made movies.

Adam took Aris to one such theater. It was small. There were only three separate theaters. With the population no longer what it once was and movies having fallen out of favor, any theater that still existed had been downsized. This was one of the bigger theaters. Most only contained one theater and it could hold, at maximum, twenty people.

"What do you want to watch?" asked Adam as he looked at the movies available. There were only three. One looked like an action movie, one a romance, and the last looked like a comedy.

"I want to watch *For You,*" Aris said.

"The romance, huh? Okay. We'll watch that."

Adam paid for their tickets and entered the theater. While small, the theater still had a concession stand, which sold popcorn and several snacks. The person standing behind the concession stand looked awfully bored since no one was coming up right now.

"Can I have popcorn?" asked Aris.

"Let's not this time." Adam gave Aris a small grin when he saw her pout. "The movie will finish around lunchtime. I bet Fayte will have lunch ready by the time we get back. I don't want you ruining your appetite—and Fayte's cooking is way better than popcorn."

"You seem to know Fayte pretty well," Aris said.

"You think so?" Adam looked away and scratched his cheek when he saw the perceptive expression on her face. "Well, she and I have been living together for about a month now. It's only natural I'd know a little about her."

"Hmm…"

"What is it?"

"Nothing. Since you don't think I should have popcorn right now, I don't mind just watching the movie with you."

Adam sighed in relief as Aris acquiesced. He never noticed the mischievous grin on her face as he pushed her wheelchair into the theater where their movie would be playing.

***

Fayte returned home to discover that Adam and Aris were still out. She slipped off her boots, set them off to the side, and slid out of her ugly brown jacket. After placing it on a coat hanger, she walked into the kitchen and started making lunch.

Her fridge had all the ingredients necessary for simple macaroni and cheese. Noodles, cheddar, Velveeta cheese, milk, and butter. She grabbed the ingredients and set them on the counter. She then took a pot, filled it with water, and turned the stove on high to bring the water to a boil.

As she waited for the water to boil, she thought about Aris and Adam. She was truly happy that Aris was now awake. She had seen the look on Adam's face when he visited Aris while she was in cryosleep, and it had torn her apart inside. He tried so hard to be strong, but she could tell he was in pain. No strong facade could disguise it.

Fayte absently placed a hand against her chest as a sharp pain pierced it. However, this pain was in no way physical. It felt like someone had grabbed her heart and given it a strong squeeze.

"They really do make a great couple," she said, wondering at the bitterness in her voice.

Macaroni and cheese was pretty simple to make. After bringing the water to a boil, she placed the noodles inside. Then she set the cheddar and Velveeta into a separate pot and began melting it. She added some milk, butter, and salt for flavor. She considered adding bacon bits to the cheese, but she didn't have any bacon.

The sound of her door opening and closing told her that Adam and Aris had returned, and just seconds later, the sounds of their voices could be heard coming from the entrance.

"I can't believe how amazing that movie was. The love between Kenichi and Amanda was so touching," Aris was saying.

"You think so? I thought Alex's love for Amanda was much stronger. He was willing to die for her sake. I feel kind of bad for him because even after being willing to go so far, she still chose Kenichi in the end."

"Dying is easy. Isn't living for someone much harder?"

"I… suppose you bring up a good point."

"Hee-hee. Of course I do. You should listen to me, Adam. I know what I'm talking about."

"I won't deny that."

Fayte froze with the smile halfway on her face when Adam and Aris came into the living room.

Aris was, of course, in Adam's arms. She looked just like a princess being carried off by a gallant prince. It was such a picturesque scene that Fayte couldn't help but feel like an intruder getting a peek at their private lives. The sharp pain in her chest returned, but she tried to rub it away and smiled at the pair.

"Welcome home, you two," Fayte said from the kitchen. "I hope you're both hungry because I made lunch."

"Hee-hee. It's good to be home. By the way, what are you cooking?" Aris asked suddenly, sniffing the air. "It smells delicious."

"Macaroni and cheese?" Adam asked, an amused smile touching his lips.

Fayte felt her cheeks grow warm at the look he directed her way, but she kept up her smile. "You can't beat the classics."

Adam set Aris on the couch, turned on the TV so she would have something to watch, and walked into the kitchen. He didn't even ask if she needed help before he started getting out the plates, forks, and cups. He got three of everything.

As he walked past her, Fayte froze when his masculine scent entered her nose, somehow overpowering the smell of cheese. He wasn't sweating, and he didn't smell like body odor. The scent was fresh and crisp, as though he had just gotten out of the shower and put on a splash of cologne. It made her heart accelerate.

"Why don't you sit down?" Adam suggested. "I'll serve the food since you made it."

Adam looked at her with that soft smile of his, the one she had been subjected to for the past four weeks, and she couldn't stop her legs from growing weak. She looked away to avoid that expression. She needed to be strong.

"Okay. Yeah, I'll go sit down."

Fayte walked to the couch on shaky legs and sat down. Aris was leaning against the armrest. She still seemed a little weak, but Fayte noticed that the girl looked much better now than she had yesterday. When she first woke up, it took all her strength just to sit straight.

"Thank you for making lunch," Aris said with her typical tender smile.

"You're welcome."

Fayte wondered if the guilt she felt was because she wished Aris wouldn't smile at her like that or if there was another reason. Bitterness once more crept into her heart as she imagined what it would be like to be in Aris's place.

"By the way, I don't know if you remember saying you wanted to play Age of Gods with Adam, but I've got your system," Fayte said. "It's in my bedroom right now."

"Really?! Thank you so much!" The smile on Aris's face became so brilliant that Fayte felt like she was being blinded. "You're such a great person! Just like a big sister!"

"You think so?" asked Fayte.

"Definitely." Aris nodded several times. "Hee-hee. If I ever had a big sister, I would want her to be just like you."

Fayte didn't know how she was supposed to feel about those words. All she knew was they made her body shiver unpleasantly. She liked this girl. It was hard not to, and yet… a part of her could not help but feel incredibly envious of her. Fayte could not deny that she was jealous of how devoted Adam was to Aris.

At that moment, the reason for her envy entered the living room and placed three plates of macaroni and cheese and three cups of ice water on the coffee table. He then sat between the two.

"Thank you for bringing out the food," Fayte said.

"Thank you for making the food," Adam replied.

"I'll just thank both of you. Now, can we hurry up and eat?" asked Aris. Her words elicited a smile from both of them.

Conversation was sparse as everyone ate. However, Adam eventually began talking about how he wanted Aris to begin her rehabilitation starting tomorrow. Since she had only just woken up, he first wanted her to get used to the changes in her body, but he eventually planned to have her begin doing basic stretches and calisthenic exercises to build up her strength.

"Once you've got a decent amount of strength built up, we can begin having you try to walk," Adam said. "It's going to be hard. You've been confined to a wheelchair for three years and your muscles have atrophied, but they fortunately haven't been ruined. They just need to be worked out. It might be a few years before you can walk normally."

"So long as I can begin walking, I don't think it matters how long it takes," Aris said. "Hee-hee. That said, I'd like to begin walking soon so we can have sex like you promised."

Fayte almost did a spit-take when Aris said those words. She could feel her cheeks burn. How could such an innocent girl be so blunt?!

"Aris," Adam said in warning.

"Hee-hee. Sorry."

Aris didn't look the least bit sorry, but that was surely Fayte's imagination. Yes, the mischievous grin—reminding her of a cat after it caught a canary—could only be a delusion, since there was no way such an innocent girl would talk like that. She coughed into her hand several times and used what she knew of keeping calm in stressful situations to rein in her blood flow.

"Let me know if you need any help," Fayte said. "I don't know much about rehabilitation, but I used to attend a calisthenics class meant for women, so I might be able to ask my former instructor if she knows any good exercises."

"That would be a great help," Adam said. "Thank you, Fayte."

"It's no trouble at all."

Fayte found it hard to look at Adam when he was staring at her like that. She felt a combination of embarrassment and pain. Her face had blood rushing straight to it, but her chest felt cold, like it had been dumped in ice water. It was a feeling she'd never experienced before. She didn't like it.

However, just as she looked away from Adam, she found Aris staring at her. There was an unusually perceptive look in the young woman's eyes that Fayte didn't recognize. All she knew was that it made her feel naked. She felt like that young girl was seeing her innermost thoughts.

"Why don't I get your system for Age of Gods now?" Fayte stood up.

"That would be great. Thank you, Fayte," Aris said.

Fayte tried to smile, but her legs were already carrying her out of the living room. Once she had entered her bedroom, Fayte shut the door and leaned against it, closing her eyes as she pressed a hand to her chest.

She could feel her heart throbbing in her ribcage. It was painful. Green envy and black self-loathing mixed together inside of her.

Aris's awakening was undoubtedly a good thing. Adam was happy... so incredibly happy. She had never seen him smile the way he did when he looked at Aris. She was happy for him. She really, truly was.

And yet...

And yet...

"Why can't he smile at me like that?" she asked herself, voice a hoarse whisper.

There was not a soul present who could answer her.

APOLOGIES

"It's been so long since we've taken a bath together." Aris sighed, her body submerged in warm water up to her modest chest. She was leaning against Adam, her back resting on his chest as he wrapped his arms around her. It was a comforting position for them both. Adam felt like it had been years since he was able to hug Aris like this.

"It has," Adam agreed. "It hasn't been that long since you were placed in cryosleep, but it feels like it's been forever."

Even before Aris contracted Mortems Disease, the two of them had been taking baths together—much to the disgruntlement of Aris's parents. The four weeks that Aris had spent in stasis made Adam keenly aware of how much they did together. Taking baths with her was just one of the things he had dearly missed.

"We shouldn't stay in much longer though," he added.

"Hmm… just a few more minutes," Aris murmured as she closed her eyes.

Adam shifted a little to adjust his erection so it wasn't pressing against Aris's back. It was hard for him to be in the bath with this girl.

"Hee-hee. Adam, do you feel like sticking that thing inside of me yet?"

And, of course, Aris did not fail to notice his growing arousal. She had always been aware of what she did to him and made it perfectly clear that she wouldn't mind in the least if he took her virginity. Were it not for the fact that her body was still weak, he would have turned her into an adult a long time ago.

"I do… but you know we can't."

"You mean 'yet'."

"Yes. Yet."

They remained in the bath for a few minutes longer, but Adam eventually had them get out. He dried Aris off with a towel, then dressed her and himself in simple pajamas. His merely consisted of gray sweatpants. He didn't wear a shirt because his companion said she liked feeling the warmth of his skin against her. Aris's pajamas were light pink shorts that stopped about halfway up her thighs and a button-up pink shirt. After dressing her, he carried her into the living room and let her watch TV as he combed and dried her hair with a portable dyer.

"In the latest news on Age of Gods, the hottest virtual reality game currently on the market, a list was recently released regarding the top five most powerful hidden classes currently available. Standing at the top of that list is, surprisingly, not Lin Akamine, the current number one gamer on the International Power Rankings. An unknown player named Adam, who was the first person to leave the Village of Beginnings, is currently the holder for the most powerful hidden class known as Seven Forms Spearman. What do you make of this, Josh?"

"Well, Drew, while Adam might seem like a new player on the gaming scene, I'm not actually sure that's true. There was a player who went by the name of Adam. I did some research and discovered that Adam was a well-known player several years ago who dominated every game he played and even defeated Lin Akamine in single combat during the International Gaming Championship."

"And you think they are the same person?"

"I think there is a good possibility that the Adam from Age of Gods and the Adam who defeated Lin Akamine in the past are one and the same."

The newscaster was a stunning woman whose beauty looked fake. It was like staring at a plastic model rather than a person. Adam thought it was all the makeup she wore, or maybe she'd gotten plastic surgery to make herself prettier. She didn't possess the natural beauty of Aris and Fayte. Her companion was a middle-aged man with a sharp beard, blue eyes, and the kind of rugged good looks expected of a male newscaster in this day and age.

"You've been busy, huh?" Aris said as she sat with only a small slouch. He was a little surprised she wasn't leaning to the side, which normally happened because her body didn't possess the strength for her to sit up on her own. Did that mean she was already growing stronger? That couldn't be it. Only two days had passed since she woke up. She hadn't even begun her rehabilitation yet.

"I've been playing Age of Gods for about twenty hours every day since you were put in that cryobed," Adam confessed. "It really helped me level up quickly and get all those accomplishments."

"I'll bet. Hee-hee. I knew my Adam was the best." Even if Adam couldn't see the smug smile on her face, he knew what sort of expression she was making. "Everyone thinks that Lin Akamine is the strongest player in the world, but that's only because you haven't been playing consistently. If you'd kept gaming back then, you would have been listed as the number one player in the entire world right now instead of her."

"I don't really care about being number one," Adam admitted. "So long as I'm your number one."

His words, spoken with complete sincerity, caused Aris's ears to turn red. She would have turned around, but he was still gently running a comb through her hair. Because her hair was fairly long, it took a while for him to completely comb it, though he honestly didn't mind. Sometimes he wished it took longer so he could enjoy this feeling of closeness and intimacy more.

As he continued combing her hair, Fayte stepped into the living room, saw them, and paused in the hallway. An uncertain look flashed across her face, but then she smiled and began walking backward.

Her smile looked fixed.

"It seems… I'm interrupting something," she said in a slow, measured voice. "Sorry. I was about to make dinner, but I'll leave you two alone."

"There's no need for that. I just finished combing her hair. Also, since you made lunch, let me make dinner," Adam said as he set the comb down and slid out from behind Aris.

With Adam no longer supporting her, Aris fell back onto the couch, though she was able to readjust herself so she didn't slide off the edge. Adam helped her keep steady. Even if she was stronger than he expected, she still wasn't very strong.

Fayte seemed hesitant about remaining in the living room. She glanced back and forth between Adam and Aris several times. In response, Aris smiled and patted the spot beside her.

"Don't worry about dinner. Sit with me. I'd like to talk to you some more."

The hesitation, while still present, was not enough to overcome Fayte's kind personality. She sat beside Aris and spoke to the girl as Adam made them a simple meal of pan-seared lemon salmon and a citrus salad. The salmon's taste was complemented by lemon dijon vinaigrette, which he made by mixing lemon juice with dijon mustard, parsley, salt, and pepper slowly whisked in olive oil. Aris and Fayte both complimented him on his food.

"Your cooking really is to die for," Aris moaned around a mouthful of salmon.

"Please don't talk with your mouthful," Adam muttered with a resigned smile.

"I have to agree with Aris. Your cooking is incredible. Even the Dairing Family's chefs are no match for your skills in the kitchen," Fayte added.

"Stop it. You're making me blush," Adam said with a smile.

Fayte rolled her eyes.

Adam, Aris, and Fayte stayed up until around 7:00 PM. Fayte was the first to retire, saying that all the excitement had made her exhausted. Adam did not think that was it, but he didn't have the heart to say anything, so he just bade her goodnight and carried Aris into their bedroom.

Once they were nestled under the covers, Aris, perhaps exhausted because of all the excitement, immediately fell asleep while snuggled against his chest. Adam tenderly stroked her hair and just watched her sleep for a while. However, he eventually closed his eyes and logged into Age of Gods. It had been more than a day now since he'd logged on, and whether he liked it or not, he did need to spend time playing.

When Adam reappeared, he was not inside of any city, but standing in the middle of a field. There was a sleeping fox yokai not too far from where he stood. There was also a very irate fairy who, upon noticing him, fluttered in front of his face and gave him a glare so harsh even the Spider Queen would have run away in fright.

"You… didn't I tell you just a little while ago that it's dangerous for us if you log off outside of a city?! What were you thinking?! Do you want us to die?!"

Even when irate, Titania was an incredible beauty. Her long hair was red and reminded him of fire, each strand catching the light and appearing like a flame; her eyes were like two emeralds that reflected a beautiful forest, and her gorgeously proportioned body was clad only in a green dress. She wasn't wearing any shoes, not even sandals. Her bare feet were tiny. That might have been due to how she was only one foot tall, but even objectively speaking, she had small feet. They reminded him of jade sculptures.

Had she been taller, Adam might have been stunned by her perfect beauty, far different from Fayte's mysterious beauty or Aris's innocent appeal.

"Ah…"

When Fayte had called him to deliver the news that Aris was awake, Adam had completely forgotten all about Kureha and Titania. Any sense of propriety he might have had flew right out the window whenever that girl was involved. Now that he was back in Age of Gods, Adam finally realized that he had made a grave mistake, which was why he didn't say anything as the woman berated him.

"Don't you realize that we're not like you? You otherworlders get resurrected when you die, but we do not. Death is permanent for us. Had we run into an enemy that neither of us could handle, Kureha and I would have died."

Kureha woke up at the sound of Fayte's shouting. The little fox unfurled herself from the ball she'd curled into and sat up. After releasing a wide yawn, the fox yokai shifted her gaze from Titania and suddenly discovered Adam. With an excited yip, she leaped to her feet and ran over to him, where she began rubbing her face and body against his legs.

Adam would normally have picked the little fox up and began petting her, but there was no way he could do that while trapped by Titania's fierce glare. She could have melted steel with those eyes.

"You're right," he said after Titania finished. He bowed his head toward her and expressed a heartfelt and genuine apology. "I'm sorry. I shouldn't have left you two like that."

Titania glared at him a bit more, but then she sighed. She felt silly being so angry at someone who was so contrite. Even though the anger she felt slowly evaporated under Adam's sincere gesture, she still crossed her arms and glared at him.

"Promise me that no matter what happens, you won't do something like that again," she said. "That's the only way I'll forgive you."

"I promise," Adam said with a fervent nod.

Once Titania accepted his apology, the three of them made their way into Solum. Adam had a huge inventory of items that he needed to get rid of. He was very fortunate that he'd mostly been hunting the same monsters. While the item pouch only allowed him to store up to ten items, he could store multiples of those items up to one hundred.

His current inventory was:

Item Pouch:
Item Name: Low-Grade Health Potion
Item Type: Potion
Grade: 1-Star
Quantity: 100
Description: A potion that restores +100 health points

Item Name: Low-grade Magic Potion
Item Type: Potion
Grade: 1-Star

Quantity: 100
Description: A potion that recovers +50 magic points

Item Name: Monster Bone
Item Type: Material
Grade: 1-Star
Use Requirements: Can only be used by crafter and
blacksmith classes
Quantity: 100
Description: A monster bone that can be refined and used
in the creation of armor and weapons
Abilities: Physical Defense+25

Item Name: Monster Core
Item Type: Material
Grade: 1-Star
Use Requirements: Can only be used by crafter and
blacksmith classes
Quantity: 100
Description: A monster core that can be used to enhance
armor and weapons
Abilities: Magical Defense+25

Item Name: Heavey Plate Armor
Item Type: Armor
Grade: 1-Star
Use Requirements: Anyone of the Warrior Class
Quantity: 1
Description: A heavy chestplate made from overlapping
steel plates
Abilities: Physical Defense+50; Speed-5

Item Name: Iron Ore
Item Type: Material
Grade: 1-Star

Quantity: 100
Description: Iron ingots that can be used by crafters and blacksmiths to create armor, weapons, and accessories

Item Name: Durability Ring
Item Type: Accessory
Grade: 1-Star
Quantity: 1
Use Requirements: Can be equipped by anyone.
Description: An enchanted ring that adds to a person's Defense and Magical Defense.
Abilities: Magic Defense+10; Defense+10

Item Name: Heavey Plate Leggins
Item Type: Armor
Grade: 1-Star
Quantity: 1
Use Requirements: Can be equipped by the Warrior Class.
Description: Heavy leggings made with overlapping steel plates
Abilities: Physical Defense+25

Item Name: Unknown Key
Item Type: Key
Grade: 4-Star
Quantity: 1
Use Requirements: Can be used by anyone
Description: This old but ornate key was discovered with the item [unknown map]
Abilities: None

Item Name: Unknown Map
Item Type: Map
Grade: 4-Star
Quantity: 1

**Use Requirements: Can be used by anyone
Description: This is a map that marks a location
somewhere on the Sun Continent**

Gold Coins: 920,000

He had a full inventory of mostly useless items. He wouldn't even call the health and magic potions useful anymore since he had way too much health and magic for these low-grade potions to help him.

However, as he looked at the inventory, Adam's eyes fell on the two items [unknown map] and [unknown key], both of which he had completely forgotten about after leaving the Village of Beginnings. Now that he was staring at them again, he could not help but be curious about them. Where did this map lead to? What did this key open? He wanted to know.

There were a lot of shops in Solum, and you could tell what they sold by the sign hanging overhead. Adam entered one that had the sign of a chair, which was the symbol used for the general stores in Age of Gods.

The shop was not large, but they did have a decent supply of items on stock. He wasn't sure if general stores like this had ever existed in ancient times, but the room only contained a few items hanging from the wall, which showed what they had in stock. When he looked at one of the items, a screen appeared that told him the name of the item and how much it cost. Because this was a general store, they sold a lot of different items, from armor and weapons to books and potions. They even had a [scan scroll] on sale.

"Hello! Welcome to Jessabelle's Emporium! What can I help you with?" A woman with a refreshing smile greeted him. She was standing behind the counter. Her face was painted entirely white with makeup, which made her look too gaudy for him to consider her attractive.

"I have some items I'd like to sell," Adam said.

"Okay! Just let me see what you'd like to sell, and I will estimate a price for you."

To show an NPC what he wanted to sell, he had to show her his inventory, but that was as easy as pressing a button. A screen appeared before him, telling him that Jessabelle wanted to see his inventory and asking if she had permission to look. He pressed yes.

"Hmm… which of these items are you selling?" asked Jessabelle.

"Everything except the [unknown map] and [unknown key]," Adam answered.

"All right! Let me calculate how much all this stuff totals up to really quick… but gosh, you certainly do have a lot of high-quality items. These monster bones and monster cores can fetch quite the high price. There are a lot of blacksmiths who would kill to get their hands on these."

Adam let the woman run her calculations. In the meantime, he searched through her inventory to see if she had anything he might want to buy. Most of the items she sold were pretty basic. She had [middle-grade health potions] that recovered +500 health points, [middle-grade magic potions] that recovered +250 magic points, and a few other potions like the [antidote] and [magic bell], which healed specific status effects like being poisoned or put to sleep. The [cure-all] healed every status ailment, but it was five times more expensive than potions that cured individual ailments. She also had [scan scrolls], but Adam didn't need those since he had Titania.

"Adam, it looks like she has an [item expansion stone]. You should buy this. It will be very useful to you," Titania suddenly said. She was sitting on his shoulder as always, while Kureha was perched on his head… also as always. He felt like his body was becoming a roost or a burrow. Fortunately, Titania and Kureha were both very light.

"[Item expansion stone]?"

Adam looked at the inventory list again. The woman had a lot of items, so he had to scroll back up before he found what Titania had spotted. It was called [item expansion stone] and had the effect of expanding an item pouch, allowing it to carry up to thirty items instead of just ten. It was currently listed at 150,000 gold coins, which was expensive, but he had 920,000 gold coins from all the enemies he had killed.

"I'm going to buy one hundred [middle-grade health potions] and another one hundred [middle-grade magic potions]. I'd also like to get this [item expansion stone]," Adam said to Jessabelle.

"Okay," Jessabelle said. "I'll just deduct the cost of the potions and the [item expansion stone] from how much I'll pay you for all of these items. After everything is subtracted, it looks like your total comes to 223,000 gold coins."

The gold coins transferred from Jessabelle's inventory to his own. Adam watched as his 920,000 gold coins became 1,143,000 gold coins. That was a lot of money considering most of what he'd been doing was killing monsters. He only earned this much because of how many monsters he killed and because he slew a lot of them solo. The [item expansion stone] was also transferred to Adam's inventory, but he used it right away, which expanded his item pouch's space, allowing him to carry thirty items instead of ten.

"Thank you for your business," Jessabelle said, waving at him.

Adam waved at the woman out of instinct as he left the store. However, his mind was no longer on the items he just sold and bought. It was on the [unknown map] and [unknown key] that he still had in his inventory.

✳✳✳

The morning after Aris and Adam went to see Dr. Sofocor found Adam in the kitchen, cooking breakfast. Aris was sitting on the couch. She was watching old cartoons. Fayte was not awake yet, but he imagined she would wake up soon. Aris was only awake because she woke up when he was getting out of bed and demanded he take her with him.

To celebrate Aris being completely cured of Mortems Disease, Adam decided to splurge. He'd gone to the nearest grocery store and bought the ingredients he needed to make cannoli-stuffed French toast. It only took eighteen minutes to make four servings worth.

Cannoli-stuffed French toast was a decadent dessert breakfast that consisted of creamy ricotta filling sandwiched between two slices of French bread. Mini chocolate chips were mixed in with the ricotta. The French toast sandwiches were cooked in sizzling butter to create a golden-brown crust, and then Adam had added powdered sugar on top.

The smell had already drifted into the living room and made Aris take several deep breaths. Adam could hear her stomach rumbling from the kitchen.

"What are you making?" she asked.

"Something delicious," Adam replied as he came out with three plates of food.

Aris saw what he set on the coffee table and began drooling. "Waaaaaaa... this looks so good!"

Adam wore a proud smile as he watched Aris drool over his breakfast; this was one of his greatest pleasures in life. He loved it when Aris enjoyed his food.

Just like Adam suspected, Fayte arrived not long after he sat down and began feeding Aris. She didn't hesitate to sit and begin eating, though he did notice that she chose to sit further away from him than she usually did. He felt like a distance had opened between them. He wanted to close it, but he sadly didn't know what he could do to make him and Fayte as close as they had been before Aris woke up.

"Mmmm."

While Fayte might have distanced herself from him, that didn't mean she appreciated his food any less, evidenced by the joyful moan she released after taking a bite of his food. Adam pretended not to notice.

"Hey, Adam? I can begin playing Age of Gods today, right?" asked Aris.

"You can," he allowed. "However, I am going to impose a few limitations on you. While virtual reality doesn't strain someone's mind like people used to think it did back when it was first introduced, your body is still weak and needs more rest than the average person's. You can only play four hours each day. Once your time is up, you and I will log off and I'll begin helping with your rehabilitation."

While Aris did pout at him a little for imposing a four-hour time limit, she didn't try to argue with him. She knew he was just doing this for her own good. He wanted her to be healthy and safe, and now that she didn't have Mortems Disease, he was even more unwilling to risk her health.

"Once your body recovers, we can increase the amount of time you play," Adam said. "But I first want your body to recover enough that you aren't exhausted by staying awake for several hours."

Mortems disease sapped a person's endurance. Their body's immune system was working overtime, which left them perpetually tired, making it so they had to take long naps throughout the day. Before Aris had gone into the cryobed, she'd only been able to remain awake for two hours tops.

"How long do you think that will take?" asked Aris.

"I'm not sure," Adam confessed. "A few months, probably, but it's not like I've ever done anything like this before. No one has ever been cured of Mortems Disease, and you had it for three whole years. That's not something you can just get over with a little bit of time."

"I guess not," Aris said with a frown.

While they were speaking, Fayte slowly ate her meal, savoring each bite. The look on her face was so mixed at this moment. She seemed incomparably happy now that her sweet tooth craving was being satisfied, but Adam knew from the scrunched up nose that something was bothering her.

"What's up, Fayte? You look like you just got sprayed in the face by a skunk," he said.

"Do I really look like that?" asked Fayte, blinking several times.

"A little. Yeah."

"Well… that is unpleasant." Fayte sighed, finished off the last bite of her cannoli stuffed French toast, and set the plate down. She observed Adam with her intelligent gaze, then slowly spoke. "It sounds to me like you will not be playing Age of Gods as much to help Aris with her rehabilitate."

"That is correct," Adam said. "Aris has always been my number one priority. Now that she doesn't have Mortems Disease, I need to help her muscles recover so she can live a normal life. However, you don't need to worry. I haven't forgotten my promise to you. I will help you win your win. Even if I spend a little less time inside Age of Gods during the day, I will make up for that by grinding my level during the night. Speaking of, do you know when the money exchange system will be implemented?"

The money exchange system was the system that allowed people to exchange in-game currency for real-world currency and visa versa. It had been introduced to virtual reality games one year after the WWIII armistice, and it was also what had propelled virtual reality to the top of everyone's priority list. There were many rich and powerful families who had risen to power specifically because of this system.

"I do not." Fayte shook her head. "There has been some speculation that it will be released within the next month, but that's all it is. Speculation. Mystique Incorporated has not announced any information regarding this subject."

Adam absorbed this knowledge as he took away the three plates, placed them in the dishwasher, and came back. As he sat down, Aris leaned into his side and he wrapped an arm around her shoulder like it was the most natural thing to do. He only paused when he saw the look on Fayte's face. At that moment, there was a conflicted expression in her eyes as she stared at them.

He suddenly felt guilty.

"I guess it doesn't matter when it's implemented." Adam tried to get back on track. "Right now, the most important thing is finding a hidden class for you. Once you have a hidden class, we can focus on grinding our levels. I think once everyone is at level 20, we should be able to take on the Spider Queen and the Undead King. They should give us a lot of money, and I bet they'll have some really amazing item drops too."

Fayte did not deny the truth in his words and instead nodded. She stood up after their conversation was over, said she was going to play Age of Gods, and then left the two of them alone.

"Is something wrong with Fayte?" asked Aris with a frown. "She seems sad…"

Adam didn't know what to tell her. He had recognized the look in her eyes, and he had a pretty good idea of what was bothering her, but there wasn't anything he could do. He could become Fayte's sword, act as her shield, and place her needs before his own, but there was one thing he couldn't do for her.

"I'm not sure. Anyway, before you log into Age of Gods, I have some advice I'd like to give you about how to play."

"Okay."

"Once you earn enough money, I want you to buy yourself a mask like mine, or a veil like the one Fayte uses. You should be able to find one at the general store. Just a simple one will do. I don't want anyone to figure out your identity. If they have your face on profile, it will be possible to look up information on you in the real world, which could lead to trouble."

While the armistice forbade people from fighting in the real world, that did not mean no one was willing to break those rules if they thought it would benefit them. This was especially true for rich and powerful families. They were not above using underhanded tactics like sending assassins after someone in the real world, blackmail, bribery, and other violence to get what they wanted.

Adam's very existence was the perfect example of this.

"I understand," Aris said with a serious look on her face.

"Good. Now, a lot of people tend to focus on grinding their levels, but that's not the most efficient way to go about playing this game. While you're in the Village of Beginning, I want you to instead focus on doing quests…"

Adam gave Aris all the information he could think of to help her succeed faster than anyone else. Aris listened to everything he said, nodding along and asking questions where appropriate. He made sure she knew his "in-game name" and told her about the player chat function. Only after he imparted all the knowledge he could think of did Adam carry her into their bedroom, lay her down, and then get in with her. He watched as she closed her eyes and logged into the game. The device around her neck lit up with a light pink color.

He watched her for a moment, making sure she was logged in, then made a cold expression as he grabbed the phone sitting on the nightstand and made a call.

"Master? Did you need something?"

The voice that spoke sounded middle-aged and firm. His voice reminded Adam of a butler character from an old TV show he used to watch with Aris, though he'd long since forgotten the name. He remembered it had been about a vigilante who fought crime in some made-up city.

"Astaroth... how many of you are still in the Village of Beginnings?"

"All of us except for Lilith, Master. We have not left, just as you requested."

"Good. Aris just logged on. I want all of you to be on the lookout for her. Tell everyone else to protect her if she ends up in their village."

"Of course, Master. Don't worry. We all know how important Miss Aris is to you. We will protect her with our lives."

"I'm counting on you."

Adam hung up the phone a moment later, set it on the nightstand, and silently contemplated his situation. Aris was going to be entering a Village of Beginnings. However, there were hundreds of thousands of such villages, which meant the chances of someone from his barely one hundred-strong group of individuals being in the same village as her was about 100,000 to 1. He could only pray that luck was with him.

Ever since the first virtual reality game experienced an in-game rape, it had become mandatory for virtual reality games to have an anti-rape feature. Any man or woman who tried to sexually assault another person was automatically ejected from the game, their account was deleted, an alert went out to the authorities, and the perpetrator was arrested and thrown in jail. While Adam was glad he didn't have to worry about someone assaulting Aris in-game, there were still other ways of harassing someone that didn't activate this feature. That was what worried him.

Settling down, Adam closed his eyes and logged into the game.

TREASURE HUNT

As had become customary, Adam, Fayte, Lilith, Susan, Titania, and Kureha were sitting at a table in the outdoor food court. They weren't the only ones. More players had arrived in Solum by now, at least several thousand, and so many of the tables were occupied. Some were eating, some were talking, and some were planning their next quest like Adam's party was.

Adam eyed the group immediately to their right for a moment. It was a group of all women. They had a good party combination, with one Mage, one Assassin, two frontline fighters, an Archer, and a Priest. One thing Adam noticed was the front-liners had different classes. One was listed as a Magic Swordsman, while the other was a Monk.

They must have changed their class by speaking to a trainer.

"You want to go on a treasure hunt?" asked Fayte, blinking several times. He was sure she was also frowning, but he couldn't see past her veil.

"That's right." Adam reached into his item pouch and pulled out the [unknown scroll], setting it on the table as he unfurled it for the others to see. "I forgot about this until just recently, but I remembered it when I was selling some of the item drops I had. I'm not really sure where it leads."

"Are you sure going on this treasure hunt is a good idea?" pressed Fayte. "I do not mean to doubt you, but it is possible we'll run into a lot of danger. You already admitted you don't know where this leads. What if the enemies there have an even higher level than the ones we fought at Suncrest Mountain?"

Adam had already thought about that and had the perfect answer. "If the area where this map is pointing to has enemies that are too strong for us to beat, we'll just retreat. I only thought it was a good idea because we don't have any leads for another hidden class. However, if this does lead to treasure, then I'm sure it will be worth a lot even if it doesn't have a hidden class, and if it's worth a lot…"

"Then it might help me earn some of the money I need to win my bet." Fayte saw where he was going and nodded along. She looked back down at the scroll.

"So you don't know where this map leads?" asked Susan, also looking curiously at the map.

Adam shook his head, but Titania, who had been eating up until this point, suddenly fluttered over to the map and landed on it. She peered at the map with narrowed eyes. No one said anything as they watched her. Kureha was the only one not paying attention… well, she was the second one. Lilith was paying more attention to Kureha than Titania, though Adam didn't doubt the woman was still aware of everything happening around them.

"I believe I know where this is," Titania said at last.

"You do?" asked Adam.

Titania nodded. "It was around… four thousand years ago, I believe. A thousand years after the war against the Demon Lord and his thirteen Lords of Chaos, a powerful mage founded an academy that taught magic. Some of the best and brightest minds of the time went there to learn, and it eventually became renowned for producing unparalleled geniuses when it came to magic. Unfortunately, the greed of men is vast and far-reaching."

"What happened?" asked Susan, her gaze hooked on Titania. She seemed to be the most interested in what the fairy was saying. Her eyes were bright and vibrant like a child being told fantastical bedtime stories by her parents.

"The academy was built in the center of three neighboring countries," Titania explained. "These countries were, at the time, the three most powerful countries on the Sun Continent. They had always been in something of a stalemate. No country could gain more power than the other. However, all sides wished to become stronger than their neighbors." Titania walked along the map, looking at it as though she was remembering something from the past. "I do not know who struck the first blow, but the three countries eventually tried to absorb the magic academy into their kingdoms. When the academy refused, all three countries attacked and burned the academy down, then began warring with each other over the remains. That is actually how the original three great powers of the Sun Continent were destroyed and the current Sun Kingdom that covers the whole continent formed."

While Susan looked like she was embroiled in the tale, Fayte merely cupped her chin and seemed to be pondering something.

"Do you remember what those kingdoms were called?" asked Susan.

Titania shook her head. "I'm afraid I do not. Those kingdoms were destroyed around the time I had just reached maturity. While we fairies had not yet isolated ourselves from the outside world, we still did not leave our home very often. I only heard about all this after it happened because a few humans passing through our village were refugees from those kingdoms. One of them had a map similar to this one. I recognize some of the landmarks on it."

"Oh…" Susan's shoulders slumped as though disappointed.

They discussed the matter a bit more and eventually decided to travel to this magic academy. Since it was a magic academy, Adam was hoping they would have a [hidden class scroll] for Fayte, who they still needed to upgrade with a new class. The Mage class was not very good, and none of the classes she could upgrade to by speaking with a trainer were good enough either—not in his mind.

To prepare for the journey, Adam took Fayte, Susan, Lilith, Titania, and Kureha to several stores. They bought [middle-grade health potions] and [middle-grade magic potions]—one hundred of each for everybody. They also bought a few scrolls that released spells like the [fireball scroll], and there was even a [tent scroll].

"That [tent scroll] is useful if you are going on a long journey," an older man called Justice said. "While there are a lot of small towns and villages spread across the Sun Continent, there are also large stretches of land with nothing but monsters. This [tent scroll] will allow you to set up a tent, which monsters cannot enter. It basically keeps you safe from any monster, and it lasts a full twenty-four hours. Just be warned: you can't set up a [tent] if there are already monsters in the area, so you'll need to clear the monsters out first."

The old man, Justice, was the owner of the equipment store, which sold all kinds of supplies necessary for travel. Adam was shocked to discover they not only sold potions and scrolls, but they also sold cookware.

Having already experienced cooking in this game, Adam knew that food had actual flavor. Most video games never bothered giving food flavor, or rather, none of the virtual reality games he had played until now had the processing ability to affect the senses known as taste and smell. Food might have a use in other games, but it was usually to replace health potions.

Of course, in-game food could not replace food in the real world. Even if they ate in Age of Gods, they would still have to log off and eat a real meal to maintain their bodies' functions.

"We should buy several of these," Fayte suggested. "They will be useful for us, especially for you two."

Adam knew she was talking to Titania and Kureha. Whenever he logged off, those two would remain where he left them. This meant they were vulnerable. If a monster or even a player with a blood-thirsty streak came by, they could easily be killed, especially since their levels were still low.

"I'll take ten [tent scrolls]," Adam said.

"Righto. With the [tent scrolls] added, your total will come to 60,000 gold coins."

Adam didn't hesitate to pay for the supplies, watching as the money in his inventory dropped. It wasn't much. Adam had a lot of gold because he constantly sold the item drops he got from monsters. Even after spending 60,000 gold coins, he still had 1,083,000 left.

After buying their supplies, they made their way to the stables and rented four horses. Because they wanted to move fast, they rented [midnight stallions], which had a speed of +1,000, which was the equivalent of a car with a maximum speed of 245 miles per hour.

Titania and Kureha both made themselves comfortable on him. The fairy sat upon his shoulder and the fox yokai turned his head into a burrow. A little ways off, Lilith's eyes burned into the back of his head. Adam still didn't know if she was jealous of him for having Kureha using his head as a pillow, or his two companions for being so close to him. Given what happened between them several nights ago, he wasn't sure he wanted to know.

According to Titania, the journey to the magic academy would take several days, provided they didn't run into any enemies. Adam was certain it would take them even longer. They couldn't focus solely on travel. Without constantly leveling up, without grinding for experience points, they would eventually fall behind everyone else's levels.

Speaking of...

"Fayte, do you know what the average level is right now?" Adam asked as they traveled across a vast plain via horseback.

"At the moment, the average level is still 10, though some people have recently broken into level 11," Fayte answered. "Lin Akamine is at level 12. I also heard the Spear God reached level 12 two days ago. They are the only ones so far."

"They're probably grinding in high-level killing fields," Adam muttered. "Or maybe they're going the more dangerous route and tackling dungeons solo."

There were always a few abnormal players who could do what many considered impossible, like doing solo raids on dungeons or defeating boss-level enemies by themselves. Adam was one such person. It was especially easy for someone like Adam, who was an experienced combatant in real life, to defeat high-level opponents in Age of Gods thanks to the additional realism. Adam was certain he would never be able to do what he did in this game if not for the fact that his virtual body moved and felt exactly like his real one.

Adam was currently at level 16. That was the highest level a player possessed in the game right now. Fayte, Susan, and Lilith were all at level 14.

The reason their levels were so high was because of the high-level killing fields they went to. The area around the Sunset Mountain Range was filled with enemies that were all between levels 30 and 40. Thanks to the unique skills possessed by Titania and Adam, they had been able to kill a number of high-level enemies, which earned them a lot more experience points than enemies closer to their levels.

The enemies they ran into on the road were between levels 20 and 25, which was still pretty high-level, but they could not compare to enemies like the ones they had fought against when they were helping Lilith become a Demon Knight Assassin.

There were four enemies that they ran into on their travels: level 20 [demon bear], level 22 [slime], level 24 [giant mantis], and the level 25 [storm wolf].

"Fayte, Susan, Titania, and Kureha! Stay back and attack from a distance. Lilith, let me pull its agro, and then attack while it's distracted!" Adam shouted as their group prepared to once again battle a [storm wolf]. However, the one they were fighting right now was not a regular [storm wolf].

The creature before them stood on four thick legs that were all muscle. Not an ounce of fat could be seen beneath that bristling fur. Sharp claws jutted from its paws and scratched against the ground, creating four gouges in the soil. This particular [storm wolf] had midnight blue fur covering every inch of its body except for the belly, which was coated in a layer of soft white fur. Odd white stripes within the fur reminded Adam of lightning bolts. With a massive horn jutting from its head, a row of sharp fangs, and vibrant blue eyes, the snarling creature before them was something that would have caused children nightmares.

Everyone listened to Adam's words. Fayte, Susan, and Kureha moved backward, while Titania flew into the air. The first thing Titania did was cast [scan] on the [storm wolf].

Name: Storm Wolf

Description: Storm wolves are evolved versions of the fire wolf. They are much stronger than dire wolves and have powers over lightning.
Class: 1-Star
Level: 25
Health: 150,000/150,000
MP: 6,000/6,000
Strength: +500
Constitution: +800
Dexterity: +500
Intelligence: +500
Speed: +500

Skills:
Skill Name: Slash
Description: The storm wolf attacks with its powerful claws
Damage = Strength + Speed
MP Cost: 40
Cooldown Time: 0 Seconds

Skill Name: Storm Flash
Description: Storm wolves can instantly teleport to anywhere within one hundred feet of their current location
MP Cost: 1,500
Cooldown Time: 30 seconds

Skill Name: Thunderstorm
Description: The storm wolf calls down a thunderstorm from overhead and damages every enemy within fifty feet of its target
MP Cost: 200
Cooldown Time: 10 seconds

Skill Name: Thunderbolt
Description: Fires a compressed bolt of lightning from its horn
Has a 10% chance of causing stun

MP Cost: 100
Cooldown Time: 15 seconds

It was a fairly powerful enemy with stats that could one-shot any player outside of him right now. That was why Adam was drawing all of its agro. He wanted to make sure the others didn't get hit by this beast.

-3,937!

A single [slash] from Adam brought the amount of health their enemy had down by almost four thousand points. Because his attack was so powerful, this also had the effect of drawing the [storm wolf's] agro, which meant it was now focused solely on him.

Titania did not sing [Song of Vigor] like she usually did, but instead began singing the steady and daunting [Song of Valor], which increased everybody's physical and magical defense by 300%. She did this was because Adam had told her not to increase their attack power. Adam wanted everyone to gain experience fighting as a unit. That couldn't happen if he kept killing their enemies in a few attacks.

-850!

Susan's [Fairy Shot] struck the [storm wolf] in the right flank. The arrow became deeply embedded into its flesh. This did not seem to bother the monster as it continued attacking Adam, who wove through the numerous claw strikes using deft footwork. He ducked underneath one massive paw, leaped over another, and then skipped back several yards to put some distance between him and his enemy. The [storm wolf] released a frustrated howl as it charged at him.

-390!

Among everyone, Fayte was still the weakest, but that was not because of her level. It was because of her class. Susan had even worse equipment than her, but she also possessed the Fairy Archer Class, which gave the girl an incredible boost every time she leveled up. Once she gained a few more levels, her current stats would no longer be able to compare to her stats now.

-4,245; MISS; MISS; MISS!

Adam frowned as three of his attacks missed, but he realized that was the difference between their stats. His Hit-Rate was at 50%, but that [storm wolf] had a high Dexterity, meaning it probably had a high Dodge-Rate.

-2,772!

While Adam was avoiding the enemy's claws, Kureha launched a [Thunder Bolt] at the [storm wolf]. Even though its name was [storm wolf], that didn't seem to give it a lightning immunity, which dealt a shocking amount of damage. The [storm wolf] howled in pain before, shifting its gaze from Adam, it glared at Kureha with hatred in its eyes.

And then it vanished with a loud crackle.

Adam was shocked at first, but he realized this was its [Storm Flash] ability at work. He spun around and shouted at the group behind him.

"Fayte, Susan, Kureha! Move!"

His words of warning came just in time. They moved barely a second to move before the [storm wolf] appeared within their midst and lashed out with a point-blank [Thunder Bolt] that slammed into the ground, splitting the earth apart and leaving a crater in its wake. The girls had fortunately dodged in time, but now they had a new problem. The [storm wolf] was in the trio's midst.

With a loud howl, the [storm wolf] raised its head to the sky. Adam did not know what it was doing, but Titania did.

"It's about to use [Thunderstorm]!" she shouted, ceasing her song.

"Keep singing! Don't stop!" Adam shouted back.

Titania seemed to realize that the best thing she could do right now was to bolster everyone's magical defense. She began singing again as Adam raced toward the [storm wolf], but he could tell from how fast the storm clouds were gathering that he would not make it in time.

-17,440!

At that moment, Lilith suddenly appeared on the enemy's back and used [throat slit] to deal a massive amount of damage. Her attack did not end there, however. After her attack ended, she leaped into the air, and then came back down and used [Pinpoint Strike], attacking the enemy's vital areas.

-4,578!

The attack disrupted the [storm wolf's] attempt at using [Thunderstorm]. It staggered back and stared at her as though it couldn't comprehend what had just happened. Adam used its distracted state to reach the creature and activated [Dance of the Sakura Blossoms]. He struck the enemy with a powerful thrust of his spear, then danced around the creature, his feet creating patterns in the grass as he attacked from the left, the back, the right, and the front. Had anyone been watching from above, they would have noticed how his movements had drawn a pattern similar to a sakura blossom in full bloom.

-2,625; -7,875; -23,625; 70,875; 212,625!

With all five attacks hitting, Adam was able to demolish its health. The [storm wolf] unleashed a frightening howl, which turned into a whimper halfway through before it slumped to the ground, never to get back up.

Ding!

[Congratulations! You have killed the 1-Star enemy [storm wolf]! [Storm wolf] has dropped the items [Storm Necklace], [Storm Wolf Pelt], [Thunder Staff], and 6,000 gold coins. +20,000 experience points! +5,000 ability points!]

Adam checked his stats after defeating the [storm wolf] and saw this his experience points hadn't risen much compared to what he needed. He only had +20,682 experience points. He needed +9,800,000 to reach the next level.

Truly ridiculous.

He also checked out the new items he got from the drop to see if there was anything useful.

Item Name: Storm Necklace
Item Type: Accessory
Grade: 1-Star
Use Requirements: None
Description: A necklace that was enchanted to contain the power of storms.
Abilities: Adds 50% lightning damage to all attacks; 50% lightning resistance

Item Name: Storm Wolf Pelt
Item Type: Material
Grade: 1-Star
Use Requirements: Must have the Craftsmen secondary class
Description: This pelt is very soft. It can be used in the creation of clothing. Offers protection against lightning.
Abilities: 40% lightning resistance

Item Name: Thunder Staff
Item Type: Weapon
Grade: 1-Star
Use Requirements: Can only be used by a Mage level 10 and above
Description: A staff that contains the power of lightning.
Abilities: Magic Attack+40; adds 10% lightning damage to all attack spells

None of the items were bad, but it wasn't what he would call great either. He would sell them when they reached Solum after their treasure-hunting mission was over.

"I think this is a good place to stop for the day," Adam said as everyone regrouped. "We've been traveling for a good four or five hours, so we should log off to get some food and maybe rest a bit. I also have to help Aris with her rehabilitation."

"I think that's a good idea," Susan agreed. "My… my dad doesn't like it when I play video games for too long, and I still have to do my studies for school."

"Then let's log off now and reconvene at a later time," Fayte said.

Everyone else agreed to log off, so Adam used one of the [tent scrolls] he had bought, which created a large brown tent in the middle of the field they had been riding through. It was as simple as unrolling the scroll and setting it on the ground. The scroll flashed, disappeared, and a massive tent took its place. The horses were still a little ways off. When they found the [storm wolf], they had tied the horses to a tree so they wouldn't run away.

They all piled into the tent, which was large enough for about ten people. Adam wondered if this size was the standard, or if the size was created based on the number of members a party had. It didn't have much in the way of amenities. There were only a few sleeping bags, but since they were only using this to protect Titania and Kureha while they were logged off, the tent did not need much.

"See you tomorrow," Adam said to Titania and Kureha.

"Yes, yes." Titania waved him off. "Go ahead and leave us here. Kureha and I shall be just fine on our own."

Everyone knew Titania hated it when they logged off or "traveled back to their world" as she so often put it, but it wasn't like they could help that. This world was just a game. Everything within it was virtual, including the food, and that meant they couldn't acquire sustenance unless they logged off.

As Adam logged off, the first thing he realized was that he felt incomparably warm. This was a feeling he had not experienced in a very long time, but he recognized the warmth being emitted by the soft body next to him.

The second thing he realized was that someone was running their hands through his hair.

Adam opened his eyes and found himself gazing into the beautiful blue eyes of Aris. She was lying on her side, but she had propped her head on her right hand and was using her other hand to run her fingers through his hair. It felt so good that he almost closed his eyes again. Only after a moment did he realize something.

"Good morning," Aris said before she leaned down and kissed him on the mouth. Adam was shocked for a moment, but after the initial jolt from her kiss wore off, he was more than happy to reciprocate the gesture. He lost himself in exploring her warm, pliant lips. It was almost to the point where he'd forgotten his initial shock over learning about what she'd been doing.

"You can move?" he asked, pulling back to look at her.

Aris's smile widened. She looked almost smug. "Are you surprised? I'm not sure why, but I feel a lot stronger now than I did before entering the game."

"Hmm… maybe that's a sign that your body is recovering…"

Adam was a bit surprised since she hadn't even begun her rehabilitation yet. When she had Mortems Disease, moving, even a little, took a monumental amount of effort. Her muscles had atrophied so badly that they were basically gone. That shouldn't have changed just because she was cured. She shouldn't be capable of holding herself up like that.

"Maybe. Anyway, Adam, I have something important to tell you."

"What is it?"

"I'm really hungry."

At that moment, Aris's stomach erupted with a loud gurgle that made the young woman look at him with a very expectant expression. It all but said, "Feed me."

Adam grinned. "Then why don't I make lunch?"

While Aris was strong enough to sit up on her own, she still wasn't able to walk on her own, so Adam carried her into the living room. Fayte was already there. She was in the process of tying an apron over her turtleneck sweater, but Adam called out to her before she could finish.

"Let me make lunch," he said.

Fayte seemed hesitant for a moment, but then she shook her head and smiled, removing the apron and hanging it back up.

"If you insist on making lunch, then I won't stop you."

"Thanks."

After setting Aris on the couch, Adam wandered into the kitchen and got started on making lunch. Fayte had recently stocked up on their supplies, so she had everything he needed to make a pasta salad with chopped chicken. Unlike Fayte, he did not wear an apron.

As he began preparing the food, Adam listened to the two women as they talked.

"You started playing Age of Gods this morning, right? What level are you at right now?"

"Hee-hee. I'm at level 4."

"Level 4? Already? I know it's easier to level up quickly near the beginning, but with so many players, it should be hard to gain enough experience points to level up. Even I needed two days to reach level 4."

"That's only if you grind levels like most people. I did what Adam told me to do and asked around for quests. So far I've completed the quests [Save Marianne's Daughter], [Defeat the Goblins], and [Protect Farmer John's Orchids]. All of them gave me a good amount of experience points. Plus I gain experience points for defeating the enemies I kill in each quest too."

"Ah. Yes, I can see how that would let you level up more quickly. After Adam told me about how he leveled up so fast, I felt foolish for grinding so much. I did a few quests as well, but my level was already around level 6 by the time I began. Oh. That's right. What class did you choose?"

"I chose the Warrior Class!"

Adam finished preparing the food just as Aris said that. He arched an eyebrow at the girl as he set the bowl of pasta salad on the coffee table, followed by the plates, forks, and Parmesan cheese. Aris and Fayte both gazed at the pasta salad like it would run away if they didn't devour it this instant. Their eyes reminded him of starving wolves seeing their first meal after months of fasting.

"Why did you choose the Warrior Class?" asked Adam.

"You thought I'd be a Priest, didn't you?" Aris asked. When Adam blushed, she giggled. "Hee-hee. I did think about choosing the Priest Class because it would let me use buffs and healing spells. If I was a priest, I could definitely help you out. But then I thought about what I really wanted, and it wasn't supporting you from the back. I want to be right in front, standing side by side with you as we confront danger and go on adventures together. The idea of watching your back as you fight didn't appeal to me."

Now that he heard her reasoning, he couldn't help but feel like her choosing the Warrior Class made more sense than choosing to be a Priest. As someone who had been crippled for so many years, of course she would want to have one of the most active roles in the game. As a Warrior, she could join him at the front lines, battling against their enemies side by side. That sounded more like something Aris, an active woman who had been confined to a wheelchair for three years, would want. If their positions had been reversed, he'd want the same thing.

"In that case, keep working hard to reach level 10, so you can leave the Village of Beginnings and join us," Adam said.

"I will!" Aris nodded with enthusiasm.

"Also, we're going to begin your rehabilitation today. We'll start with simple stretches right now to get the blood circulating to your limbs."

"Okay!"

Once lunch was finished, Fayte washed the dishes while Adam cleared some space on the floor for Aris so they could begin doing simple stretches that would allow her damaged muscles and tissue to heal. They didn't log into Age of Gods for the rest of the day.

DERELICT MAGIC ACAD-EMY

It took a lot longer to reach the magic academy on the treasure map than Adam would have thought possible. Four days, in fact. It took exactly four days to reach the academy, and this was not in-game days like some video games where the time in the game was faster than the time outside of the game. Four days in this game meant four days in real life.

They probably could have gotten there sooner, but Adam and Fayte made it a point to have everyone grind their levels. Lin Akamine had already reached level 13 and many of the higher level members of guilds like Daggerfall Dynasty and the Pleonexia

Alliance had reached level 12. If they wanted to keep their edge over the larger guilds, they needed to maintain a higher level.

Adam was now level 17. His level was still the highest so far, but that was because he spent more time in the game than anyone else. He required very little time to sleep. By sleeping for only two hours, he could spend at least twelve to fourteen hours playing the game, even after cutting back on his playing time thanks to how he spent time with Aris outside Age of Gods. His time was currently divided between grinding his levels on his own, partying with Fayte and the others, and helping with Aris's rehabilitation.

Not only had he leveled up, but his spear had also leveled up. Now at level 11, the [Goddess of Creation Spear] added a +110 bonus to both his Strength and Physical Attack. This boost was insane and meant his current abilities were easily among the best in the game. He didn't think there was anything outside of a level 90 boss like the [Spider Queen] who could cause him trouble.

Aris had already reached level 9, and he suspected she would reach level 10 either sometime today or tomorrow. He was really surprised. She would have reached level 10 long before now, but Adam had her on a strict four hours of gameplay a day regiment to keep her from exhausting herself. Given how high her level was, anyone else would have assumed she was secretly spending more time in the game, but Adam knew Aris. She would not go against him, especially when he was only doing so because he was looking out for her safety.

Fayte, Susan, and Lilith were all on the cusp of reaching level 15. They only needed one hundred thousand more experience points.

They probably would have acquired the needed experience points if they played eight extra hours like Adam did every night, but he was holding off on having them grind to reach that level. He wanted Fayte to have a good class that would significantly increase her stats before she leveled too much.

He also didn't think they could play fourteen hours a day like he did.

Kureha and Titania had also reached level 17 like him, but thanks to the insurmountable number of experience points needed, neither of them had been able to get even close to reaching level 18. While reaching the next level was indeed going to be difficult, Adam was not too worried. At present, there wasn't a single player who could threaten them.

"Is that the magic academy?" asked Susan.

Titania flew off Adam's shoulder and created a visor out of her hand to protect her eyes from the sun as she squinted into the distance. After a moment, she lowered her hand and nodded.

"That should be it," she said. "I have never seen the magic academy myself, but I remember reading that it was located at this spot. It can't be anything else."

Their group was currently standing on a bluff overlooking a city with a large tower in the center. The magic academy was several miles out and below the cliff they were standing by. From a distance, the academy looked like a massive tower so tall it could pierce the sky. Despite being located beneath them, the tower was taller than the bluff and extended into the clouds—black storm clouds that surrounded the tower and made it look dark and ominous. Adam had to admit, it was odd seeing a single spot with dark clouds swirling around it while there wasn't a cloud in the sky anywhere else.

"Those storm clouds look... ominous," Fayte murmured, saying the same thing he was thinking.

"Those storm clouds are formed by the residual magic and negative emotions the mages at this academy must have felt at the time of their deaths," Titania explained. "When the three kingdoms attacked, they attacked from all sides and slaughtered their way through the academy. I was told that at the very last moment, the academy's dean used her own life as a catalyst to cast a curse on the kingdoms, which killed the environment to prevent crops from growing. This is why the area around here is so desolate."

Adam studied the tower from this distance, his eyes narrowed as he used his unique abilities to enhance his eyesight. For whatever reason, it was easier to channel his energy in this game than it was in real life, which shocked him more than he cared to admit. Whoever heard of being able to use esper powers in a game?

Circling the tower near those black clouds were several massive birds. They didn't look like much from a distance, but when he zoomed in with his enhanced vision, he saw that each bird was pitch-black, and seemed to have evil red eyes and a wingspan of at least two dozen feet. They were huge birds of prey.

"We arrived pretty early today so there's still plenty of time," Adam said. "Let's head down there and explore the area around the tower."

"That's a good idea," Fayte said.

Their horses were stationed only a few yards from the bluff. Adam, Fayte, Lilith, and Susan each mounted their own horse, while Titania and Kureha perched themselves in their usual places on Adam's shoulder and head respectively. Like that, the group began looking for a way down the bluff.

***

-300; -300; -300; -300; -300; -600!

Aris wore a bright, big smile as she danced around the [giant minotaur], which was a massive mountain of muscle that had the head of a bull and the body of a man. The creature was wielding an axe in one hand and a sword in the other. Both axe and sword were nearly as big as adult humans. However, the ease at which this enemy swung those two weapons was enough to shock the pair of players standing naught fifty yards from where the battle was taking place.

Astaroth and Abaddon had been lucky enough to wind up in the same Village of Beginnings as Aris. As per the instructions of their master, they had been following the young woman, secretly protecting her. Any player stupid enough to get close with evil intentions was killed without mercy. Fortunately, not many players had bothered Aris after she bought a veil, and even fewer bothered her when she began taking quests.

To be honest, these two men were beginning to question why they were even protecting her. This woman could obviously take care of herself.

-600; -600; -300; -300; -300!

Aris was constantly dancing around the level 25 lord class [giant minotaur]. Asteroth did not know how much health it had, but with the amount of damage Aris was dealing, it wouldn't be long before the enemy's health was reduced to zero.

Asteroth felt a sense of awe as he watched the young woman dance along the ground with unparalleled grace, avoiding the swings of the [giant minotaur] like it was moving in slow motion. Even more than her grace, however, was the way she ruthlessly whittled away its health even as it continued to attack her with reckless and enraged swings. As the amount of health it lost dropped lower and lower, the [giant minotaur] became more and more desperate. Its swings became faster and more vicious, but that only made it easier for Aris to dodge.

Finally, with a cry of despair, the [giant minotaur] dropped onto its back.

"I did it! I defeated the [giant minotaur], and I reached level 10! Hee-hee! Wait til Adam hears about this! I'm gonna shock the pants off him!"

Aris jumped up and down, cheering excitedly and throwing her hands into the air. Asteroth glanced bemusedly at Abaddon, who looked like he didn't know what to think either. They were both experienced gamers. However, from the moment they began watching this girl in secret to now, they had consistently been shocked by the things she had done.

"Oh?" Aris's suddenly questioning tone made them look at her again. She was flipping through a popup screen they couldn't see, muttering to herself. "It looks like I have some new items, but… hmm… they all seem pretty useless. I guess that means I can just sell them."

With a shrug, the girl continued walking. Asteroth and Abaddon silently followed her.

The area they were walking through looked like an underground passage. It was dark and gloomy. The air smelled of dust. Asteroth was reminded of a story he'd once read about a young man who traveled into an underground labyrinth to rescue a queen. At least, he thought that was how the story went. It was hard to remember anything from before his time in Eden.

Aris did not run into any more monsters and eventually reached the end of the labyrinth, which only contained a small pedestal with a treasure chest sitting on it. Where experienced gamers like Asteroth and Abaddon would have been cautious, this young girl threw caution to the wind. They wanted to yell at her for being so naive. Did she not know that any treasure chest might be a [mimic]?!

However, the treasure chest was not a [mimic] and contained a pair of short swords, clothing that looked like a belly dancer's outfit, and a scroll. Aris took each item from the chest and inspected them. While the clothing and weapons went into her inventory, she kept the scroll in her hands and studied it.

"Blade Dancer Class?" she questioned the thin air. "I wonder what this is?"

***

The area surrounding the magic academy was a city—a completely ruined city that had been abandoned four thousand ago, but a city nonetheless. It must have been where the people who didn't attend the academy but helped run the place lived. He imagined tourists also stayed inside of the city.

Adam could not tell what kind of architectural style had been used in the construction of these buildings. They were all burned out. Many of them were missing walls and roofs, and a few were just piles of rubble. Even though the battle that had destroyed this place happened over four thousand years ago, the battle scoring from spells and weapons still existed. No one had ever come back to reclaim this place.

"This city reminds me a little of the towns and cities that were abandoned after World War III," Fayte said in a soft voice.

"I didn't know you traveled to places like that," said Adam.

"I have only passed through them," Fayte admitted. "Though I used to think it would be interesting if I could stay the night in one. I tried to convince Su to spend a night in a ghost town with me, but she refused."

"S-sorry," Susan mumbled an apology.

Fayte rubbed Susan's head like an affectionate older sister. "There's nothing to be sorry for. If anything, I should be sorry for trying to convince you when I know you hate anything spooky."

"You two should try to be quieter," Titania muttered in a whisper. "There is no telling what kind of monsters lurk in this place."

Her words caused Fayte and Susan to go silent, and the group continued walking down the abandoned street.

Their formation was pretty standard. Adam once again took point, Lilith was taking up the rear, and Fayte, Susan, Titania, and Kureha were in the center.

The sound of their footsteps echoed ominously loud as they meandered through the abandoned streets, though maybe that was because they were the only people present. That was how it felt to him at least. Even Adam, who kept his senses extended in all directions, could not sense anything.

"It doesn't look like there are any enemies," Adam whispered.

"No. There are definitely enemies nearby," Titania corrected him.

Adam wanted to ask her what she meant by that, but a howl echoed around them seconds later. A chill suddenly ran down his spine. Of course. Not all enemies were human. In fact, most of them were monsters.

"Everyone, be on guard!"

His orders weren't needed. Everyone was already closing ranks. Adam and Lilith moved in close to Fayte, Susan, Kureha, and Titania. Adam did not activate [Blood Sacrifice] yet, and Titania was still waiting to see what kind of enemy they were facing before she decided on a song to sing.

Just as Adam was about to suggest they keep moving, several dozen figures rushed out from around the corner of a ruined building. These creatures raced toward them on four powerful legs. Their bodies were covered in sleek black fur the color of midnight. Only their white bellies and areas around their eyes were a different color. Adam recognized them for what they were.

[Dire wolves].

While not as powerful as the [storm wolf] they had fought before, [dire wolves] were still a serious threat, especially in large numbers like this. It looked like they were part of a pack. He didn't know what level they were at since Titania had not cast [scan], but he imagined it would be much higher than theirs. There were also more than two dozen of them, which meant there were far too many for their group to handle.

"I… uh… I think we should run," Fayte said.

"I second that," Lilith agreed.

"Um… how can we?" asked Susan. "We're trapped."

Adam quickly considered the situation as he looked at the ring of [dire wolves] surrounding them. This encirclement was impressive. It looked like these [dire wolves] were somewhat intelligent. Not only were there a lot of them circling his party, but there was another [dire wolf] further away. It was bigger than the others and had glowing yellow eyes. It stood on the roof of a building that hadn't collapsed and stared down at them with a triumphant snarl on its face.

That one must have been the pack leader.

"Titania, use [Song of Vigor] to increase my attack power please," Adam began in a calm, collected voice. "I'll carve a path for us. Once I do, I want all of you to run through that path. Don't worry about anything else. Just run."

Nobody said anything, but Titania started singing, and Adam suddenly felt like he could take on the entire world. The [Song of Vigor] did exactly what it sounded like, invigorating him. Taking a deep breath, he also activated [Blood Sacrifice] to further increase his attack power, then counted down from three, two, and one.

Pushing off the ground with his toes, Adam burst forward at a speed far quicker than his in-game stats seemed to suggest he could move. He was on the first [dire wolf] before it could attack, activating [Dance of the Sakura Blossoms] and attacking. He swung his blade with the elegance and grace expected from a dancer instead of a warrior. If someone were to look at the pattern his feet made as he shuffled across the ground, they would have noticed that it looked like he was making a giant sakura blossom.

-23,940; -71,820; -215,460; -646,380; -1,939,140!

Adam's continuous stream of attacks flowed together. The first two attacks didn't instantly kill a [dire wolf] in one hit, but every swing after that was a killing blow. The amount of damage he could deal was incredible. With [Blood Sacrifice] tripling the damage he did, and then Titania's [Song of Vigor] further tripling the amount of damage he could inflict, Adam's already high Physical Attack stat had reached a hitherto unheard-of level. He was like a one-man army.

Of course, Adam was still just one person, and he couldn't defeat so many enemies at once. He carved a path through the [dire wolves]. Following right behind him were Titania, Kureha, Susan, Fayte, and Lilith. Thanks to his sudden surprise attack and the series of quick deaths he had inflicted, the [dire wolf] pack couldn't respond right away, but upon seeing their prey escape, they howled and chased after him and his party.

They raced through the city, the [dire wolves] hot on their heels. Up ahead was the magic academy. It was getting closer and closer, the tower growing larger and larger in their vision. Now that he was so close to it, Adam could appreciate just how massive the magic academy was. Even the tallest skyscraper in the real world could not match up to this monstrosity.

"Ahhh!"

As they were nearing the tower, Adam heard a scream. He recognized Susan's voice!

He spun around and ran over to Susan, who had fallen onto the ground, lifted her into his arms, and stood back up. A [dire wolf] got close and tried to snap at him, but Lilith swooped in and activated [Pinpoint Strike] to attack the [dire wolf] where it was weak. She buried her dagger into its neck. The creature howled in pain and threw her off as a large damage sign floated over its head.

-13,734!

Lilith landed on her feet, spun around, and began running right behind Adam. Her attack had done what it needed to. The [dire wolf] who had attacked him was no longer close and they were putting distance between themselves and it.

Susan, now in Adam's arms, was blushing red as a tomato as he raced toward Fayte, Titania, and Kureha, who were already at the massive double doors to the magic academy. Fayte was waving at them to hurry up.

The doors were locked, but Adam used the [unknown key] to open them. They raced through the doors. Then Fayte and Lilith pushed them closed behind their party. A loud *bang!* echoed around the room and the doors shook as something struck them. Susan squeaked in fright, and for a moment, Adam thought the door might break. Several more banging noises echoed around them as the [dire wolves] slammed into the door, but then it grew silent.

Adam sighed in relief and turned to observe their new surroundings.

This room reminded him of an atrium. It looked like the central hallway to a massive building that branched off into more hallways. Far in the back was a split staircase. Columns jutted from the ground and stretched up to the ceiling. When he looked down, Adam realized the floor was made of granite and was in surprisingly decent shape for something that had not been maintained for thousands of years.

Of course, there was a lot of battle damage too. Some of the columns had been destroyed, a few sections of the ceiling had collapsed, and there were a variety of skeletons dressed either in armor or the ragged robes of mages littering the ground.

Adam set Susan on the ground and she jumped away like she'd been scalded. Her face was beet red. It was kind of cute if he was being honest, but Adam didn't have time to focus on her because, at that moment, several announcements appeared before them.

Ding!

[Congratulations! You have killed 15 [dire wolves]. [Dire wolves] dropped the items x10 [Dire Wolf Pelt], [Speed Ring], [Wolf

Pelt Gauntlets], and 150,000 gold coins. +1,150,000 experience points!]

Ding!

[Congratulations! Changing_Fayte has leveled up! She is now at level 15! +60 HP! +120 MP! +5 SP!]

Ding!

[Congratulations! Little_Su has leveled up! She is now at level 15! +125 HP! +10 MP! +5 SP!]

Ding!

[Congratulations! Lilith has leveled up! She is now at level 15! +195 HP! +10 MP! +5 SP!]

"Looks like... we made it," Fayte said between gasps for breath.

"It was a close call." Titania crossed her arms. "We are lucky that Adam has such a ridiculously high Physical Attack stat and that broken ability of his, or not even my [Song of Vigor] would have changed the outcome."

While Fayte and Susan were both breathing hard, one from running and one from a combination of fear and embarrassment, Lilith stood off to the side with her arms crossed. She said nothing, but she was looking at him.

"Thank you for the quick save, Lilith," he said.

"You're welcome." While Lilith's reply was simple and her voice cold, Adam thought she sounded happy just then. For some reason that was beyond him, he thought he could see a tail wagging behind her. He was tempted to rub his eyes.

"A-Adam," Susan said suddenly, clutching the fabric of her clothes and biting her lower lip. "Th-thank you very much for saving me. And... sorry for being such a burden to you."

"Silly girl." Adam flicked her forehead, though he didn't apply any force. "Why are you apologizing? The only thing you need to do when someone helps you is say, 'Thank you'. That's what people want to hear. Not apologies."

Susan's cheeks grew even redder, until it looked like they might explode with fire, but she was still somehow able to find her voice and say, "Uh, right. Th-then... thank you."

"You're welcome."

"What should we do now?" asked Fayte.

"It's getting pretty late, so we should probably—"

Just as Adam was about to speak, a ringing noise let him know that someone was calling him. Since there was only one person on his friend's list who wasn't with them, Adam already knew who it was.

"Aris?" he asked after activating the player chat function.

"Adam! Guess what! I reached level 10!" came the excited voice of Aris.

"Wait. Already? That's amazing!" Adam said, and he meant it. "I think you've managed to reach level 10 in the same number of days that I did!"

And to think she had played fewer hours each day than he had. If she'd been allowed to play twenty hours a day like him, it wouldn't have taken more than maybe two days for her to reach level 10 at her pace.

"Hee-hee. I'm awesome, right? I just did what you told me to and took on lots of quests. Also, listen to this. When I was on my last quest, I went into this labyrinth that had all kinds of treasures. Not only did I pick up some really cute clothes that increase my speed, but I also got two new weapons and a hidden class scroll."

Adam was not the only one shocked by what Aris was saying. The others could all hear her as well, though they were unable to speak back. Members of his party could listen, but unless Aris was also a part of their party, they could not speak to her. All of them were gazing at Adam with wide eyes.

"What is the class name?" he asked.

"It's called Blade Dancer," Aris answered. "It's an amazing hidden class that increases my Speed and Movement and lets me use two weapons at the same time. Just watch, Adam! I'm gonna become the best dual-wielding badass this game has ever seen!"

Another dual-wielding class, huh? Adam glanced at Lilith, who possessed a class that let her use two weapons as well. Hers was an assassin class, though, which had a heavy focus on attack power. It sounded like a class focused on speed.

"Anyway," Aris continued, "I'm about to leave the Village of Beginnings."

"Ah. Wait." Adam knew he needed to stop her before she did that. "I'm actually in the middle of something right now. Could you hold off on leaving the Village of Beginnings until I'm finished? Then I can meet you when you arrive in Watershore."

"Hmm… okay. I can do that. In that case, I'll log off for now."

"Thanks, Aris."

"Hee-hee. You're welcome. Get off the game soon so I can kiss you."

Adam ended the call and spoke with Fayte, Susan, Lilith, and Titania. They decided to end their session here. It didn't look like there were any enemies in this atrium, so while it was certainly creepy, Titania and Kureha shouldn't be in any danger.

Before he logged off, Adam decided to check the stats of his party, and, just as he suspected, they needed to get Fayte a better class.

Name: Lilith
Class: Demon Knight AssassinsLvl: 15
SP: 0
AP: 17,020
Experience: 1,025,500/2,2457,600
Reputation: 63,000
Strength: +110
Constitution: +60
Dexterity: +125
Intelligence: +5
Speed: +100
Physical Attack: +1,170
Health: 595/595
Hit-rate: ???
MP: 85/85
Movement: +200
Defense: +405
Magic Defense: +405
Dodge-Rate: 5,000%
Magic Attack: +10

Name: Little_Su
Clas: Fairy Archer
Lvl: 15
SP: 0
AP: 15,150
Experience: 1,017,460/ 2,457,600
Reputation: 70,000
Strength: +35
Constitution: +30
Dexterity: +20
Intelligence: +5
Speed: +50
Physical Attack: +195
Health: 720/720
Hit-rate: 400%
MP: 90/90
Movement: +200
Luck: +1
Defense: +185
Magic Defense: +125
Dodge-Rate: 300%
Magic Attack: +25

Name: Changing_Fayte
Class: Mage
Lvl: 15
SP: 0
AP: 35,200
Experience: 1,028,050/2,457,600
Reputation: 45,000
Strength: +5
Constitution: +25
Dexterity: +10
Intelligence: +70

Speed: +5
Physical Attack: +5
Health: 510/510
Hit-rate: 10%
MP: 915/915
Movement: +5
Defense: +46
Magic Defense: +90
Dodge-Rate: 10%
Magic Attack: +195

ACADEMY
RUINS

"How does that feel? Does it hurt anywhere?"

"No… but it does feel a little tight."

"That's good. It should feel like that. It's proof that you're regaining feeling in your muscles."

Aris was lying on the floor as Adam knelt above her. He had one hand on her left leg, holding it up so her leg was perpendicular to the ground. He maintained that position for several seconds, then moved it backward until her knee was touching her chest before bringing it back to its original position. He moved slowly, asking her to let him know if she felt any pain.

"Maintain your breathing. Breathe in. Breathe out. Slowly now."

"I know. Haaaaah. Hoooooh. Haaaaah. Hooooh. I got this."

It was the morning after Adam, Fayte, Lilith, Titania, and Kureha entered the magic academy. They would be logging onto the game soon, which meant Aris would be alone since he had asked her to not leave the Village of Beginnings until he could be there when she left.

He was, at this moment, helping her do some simple stretches to get the blood flowing back into her legs. Aris's thighs and calves were smooth like fine silk and more supple than most people would have expected from a woman who once had Mortems Disease. Adam had been constantly infusing his own energy into her body to stimulate her muscles and nerves. That and his blood were the reasons her body hadn't deteriorated like everyone else who got this disease.

Being able to freely touch these amazing legs was Adam's blessing and something he admittedly took guilty pleasure in. He was the only person Aris would let touch her. Of course, he knew part of that reason was that she'd had Mortems Disease until recently. Since it was highly contagious, very few people would be willing to go near someone who had it, but Adam liked to think that even if she never contracted it, she still would not let any man except him touch her.

Now that he was thinking about it, Fayte was pretty abnormal as well. She was not immune like him. Even so, she still allowed Aris to live with her.

Aris suddenly made a slightly squished face as Adam put more weight on her leg than he intended.

"Adam, that hurts."

"Does it? Sorry."

He eased off. He didn't want to hurt her, but he did want to know how limber she was since it would help him determine what stretches she could and couldn't do in the future.

At that moment, Aris was still dressed in her pajamas. The pink pants were very cute on her slender hips and supple thighs, and the button up pink shirt covered her modest chest. As he pushed her right leg down until it touched her chest, he grabbed her small foot, which was no bigger than his hand, and rolled it a little.

"How does that feel?"

"Mmm. It feels fine... I think? It doesn't hurt if that's what you're asking."

"Okay. Let's do a few more stretches then. We've got time.

"Hee-hee. I think you just enjoy manipulating my body. Would you like to make me do some lewd poses? It's okay. You can do it if you want."

"...That's enough out of you."

They went through several more stretches. There were some that she couldn't do yet, like the lying pectoral stretch, which was where a person laid on their stomach with both arms extended to the sides, then pushed off the ground with the left hand, bent the left knee for balance, and rolled onto their right side. Her muscles simply weren't developed enough for such extraneous movement. Adam cataloged what she could and couldn't do and composed a routine they could follow.

"Breakfast is ready, you two," Fayte called as she walked into the living room.

While Aris was still dressed in her pajamas, Fayte was wearing her usual jeans and a turtleneck sweater. She wore an apron over her turtleneck. It was white with pink polka dots.

"Ah! Breakfast!" Aris's eyes lit up like twin bonfires at a festival. She looked at Adam and held out her hands. "Adam, can you help me up?"

Adam reached out and grabbed her soft hands. She had delicate fingers, which she curled around his as he pulled her up. She was able to stand with his help but leaned into him immediately after. Standing up still took a lot of effort. She couldn't stand for long, much less walk, so Adam carried her to the couch.

That said, it's amazing that she can stand so soon with or without aid. I didn't expect her to be capable of this for at least another week.

A sweet cinnamon scent wafted through the air as Fayte put three plates and a large serving tray on the coffee table. Aris stared at the pan filled with French toast made from thick cuts of Texas toast. Adam needed to look at her a second time because it looked like she had hearts in her eyes for a moment, but... yeah, it must have been his imagination.

"This looks delicious! Fayte, you're such an amazing cook!" Aris complimented the woman.

Fayte smiled, and because she never wore her veil at home, they were able to see the truly wondrous way her gently curved lips lit up the entire room. Adam likened Fayte's smiles to the gentle blooming of a red rose illuminated by the first rays of the morning sun. It was breathtaking. Even Aris found herself staring in stunned silence at it.

"Thank you. I hope you enjoy its flavor as much as its presentation."

"I'm sure I will!" Aris said with an enthusiasm she didn't bother to hide.

Maybe it was the result of his blood helping her out, but while Aris still couldn't walk, she could do many other things she had not been able to do before. One of those was eat by herself.

The plate of French toast that Fayte served Aris sat on her lap, and she was using a fork to cut the food into smaller bites. This French toast was fairly soft because it had been soaking overnight. That meant it was much easier to cut into smaller bites and didn't require a knife. As she stuck the first bite into her mouth, stars appeared to burst from Aris's eyes as a delirious moan escaped her pink lips.

"Thish ish sho good! Sho good! Oh ma gawd! Ish feelsh like ish melhing in my mouth!"

Adam and Fayte looked at each other from over Aris as she enjoyed the food and shared a smile. While Fayte still acted oddly around them when he and Aris were acting like a couple, she seemed to enjoy it when Aris complimented her cooking.

"How do you like it, Adam?" asked Fayte.

Taking a bite, Adam responded with a lot more restraint than his lover. The combination of cinnamon and sugar was present in every bite, but it didn't overpower the flavor from the eggs and milk. There was just the right amount of sweetness. He also detected a small hint of cream, which he thought brought the two separate flavors together in harmony.

"Aris was right. This is delicious," he said at last. "I couldn't have made it better if I tried."

Fayte's smile grew even wider as a soft warmth spread across her cheeks. "I'm very happy to hear that."

Adam wouldn't say he found himself mesmerized by Fayte's smile, but he did find it hard to look away. No matter what he said and no matter how much he loved Aris, he still could not deny that Fayte was an attractive woman. It didn't help that he'd gotten to see so many sides of her during their time cohabitating.

Aris seemed to notice him and Fayte staring at each other. There was an odd look on her face, like she was thinking hard about something, or maybe like she wanted to say something but was holding back. Seeing that expression made Adam realize what he was doing and look away.

He coughed into his hand. "Anyway, are you about ready to explore the magic academy?"

"I am," Fayte said, taking a deep breath. "I just hope we find what we're looking for in that academy. The last thing I want is for us to spend several days fruitlessly searching for something that doesn't exist."

"Even if we don't find a hidden class, I believe we'll at least find some items that will make it worth our while," Adam said.

"You two are so lucky." Aris pouted at them. "You get to play Age of Gods. Meanwhile, I'm going to be stuck here for several hours."

"I'm sorry," Adam said.

He did feel guilty about telling her not to play, but Adam wanted to be the person she did everything with. He wanted to be there when she arrived in Watershore, wanted to join her when she went on the mayor's quest, and wanted to spend the rest of his time in the game with her. It was selfish of him. He knew that. Just like he knew Aris would listen to him if he told her not to play.

I feel like I'm taking advantage of her, and yet I know that won't stop me. Does that make me a bad person?

"If you're really sorry, then you'll take a bath with me after you finish playing," Aris said with a narrow-eyed smile.

Fayte looked away when she heard those words, a small frown on her face. Adam tried to ignore that and the way his chest fluttered as he nodded.

"Deal."

With the deal between him and Aris sealed, Adam decided to play Age of Gods in the living room instead of his room. He didn't have any entertainment in his bedroom. Aris could watch TV, play video games, and enjoy the sun streaming in through the window if they were in the living room. Fayte went to her bedroom. She claimed that she wasn't comfortable leaving her body vulnerable like this.

The body was more or less unconscious whenever people played VR games. That was one of the dangers of playing. There had once been a report about a man who raped his roommate while she was playing VR games, which had caused a huge backlash at the time, though this had not been a major problem for the last ten years.

Ten years ago was when the new lock systems had been installed. Now only people who had access to a room were capable of entering. Of course, it was still possible for someone to assault a person while they were playing VR games, but reports of it happening had gone down from several dozen a year to just one or two.

On that note, Fayte had programmed him into every room, including her own, which went to show the level of trust she had in him. Adam would make sure to never betray her trust.

"Lay down." Aris, sitting up straight instead of slumping over like she had the day before, patted her thighs and smiled at him.

"You're gonna let me use your lap as a pillow?" Adam raised an eyebrow.

"Hee-hee. I've always wanted to do this for you. Normally, you're the one letting me rest on your thighs, but this time, I get to return the favor."

Aris was so excited about letting him rest on her lap that even if he was inclined to say no—and he wasn't—he didn't think he would be able to resist.

He laid down on his back and set his head on her thighs. They were soft and squishy. Adam believed they should be a little firmer and worried that it was because of how badly her muscles had atrophied, but he shook the thought off. They were doing all they could to get her body back in shape. He was just being paranoid.

The last thing Adam felt before he logged onto Age of Gods was Aris gently running her hands through his hair.

✳✳✳

When Adam appeared in the game, he was standing in the middle of the atrium of the ruined magic academy. The tent was still there, but Titania and Kureha were not using it right now. Kureha looked like she was chasing after a cricket, but Titania was sitting against a destroyed column with her knees drawn up to her chest. She looked up when he appeared.

"You have finally arrived."

"Yeah. Sorry. I know you had to wait for a long time."

"It is fine. Now we just need to wait for the others."

Fayte was the first one after Adam to arrive. Lilith and Susan logged on not long after she did. With everyone present, they finally set off in a standard diamond formation with Adam in the front, spellcasters in the middle, and Lilith in the rear.

The magic academy was extravagantly large, to the point where Adam felt like it was impractical. After ascending the first flight of stairs, they ran into a moving staircase that caused them no end of trouble. They ended up having to double back several times as the staircases moved on them. There were also several enemies on this staircase that were even harder to kill than the [dire wolves] outside.

Name: Vengeful Spirit
Description: The vengeful spirit of a student who died at the academy during its sacking.
Class: None
Lvl: 35
Health: 150,000/150,000
MP: 180,000/180,000
Strength: +50

Constituion: +800
Dexterity: +100
Intelligence: +1,000
Speed: +50

Skills:
Skill Name: Fireball
Description: The vengeful spirit shoots a fireball from its staff
Damage = Intelligence
MP Cost: 30
Cooldown Time: 5 seconds

Skill Name: Thunderbolt
Description: The vengeful spirit fires a thunderbolt from its staff
Damage = Intelligence * 180%
MP Cost: 50
Cooldown Time: 5 seconds

Skill Name: Curse
Description: The vengeful spirit has a 15% chance of casting
Curse
When someone is cursed, they have 100 seconds to kill the
vengeful spirit, or they will die
MP Cost: 1,500
Cooldown Time: 60 seconds

While the [vengeful spirit] wasn't much stronger than the [Dire Wolf], it was also floating in the air, making it much harder to reach. It looked like a classic grim reaper. Ragged robes covered its body. It didn't have any legs, but the robes became more translucent near the bottom. Its head wasn't covered by the hood of the robe, meaning they could see the terrifying skeletal face and blood-red orbs filled with resentment as it glared at them from its empty eye sockets. A gnarled staff was gripped firmly in its left hand, which was pointed at them.

"Kureha! Fayte! Susan! Fire at will! Titania, sing the [Song of Valor]!"

Adam gave orders immediately and strode in front of the girls as they moved to the back of the moving staircase. Titania hid behind his back and began singing. He instantly felt his body become lighter, stronger, sturdier, and he glared at the [vengeful spirit] as lightning burst from the tip and struck him in the chest.

-600!

Adam was very glad he had a lot more health than he used to. With nearly four thousand health, being dealt six hundred points worth of damage wasn't much. What got to Adam was not the damage but the pain. His entire body felt like it had been struck by real lightning. His muscles seized up, his nerves flared with agony, and his body shook as he withstood the damage. Even though he only felt 15% of what he would feel in real life, that was still a lot. Honestly, he thought even 15% might be too much for a game.

The first person among his party to launch an attack was Kureha, who fired off a bolt of crackling lightning from her second tail. It struck the [vengeful spirit] and sent it soaring backward. A large number sign also appeared above it. She didn't just stop with [Thunder Bolt] either, but cast [Fireball] soon after.

-3,036; -2,300!

After Kureha brought the [vengeful spirit's] health down by around -5,000 points, Susan pulled back the arrow notched in her bowstring as a bright, incandescent light flared from the tip. Light energy swirled around the tip and gathered. It felt holy, pure, like a blade of divinity cutting through the darkness of this academy. Once her attack was ready, she released it.

-1,170!

[Light Arrow] was a skill that dealt six hundred percent damage to undead and enemies with a darkness element. The [vengeful spirit] was classified as an undead enemy, which meant her arrows effect was six times greater than if this had been a regular enemy. Sadly, the bow she was using didn't grant her that big a bonus to her Physical Attack, so the attack still did less damage than Kureha's magic.

-390!

Fayte was the last to launch her attack. [Energy Bolt] was the weakest among all the attacks so far, which was due to a combination of her normal class and lack of powerful weapons. Adam didn't have a staff that could let her deal more damage than the one she already had.

Things would have been a lot worse for them if Kureha hadn't been present. She was their heavy hitter when it came to long-range attacks. After her cooldown time ended, she launched two more attacks that dealt another five thousand points of damage. Of course, even with all that, they still only managed to deal about fifteen thousand points worth of damage. This [vengeful spirit] had +150,000 health.

Then Adam remembered he had two unique abilities thanks to his [Goddess of Creation Boots]. He had forgotten them because he didn't have much use for them until now. They were [Flight] and [Double Jump].

He used both skills without hesitation to reach the [vengeful spirit] and attacked several times with [thrust] and [slash].

-3,990; -4,256; -3,990; -3,990; -3,990!

He only managed five attacks before his [Flight] ability ended and forced him to land back on the staircase. His attack also pulled the monster's agro, but that was a good thing. Fayte, Susan, and Kureha were able to launch several attacks without being targeted as he downed a [middle-grade magic potion] to replenish his lost mana.

-3,036; -2,300!

-1,170!

-390!

-3,036; -2,300!

-1,170!

-390!

-3,990; -4,256; -3,990; -3,990; -3,990!

The four of them continued to trade attacks, using long-distance magical attacks mixed with hit and run tactics. Because she didn't have a skill that would let her attack something floating so high above them, Lilith was the only one unable to contribute in this battle. Adam felt a little bad for her. However, he put those feelings out of his mind and focused on battling this enemy until the [vengeful spirit] was killed.

Ding!

[Congratulations, you have killed a [vengeful spirit]! [Vengeful spirit] has dropped the items [Robes of Despair], [Ring of

Darkness], [Cursed Staff], and 20,000 gold coins. +40,000 experience points!]

The experience points they gained were not much (at least to them), but that was because they were sharing it between themselves. Six times 40,000 was 240,000. Had Adam been fighting alone, he would have gotten a lot more experience points.

Since it looked like they had a few new items, Adam looked at their spoils to see if anything might be useful.

Item Pouch:
Item Name: Robes of Despair
Item Type: Clothing
Grade: 1-Star
Use Requirements: Can only be equipped by Mages over level 15.
Description: These robes Grant the wearer basic defense and resistance to magic-based status effects.
Abilities: Magic Defense+25; Defense+25; 15% defense to fear, blind, confusion, curse, disease, disable; debrave, patrify, and charm

Item Name: Ring of Darkness
Item Type: Accessory
Grade: 1-Star
Use Requirements: Can only be used by Mages over level 15.
Description: This ring grants the wearer protection against the darkness element.
Abilities: 30% resistance to darkness element

Item Name: Cursed Staff
Item Type: Magic Staff
Grade: 1-Star

Use Requirements: Can only be equipped by Mages level 15 and above.
Description: This is cursed staff has decent attack power and grants a boost to all darkness related magic.
Abilities: Magical Attack+50; increases damage done by darkness magic by 150%

While the items didn't seem all that good, they were better than the equipment Fayte currently possessed, so Adam gave them to her. All of her stats received an increase after she put them on, though the new robes did make her look like an evil mage.

"Let's keep going," Adam said as the staircase began moving again.

"This staircase is going to be a huge problem," Fayte mumbled.

"I'm not even sure where this staircase is going," Titania added with a frown.

"Hopefully, it will lead to the top of this tower or at least the dean's office." Adam ran a hand through his hair and released a deep breath. "That should be where the treasure is."

"You mean if there is any treasure," Fayte corrected.

Adam shrugged his shoulders and didn't say anything further.

They continued to climb up the stairs and were forced to fight twelve more [vengeful spirits]. They used the same tactics they had in the previous battle to defeat them and thus earned another +240,000 experience points.

"Your [Flight] ability certainly is useful," Titania muttered.

"I didn't realize you could fly," Fayte added.

"I had forgotten about it until we began fighting these [vengeful spirits]," Adam admitted with some reluctance. "I haven't needed it yet, so I kinda just forgot it existed."

"I wish I could fly like that," Susan said in a shy voice.

"I'm sure we'll be able to find some equipment with the [Flight] ability for you," Adam said with a smile.

After exiting the moving staircase, they found themselves in what appeared to be a library with three levels. Dust covered much of the floor, the bookshelves, and the tables scattered around the room. The second floor was made up entirely of a balcony that went around the entire interior. Catwalks moved across the second and third floors as well, held up by colonnades that were evenly spaced apart.

The group kicked up dust as they walked in. Adam coughed several times and waved the dust away. He wasn't the only one, as Fayte, Susan, and even Kureha were releasing coughs. Lilith did not and Titania flew into the air to avoid being caught within the dust cloud.

They continued moving as the dust settled. Adam walked up to one of the bookshelves and ran his fingers along the spines. There were many titles such as *An Introduction to Magic, Magic for Beginners,* and *Intermediate Magic for Spellcasters.* He grabbed one of the books, but could only watch in shock as it crumbled into dust.

"These books are pretty old. I've never seen that happen before."

"They probably don't contain any useful knowledge, which is why they are designed to self-destruct like that," Fayte guessed.

"My guess is the creator didn't want to create too much complicated content, so he programmed them to crumble the moment someone tries to pick them up."

"I guess that does make sense," Adam said with a slow nod.

"Do you think there might be some treasure in this library?" asked Susan.

"I'm not sure, but I think we should at least search the area to find out," Adam said.

They searched the library for what felt like an hour at least, but while Adam found nothing, Susan somehow discovered a hidden room with a treasure chest. It was one of those standard rooms that could be accessed via a hidden door when you pulled back one of the books on a shelf. He had no idea how she had discovered this. He assumed it was her Luck stat at play. Either way, they ended up gaining several new pieces of equipment meant for Mages.

Item Pouch:
Item Name: Magical Raiment
Item Type: Clothing
Grade: 2-star
Use Requirements: Can only be equipped by a Mage level 20 and above.
Description: These raiments have high defensive power and offer resistance to all the elements.
Abilities: Magic Defense+150; Defense+150; 30% resistance to fire, wind, lightning, earth, water, holy, and darkness elements

Item Name: Elemental Ring
Item Type: Accessory
Grade: 3-Star

**Use Requirements: Can be equipped by any class over level 20.
Description: This ring was enchanted by a student who
specialized in elemental magic.
Abilities: 20% resistance to fire, wind, lightning, earth, water,
holy, and darkness elements; 20% boost to fire, wind, lightning,
earth, water, holy, and darkness spells**

The two items located inside of the treasure chest were impressive, but sadly, no one had the level to equip them. Even Adam was still trying to reach level 18.

Since there was nothing more inside of the library despite its size, they left and continued traveling down a large hall, eventually reaching a circular stairwell that led up. The inside of this stairwell was much more cramped than the moving staircase. On the plus side, they didn't have to worry about the stairs moving on them.

After reaching the end of the stairwell, they ended up in another hallway. This hallway was long, had numerous locked doors, and featured suits of armor that were holding large weapons in their wrought-iron gauntlets. The armored suits were covered in rust stains. As their group walked down the hall, Adam could swear he saw one of those suits turn its head to watch them as they walked past it.

"I-I… is it just me, or are the suits of armor moving?" asked Susan.

"So I am not the only one who saw that," Fayte murmured. Unlike her stuttering friend who sounded frightened, she seemed relieved to know she wasn't hallucinating.

"Be careful," Titania warned them. "These suits of armor are actually a type of monster. They have been enchanted to attack intruders."

Just as she said that, one of the armored suits stepped away from the wall and stood before them. A loud clanking sound from behind alerted Adam to another suit of armor doing the same, essentially pinning them in place. Titania floated above them and cast [scan].

Name: Cursed Armor
Description: This suit of armor has been enchanted by the teachers of the magic academy to act as a last line of defense and protect the students in the event of an invasion.
Class: None
Lvl: 35
Health: 350,000/350,000
MP: 500/500
Strength: +1,200
Constitution: +1,500
Dexterity: +100
Intelligence: +10
Speed: +50

Skills:
Skill Name: Slash
Description: The cursed armor can wield the claymore in its hand with ease, dealing incredible damage with one swing.
Damage = Strength
MP Cost 10
Cooldown Time: 1 second

Skill Name: Impale

**Description: With a single thrust of its sword, the cursed armor
can impale an enemy and throw them aside.
Damage = Strength + Critical Hit
Causes bleed status effect
MP Cost: 20
Cooldown Time: 5 seconds**

These enemies were at about the same threat level as the
[vengeful spirit], but they dealt physical damage instead of magical
damage. Adam felt better about fighting these things than he did the
spirits.

"Titania, sing [Song of Vigor]. Lilith, Fayte, Susan, and
Kureha, attack the [cursed armor] behind us. I will take care of the
one in front of us," Adam gave the orders and everyone quickly
followed through.

Because he wanted to take this thing out quickly, Adam
activated [Blood Sacrifice] as he charged forward. The [cursed
armor] raised its weapon and swung down as he reached it. Adam,
however, had already anticipated this and moved aside, barely
glancing at the sword as it struck the ground with a loud clash and
shower of sparks. Now that he was so close, Adam swung the spear
with all his might and activated [Dance of the Sakura Blossoms].

-23,940; -71,820; -215,460; MISS!

Adam's base Physical Attack was at +2,660. [Blood Sacrifice]
was a skill that increased this stat by 300%, while [Song of Vigor]
caused a further 300% boost to it. That was three times three. The
massive increase was enough that just a single attack from him
could instantly kill the [cursed armor], so long as he used [Dance of

the Sakura Blossoms] to unleash several continuous attacks that multiplied the amount of damage dealt with each successfully executed attack.

While Adam killed the suit of armor in a single attack, Lilith struck her enemy with [slash].

-5,265; -5,265; -5,265; -5,265!

Her newfound power as a Demon Knight Assassin meant she had a much higher attack power than before. She danced around the [cursed armor] and launched attack after attack, drawing all of its agro to her. The [cursed armor] tried to slice her apart with several vicious swings of its claymore, but Lilith would duck under or leap over each [slash] it sent her way. When it used [impale] to attack her, she used [counter] to devastating effect.

-15,000!

Thanks to her constant attacks, the [cursed armor] lost a good deal of health by the time Kureha unleashed her first attack. A [Thunder Bolt] blitzed through the hallway and slammed into the [cursed armor] with incredible force, pushing it back several steps.

-9,108!

With smoke still rising from its breastplate, the [cursed armor] could do nothing as Fayte and Susan fired their respective attacks. Fayte pointed the staff in her hands and launched [Energy Bolt]. Susan released the bowstring and fired off a [Fairy Shot]. Both attacks struck hard.

-1,170!

-2,925!

Once Kureha, Susan, and Fayte launched their respective attacks, Lilith came back in and finished the enemy off with [slash]. She swung her blade across its breastplate. A line of light appeared where her blade left as though it was slicing through the armor. Then she drew the blade back in and used [slash] once more before repeating the process for a total of -26,325 damage.

-5,265; -5,265; -5,265; -5,265!

-9,108!

-1,170!

-2,925!

-5,265; -5,265; -5,265; -5,265!

The four continued to attack, and Adam stood back and watched, ready to step in if they needed help, only to realize there was no need. Ten minutes after the battle began, it ended in the girls' victory. Fayte fired off her last attack, an [Energy Bolt] that slammed into the face of her opponent and sent it clattering to the ground, where it remained after its health was depleted.

Ding!

[Congratulations! You have defeated 2 [cursed armors]! [Cursed armors] have dropped the items [Enchanted Breastplate], [Enchanted Claymore], [Enchanted Leggings], and 50,000 gold coins! +60,000 experience points!]

KILLER GAR-GOYLE

There were four different types of enemies located inside of the magic academy: [cursed armor], [vengeful spirit], [undead mage], and [golem]. Each enemy was at level 35, though they had run into a few 1-Star enemies that were at level 40. No matter what sort of enemy they faced, however, none of them could defeat their group, and they continued to ascend level after level.

Lilith, Fayte, and Susan had all leveled up thanks to the massive influx of experience points they'd been gaining. All of them were now at level 16, which was both good and bad. While Adam was pleased to see how Susan's and Lilith's stats were shaping up, he was still very worried about Fayte's stats. They were just too low for his taste. He didn't want her leveling up too much until she had a hidden class to give her stats a more significant boost per level.

By now, it felt like many hours had passed since they entered the magic academy. This place was like a maze. It was filled with hallways, secret passages, locked doors, and puzzle rooms. Sometimes they would have to solve a specific puzzle to proceed to the next area. There had been one room where they were forced to recreate the image depicted on a portrait by pushing square blocks across the ground. In another room, they were separated from each other and forced to individually solve a number of riddles and logic games. They hadn't been allowed to help each other either. The roaring of the flames had prevented them from communicating. Not even their player chat feature had worked. At other times, they would have to battle against what Adam took to calling a sub-boss. These were the 1-Star enemies they were forced to fight.

And they were fighting one of those sub-bosses right now.

At the moment, they were standing on a series of stone platforms located high above the ground. These platforms had jutted into the sky after they stepped on them. Now they were at least a hundred yards above the floor.

The platforms were not big. They were large enough for two people to stand on if they stood with their backs pressed together, and there was one for each of them. It seemed the room was specifically made to work with however many people were in their party. Adam assumed if there had been eight of them, there would have been eight platforms.

That was not the problem.

The problem was the enemy they were fighting.

Name: killer gargoyle
Description: A gargoyle that has been brought to life using magic. This creature is a guardian that protects the magic academy.
Class: 2-Star
Lvl: 45
Health: 996,000/1,435,000
MP: 16,200/30,000
Strength: +2,000
Constitution: +1,000
Dexerity: +50
Intelligence: +50
Speed: +50

Skills:
Skill Name: Dive
Description: The killer gargoyle swoops down and attacks its enemies with claws and feet.
Damage = Strength * 150%
MP Cost: 1,000
Cooldown Time: 10 seconds

Skill Name: Tail Whip
Description: Using its tail to attack, the killer gargoyle does x2 damage
Attack will always knock opponent off their feet
MP Cost: 1,200
Cooldown Time: 10 seconds

Skill Name: Rend
Description: Using its sharp claws, the killer gargoyle will rend flesh from bone
Damage = Strength
MP Cost: 200
Cooldown Time: 0 seconds

**Blitzkrieg: The killer gargoyle attacks fast and hard, swooping
in and slicing into opponents with its claws consecutively
Each attack does x2 damage
Attacks do not stop unless the killer gargoyle's attack pattern is
disrupted
MP Cost: 10,000
Cooldown Time: 120 seconds**

The [killer gargoyle] was a lot more powerful than anything else they had faced so far, but more than that, what made this situation difficult was how they were forced to fight on these stone pillars. If it wasn't for the fact that Adam's [Goddess of Creation Greaves] could use the [Flight] skill, they would have long since been finished.

-MISS!

At that moment, Adam was already flying around their tricky foe, swinging his spear down to use [slash] as he passed by. Sadly, his attack missed because the [killer gargoyle] was a lot more versed at flying than him and deftly dodged the attack. Even though his attack didn't hit, he still pulled its agro by being the aggressor. The [killer gargoyle] very quickly locked onto Adam as he landed back on an unoccupied pillar and charged in.

-9,108!

-1,170!

-3,300!

Not long after the [killer gargoyle] tried to attack him, Kureha, Fayte, and Susan all launched their own attacks. Kureha's [Thunder Bolt] struck the [killer gargoyle] in the back, blasting a chunk of stone off its body. Fayte fired an [Energy Bolt] that struck it again. Her attack smacked it in the chest, knocking it back and making it swerve. Seconds after their attacks struck, Susan's [Fairy Shot] landed a critical strike between its shoulder blades.

Because Kureha had done the most damage, the [killer gargoyle] turned to her. It released a furious shrieking sound that was like rocks grinding together and shot forward with a flap of its wings.

Adam did not let it go far. He pushed his toes off the platform and flew forward, once more swinging his spear in a powerful arc that activated [slash].

-36,720!

Perhaps it was because the [killer gargoyle] was distracted and couldn't dodge, but Adam's attack tore into its back and a large damage number appeared above it. Adam chuckled as the enemy turned to him with its glowing eyes the color of blood. Its stone body was already badly damaged, with cracks traveling along its torso, arms, and face, and several chunks having broken off long ago. Three of its fingers were now missing.

-36,720; -36,720; MISS; -36,720; MISS; MISS; MISS; MISS!

After attacking several more times and only landing three hits, Adam landed back on his platform, pulled a [middle-grade magic potion] from his item pouch, and downed it in one gulp. The [killer gargoyle] chased after him again, but once more, Kureha, Fayte, and Susan attacked it while it was distracted. Their combined efforts knocked off another -13,578 from its health. With a fierce snarl, it turned to them, and then Adam attacked again.

This was the strategy they had come up with. Adam would pull its agro, then they would attack while it was chasing him, and then when it tried to attack them, Adam would attack again. Meanwhile, Titania floated high above their heads and sang the [Song of Vigor] to increase their physical and magical Attack Power. In this way, they managed to quickly reduce its HP by half over the course of maybe ten or fifteen minutes.

Unfortunately, the battle became tricky once its health was reduced to seven hundred thousand.

"It's about to use [Blitzkrieg]!" Adam shouted as the air around the [killer gargoyle] burst. A loud sound like something had exploded rang in his ears. That was the noise of the sound-barrier breaking. The [killer gargoyle's] target was, unfortunately, not Adam but Kureha, who had unleashed the last attack.

Adam's platform was on the other side of the room, which meant he had no chance of reaching Kureha in time to save her. All he could do was watch as time seemed to slow down. The [killer gargoyle] continued to advance, closer and closer, its claws outstretched as though it could already feel Kureha's flesh being torn from her bones. It was enough to make him sick with helplessness.

However, what Adam thought would happen never came to pass.

Just before it could reach Kureha, a figure appeared on top of the [killer gargoyle]. It was Lilith. Adam had no idea how she managed to get there, but he wasn't about to question it. The woman's eyes, her only visible feature, were narrowed as she slid her weapon along the enemy's throat. Then she swung her weapon against its back several times. Each attack produced a series of sparks. She finished her attack by stabbing her weapon between its shoulder blades.

These attacks were [Throat Slit], [Slash], and [Pinpoint Strike].

-58,080; -5,445; -5,445; -15,246!

Because her attacks disrupted its [Blitzkrieg], the [killer gargoyle] not only stopped aiming for Kureha but also swerved off course. It crashed headfirst into a pillar, which didn't do any damage but did stun it. Lilith waited until the very last second before leaping off the [killer gargoyle] and landing back on her platform.

"Great job, Lilith!" Fayte shouted.

Lilith nodded but said nothing. Her gaze was locked on the [killer gargoyle] as it flapped its wings and hurried back toward the center between all the pillars.

The two attacks they needed to worry about the most was [Dive] and [Blitzkrieg]. Both attacks were fast and hit hard. Fortunately, [Blitzkrieg] required a lot of MP to use and therefore couldn't be done on a whim. This was only the second time it had used that skill. It had used this skill at the start of the battle, which was how Adam recognized what it was about to do. Since it only had thirty thousand MP to begin with and couldn't regain any of it during combat, Adam believed they were safe. He didn't think it would or even could use it again since it had already used so much MP during this fight.

After seeing what Lilith had done, Adam got another idea and used the [Goddess of Creation Greaves'] ability—[Flight]—to land on the [killer gargoyle] like her and attack it with his spear. Sadly, he soon found a problem with that. The reason Lilith could attack at this range and position was that her dagger was small and could be wielded with one hand, while she gripped the [killer gargoyle] with the other hand. His spear was long and unwieldy. Not good for attacking from this position.

He lost his balance and fell off the enemy's back, though he used [Double Jump] to keep himself from falling and landed back on his platform. Of course, he did not fly back before at least dealing another large slice of damage to his opponent. He managed to hit it once with [Slash].

-36,720!

Their tactics continued like this until Kureha's [Thunder Bolt] and [Fireball] combination reduced the [killer gargoyle's] health to zero. The enemy let out a mournful shriek as it fell from the sky, striking the hard stone floor below and shattering against it.

Ding!

[Congratulations! You have defeated the 2-Star enemy [killer gargoyle]! [killer gargoyle] has dropped the items [Gargoyle Core], [Stone Tablet], and 60,500 gold coins. +300,000 experience points! +30,000 ability points! +15,000 Reputation!]

After the announcement was made, the pillars they had been standing on slowly lowered until each one was embedded into the ground again. Adam looked at his skill list and decided to use four thousand ability points on [Energy Thrust] and eight thousand on [Energy Sweep], bringing them both up a level.

His current skill set was pretty impressive. The only abilities he hadn't maxed out were [Dance of the Sakura Blossoms], [Energy Thrust], and [Energy Sweep], but all of his other abilities had become as powerful as he could make them. He could have maxed out [Energy Sweep] right now if he wanted to, but he honestly wanted to save as many ability points to max out [Dance of the Sakura Blossoms] first.

Adam also looked at the two new items in his item pouch.

Item Pouch:
Item Name: Gargoyle Core
Item Type: Material
Grade: 2-Star
Use Reuqirements: Can only be used by crafting classes like Blacksmith and Craftsman.
Description: Gargoyle Cores are magical cores that can be found inside of gargoyles. They can be used to create various effects in armor, weapons, and items.
Abilities: Boosts Magic Attack proportionate to the Craftsman's or Blacksmith's level.

Item Name: Stone Tablet
Item Type: Key Item
Grade: 3-Star
Use Requirements: None
Description: This stone tablet emits a mysterious energy. Its use is currently unknown. Cannot be traded, sold, or discarded.
Abilities: None

Neither item was something that Adam or anyone else could use. None of them had the Blacksmith or Craftsman class to begin with. Those were secondary classes and they were not able to gain them yet. That said, Adam did wonder when he would be able to gain a secondary class. Could they only be gained upon reaching a certain level? Did he need to complete some secret quest to gain a secondary class? He had no idea.

The item [Stone Tablet] was something else he knew nothing about. Adam guessed it the kind of item used to advance a story quest. They were not on a quest right now, which might have negated the idea, but he believed that like his spear, there was some kind of significance in holding onto this tablet.

"We defeated the [killer gargoyle]," Fayte said with a relieved sigh. "What should we do now? Do we press forward or take a break here?"

Now that they had defeated this floor's guardian, they could move onto the next floor by entering through the large double-doors on the opposite side they had come in through. It would probably lead to another staircase. Then they would reach the next level.

Susan suddenly raised her hand like she was in a classroom. "Um… I'm actually a little hungry, so…"

Fayte nodded. "Hmm… I guess it would be a good idea to take a break and get something to eat. What do you two think? Adam? Lilith?"

"I am fine with whatever decision Ma—with whatever Adam decides," Lilith said, quickly changing the word she'd been about to call him.

Adam gave her an aggrieved look, wondering if she'd done that on purpose, but then he sighed and looked at Fayte.

"I agree with you and Susan. It's probably around lunchtime right now, and anyway, I'm worried about Aris."

"She's probably bored sick by now," Fayte agreed with him. He thought she might be smiling beneath that mask. "Okay. Let's all take a break, get something to eat, and then we can come back here in… two hours."

✳✳✳

The first thing Adam saw after logging off was lustrous brown hair. The first thing he felt was a pair of soft lips over his. It took him a moment to realize the person kissing him was Aris, but once this realization set in, he placed his hand behind her head and pulled her deeper into a kiss. He pushed his tongue into the surprised girl's mouth, eliciting a squeak from her. Her surprise, however, did not mean she was going to stop. If anything, suddenly being kissed like this caused her to moan around his tongue and kiss him harder.

"Hee-hee. Did you like my surprise?" asked Aris after pulling back. Her cheeks were flushed and her breathing a little heavy. She licked her slightly bruised lips. They were redder than normal.

"Have you been kissing me while I was logged into the game?" asked Adam as he sat up.

"Maybe," Aris admitted with a catlike smile.

Aris had, at some point, moved off the couch. She was kneeling on the floor next to where his head had been. Several pillows were arranged behind him. Aris must have placed the pillows there to replace her thighs.

"You're such a minx."

"Why, thank you."

"Were you okay on your own?" asked Adam as he playfully rolled his eyes.

Aris's smile evaporated as a cute pout took its place. "I was bored."

Adam reached out and caressed her cheek. "I'm sorry."

"Hee-hee. It's okay." Aris placed her hand against his to keep it pressed against her soft cheek. Her eyes were gleaming like a pair of moons. "You can make it up to me later."

The implication was not lost on Adam.

"I will."

Since he was up, Adam decided to help Aris do some simple stretches and exercises. Her body was surprisingly stronger this afternoon than it had been this morning. He was more than just a little shocked when, after stretching out her legs with some basic exercises, she was able to stand on her own for nearly a full minute. Adam might not be a doctor, but he understood the human body well enough to know that gaining strength this fast should have been impossible.

It must be my blood. She's been ingesting it for several years. Perhaps the effects of my blood have activated now that she no longer has Mortems Disease, or maybe its effects are just showing themselves differently now that it's not keeping her disease in check. Should I see a doctor about this? I'm a little worried, but... it should be fine. I'd rather not have her see a doctor if I don't have to.

Doctors were required to keep the personal information of their patients on file, which meant they could also be accessed by others. Someone with a lot of influence like Levon Ploenexia could find information on her if they knew what she looked like. All they would have to do was exert their influence and power to force the hospital to give them whatever information they wanted. In truth, Adam would have never taken Aris to Dr. Sofocore if there had been any other choice.

Fayte arrived just as Adam was helping Aris walk. She watched them from the entrance to her hallway, a soft but funny smile on her face, then walked in.

"Since you're so busy, would you like me to make lunch?" she asked.

"I would appreciate that," Adam said with a smile.

"Thank you, Fayte," Aris said with her own bright and wonderful smile.

Fayte returned their smiles with one of her own before heading into the kitchen. While she made simple grilled cheese sandwiches and tomato soup, Adam held Aris by both hands and walked backward as he led her around the room. Her legs shook with every step she took. Sweat formed on her forehead. It was clear from the redness of her face and the way her teeth were grit that walking was still difficult, still tiring, but Aris didn't stop, even when Adam asked if she wanted to take a break.

"I'd like to keep going," she said through clenched teeth. "I want to be able to go on walks with you, to spend time outside with you. I don't… haaah… haaah… I don't want to be a burden anymore."

Adam wanted to tell Aris that she had never once been a burden to him, that he'd never considered her as such, but they'd had this conversation before, and he knew that her feelings wouldn't change just because he said so. He had given her three years of his life. How could she not think of herself as a burden when he dedicated every waking second to her? If their positions had been reversed, he would have felt the same way.

"Ah…"

Aris's legs finally gave out. She pitched forward into his chest, and Adam wrapped his arms around her, holding her up as her legs shook.

"You're already a lot stronger than I expected you to be after going so long without walking." Adam leaned down and buried his nose in her hair. "Aris, I know you want to get better faster, but you're already doing a great job. Please don't rush this. Rushing to grow stronger could prove detrimental and actually set you back. You don't want that, do you?"

"I don't. Sorry," Aris said with a sigh. Her body fully relaxed into his embrace. "It's just so frustrating. I'm finally cured, but it's still impossible for me to do anything on my own."

"Are you saying you don't want me doing everything for you? I thought you liked it when I spoiled you." Aris pinched his waist. "Kidding. Kidding. No need to get violent."

"Hmph. Just wait until I'm strong enough to really move. Then I'll show you violence."

As Adam and Aris joked around like they used to when they were younger, Fayte wandered out of the kitchen with three plates balanced perfectly on her arms. She looked so graceful even while carrying plates that Adam was stunned for a moment.

"Adam, could you bring in the tomato soup and some drinks?" Fayte asked him with a sweet smile.

Adam could only agree.

After setting Aris on the couch, he hurried into the kitchen, grabbed three cups and filled them with ice water, then brought the cups and three bowls of tomato soup into the living room.

While they ate lunch, Fayte pulled out a tablet and accessed the web. She began searching through forums related to Age of Gods. This was something she did every day so they could keep up to date on everything happening with other prominent players.

"It looks like Lin Akamine has reached level 16," Fayte murmured. "I don't understand how she can level up so quickly. We've been fighting against enemies far stronger than our current levels, but we haven't gained that many experience points in so little time."

"Don't forget that Lin is a solo player," Adam said as Aris dipped her grilled cheese sandwich into the tomato sauce and took a big bite. Her face flushed with pleasure as she chewed with her tiny mouth closed. "You gain more experience points when you play solo. If you or I were to defeat the [killer gargoyle] we fought on our own, we would have gained +1,800,000 experience points. You might have gained even more since your level is lower than mine. While I don't think Lin can kill monsters at that level, I'm sure the ones she is killing are at least around level 20 or 30."

The experience points earned while in a party was based on the highest leveled player. If a player at level 16 earned thirty thousand experience points by defeating a level 28 enemy, and a player at level 20 only gained twenty thousand experience points from defeating the same enemy, the number of experience points earned if those two formed a party and defeated the same enemy would be equal to the number of experience points earned by the level 20 player. By that logic, if Fayte fought against and defeated the [killer gargoyle] when playing solo, she probably would have earned two million experience points or more.

As they were talking, Adam noticed that Aris had some tomato soup on her chin, so he grabbed the napkin and wiped it off just like he always did. She pouted at him, as though to say she could do it herself, but he merely smiled at her.

"I guess that is the benefit of being a solo player," Fayte said with a sigh, though whether she was sighing at her own words or the byplay between him and Aris was unknown.

Adam nodded. "What about the members of the Pleonexia Alliance? Are there any players from them who have reached level 16?"

"Not yet." Fayte shook her head after a moment of scrolling. "It looks like the highest level player right now outside of Lin Akamine and us is the Spear God, who is at level 15. Everyone else is still at level 14."

There seemed to be a hierarchy to the players who leveled up. He was currently the highest leveled player at level 17. Lin Akamine was at the same level as Fayte, Lilith, and Susan. Lin Akamine was number one on the International Power Rankings, so while her level was the same as theirs, she was considered a higher ranked player. The Spear God was immediately after them. Adam didn't know how the Spear God leveled up, but Adam's party had been gaining a lot of experience points because they had been constantly battling against enemies with a far higher level than themselves. He assumed the Spear God had been doing the same, but she leveled up more slowly because she was in a party with the leaders of the Daggerfall Empire.

"What are some of the players we need to watch out for?" asked Adam.

"I assume you're talking about the players belonging to the Pleonexia Alliance," Fayte said before calling up all the information she had off the top of her head. "Aside from Levon Pleonexia himself, there's also his Four Elements and the Sword King, Connor Sword. They're called the Four Elements because in every game they play, each one masters a specific element. There's the Flame Emperor, the Ymir, Thor God of Thunder, and Gaia. Gaia is the only woman among the Four Elements. Her name is derived from the ancient Greek Primordial Earth Goddess."

"So she specializes in earth magic," Adam murmured.

"Yes. Though I suppose she doesn't right now. Age of Gods is still new, so it will take a while before they can learn all the necessary spells and get them each one up to snuff."

"I doubt these element people will be much trouble right now," Aris said with crossed arms.

"Why is that?" asked Adam.

"Because I met one of them when I was in the Village of Beginnings," Aris stated. "I think it was that Thor God of Thunder guy. That is what his information screen said."

"You met Thor God of Thunder at the Village of Beginnings?" Fayte blinked several times. "That can't be right. He should have left a long time ago… although, I haven't heard much about him on the forums yet…"

Fayte trailed off as she went into thought. Adam, on the other hand, could not help but look at Aris with a concerned gaze.

"He didn't try to cause any trouble for you, did he?" asked Adam.

"Hee-hee. Well, he did see me without my veil. It was when I first entered the village. He was already at level 10 at the time, so I'm guessing he was planning to leave, but then he saw me and came right up and asked me to become his woman." Adam twitched several times when he heard this, which caused Aris's eyes to brighten like stars in the night sky as a mischievous smile crossed her face. "Are you worried? Don't be. I told him I already have someone I love. Though he was kind of persistent. He kept tailing me every day for several days…"

She trailed off and went into what he recognized as her "thinking mode." With her arms crossed, face scrunched up, and head tilted down, she looked adorable. Adam wanted to kiss her, but he held back.

"What is it?" asked Adam.

"Um, it's nothing important," Aris said at last. "It's just that, after the first three or so days of him following me around, he just stopped. It was kind of strange. I guess maybe he got sick of constantly being rejected and left the Village of Beginnings."

Adam didn't say anything, but he decided he was going to speak with Asteroth about this and ask why they hadn't informed him of this Thor player harassing his Aris.

After lunch was over, Adam washed the dishes and the three friends talked and played some simple console games together for at least an hour or so. Then Adam and Fayte once more entered Age of Gods. They appeared next to each other inside of the large room where they had battled against the [killer gargoyle]. Lilith was already there. She was petting Kureha, seeming to enjoy the way the little fox yokai's hind leg twitched in the air as she scratched behind her ear.

"Welcome back, you two," Titania said from where she stood. There was a slice of bread in her hands, which she periodically nibbled on.

"It looks like Susan is the only one we're waiting for," Adam said.

He couldn't see her face, but Adam could tell Fayte was smiling as she said, "Susan is probably in lessons right now. She is home-schooled by some of the best tutors in the world, and sometimes her classes run late."

"What is this 'home-schooled'?" asked Titania as she floated over to them and landed on Adam's shoulder.

"It's when someone is taught at home instead of going to school," Adam answered.

"So I see. And what is school?"

Adam knew what school was even though he had never attended before, but he didn't have the patience to tell Titania. He looked at Fayte, who interpreted the request with eye contact alone, and while she explained the concept of school to the fairy (she explained that it was like this magic academy), Adam walked over to Lilith.

"Master," Lilith greeted in a soft voice, though she did not stop petting Kureha. Her love for cute things had been outed a long time ago. There was no longer any need for her to hide her obsession.

Adam did an admirable job of hiding his grimace. "After we finish things here, I want you to get in touch with Astaroth and the other members of the Soul Reapers. Tell them to find Thor God of Thunder, and kill him until his level drops back to 1."

Lilith tilted her head in obvious confusion, but she didn't question his orders and instead nodded once. "It will be done."

Susan appeared several minutes after his conversation with Lilith. She apologized profusely to all of them for being late, bowing repeatedly. Everyone told her not to worry, but the girl still seemed more contrite than simply being a little late warranted. After they had gotten her to calm down, the group of six found themselves standing in front of the massive double doors.

"Is everyone ready?" asked Adam. Everyone nodded. "Then let's keep going. I'd like to conquer this academy before dinner."

Adam inserted the [stone tablet] into a relief on the massive double door, which caused the entire door to light up with runes. A loud creak echoed around them. The sound of stone grinding against stone was ear-piercing. Adam, Fayte, Lilith, Susan, Titania, and Kureha remained silent as the door opened, revealing a large staircase that curved upward.

The six stepped passed the door and continued on their journey.

ELEMENTAL
MASTER

Something Adam discovered was that the higher they climbed up this tower, the stronger the enemies became. In the first ten floors, enemies were all at level 35. After reaching the eleventh floor, their enemies became level 40. That was a five-level increase.

At present, Adam and his party were on the fortieth floor, which meant all their enemies were at level 55. That was about the limit to what they could win against. Even Adam found himself struggling against enemies that had on average +1,000,000 health, never mind the fact that most of the time when they ran into enemies, there were always groups of them.

On the plus side, they ran into so many enemies that all of them had gained +4,000,000 experience points. Kureha and Titania had reached level 18.

Kureha's and Titania's levels had finally surpassed Adam's. The reason for this was just simple math. When Kureha and Titania were at level 1, they only needed +100 experience points to reach level 2, whereas Adam needed +150. Each level they gained still required fewer experience points than Adam, so at level 17, they only needed 6,553,600 experience points to reach level 18. On the other hand, Adam needed 9,830,400.

"I'm not sure how much longer we can keep going." Fayte's voice was not at all muffled by her veil as she spoke. She sounded worn out. "We've been traveling for a long time now, but we haven't found anything that would suggest there is a treasure, much less a [hidden class scroll] here."

"If we want to find a [hidden class scroll], then we will need to travel until we find a magic vault," Titania said. "I heard this place had a massive vault where all their most powerful items were stored."

"Are you sure the vault has any treasure left?" asked Fayte. "It looks like this place has been ransacked."

"I'm sure," Titania said. "Do not forget this magic academy was the most prominent institute on the continent at the time. They would have completely sealed off the vault and all of their most important rooms with magic and seals. Even if several armies stormed this place, they would not be able to break the seals on these doors so easily."

Since Titania was the closest thing their group had to an expert on this world, nobody denied her words, but all of them were feeling the effects of traveling up this tower for several hours. Even Adam and Lilith displayed their tiredness in the way their shoulders slouched. It was fortunate they were wearing masks so no one could see their haggard faces.

Their group was traveling in the same formation as always, with Adam in front and Lilith taking up the rear. The floor they found themselves on looked a lot like a series of classrooms. There were a lot of lecture halls with tertiary seating. Adam could imagine students sitting in the seats while their magic teacher lectured them from the podium. Of course, most of the seats had long since broken down and even the stone tables had numerous cracks running across them.

After constantly traveling without rest and fighting the enemies located in the halls and rooms, the group eventually reached another massive door. This one was even bigger than the previous ones they had entered. Made from a type of metal, Adam was shocked to find that this door, unlike all the others, still appeared to be in pristine condition. Majestic and imposing, the door's primary feature was the magical seal in the center. It was the coat of arms for this academy.

"Should we… go in?" asked Susan.

"I'm not sure." Fayte turned to Adam. "What do you think?"

"How many hours has it been since we started playing?" asked Adam.

Fayte tilted her head and Adam knew she was calculating the passage of time. She had a perfect memory and possessed an impeccable internal clock, making it easy for her to figure out how much time had passed.

"I would say we've been playing for about three hours, give or take a few minutes," she answered at last.

Adam nodded. "We'll go in, but this will be our last door. If we don't find any treasure or a [hidden class scroll], we'll stop for the day and begin again tomorrow."

Everyone agreed and together placed their hands on the door and pushed. Nothing happened at first, but then the door released a low creaking sound before, like magic, it swung wide open. Adam counted their blessings. He'd been worried this door would be locked.

The room on the other side of the door reminded him of a stadium. A high wall rose all around an oval-shaped space. Behind the wall were several rows of seats where people could watch whatever was happening down below. As they walked forward, he twisted his head, picturing the many students sitting in this place and enjoying death matches against ferocious monsters.

Not that he thought this place would allow their students to fight to the death against ferocious monsters or anything.

In the center of this stadium stood a silent figure. Adam could not tell what their gender was from so far away, but they were dressed in a dark robe with gold lining the hems. As they got closer, he noticed this person had long, dark hair tied together at the back with a leather band, and they were somewhat translucent. He could see the other side of the stadium through their body.

In other words, this person was a ghost.

The figure turned around as they got closer, and their group was met with purple eyes, a pale face, and beautiful features. A woman. Adam could now see the full figure concealed by this person's robes, though it was just a hint. Those robes were thick enough to hide most of her figure from view. Her pale face was framed by strands of hair. In her left hand was a black and gold staff, odd symbols running up its length.

Her face was scrunched into a vicious snarl.

"Foul invaders! Do not think my academy will be so easily brought down by the likes of you!" she shouted at them.

Fayte, Titania, and Susan jumped at the sound of her voice, harsh and grating like nails against a chalkboard, but Adam and Lilith merely stared in silence. This woman was a ghost. Adam had once read a spiritualistic article about how ghosts that were stuck on the mortal plane would sometimes relive their last moments. The article had been utter garbage, completely unbelievable since spirits and ghosts didn't exist, but seeing this woman and her expression reminded him of that article. He wondered if this character's creator had read it as well. In either event, she was probably reliving the time when she defended this academy from the three armies that destroyed it.

"It looks like we have no choice but to fight this woman," Adam said. "Let's get in formation. Long-range fighters in back. Me and Lilith in front. Titania, give me her stats."

Having worked together for several days now, Adam gave his orders smoothly and the others got in formation as if they had been anticipating them. Lilith stepped up to his right and held her dagger in a reverse grip. Her dark eyes were narrowed. Titania, meanwhile, fluttered behind Fayte, Susan, and Kureha as she cast [scan] on the woman.

Name: Alexandra Mystique
Description: Alexandra Mystique was a young woman with an unprecedented talent for magic. She went on to found the Advanced College of Magic, but she was killed when the kingdoms of Friedonia, Slaveon, and Malroc attacked her academy.
Class: 4-Star
Lvl: 50
Health: 5,000,000/5,000,000
MP: 10,000,000/1,000,000
Strength: +50
Constitute: +1,500
Dexterity: +500
Intelligence: +5,000
Speed: +50

Skill List:
Skill Name: Fireball
Description: Shoots fireball from staff
1,000% damage
MP Cost: 2,000
Cooldown Time: 15 seconds

Skill Name: Firestorm: Releases a wave of flames that sweeps over every enemy within a 50 yards of target
1,000% damage
MP Cost: 4,000
Cooldown Time: 20 seconds

Skill Name: Thunder Bolt
Description: Fires a bolt of lightning from staff

6,000% damage
MP Cost 4,000
Cooldown Time: 15 seconds

Skill Name: Chain Lightning
Description: One bolt of lightning is fired from staff and attacks
multiple targets, linking them together like a chain
Can hit up to 100 targets
3,000 damage
MP Cost: 5,000
Cooldown Time: 30 seconds

Skill Name: Wind Blade
Description: Fires a single blade of wind from staff
600% damage
Has a 50% chance of removing a limb
MP Cost: 2,500
Cooldown Time: 15 seconds

Skill Name: Wind Hammer
Description: A massive hammer of wind is formed and slammed
into the ground, releasing all the compressed wind to blast
enemies away
400% damage
100% chance of causing stun
MP Cost: 1,000
Cooldown time: 15 seconds

Skill Name: Earth Wall
Description: A defensive technique that causes the earth to rise
from the ground and form a defensive wall to block attacks
The wall lasts for 60 seconds
Can create a maximum of ten walls.
MP Cost: 500
Cooldown time: 60 seconds

Skill Name: Quicksand
Description: The earth around the enemy turns into quicksand,
trapping them for 230 seconds
This spell can effect enemies 15 yards from targeted enemy
MP Cost: 500
Cooldown time: 40 seconds

Skill Name: Water Bullets
Description: Multiple bullets made of water are rapidly fired
from Alexandra's staff
Attack lasts for 60 seconds and does 100% damage
Can be used to attack one target only
MP Cost: 1,000
Cooldown time: 30 seconds

Skill Name: Water Dragon
Description: An ultimate attack that creates a dragon made of
water
This attack will act independently of its user to attack enemies
It has 300,000 health points and is immune to water attacks
MP Cost: 50,000
Cooldown time: 120 seconds

Skill Name: Resurrection
Description: Resurrects a single person from the dead
Only works if used before one hour has passed
Can only be used once per day
MP Cost: 20,000
Cooldown time: 120 seconds

Adam felt his blood run cold when he saw how powerful this enemy was. Disregarding her level 50 and 4-Star class, she had a health of 5,000,000/5,000,000 and any one of her attacks would kill them in one hit. Even Adam would not survive taking a single hit from this woman. This meant they would need to be very careful when dealing with her. Even if they were as careful as possible, there was no guarantee they could defeat an enemy who was this strong. She was, without a doubt, the strongest enemy he had run across since his meeting with the Spider Queen and Undead King.

But Adam had never been the kind of man who gave up.

"Lilith!"

"..."

Lilith didn't speak a single word, and her body suddenly vanished as Adam raced forward. As he heard Titania begin singing [Song of Vigor], he activated [Blood Sacrifice], and then began swinging his spear in the pattern needed to activate [Dance of the Sakura Blossoms]. He danced around the woman, thrusting and slashing out. If someone were to look at his attack pattern with a bird's eye view, they would have seen that the movement of his feet created an outline in the general shape of a sakura blossom.

-24,480; -73,440; -220,320!

Adam was forced to back off when Alexandra spun around and swung her staff in his direction, light flashing near the tip as electricity crackled out in arcs. Lightning condensed into a sphere before it was fired as a bolt that soared past his head. Adam barely dodged the attack, which struck the wall behind him.

A massive burst exploded from where the [Thunder Bolt] struck. The attack left a large black mark on the wall, but that was it. Adam was surprised the wall had been able to withstand it. He'd already seen how much damage could be done by enemy attacks.

The [Skeleton Dragon] back in the Village of Beginnings had carved trenches in the ground. These walls must have some kind of magical protection to keep them from being too damaged, or maybe they were made from a material that absorbed magical damage.

-58,080!

Lilith suddenly appeared behind the woman like a mirage, placing her dagger against Alexandra's throat, and sliding it across the surface. No blood emerged. However, a thin line appeared, as though she was a hologram that someone had interfered with.

The moment the attack landed, Alexandra's eyes turned red with rage. She spun around and prepared to attack Lilith.

-1,170!

-9,504; -7,200!

Before she could unleash her attacks, Fayte struck her in the back with the magic spell [Energy Bolt], and then Kureha launched an attack from each of her tails. The first was [Thunder Bolt], which slammed into the woman with enough force to make her stumble. The second attack was [Fireball]. That one struck the woman in the face and seemed to light her hair on fire.

"Unfilial bastards!" Alexandra shrieked. "How dare you and your kingdoms bare your fangs against me! Do you think you can kill me with such pathetic magic?! Let me show you what real magic is!"

Adam was surprised this boss-level opponent could still talk. That was something that had never happened during boss battles in other games.

Alexandra pointed her staff at the three long-range attackers and Titania. Adam grimaced as he realized what was about to happen.

"You four need to scatter!" he shouted.

[Chain Lightning] was an AOE skill with a decent range. It targeted a specific opponent, then leaped from one enemy to another once it struck. The good thing was it moved linearly when first released and couldn't track enemies if they moved out of the way. This meant it was perfectly possible to evade the attack.

Fayte, Susan, Kureha, and Titania all scattered, not even bothering to remain together when they ran away. Seconds after they raced from the spot where they had been standing, a powerful bolt of lightning shot from the staff and slammed into the floor. Lightning crackled and the room shook. Light flashed. It was blinding. Even Adam had no choice but to close his eyes to save himself from being blinded. When the attack ended, the stone floor featured a massive scorch mark where the lightning bolt struck.

Adam downed a [middle-grade magic potion], raced forward once again, and attacked. [Blood Sacrifice] had worn off and was cooling down, which meant he could no longer ignore the cooldown times for his other skills—that meant he couldn't use [Dance of the Sakura Blossoms] either—but Adam needed to draw this woman's agro. That was why he used [thrust] and [slash] to attack even if the damage he did wasn't as good.

-13,056; -12,240; -12,240; -12,240; -13,056!

Of course, while Adam didn't think the amount of damage he did was that great, he understood this was just his perspective.

Anyone else would have screamed in a fit of jealous rage if they saw the damage his single attacks did. No other player could deal this kind of damage right now, after all.

"Cretin!!!"

Alexandra once more tried to attack him. This time she swung her staff, which launched a [Wind Blade] at him. He couldn't see the attack. All he could see was a ripple in the air, but that was enough to let him lean his body to the side and dodge. When it struck the wall, the damage done was impressive. A long scar at least 2 yards in length ran across the wall.

-14,520; -5,040; -5,040!

Lilith once more attacked Alexandra with [Throat Slit], but because Alexandra was now aware of her, the attack didn't deal critical damage like it had done last time. The Demon Knight Assassin made up for her lack of damage by swinging her dagger into the woman's back. Each [slash] dealt around five thousand points of damage. Sadly, she was only able to attack twice before the woman slammed her staff into the ground.

Leaping backward as a wall formed between her and Alexandra, Lilith prepared to use [hide] again, but she found herself unable to move. A glance down revealed the reason. Her feet were stuck in quicksand! This was the [Quicksand] skill. She grabbed her right leg and tried to pull it out, but it was no use.

"Not so stealthy now!" Alexandra screeched as she raised her staff. "Let's see how you deal with my lightning!"

With Lilith unable to move, Adam knew she would be done for if they didn't disrupt this woman's attacks now. Fortunately, [Blood

Sacrifice] and [Dance of the Sakura Blossoms] had become usable again, so after activating his physical enhancement skill in exchange for half his health, he raced forward and began swinging his spear as he danced along the floor to form the shape of a sakura blossom on the ground with his feet.

-24,480; -73,440; -220,320; 660,960!

[Dance of the Sakura Blossoms] was Adam's strongest attack, and the large numbers floating over Alexandra's head proved why. Each attack did three times more damage than the previous attack. With just a single skill, Adam was able to deal about twenty thousand points short of one million points of damage to Alexandra's health.

Of course, this meant Adam had become the focus of Alexandra's spell.

He was very lucky he was so fast.

Adam leaped backward for several meters and dodged as a bolt of lightning flashed from the woman's staff. It missed him and struck the wall again, but this was not the end of Alexandra's onslaught as she launched [Wind Blade], [Fireball], and [Water Bullets] in quick succession.

Adam found himself relying on his incredible reflexes born from years of combat training and death to avoid being struck. Sweat formed on his forehead as each attack came within inches of killing him. The [Wind Blade] carved into the ground mere inches from his feet. When the [Fireball] struck, it created an explosion so massive that Adam was sent sailing and still received one thousand points of damage from being burned—and this was despite not actually getting hit. As he quickly downed three [middle-grade health potions] to recover, several hundred bullets composed of water flew from Alexandra's staff and nearly blasted his body full of holes.

Just as Adam was beginning to worry he might be hit, Susan came racing in from the left. She skidded to a stop, took aim with her bow, knocked back an arrow, and fired. She then fired another arrow, but this one whistled as it approached. Adam recognized the two skills she used.

[Deadeye] and [Fairy Shot].

-1,320; -3,300!

Neither attack did much damage, but perhaps through some kind of miracle, one of Susan's arrows pierced Alexandra's right eye. There was no blood, but Alexandra screamed in agony. Her attacks stopped as she stumbled backward, one hand moving toward where the arrow was protruding.

Susan looked a little green as the woman tore the arrow out and turned to her. Adam couldn't blame her. Even though this game didn't show any blood, there was now a black mark all around Alexandra's eye to show that it was no longer there.

Adam was a little surprised that attacks like that worked, but he didn't give it a second thought. Lilith had recovered from the quicksand attack, and so before Alexandra could attack Susan, he and she raced forward and launched simultaneous attacks on the mage. Even with [Blood Sacrifice] no longer active, the damage dealt was impressive.

-12,240; -12,240; -12,240; -12,240; -13,056!

-5,040 ; -5,040 ; -5,040; -5,040!

-1,170!

-9,504; -7,200!

-1,320; -3,300!

-12,240; -12,240; -12,240; -12,240!

Their combined attacks forced Alexandra to look away from Susan and glare at them. Not only did Adam and Lilith launch consecutive strikes without pause, but Fayte and Kureha launched several magic spells from afar. The combined damage they did to this woman was staggering, though it was a mere drop in the bucket for her.

Madness and rage filled her eyes as she swung her staff in their direction and fired several [Wind Blades] with reckless abandon like she was hoping one of them would cut either him or Lilith in half. The two of them moved away from each other. As the wind blades tore through the ground, Alexandra looked back and forth between the two of them like she wasn't sure who to attack.

By now, their group had shaved off over two million points of Alexandra's health, and they were continuing to do more damage. Adam and Lilith pulled as much agro as possible. Through experimentation, they learned that Alexandra would not use AOE skills if people were not grouped. This meant they didn't have to worry about those so long as the long-range attackers split up.

Titania was the only one Adam had to worry about. This Alexandra wasn't a standard enemy who attacked without intelligence. She soon realized the fairy was the reason for their incredible attack power and began targeting her with extreme prejudice. She sent several [Wind Blades] and [Water Bullets] at the fairy. While they were all dodged as Titania flitted through the air, it was only a matter of time before she was hit by a lucky strike.

Adam would not let this woman's attack his companion so easily. After drinking another [middle-grade magic potion], he activated [Blood Sacrifice] when the cooldown time ended and once again used [Dance of the Sakura Blossoms] to deal an extravagant amount of damage.

-24,480; -73,440; -220,320; 660,960!

Because Alexandra had been so set on taking out Titania, she completely neglected Adam, who used her one-track mind to deal close to a million points worth of damage before she could even respond. Now she had lost almost one-fourth of her health. His attack staggered her, but she recovered too quickly for him to deal more damage.

"Damn you! This is why I hate melee combatants!" Alexandra cursed Adam as she turned around and launched another [Wind Blade]. Sadly for her, this left her back exposed to Kureha and Fayte's magic attacks.

-1,170!

-9,504; -7,200!

-1,320; -3,300!

Before the woman could swing her staff to launch magic at the two, Lilith came in. Her dagger flashed as she struck the woman with a series of attacks.

-5,040 ; -5,040 ; -5,040; -5,040!

Alexandra screamed in range and tried to attack Lilith, but Adam chose to hit her at that moment. [Blood Sacrifice] had already run out, so the damage he did was cut by three.

-12,240; -12,240; -12,240; -12,240!

"Damn you! Damn all of you!!!"

With a shriek of outrage, Alexandra slammed her staff into the ground, creating walls that surrounded her on all sides. There was no way for any of them to attack now.

Water swirled around them, gathering together in front of the four walls. Four massive limbs jutted from the swirling water, which changed from an undulating mass into a body packed full of muscle. Pinions at least twelve feet in length exploded from its back. A long neck formed near the front before a reptilian muzzle filled with sharp teeth grew from the end. Near the back, a tail at least eight yards long formed, swinging back and forth. This was Alexandra's most powerful skill.

[Water Dragon].

"Lilith!" Adam shouted.

"Yes, Master!"

Adam had no time to scold her as they rushed forward and began attacking. He still couldn't activate [Blood Sacrifice] yet, but his incredible attacks pulled this monster's agro like nobody's business, which allowed Lilith and the long-range attackers to fight without worry.

-12,240; -12,240; -12,240; -12,240!

-5,040 ; -5,040 ; -5,040; -5,040!

-1,170!

-9,504; -7,200!

-1,320; -3,300!

The [water dragon] slammed its tail into the ground at Adam, nearly crushing him, but he rolled out of the way and attacked the tail. He spun the spear in his hands and used [slash] without reserve—or he would have, except he'd run out of MP.

-1; -1; -1!

His eyes went wide. This had never happened before, but he soon realized that in his effort to pull this monster's ago, he had used up all of his MP attacking.

"Crap! Lilith!"

"I'm here!"

Adam leaped back as Lilith jumped onto the [water dragon] and began attacking with [slash] and [pinpoint strike]. Damage signs appeared above the monster's head as Adam took a [middle-grade magic potion] from his item pouched and downed it.

By the time he'd recovered, Lilith, Fayte, Kureha, and Susan had dealt around one hundred thousand points of damage on their own. Adam finally activated [Blood Sacrifice] and attacked with [slash] and [thrust] once again.

-39,168; -30,645; -30,645!

Adam's last attack destroyed the [water dragon], causing it to explode into droplets of water. At that moment, the walls surrounding Alexandra crumbled, and the woman herself attacked the moment she became visible. A [wind blade] tore through the air toward Titania.

"Move, Titania!" Adam shouted.

Despite his warning, Titania did not have any time to dodge. She had only just turned around to see the attack coming toward her. Her eyes widened, her body froze, and the blood drained from her face.

Just as the [wind blade] was about to tear her body apart, Lilith appeared in front of the tiny fairy and took the attack in her place. Adam stared in horror as a massive damage sign appeared above her head.

-29,500!

Lilith's body hit the floor with a heavy thump and didn't get back up. She was dead. It was obvious she had died. Her health was at 0. Adam felt a sharp pain slice into his chest like a bladed weapon cutting his heart open. He knew that she was not really dead, that she'd resurrect back at the cathedral in Solum, but just seeing Lilith's body lying there sent his mind into a spiral.

His vision became filled with red, but his heart grew cold.

"Ha ha ha! How do you like that?!" Alexandra laughed as she swung her staff around, prepared to hit Titania with a magic attack again.

-5,040 ; -5,040 ; -5,040; -5,040!

-1,170!

-9,504; -7,200!

Susan, Fayte, and Kureha attacked the woman, but it seemed she would not be deterred. Now that she understood who the most dangerous person in their group was, she had no intention of letting Titania go.

But Adam also had no intention of letting her continue to attack Titania. He activated [Blood Sacrifice] and charged forward, swinging his spear to use his most powerful attack once more. [Dance of the Sakura Blossoms] activated as he went through the familiar steps.

-24,480; -73,440; -220,320; -660,960; -1,982,880!

Adam demolished the rest of Alexandra's health, even going so far as to unleash the last of his five-petaled attack, despite how it wasn't needed. He'd never been able to release all five attacks before. Alexandra kept disrupting his attack pattern, but she was unable to do that this time. The vengeful dean screamed in shock, anguish, and rage before disappearing.

"Haa... ga... hoo..." Adam took several deep breaths as he hunched over. Sweat formed on his forehead and got into his eyes, stinging them.

"We... we did it," Susan mumbled like she couldn't believe it. As the seconds passed, her eyes began shining. "We did it!"

"Yes, we did," Fayte smiled. Then she shifted her gaze to Adam. "Though I suppose we have you to thank for that."

Adam shook his head. "I did deal the most damage, but if this had been just me fighting, I would not have been able to win. This victory belongs to us. All of us/"

The group of five—three humans, one fairy, and a fox yokai— gathered together and smiled at each other, though the smiles soon left as they looked over at Lilith's corpse. Adam parted from the group, walked over to Lilith, and knelt. There was no blood to be seen. However, Lilith's dull eyes were wide open in surprise. Seeing her eyes like that caused his heart to clench as if the Frost Giants of Norse mythology were squeezing it to a pulp.

"I can't believe Lilith died," Fayte mumbled.

"She sacrificed herself for me." Titania's expression was guilt mixed with gratitude. Her eyes shone with unshed tears. "I cannot believe she did that."

Adam took a deep breath. "Lilith sacrificed herself because she knew you'd die if she didn't. She understood that you were the most important factor in this battle and decided to give up her own life so we could achieve victory."

"But her level..." Susan began.

Adam smiled and placed a hand on Susan's head. "I will help Lilith get her level back up. No—I'll make sure her level is even higher than it was before she died."

Susan froze when Adam placed his hand on her head, and Adam, realizing what he had done, jerked his hand away from her as if scalded.

"S-sorry," he said. "I'm not sure what possessed me to do that."

"N-no. It's okay. It isn't like I… disliked it or anything," Susan muttered, her cheeks turning a deep red.

Fayte and Titania looked at the two as they stood there in awkward silence. While Fayte's expression was hidden, Titania clearly wanted to say something. Her face was scrunched like a pug.

"You six did a rather magnificent job defeating me, but please don't think this means you're actually powerful," a voice suddenly said, causing their blood to run cold. "If I was actually alive and in top shape, there's no way you would have won."

Everyone spun around in shock. Adam held his weapon at the ready, prepared for combat. Titania fluttered behind Adam as though seeking his protection. Fayte and Susan merely stood there in stunned silence. The only one who didn't seem too surprised was Kureha, but Adam thought that was because he wasn't well-versed in fox facial expressions. For all he knew, she could have been so shocked she had a heart attack.

Floating several yards away from them was none other than Alexandra, but her body seemed more ethereal than before, and she was floating instead of standing. Her appearance wasn't much different from when they were fighting her. However, the enraged look on her face was no longer present.

Alexandra smiled when she saw at least one of them prepared for combat. With a soft chuckle, she raised her staff in a gesture of defeat.

"Relax. I do not have any intention of harming you now."

"How do we know that's true?" asked Adam.

"You're a suspicious one, aren't you?" Alexandra rolled her eyes, then shrugged as though it didn't matter to her whether he believed her or not. "You have already defeated me. This spirit body of mine can no longer retain its physical shape. I'll be disappearing soon… but I wanted to speak with the ones who defeated me before I go. Oh! Right. How about I revive your friend to show my sincerity?"

None of the players present were sure they could believe her words. Susan looked the most uncertain, like she was tempted to believe this woman despite her distrust, but Adam and Fayte still stared at her suspiciously.

As if to dispel their distrust, Alexandra waved her staff at Lilith's body. Motes of light emerged from the staff and floated over to it. The body was soon surrounded by hundreds of tiny motes, which were absorbed into the body. One second passed. The motes disappeared. Then Lilith stirred. Adam, Fayte, and Susan watched in shock as the woman stood up, shaking her head as though to clear it.

Adam quickly checked Lilith's stats. He was relieved to see that she hadn't lost a level—he guessed being revived through magic allowed players to keep their level—but all of her experience points, ability points, and reputation was gone. That must be the price one paid for dying. Adam supposed if she had died and been resurrected at a cathedral, she'd have lost all of that and her level would drop by one.

"Are you okay, Lilith?" Adam asked.

"Yes, Mas—I mean, Adam," Lilith said.

Adam flinched, but then cast a glance at Fayte and Susan to see if they had noticed the woman's slipup. They hadn't. He heaved a sigh of relief.

"I guess this means… we can believe her?" asked Fayte like she still didn't know whether to trust this woman or not.

"It should be fine," Titania suddenly said as she fluttered out from behind Adam. "I do not sense any malicious intent from her anymore. That means she does not want to harm us."

Adam and the others relaxed when they heard Titania's words. She was the only one they could count on for advice and information about all things relating to Age of Gods, so they had a great deal of trust in her. However, while their reaction was to relax, Alexandra gawked when she saw the tiny woman now sitting on Adam's shoulder.

"I didn't realize this before, but you're a fairy, are you not?! Why the fuck are you so tiny?!"

"Do not call me tiny!" Titania snapped like it was an inborn reflex. Her face had turned bright red like a volcano ready to explode. "I don't want to hear someone who died several millennia ago calling I'm tiny! Say it again, and I'll curse you!"

"Okay. Okay. I'm sorry." Alexandra raised her hands in a gesture of surrender. "I apologize. I did not mean to offend a member of the Fairy Clan. I was just shocked. I've met a fairy once before, you know, and she was the same size as a normal human."

Titania glared at the woman but didn't say anything further.

"What did you want to talk to us about?" asked Fayte.

Alexandra recovered from her previous shock and smiled at them. "When I was alive, I had been considered by many to be a magical prodigy. Rather than go to an institute, I traveled the world, learning magic from various places and helping people in need. I soon created my own branch of magic called Elemental Magic, which is how the Elemental Master Class was created. You could say it is the culmination of my work. To be honest, the skills I currently have right now are pathetic compared to when I was still alive."

Nobody said anything as the woman looked at her own hands with a self-deprecating smile, like she was reprimanding herself for being so weak.

"Being a ghost has made me lose a good portion of my spells. The longer I exist here, the less I remember," she admitted, dropping her arms to her side. "I don't want the magic I so carefully cultivated for so many decades to go to waste. The magic academy I created to teach others is done for, but that doesn't my work has to cease. You." She pointed at Fayte. "You are a Mage, yes? Will you allow me to pass down my knowledge to you? I promise you won't regret it."

Ding!

[Alexandra would like to pass her skills on to you. Do you accept? Yes or no?]

A window appeared in front of Fayte, who glanced at it before looking back at Alexandra. The excitement in her eyes was visible—and why wouldn't it be? It sounded like this woman was offering to turn her into Elemental Master, and finding her a suitable hidden class had been their entire reason for coming to this academy.

"I accept," Fayte said with a bright smile as she pressed the "yes" option.

"Good. Then be sure to learn these skills well. Also, make sure you show these skills off in front of everyone. Let the entire world know the power of an Elemental Master, someone who has mastered all the elements."

With a satisfied nod and a bright smile, Alexandra burst into particles of golden light, which floated over to Fayte and engulfed the woman. Susan released a startled scream as light erupted from Fayte's body. Adam, Lilith, Kureha, and Titania were forced to look away. The light eventually died down, however, and everyone looked at Fayte to see her staring at her hands in awe.

"Did it work?" asked Adam.

Fayte looked up. "It worked. My class changed. It's now Elemental Master."

"That's great!" Susan cheered. Everyone seemed excited. Even Kureha was running around and yipping in excitement.

At that moment, another flash of light appeared in the middle of this stadium. What appeared before them was a treasure chest. Simple, unadorned, but well-crafted. Adam walked over and opened it up. A smile appeared on his face as he reached in, grabbed the items, and held them out to Fayte.

"I think these are meant for you."

What Adam held in his hands was a set of clothes and a staff. The clothes consisted of a black robe with gold adorning the hems, black pants, a black shirt, a black veil with gold around the edges, and black boots with golden lines running across them. The staff was the same one that Alexandra had used against them. What impressed Adam more than their appearance was their abilities. Each piece of equipment seemed better than the last.

Item Name: Alexandra's Staff
Item Type: Magic Staff
Grade: 4-Star
Use Requirements: Can only be used by Elemental Masters
Description: This staff was carved by Alexandra herself. When

she was young, she discovered the fabled Tree of Life and was gifted one of its branches by the tree itself. This staff was carved from that branch and contains incredibly potent magic.
Abilities: Intelligence+200%; MP+250%; Magic Attack+200%

Item Name: Enchanted Elemental Robes
Item Type: Clothes
Grade: 4-Star
Use Requirements: Can only be used by Elemental Masters
Description: These robes were created from threads of magical silk and enchanted with incredible defensive powers.
Abilities: Constitution+100%; Defense+200%; Magic Defense+200%; 75% damage resistance for all elements

Item Name: Enchanted Elemental Shirt
Item Type: Clothes
Grade: 4-Star
Use requirements: Can only be used by Elemental Masters.
Description: This shirt was created from threads of magical silk and enchanted to protect people against elemental attacks.
Abilities: Magic Defense+300; Defense+300; 15% damage resistance for all elements

Item Name: Enchanted Elemental Pants
Item Type: Clothes
Grade: 4-Star
Use requirements: Can only be used by Elemental Masters
Description: A pair of pants created from threads of magical silk. They provide a boost to one's magic defense and elemental resistance.
Abilities: Magic Defense+150; Defense+150; 10% damage resistance for all elements

Item Name: Enchanted Elemental Veil

Item Type: Clothes
Grade: 4-Star
Use requirements: Can only be used by Elemental Masters
Description: This veil was made from threads of magical silk. It doesn't just hide your face. It also provides you with a unique skill and defense against magic.
Abilities: Magic Defense+50; Defense+50
Unique Ability: Mind Reading

Item Name: Enchanted Elemental Boots
Item Type: Clothes
Grade: 4-Star
Use requirements: Can only be used by Elemental Masters.
Description: These boots were made from the leather of a dragon and enchanted to offer a boost to the wearer's physical and magical defense, as well as resistance to elemental damage.
Abilities: Constitution+100; Defense+100; Magic Defense+100; 50% damage resistance to all elements

Fayte quickly equipped the new equipment. Adam thought they looked good on her. The black and gold of the outfit made her seem enchanting and mysterious, which fit her personality. The addition of the veil also added to her mystique. However, while the outfit certain gave her that aura of mystery, it also outlined her figure and made her more notorious assets stand out that much more prominently. Adam was sure men everywhere would be going insane once they saw her dressed like this.

Since he was curious, Adam opened her stats.

Name: Changing_Fayte
Class: Elemental Master
Lvl: 16

Experience: 4,660,450/4,915,200
Reputation: 90,000
Strength: +5
Constitution: +350
Dexterity: +10
Intelligence: +225
Speed: +5
Physical Attack: +5
Health: 560/560
Hit-Rate: 200%
MP: 1,125/1,125
Movement: 5
Physical Defense: 3,750
Magical Defense: 6,200
Dodge-Rate: 200%
Magic Attack: +5,400

The upgrade to her stats was impressive—ridiculously so—particularly the increase to her Physical Defense, Magic Defense, and Magic Attack. With this, it was unlikely there was a single player outside of himself who could harm her. This hidden class officially made her one of the strongest players in the game.

Ding!

[Congratulations! You have defeated [Alexandra the Elemental Master]! [Alexandra the Elemental Master] has dropped the items [Heart of Magic], [Dean's Key], [Teleportation Scroll], [Guild Creation Token], and 900,000 gold coins. +2,000,000 experience points! +200,000 ability points! +60,000 Reputation!]

Ding!

[Congratulations! You have leveled up! You are now at level 18! +1,500 HP! +400 MP! +5 SP!]

Ding!

[Congratulations! Changing_Fayte has leveled up! She is now at level 16! +1,400 HP! +1,800 MP! +5 SP!]

Ding!

[Congratulations! Little_Su has leveled up! She is now at level 16! +150 HP! +20 MP! +5 SP!]

Ding!

[Congratulations! Your party is the first one to defeat a 4-Star enemy. An international announcement will be made regarding your accomplishments and a suitable reward will be given. Because your party has defeated an enemy far above your levels, it has been decided that you will get to choose your reward. You can choose between +10,000,000 experience points, +1,000,000 ability points, or +1,000 status points.]

As the announcement was made, Adam, Fayte, Susan, and even Lilith could not stop their eyes from widening.

IT'S ALL ABOUT SP

Adam was so shocked he felt as if someone had shoved his finger into an electric socket. The rewards they could choose from were some of the best he'd seen from any game ever. It was almost like the creator was begging them to become the most broken characters in the entire game.

"Is this what it means to be the main protagonist?" asked Adam.

"Excuse me?" Titania turned to him with a blatant look of confusion on her face.

"Nothing." Adam shook his head.

"Am I... am I seeing this right?" asked Fayte.

"I think you are... maybe?" Susan didn't sound very sure of herself.

"Those rewards are quite substantial." Titania was back to sitting on Adam's shoulder, so she could see the announcement screen just fine. "It looks like whatever reward you choose will be what I receive as well, Adam. Kureha will also receive the same reward."

"Huh… is that because I'm the party leader?" asked Adam.

Titania shrugged. "How should I know? Well, for Kureha, it is probably because she is your pet."

"Does that mean you're also my pet?"

"Absolutely not!"

"I believe we need to think about this carefully," Fayte said at last. "These rewards are all very impressive. It's not something we can decide on a whim."

"Actually," Adam began, "I think we should all choose the status points as our reward."

His words caused Fayte, Susan, and Lilith to turned toward him. The sense of curiosity coming from them made Adam straighten his spine like a soldier in front of his commanding officer.

"Can you tell me why you believe we should choose status points?" asked Fayte.

"Because status points are the hardest type of points to come by," Adam said simply. "Think about it. How many ability points have we gained just by tackling this magic academy? How many experience points? We can get ability points and experience points whenever we want, but we can only get status points when we level up, and we only get five status points per level. If we have a thousand status points to allocate to our various stats, think of how incredible we can make our current levels. You could dump all one thousand of those status points into your Intelligence and raise your Magical Attack to over +20,000. With that kind of firepower, none of the other players will be able to threaten you."

The other three listened to him with rapt attention as he explained his reasons, and none of them could find a flaw in his argument. He was right. They could gain experience points by killing enemies, and ability points by killing enemies that were 1-Star and above, but they could only gain status points by leveling up.

Lilith reached out and placed her hand on the announcement.

Ding!

[Congratulations, Lilith! You have selected the reward [+1,000 status points]! Please allocate those status points wisely!]

"Lilith, don't you want to think about this a bit more before you select your reward?" It was hard to tell because her voice was so mild and her face covered with a veil, but Fayte seemed genuinely shocked that Lilith hadn't even considered the reward before selecting the one Adam suggested.

"There's no need," Lilith said in a cool voice. "Adam's reasoning is perfectly sound. I agree with everything he said."

Adam was glad he was wearing a mask so no one could see the pained smile on his face. This woman would do anything he said. no matter how stupid it sounded. Even so, he was also grateful that she trusted him so much, even if her absolute faith in him made Adam feel soul-crushing guilt.

"I actually… agree with Adam and Lilith," Susan said after hesitating for several seconds.

"You too, Su?" Fayte turned to Susan, only to see a somewhat resolute expression on the girl's normally meek face. After another second passed, she sighed. "All right. All right. I also agree with Adam. We can gain experience and AP on our own time, but we can't always gain status points, especially not this many."

With everyone in agreement, the entire group chose to select the status points reward.

Ding!

[Congratulations, Adam! You have selected the reward [+1,000 status points]! Please allocate those status points wisely!]

Ding!

[Because you have selected [+1,000 status points] as your reward, Kureha and Lilith have both received +1,000 status points as well!]

Ding!

[Congratulations, Changing_Fayte! You have selected the reward [+1,000 status points]! Please allocate those status points wisely!]

Ding!

[Congratulations, Little_Su! You have selected the reward [+1,000 status points]! Please allocate those status points wisely!]

Ding!

[We have an international announcement to make! As of 5:46 PM Standard Eastern Time, the party consisting of Adam, Changing_Fayte, Lilith, and Little_Su have defeated the first 4-Star enemy. They have received a suitable reward of one thousand status points. We hope that this knowledge will cause all of you will strive

your hardest to earn fame, fortune, and glory as you traverse the ancient and mysterious Forgotten Realm.]

Once all of them had received their one thousand status points, the group decided it was time to leave. Adam planned on going over the items they had acquired during their fight later. All of them were tired, and according to Fayte, it was around 6:00 PM, which meant Adam had left Aris alone for about four hours. He'd never left her alone for anywhere close to that length of time, and being away from her for so long made him nervous.

Fortunately, this room had a teleport pad that took them back to the first floor. Once they arrived on the first floor, Adam and the others logged off.

"You mean it?! I can finally leave the Village of Beginnings?!"

Aris looked at Adam like he'd just told her that every day was going to be her birthday from this moment onward. She and Fayte were sitting on the couch, playing old-school console games. The game they were playing was not the fighting one that Adam and Fayte so often played, but a racing game. Adam did not know what it was called since he had never played, but the game featured a host of unusual characters, including a fat plumber in a red suit, a skinny plumber in a green suit, and a blonde princess dressed in pink.

There was also a green lizard.

And an evil-looking turtle who transformed into a hot babe when he wore a princess crown.

"Of course I mean it. Also, your character just crashed."

"Wha—oh, no!"

Because Aris had whirled around to look at Adam when he said she could leave the Village of Beginnings, Aris had not been paying attention to her character. The green lizard she was playing had driven off the road and crashed into a lake.

Adam had decided it was his turn to cook tonight. He was going to make chicken scampi pasta. His original idea was to make shrimp scampi pasta, but Fayte did not have any shrimp in her fridge.

It was an easy dish to make, taking only around twenty-five minutes, and Fayte fortunately had all the ingredients he needed. She even had the dry white wine used for cooking.

That said, he had been forced to switch from using angel hair pasta to linguini because Fayte didn't have that particular type of pasta, but it wasn't like thicker noodles would change the flavor. Sometimes you had to get creative when cooking.

Dinner was made and Adam brought the plates, forks, napkins, and everything they would need to the coffee table.

"Thank you, Adam!" Aris leaned over and kissed him right on the mouth. Adam only felt a little awkward at the show of affection because of Fayte's presence. While Fayte retained her smile during their kiss, the upturned lips looked just a little brittle.

"You're welcome," he mumbled as Aris and Fayte stopped their game to eat.

Dinner was nice after that. Aris excitedly talked about how much she was looking forward to meeting everyone in their party.

Even Fayte's stiff smile evaporated as she listened to the excitable girl talk nearly non-stop.

"One of the things I'm really looking forward to is going on quests with everyone! Adam and I used to play World of Wargcraft when we were younger, and one of my favorite activities was quests and dungeon raids. Fighting a raid boss was always exciting. You should have seen us, Fayte. You might think Adam was the best player among us because of that silly title he earned during his stint as a VR gamer, but I was way better than him."

Adam rolled his eyes. "You say that, but how many times did I have to save you when we played the Frozen Winter expansion?"

"And how many times did I save you when you first began playing?" shot back Aris.

"What can I say? I was a noob back then." Adam shrugged.

"I did actually play World of Wargcraft when I was younger." Fayte smiled, though it was tinged with sadness. "Father didn't approve though. He said girls shouldn't be playing games and demanded I focus on learning etiquette and how to act like a proper woman."

"Screw your dad. He doesn't know what he's talking about," Aris said with a huff before she shoved some chicken into her mouth.

Aris was becoming a lot more animated as time passed since her recovery, but Adam considered that a good thing. No, it was the best possible outcome. This was the Aris from before she got Mortems Disease, before her body had started atrophying and her physical weakness left her exhausted most days.

Back during the year when Adam had first met her, Aris had been a rough and tumble girl. When she wasn't playing video games, she was getting filthy playing around in the dirt. They used to live in the countryside. The town they lived in was small, with a population of no more than maybe two or three thousand people.

Towns and cities the world over had experienced a massive population decrease thanks to World War III and Mortems Disease. Cities like New York City, Los Angeles, and Hong Kong had been reduced to nearly half of their original population. Towns like the one Aris grew up in had become the norm.

As dinner continued, Fayte ended up flicking through her tablet. Adam was closest to her, sitting between her and Aris, so he could see that she was looking at online forums regarding information on Age of Gods. There were still mostly just rumors, but there were also a few national announcements from other countries. There was even one international announcement that happened about one hour after they logged out.

"It looks like Lin Akamine has conquered the first dungeon in Age of Gods," Fayte said. "I expected nothing less from the woman who is hailed as the greatest VR player in history."

That reminded him that his party had not conquered the magic academy. They had only managed to reach the first forty floors. He wondered how many floors they would have to travel up to conquer it. Also, was the magic academy even considered a dungeon? He wasn't sure.

"She is pretty impressive," Adam said. "It sounds like she's gotten stronger too. I kind of wish I could battle her again."

"Didn't you fight against her when you took first place in the International VR Championship three years ago?" asked Aris. "I remember watching you, but I can't remember everyone you fought."

"Lin Akamine was one of them," Adam said with a nod. "She was easily the toughest opponent I've ever fought, especially since I was still not used to virtual reality at the time."

While many virtual reality games did their best to simulate reality, that did not mean they did a perfect job. Aside from Age of Gods, all other VR games had issues that made using skills picked up in real life difficult inside of the game. The avatar bodies he used also never felt like his own body. That was one of the areas where Age of Gods differed.

Fayte suddenly paused after scrolling through the information. Her hand trembled a little. Concerned, Adam leaned in to look at what her tablet said and noticed that she had switched to a chatroom and was staring at a name on the screen.

Flame Emperor.

"Isn't he one of the Four Elements you told me about?" Adam asked. "Do you know him?"

"Flame Emperor. His real name is Mason Dairing." Fayte gave him and Aris a thin smile that looked like it might break at any moment. "He's my older brother."

Now Adam understood why she reacted that way. Her older brother was one of Levon's Four Elements—one of his generals, in other words—which meant he probably had a very tight relationship with Levon. The Four Elements were, according to Fayte, the most powerful group after Levon and his vice-commander, Connor Sword.

"I take it you and your brother don't get along?" Adam said.

"Yes." Fayte sighed as she set down the tablet. "My brother was very happy when Levon expressed an interest in marrying me. In fact, it was Mason who introduced me to Levon. When I publicly rejected Levon at the party, I believe Mason felt as if I had disgraced him. He's been very... harsh to me ever since."

"Sounds unpleasant," was all Adam could say.

"That sucks," Aris added with an intense frown that looked out of place on such a cute face.

Tucking a strand of hair behind her ear, Fayte gave Adam a humorless look. "Unpleasant is greatly understating the matter."

Adam could say nothing to that. An awkward feeling settled between him and Fayte for the rest of dinner.

When dinner ended, Aris held out her hands to Adam and smiled. "I want to take a bath. Help me walk?"

"So demanding," Adam mock grumbled as he took her hands, grinning as he pulled the girl to her feet. "Since when have you been so impetuous?"

"Hee-hee. Haven't I always been this way?"

It was true. Aris had been this way until she got sick. Now that she was recovering at an astonishing pace, her original demeanor was returning. It warmed his heart. He never thought that playful and mischievous girl from back then would come back to him.

With Adam's help, Aris walked into the bathroom. He had Aris hold onto the counter as he stripped off her clothes. She was dressed in the pajamas she'd been wearing since last night. He slid the pink pajama bottoms off her hips, then removed her cotton white panties, slowly moving them down her ankles.

"Lift your left foot, please. Now the right."

Aris struggled to lift her feet so he could slide her clothing off, but she still managed it after a little difficulty. Adam took careful note of how her legs were shaking from the exertion.

As Adam came back up, he found himself stopping halfway. Aris's butt was in his face right now. While it looked a little soft because she had been unable to exercise for so long, it was still a beautiful and pert butt. Each cheek was shaped like a perfect oval, and the overall contours of her hips and ass formed a lovely heart shape. Once she toned up, this would become an even more magnificent rear end.

Of course, what really caught Adam's attention was not her butt.

Adam had seen Aris naked many times in the past, but he had never given any thought to it because she had Mortems Disease. Her body would never be able to withstand the rigors of sex. He didn't want to harm her, so he always kept his desire on a tight leash.

Now that she was recovering, Adam found the sight of her hairless mound arousing, and he was now very, *very* horny.

"Adam?" asked Aris.

He took a deep breath and tried to settle down his racing heart. "Yes?"

"I have to pee."

"Oh…"

Trying to keep his cheeks from flushing, Adam had Aris turn around and removed her shirt, then helped her sit on the toilet. As she was going to the bathroom, Adam turned on the bath. He wasn't sure how well her body could hold up to heat right now. That was why he only turned it onto a medium-high setting, enough to make the water warm but not produce steam.

After she went to the restroom, Adam used the same disinfectant wipes to clean Aris's body the way he always did before helping her into the bath.

"Aren't you going to join me?" Aris asked.

Adam hesitated. He wanted to join her, but he was worried he wouldn't be able to control himself.

"I'm not a glass figurine, you know." Aris pouted at him as if she knew exactly what he was thinking. "I know we can't have sex yet, but we can at least do other things, can't we?"

"I… yes. You're right." He smiled. "Sorry. I was letting my worry get the best of me."

"Hee-hee. You're always worrying about me. It's one of the things I love about you."

Adam removed his clothes, wiped himself down, and sank into the warm tub behind Aris. She immediately leaned back against him. As her soft back came into contact with his chest and her butt with his crotch, Adam experienced the same thrill he always did, only it was magnified a thousandfold.

His breathing became just a little heavy.

"You can touch me if you want," Aris murmured softly.

Even though she said he was allowed to touch her, Adam still hesitated. Was it really okay? He'd been resisting his urges for so long that he was worried about what would happen if he gave in. The last thing he wanted to do was hurt the woman he loved.

Whether Adam was worried or not, Aris seemed determined to get something from him. She grabbed his hands and raised them to her chest. As his fingers brushed against the soft plumpness of her chest, Adam sucked in a breath. Aris did not have a large chest. She was only a 31B, but the softness of her breasts, the elasticity he felt as he touched her, and the soft nubs that were already growing stiff, caused his mind to blank.

"Mmm…"

Aris's soft moan as he began rubbing her chest only served to further drive Adam down a hole he could not crawl out of. He started softly, but his rubbing soon became more vigorous as time passed. Only his concern for Aris's well being, which was more powerful than his desire to claim her body, kept him from being rougher.

"Haaah… haaaah… I-I think… my boobs are more sensitive than they used to be," Aris panted as he began lightly teasing her nipples. He traced his fingers around them, flicked them up and then down, and ever so gently pulled on them. Aris released a louder cry at his tug.

"It's probably because your nerve endings have recovered," Adam theorized. "Mortems Disease kills everything, including your nerves. Since your nerves were dying, you couldn't feel much. That was good at the time since it meant you wouldn't feel pain, but now that you're healed, your nerves have also become active. I imagine these heightened sensations will stop once you grow accustomed to having active nerves ending."

"I'm not sure… haaah… mmmm… ahn… I'm not sure I want to get used to it," Aris admitted.

Adam could not stop himself from smiling wryly, but then he leaned down and pressed his lips to her neck. Aris's breathing hitched as his lips branded her slender, beautiful neck, causing her to tilt her head and grant him better access. He traced his lips across her skin. It was perhaps the result of her overstimulated nerve endings, but Aris was sensitive everywhere.

As he kissed her neck and shoulders, Adam finally could no longer resist his impulses and desires, and so he removed one of his hands from her breasts and trailed it across her stomach. The way her soft belly twitched when he glided his fingers across her skin spurred him on. Her breathing grew increasingly heavier the longer he kept this up, until, finally, he reached the most sacred place on her body.

"Oh…"

Aris's eyes went wide as Adam pressed his finger between her thighs. He didn't insert it. He rubbed his finger against her lips, enjoying the way her thighs squirmed against him, then found the hood of flesh hiding her pearl. He worked out that little bundle of nerves and slowly stroked it.

"Oh! Adam! That feels… haaah… mmm… that feels… like I'm being shocked…"

"So it's electric?"

"Verily."

"What does that word even mean?"

Aris could not answer Adam as he rubbed her small clitoris with his index and middle finger. It was tiny—small and cute like her. Adam enjoyed the way it pulsed as he rubbed it.

"A-Adam… I feel something… ah… something's coming!"

"Mmm. Let it come. Don't resist."

"!!!"

Aris opened her mouth in a soundless screamed and arched her back. She stretched out her legs and feet as far as they would go, toes curling as her body twitched several times. Adam could not feel her juices staining his hand, but that was only because they were in the bath. He might not be the most experienced guy around, but he knew an orgasm when he saw one.

"Haaah… haaaah… haaaaaaaaaah…"

Adam looked at Aris as she breathed hard. Now that she'd orgasmed, he was a little worried. Her body was still weak. What if this caused her to weaken further?

"How are you feeling? Everything all right?" he asked.

"Haaah… hmmm… Adam?" Aris was still breathless as she turned her head to look at him.

"Yes?"

"That felt great."

He almost snorted but settled for a smile instead. "I'm glad you liked it."

"I want you to do that again."

"Once is enough for now. I'm still worried you might not be able to handle more."

Aris looked like she wanted to pout, but then she noticed something sticking out of the water. Adam noticed it at nearly the same time as her.

"Then… should I take care of you instead?"

Adam considered accepting her offer. It would be nice to have someone other than himself take care of this problem, and just imagining Aris's soft hands wrapped around his hot, throbbing flesh was enough to make him twitch. But then another thought occurred to him.

He shook his head. "Not yet. I want my first experience with you to be when you're body is fully recovered so I can have all of you. I don't want to stop halfway." He paused. "Besides, it will make the bathwater dirty."

"The bathwater is already dirty," Aris pointed out.

"It will make the bathwater dirtier."

"That sounds like an excuse to me. Are you trying to blue-ball yourself?"

"I have no idea where you learned that word, but you're forbidden from using it from now on."

"Hee-hee. Don't be like that."

It was later at night and Adam was lying in bed. Aris was lying on top of his chest, her body covered with a blanket and blue pajamas. Adam was, of course, bare-chested so Aris could enjoy the feeling of his skin.

As he stroked her back, enjoying the sensation of her body even though it was through her clothes, a soft vibrating sound reached his ears. He turned his head to find the phone on his wireless charger vibrating. Reaching out with one hand, he looked at who was calling, then accepted the call.

"Astaroth, what is it?" he asked.

"I wanted to let you know that we have consistently killed Thor God of Thunder and his level is now back to 1," the gruff voice of Astaroth came from the other end.

"Hmm. Good. You can let him go for now, but I'd like you to find out his identity in the real world."

"Are you planning to kill him?"

"I haven't decided yet."

While Adam did not like anyone hitting on Aris, he also wasn't so unreasonable that he'd kill someone just for trying to flirt with her. At the same time, this man was a member of Levon Pleonexia's Four Elements, which already made him an enemy. Killing him would reduce Levon's overall fighting strength. It was something to consider.

"This guy is probably from a rich family. If we kill him, there will definitely be an investigation. I've no doubt the police will be involved, and depending on how powerful his family is, they might decide to get the American Federation's government involved as well. We would also have to consider Levon's response."

There were a lot of factors to consider when killing someone. The first issue was, of course, the fact that killing was the highest crime a person could commit in this day and age where every life was considered precious. With the Earth's population reduced to about a third of what it had been, every government in the world had not only banned fighting but punished killing with the heaviest punishments available.

Slave labor.

Because killing was frowned upon no matter who you were or what you had done, no government would mete out the death sentence. They would instead force a shock collar on you and then make you work for them for the rest of your life. You would forever be a slave to the government, working on the most menial of manual labor until your body gave out and you died miserably.

"I understand, Master. We will have the information back to you in a few days' time," Astaroth said.

"Keep up the good work."

Adam thought this was all Astaroth wanted from him, but the other man did not hang up.

"Also..."

"Was there something else?"

"We received a request from Levon Pleonexia last week."

"Oh?"

Adam wished he could sit up, but with Aris pressing her entire body onto his chest, he could barely even shift, lest he woke her. His fingers clenched the phone. He was glad his phone had some armor plating to protect it, otherwise it would have broken under his grip.

"They want us to find out who you and Lilith are in real life."

Now that was interesting. He knew the Soul Reapers had done business with Levon Pleonexia before. Their motto was that they would work for anyone so long as the said person was willing to pay their price. With this motto as their main slogan, even if they wanted to deny Levon, they could not because it would look strange and might ruin their reputation. Also, there was nothing wrong with leeching that man of his money.

"Accept the contract, but don't do anything with it yet," Adam decided at last. "If he ever asks if you've found anything, remind him of our rules and tell him that you'll cut ties if he continues to question you."

"Yes, Master."

Astaroth finally hung up and Adam set his phone, now with new finger-shaped indents on the metal casing, back on the wireless charger. He looked back at Aris to make sure she was still asleep, but it was obvious she was because her breathing and heart rate had not changed at all. It was impossible to wake up and not at least show some signs unless you were trained to do so like him.

Once he was certain Aris was still sleeping peacefully, Adam shut his eyes and went to sleep as well.

IN-GAME
ARIS

Watershore's docks were not what Adam would consider big, but there was at least enough room to fit several medium-sized boats that were about fifty yards long from bow to stern. All the ships were made of wood and looked like ancient vessels from a bygone era, which fit with the fantasy setting. As the breeze caused his hair to billow, carrying the salty scent of the sea to his nose, Adam nervously tapped one foot impatiently on the wooden dock as he waited for Aris to arrive.

"Where is she?" he asked himself.

He wasn't looking for an answer, but he got one anyway.

"She will arrive when she arrives. Be more patient. It takes six hours to reach Watershore from the Village of Beginnings, and the one we came from was probably one of the closer ones. If she came from a village that is further away, it will take even longer," Titania said.

Adam wanted to scowl at the little fairy sitting on his shoulder, but he knew this wasn't her fault. He cursed the game mechanics that dealt with travel. Why did traveling take so long? It took several real-life days just to reach the magic academy, and now he was learning that it took them six hours to get from the Village of Beginnings to Watershore?

"Come to think of it, I did log off for several hours when I was in that boat," Adam muttered.

"And then we were attacked by pirates while you were in your original world," Titania said with a scowl.

Adam couldn't do much more than smile helplessly at the now irate fairy, whose glare was pretty potent for such a tiny woman.

Today was the day that Aris would be leaving the Village of Beginnings and traveling to Watershore. The other members of his party had wanted to be present, but Adam asked them to wait for him at Solum. It was selfish. However, Adam wanted to be the first person who Aris saw, and he wanted to form a party with her by himself.

Well, that was the plan, except Kureha and Titania could not actually be away from him. Kureha was his pet and Titania could not be removed from his party. He was making exceptions for them out of consideration for their circumstances.

"It's already been several weeks since we first arrived here in Watershore," Adam muttered. "It's kind of crazy when you think about it."

"It does not feel like much time has passed, does it?" asked Titania.

"You're right about that. It feels like only a few days have gone by, but it's actually been more than a month since I first started playing Age of Gods."

"Age of Gods?" Titania questioned with a tilted head.

It took Adam a moment to realize that she didn't know that Age of Gods was the name of this game, which made sense. NPCs weren't supposed to know they were just creations in a video game. Titania was also so realistic that he sometimes forgot she wasn't real.

"Yip! Yip!"

As Adam was debating what he should tell Titania, Kureha began excitedly yipping. She was sitting by his legs. He leaned down and began stroking the fur on her head, which she seemed to appreciate because she nuzzled his hand and made several mrring sounds that were like happy fox noises.

"What is it, Kureha?" he asked.

"Yip!"

Kureha raised a paw and pointed at something in the distance. Outlined by the setting sun, an object was approaching them from the ocean. Adam raised his head, placed a hand over it to shield his eyes, and squinted. The object was, of course, a small vessel made of wood, with a black sail that had... a pirate symbol on it?!

"Is that a pirate ship?!" Titania asked in alarm.

"It looks like it," Adam muttered. "Are pirates allowed to dock in Watershore?"

"Of course not!" Titania scowled. "You think any respectable city would let a pirate ship dock with them? Not only would they lose all their business, but they would probably lose their lives as well."

"So what is this about?"

"How should I know?!"

While Adam and Titania were talking, the many people who manned the docks were panicking. Dockworkers were running all over the wooden deck and some had rushed into town. Adam heard the scream of "Pirates!" from more than a few people. A few minutes later, a large group of soldiers gathered. All of them were dressed in steel armor, were at level 30, and were armed to the teeth.

As the pirate ship came closer, Adam was able to make out the ship's features in greater detail—the black scoring from what must have been a fire or some other form of damage on the hull, and the small tears in the sails like someone had sliced through them with a knife. There was also a person standing at the very bow. The closer the ship came, the more distinct that person became.

"Hold on… that's…" Adam's eyes widened.

The person standing near the ship's bow was a young woman dressed in clothes that didn't resemble armor at all. It looked more like the kind of outfit a belly dancer might wear. Her skirt traveled down to her ankles, but slits were traveling up both sides, revealing a good amount of leg. Likewise, her top looked like classic bikini armor, the kind found in games that were popular during the early 2000s. It didn't cover her soft stomach at all, and it showed a more than generous portion of her cleavage and underboob. Strapped across her back was a pair of curved swords. The only reason Adam even knew this person was because of the veil she wore to hide her face.

"Adam! Hey, Adam!"

She was also yelling his name and waving at him.

"Is that Aris?" asked Titania as she placed a hand over her eyes to shield them from the sun.

"It is!" Adam exclaimed in surprise, though he frowned at her wardrobe. "What is she wearing?"

The ship soon came into the dock. All the soldiers gathered around, swords at the ready. Adam, Titania, and Kureha stood on the dock near where the ship had stopped and watched silently as a boarding plank was extended. In the next moment, what appeared on top of that boarding plank was not a pirate, but a young girl rushing down on swift feet.

"Adam!!!"

Aris moved so fast that Adam barely had time to catch her. Even when he did, she plowed into him so hard he was nearly knocked off his feet. She moved in practically a blur! One second was on top of the ship, and the next she was in his arms, her own wrapped tightly around him.

"Aris," Adam muttered as he realized this truly was his Aris. Adam was able to recognize Aris by her body alone. He had held her, dressed her, bathed her, and massaged her body for years. There was not a single spot on her body that he had not touched. If a thousand veiled women were to gather together, he was confident he'd be able to pick her out of the crowd.

Not only did he recognize Aris by her figure, but he recognized the scent of her hair. It was the same scent she had in real life. In fact, the Aris in his arms right now was indistinguishable from her real-life self. Scent, figure, feel. Everything about her was the same.

It's unbelievable that this game can create someone with such an astounding degree of accuracy and realism.

"I can't believe I finally get to see you in the game," Aris said, setting her chin on his chest to look at him. He could not see her face, but he knew she was smiling. "Hee-hee. Isn't it exciting?"

"It's very exciting," Adam said with a smile of his own.

The world felt like it had disappeared around the two as they gazed into each other's eyes. It was the only part of them that was visible behind their headgear, but Adam could recognize Aris's beautiful blue eyes anywhere. He was sure they would have kissed by now if she wasn't wearing that veil and him a mask.

However, as with all good things, this reunion had to eventually end.

"Ahem. Ah. Miss Aris—er, no, Lady Aris, do you require our assistance for anything else?"

A voice spoke up from somewhere, and Adam looked up to realize a pirate was standing on the boarding plank. He was a tall, gangly man. His beard was thick, but not to the same thickness as the pirate that Adam fought and killed. He had a black and white coat, wearing what could be considered the quintessential pirate garb. He even had a hook for a right hand.

The information screen above his head said his name was Davy Jones.

"Oh!" Aris removed herself from Adam's embrace and looked at the pirate. "I don't need any more help. Thank you. You can leave now." After speaking, Aris narrowed her eyes, spread her feet shoulder-width apart, placed her hands on her hips, and thrust out her chest. "However, if I hear about you attacking ships again, I am going to be very upset with you."

"D-d-don't worry, Lady Aris!" The pirate waved both hand and hook back and forth in a panicked gesture. His face looked to have had all the blood drained from it. "W-we already promised you we was going to turn over a new leaf, arg? I'm a man o' me word."

There was something odd about this man and his reaction. Maybe it was the blush on his gnarled cheeks. Maybe it was the infatuation in his eyes. Maybe it was just a whole bunch of things. Call Adam crazy, but he was almost positive this pirate wannabe NPC was gazing at his Aris as if she was the sole center of the universe.

He narrowed his eyes at the man.

"Good," Aris said with a decisive nod. "Then you can go."

Adam had no idea what was going on, and neither did the confused soldiers, or the equally curious Titania and Kureha. All they could do was watch this interaction between Aris and Davy Jones. When the pirate captain went back into his ship and began shouting, "Ye heard the lass, ya scurvy curs! Get yer useless arses moving!" Adam finally couldn't withhold his curiosity.

"What was all that about?" he asked.

"Hee-hee." Grinning as she spun around to face him, Aris placed her hands behind her back and leaned forward. "When I was on my way here, that group of pirates attacked the ship I was on, so I beat them up."

There was silence. Adam thought he heard a seagull cry out in the distance.

"You... beat them up?" Adam asked dully.

Aris nodded. "Uh-huh. And then after I beat them up, they all got down on their knees and begged me for mercy. They said they would do anything I asked if I stopped beating them, so I asked them to send me to Watershore and give up their pirating ways." She paused, looking thoughtful. "They didn't start calling me Lady Aris until about halfway here though. I'm not sure what that was about."

Adam had no response to her words, but when he thought about it, this did sound kind of like something she would do. The Aris he knew from before she got Mortems Disease was adventurous, mischievous, and not someone you crossed unless you were stupid. While she never picked fights, she was the kind of girl who'd never stand for someone bullying others and would always intervene. It had gotten him into a lot of trouble on any number of occasions.

He still remembered how some boy's parents had complained because he'd broken their son's arm. As if that was Adam's fault. That boy should not have tried to touch his Aris.

Aris also had a mysterious air about her. People who got to know her couldn't help but become enamored. It was that very atmosphere she surrounded herself with, albeit unknowingly, that had drawn Adam to her.

Before doing anything else, Adam and Aris explained the situation to the soldiers who had arrived. The soldiers all stared at Aris like she wasn't human. Of course, quite a few of them gulped when they noticed how skimpy her clothing was. Adam scowled when he noticed a number of them looking at Aris's chest, stomach, or legs. Once that was done, it was finally time for introductions.

"Aris, this is Titania," Adam said with a gesture toward the little fairy fluttering above them. She had been forced to leap away when Aris glomped him.

"It's very nice to meet you," Aris said.

"It is a pleasure to meet you as well," Titania replied. "Adam has told me a lot about you."

"Ah? He has?" Aris looked from Titania to Adam.

"He has spoken about the woman he loves many times," Titania confirmed.

"Hee-hee. That makes me kind of embarrassed," Aris admitted, though it was hard to tell if she was actually embarrassed. If he didn't want to keep players seeing her face, he would have already asked her to remove that veil so he could see whether she was blushing or not.

"And this little fox right here is Kureha," Adam said, pointing at the fox yokai sitting at his feet and wagging her two tails.

Aris looked down at the fox. There were exactly five seconds of silence. Then she squealed.

"Awww! She's so cute! You said she's a fox yokai? That's like those Japanese shapeshifters, right? Does that mean she has a human form? What does her human form look like? Is she a beautiful young woman or a little girl?"

Scooping the fox into her arms, Aris bombarded Adam with all kinds of questions. She was so excited that Adam thought he saw stars in her eyes.

"Calm down." Adam raised his hands in a gesture to make her settle down. "I can't answer those questions if you don't let me." Aris calmed down immediately after he spoke, but she kept her gaze locked firmly on him. "Yes, she is a fox yokai like the kind from those Japanese cartoons we used to watch. She does have human form, but her level isn't high enough for her to transform, so I don't know what it looks like. Anyway, now that you're here, we should head over to the mayor's house so you can receive a request."

"Ah. Right. Okay. Yeah, let's do that." Aris nodded several times. "We can keep talking on the way to visit the mayor."

"Maybe you should add her to your party first," Titania suggested.

"You're right. I should do that."

Nodding at the woman's logical suggestion, Adam sent Aris an invitation to join his party, which she accepted immediately, and then the two of them were off. Kureha leaped from Aris's arms and made herself comfortable on Adam's head. Aris pouted a little, but then she became enamored with their conversation as the two of them shared their in-game experiences so far.

Adam enjoyed the way Aris looked around at the village with her sparkling blue eyes. It was so refreshing to see her acting excited and jovial instead of the soft-spoken and delicate girl she was before.

"I almost forgot, you mentioned you gained a new class. Mind if I see it?" asked Adam.

Aris beamed at him. "Of course you can. Do you mind if I look at your class?"

"Feel free."

Now that he had her permission, Adam opened his in-game window and clicked on his party members. He scrolled down until he reached Aris's name and pressed it to bring up her stats.

What he found was shocking.

Name: Aris_Lancer
Class: Blade Dancer
Lvl: 11
SP: 0
AP; 6,000
Experience: 64,890/153,600
Reputation: 15,000
Strength: +60
Constitution: +95
Dexterity: +100
MP: +20
Speed: +6,400
Physical Attack: +635
Health: 660/660
Hit-Rate: 100%
MP: 240/240
Movement: +51,200
Luck: +10
Physical Defense: +290
Magical Defense: +290
Dodge-Rate: 100%
Magic Attack: +20

Skills:
Skill Name: Slashing
Description: A basic skill where the player swings his or her sword and attacks the enemy!
Current lvl: 5 MAXED
Ability: Causes 150% damage to enemy if it hits
MP Cost: 1
Cooldown time: 0 seconds

Skill Name: Thrust
Description: A basic skill where the player thrusts his or her sword at the enemy!
Current lvl: 5 MAXED
Ability: Causes 160% damage with a 10% chance at getting a critical hit
MP Cost: 5
Cooldown time: 1 second

Skill Name: Blade Dance
Description: A skill unique to the player Aris_Lancer. Allows for continuous attacks without pause.
Current lvl: 5
AP needed to reach lvl 6: 64,000
Ability: Can constantly attack and hit every time without pausing to use another attack
Chances of landing a critical strike is 25%
MP Cost: 5 MP per attack
Cooldown time: 30 seconds

Skill Name: Double Slash
Description: User attacks with both weapons at the same time.
Current lvl: 1
AP needed to reach lvl 2: 4,000
Ability: Deals x2 damage

MP Cost: 100
Cooldown time: 15 seconds

Skill Name: Tornado Dance
Description: A sword technique where the player spins around
and attacks everyone surrounding them.
Current lvl: 1
AP needed to reach lvl 2: 3,000
Ability: 100% damage all enemies surrounding player
MP Cost: 50
Cooldown time: 20 seconds

Skill Name: Dancing Swords
Description: A sword technique that lets the user attack with
four thrusts one after the other in quick succession.
Current lvl: 1
AP needed to reach lvl 2: 4,000
Ability: Deals 200% damage with every successful attack
Damage is stacked
MP Consumption 50
Cooldown time: 15 seconds

Equipment:
Item Name: Blade Dancer Falchions x2
Item Type: Sword
Grade: 4-Star
Use Requirements: Can only be equipped by Blade Dancers
Description: These swords were once wielded by an aspiring
hero. They were forged by the dwarves and given to a man who
aided them in their time of need.
Abilities: Physical Attack+200 x2; Speed+200 x2

Item Name: Blade Dancer Sandals
Item Type: Clothing
Grade: 4-Star

Use Requirements: Can only be equipped by Blade Dancers
Description: The sandals of a Blade Dancer do not provide much protection, but they do provide a boost to speed.
Abilities: Defense+50; Magic Defense+50; Speed+200%

Item Name: Blade Dancer Top
Item Type: Clothing
Grade: 4-Star
Use Requirements: Can only be equipped by Blade Dancers
Description: The Blade Dancer shirt does not have a high defense, but it boosts speed by a lot.
Abilities: Defense+50; Magic Defense+50 Speed+200%

Item Name: Blade Dancer Gloves
Item Type: Clothing
Grade: 4-Star
Use Requirements: Can only be equipped by Blade Dancers
Description: Blade Dancer gloves offer a speed boost and some basic protection.
Abilities: Defense+50; Magic Defense+50; Speed+200%

Item Name: Blade Dancer Skirt
Item Type: Clothing
Grade: 4-Star
Use Requirements: Can only be equipped by Blade Dancers
Description: A skirt worn by Blade Dancers. Gives a significant boost to speed.
Abilities: Defense+50; Magic Defense+50; Speed+200%

Item Name: Veil
Item Type: Accessory
Grade: 1-Star
Use Requirements: Can be equipped by anyone
Description: A simple cloth veil.
Abilities; It can hide your face from view

Because she had a hidden class, it was only natural that her stats would be much higher than someone who had a normal class. At the same time, while Aris's stats were relatively high, what made him gawk was her Speed and Movement stats. They were the highest number he'd seen so far. His own stats were rather impressive, but he had nothing on those two particular stats.

"She's as ridiculous as you are," Titania said. Her words were very apt.

"I expected nothing less," Adam replied.

Adam, Aris, Titania, and Kureha traveled up the mountain and to the mansion sitting on the bluff. Adam was already known to the guards because of the quest he'd done for the mayor. They didn't even need to say anything before the four of them were directed to the Watershore mayor's office.

"Welcome back, young hero." The mayor smiled at him. "What can I do for you?"

"My girlfriend just came from the Village of Beginnings," Adam explained, getting straight to the point. "I was wondering if you had any quests we can take together."

"Hmm…" While the Watershore Mayor gave his girlfriend's flat stomach and modest chest an appreciative glance, Adam was pleased to see the man didn't focus on it for long. "I do have a few tasks that require someone of strength. I'd normally never give them to someone who hasn't already proven themselves, but since you are the one asking, I don't mind giving you this one. We received a request for aid from a village several miles away. There is a powerful beast rampaging there. I was about to send my soldiers, but since you came along, would you like to go in their stead?"

Ding!

[You have been offered a new quest: [Slay Mythical Beast!] Do you accept? Yes or no?]

Adam was a little startled when the quest name was [Slay Mythical Beast], but he decided to accept the quest. This would be a good chance to see how well he and Aris worked as a team.

***

The village they were asked to travel to was called Llyn. It was not as far away as the Deadlands, but it still took half an hour to reach on horseback. When they arrived, Adam, Aris, Titania, and Kureha were shocked to discover that the village really was under attack by a monster.

In most video games, villages and towns were places monsters couldn't enter. This was usually explained with some in-game lore like "there is a barrier that protects the town" or some such, which most players just bought into because thinking about it wasn't worth the effort or the headaches it would cause. Of course, some towns were attacked, but they were always attacked as part of the in-game story.

It seemed like in this game, villages could be attacked at random.

The creature attacking Llyn released an earth-shattering roar as it raised its scaled muzzle into the sky and breathed out several streams of fire. Red scales glistened in the sunlight. Two leathery pinions jutting from its back generated an incredible gust of wind with each flap. It walked on four massive legs, had a tail that swept several soldiers away with every swing, and clawed feet that could easily rend flesh from bone. At present, it was smashing that several yards-long tail into a building, decimating it.

"Is that a dragon?!" asked a shocked Aris.

"No," Titania answered. "That is just a wyvern. They are related to dragons, but they are much weaker. Of course, this is all relative. A single wyvern is generally powerful enough that it requires an entire squadron of humans to kill. Hold on for a moment. Let me [scan] it for you."

Name: Flame Wyvern
Description: A wyvern with a fire affinity. It typically ignores human settlements, but they will come down and cause havoc when hungry.
Class: 1-Star
Lvl: 40
Health: 500,000/500,000
MP: 50,000/50,000
Strength: +1,000
Constitution: +2,000
Dexterity: +500
Intelligence: +500
Speed: +100

Skills:
Skill Name: Fireball
Description: The wyvern shoots a large fireball from its mouth.
MP Cost: 150

Cooldown time: 10 seconds

Skill Name: Firestorm
Description: Releases a wave of flame that sweeps over every
enemy nearby
200% damage to all enemies within 50 yards
MP Cost: 1,000
Cooldown time: 10 seconds

Flame Bullet: Fires a series of small flame projectiles from its
mouth.
Damage = Intelligence
MP Cost: 100
Cooldown time: 1,000 seconds

Tail Sweep: Attacks enemies with its tail.
Damage = Strength + Speed
There is a 65% chance of enemies getting knocked over
MP Cost: 200
Cooldown Time: 0 Seconds

law Swipe: The wyvern swipes at enemies with its claw.
Damage = Strength
MP Cost: 100
Cooldown time: 0 seconds

"This thing looks pretty strong," Aris muttered.

"This is actually pretty weak," Adam countered, recalling some of the monsters he'd already slain. "You ready?"

"Of course I am!"

"Then let's do this."

With a smile on their faces, Adam and Aris led Kureha and Titania into battle against the [Flame Wyvern].

✳✳✳

"You're right. That was easy," Aris admitted as they neared Solum.

While the [Flame Wyvern] did have a relatively high level, Adam and Aris had defeated it within just a few short minutes. Adam's ridiculous Physical Attack stat combined with Aris's speedy combination attacks had demolished its health within maybe five minutes or less. Adam honestly couldn't say how well he and Aris worked together as a team because the enemy died too quickly for him to gauge their combat compatibility.

Of course, being able to kill a level 40 1-Star enemy in just a few seconds probably showed they worked well together. Maybe.

"It was even easier than I thought it would be," Adam admitted.

"I keep telling you, the only person who would find defeating a level 40 [Flame Wyvern] at your level easy is you." Titania released a long suffering sigh as if they had been over this before, which they kind of had. She often complained about how ridiculous it was to watch someone with such a low level kill creatures ten or even twenty levels above him.

"Looks like we're coming up on Solum," Adam said as he saw the city gates getting closer. "I've already let Fayte, Susan, and Lilith know we're coming. They should be at the food court."

"Do you think… Susan and Lilith will like me?" asked Aris, sounding nervous.

Adam reached out and grabbed her hand. "Of course they will. I'm certain both of them will love you."

His words didn't seem to reassure her, but Aris nodded anyway. This would only be the second time she'd met someone whose name wasn't Adam in the last few years. Because of her Mortems Disease, everyone had avoided her like the plague, and now that she was finally cured, she wanted to make friends. Her nervousness was understandable.

They reached the gate and were let through after Aris showed her Letter of Recognition to the guards and Adam paid a fee. Aris was enamored with the ancient-looking architecture. He let her look around as he led her to the food court, which was already filled with thousands of players, all looking to form parties or discussing their next quest.

Adam's group of three was sitting at their usual table. Several men were surrounding the table like vultures waiting for a free meal, but none of those men had the guts to walk over and engage the women in conversation. Adam held Aris by the hand and came over without a second thought. His actions seemed to shock the men.

"Who the hell is this guy?!"

"Does he think he can just waltz over to a couple of beauties and expect them to pay attention to him? Get in line, you bastard!"

"You know what makes it even worse? It looks like he already has a girlfriend!"

"I hope you choke on a cock, you damn normie!"

Adam only sighed at the insults being hurled at him before stepping up to the table.

"Adam," Fayte said as she turned to face him. "We've been waiting for you." Her eyes shifted from Adam to Aris standing beside him. "Aris, it's good to see you."

"Hm. It's good to be here," Aris said in a soft voice, now nervous at being surrounded by so many people she didn't know. It really had been too long since she'd spent any length of time within a group. She tried to hide behind Adam, but he was having none of that. He grabbed her arm and pulled her to the front.

"Everyone, this is Aris," Adam introduced.

Of course, the one Adam was introducing Aris to was Susan. They were already living with Fayte and saw her every day, and while Aris and Lilith had never been formally introduced, the assassin was perfectly aware of who this girl was. Only Susan did not know her.

"Um… it's very nice to meet you!" Susan stood up and bowed slightly. "I look forward to gaming with you."

"M-me too." Aris, perhaps influenced by Susan's politeness, also bowed. "Please take care of me."

Such a polite response…

While Lilith did not speak, she did nod once in Aris's direction. Adam only frowned a little. He knew Lilith was not inclined toward talking, but he wished the woman would say something. It wouldn't kill her to be polite to others every now and again.

In either event, with that, Aris's induction into their party was officially complete.

THE GUILD TOKEN

Adam did not speak much as he sat surrounded by women. He was content to let them talk amongst themselves. More importantly, he wanted Aris to interact with these women so she could grow more accustomed to everyone. Fortunately, Aris had always been an adventurous spirit. It didn't take long before she was over her nervousness and enthusiastically talking to the others.

"Ah! Y-you like playing console games too?!" Susan asked when Aris finished telling them about the games she and Adam used to play.

Aris nodded. "Mm. I love old-school console games, especially for systems back in the early 2000s like the PS22 and the XR35."

"I have both of those systems!" Susan exclaimed.

"Really?!"

"Yes! I'm currently replaying Tales of Alexandria on the PS22 and Curse of Malum for the XR35! I probably would have only bought one console, but they each have their exclusive games that I wanted to play."

While it was impossible to see her expression because Aris was wearing a veil, Adam knew there was an excited smile on her face and stars in her eyes. Her enthusiasm didn't need facial expressions to adequately convey. She leaned over and clasped Susan's hands.

"My new best friend!"

"You realize I also have the PS22 and XR35, right? We were just playing games on the XR35 the other day," Fayte said dryly. She sounded amused.

"Of course I know." Aris looked at Fayte and nodded. "You are my first best friend, and Susan is now my second best friend."

"I suppose I can accept that," Fayte said with a tinkling laugh that sounded like wind chimes.

"Excuse me, but what are these 'vee-dee-o games' you speak of?" asked Titania.

"Ah. Video games are…"

Adam stopped paying attention as Aris tried to explain the concept of video games to Titania, treating the fairy like she was just another member of their party. He instead looked at Lilith. The young woman had not said a single word since he introduced Aris. Of course, she seldom spoke anyway, but, perhaps because of how much the others were talking, she seemed exceptionally quiet right now.

"Are you not going to join them?" he asked the woman as she pet Kureha's two fluffy tails and fox ears.

Lilith shook her head. "I am too different from them. You know that. It is better if I remain in the background."

Adam felt an imperceptible frown tug at his lips. "I know you haven't had the most... conventional of lives, but you're here now, and you have four great women who would make good friends. Shouldn't you at least try to make an effort to befriend them?"

"Is that an order, Master?" asked Lilith.

"Do you want it to be?"

Adam and Lilith stared at each other for several seconds. The silence seemed to stretch on. It wasn't long before Adam realized the conversation between the four women had died down and they were now staring at him and Lilith. He looked at Aris as she tilted her head, then Fayte whose narrowed gaze said she saw something he might not be comfortable explaining. Only Susan seemed to have not noticed.

"I have noticed this before, but... you two seem awfully close," Fayte said.

"I was about to say the same thing," Aris added with a nod. "Do you two know each other?"

Adam briefly considered lying, but he could never lie to Aris. It was not something he ever wanted to do.

"We are acquaintances," he allowed. "I've known her for about..." He glanced in her direction. "Eleven years now."

"Ah! That means you knew Lilith before meeting me!" Aris exclaimed in shock.

"I had not realized you two had known each other for such a long time." Adam thought he heard a frown in Fayte's voice, but he could not tell for sure. She was excellent at masking her emotions. The veil didn't help. At the same time, that tone made her sound colder than he was used to.

"That's all in the past." Adam shook his head. "Anyway, since all of us have gathered, there's something I wanted to discuss with you."

"W-what is it?" asked Susan.

He looked at the youngest of their group. Susan's innocent brown eyes were larger than even Aris's beautiful blues, so big they reminded him of a puppy. However, beyond her adorable appearance was a perceptiveness that shocked him. She seemed to recognize that he wasn't comfortable talking about his and Lilith's past (he now realized she had probably noticed his interaction with Lilith too, but she did not say anything out of consideration for him), so she was allowing him to change the subject.

He would have to reevaluate his opinion of her. She was meek, but she was also observant.

"Not here. Too many ears. Let's find a more suitable location to talk."

While the ladies all looked at each other, no one said anything as they stood up as one and headed off. Kureha climbed onto his head, Titania sat down on his shoulder, and the group gathered around him under the intense scrutiny of nearly every player in the food court. Of course, the reason Adam had decided not to talk there was because of the people who had been staring at them this whole time.

There were a lot of other areas they could speak in Solum, but for the sake of privacy, Adam decided to get a room at an inn where they could talk.

Unfortunately, they ran into another problem.

"All six of you are sharing a room?! Do you think my inn is a brothel?!"

The owner of the inn that Adam tried to rent a room from stood behind the counter, her somewhat large and masculine face bright red, eyes narrowed in anger. She was a big woman, which made her more intimidating than your typical hotel clerk.

"We're not actually here to sleep," Adam tried to tell her. "We just want to—"

"So you're not here to sleep, are you?! Planning to keep these girls up all night, huh?! Listen here, young man, I won't tell you and these women how to live your lives, but in my inn, there will not be any debauchery allowed! Do you understand me?!"

Adam was glad no one was inside this inn aside from them right now. The wide, open space near the front was bereft of other people. He didn't think he would ever be able to live it down if someone was present and heard what this woman was saying. At the same time, he was wondering what he should say to get out of this situation.

While he was debating with himself, Fayte stepped forward. "Excuse me, ma'am. I think you have the wrong impression here."

"Oh? Who are you? You think I'm going to listen to someone who hides her face behind a veil?"

Adam flinched at the rancor in the woman's voice. He'd never met such a belligerent NPC before. It made him wonder which crackpot AI developer had a hand in her programming.

Whether Fayte was upset with the woman or not, she never let on, instead nodding her head. "You are absolutely right. Hiding behind a veil is rude when you are trying to speak with someone as their equal. Allow me to rectify that."

"Ah?"

The inn owner became shocked when Fayte removed her veil, revealing a face so beautiful that even Adam was tempted to believe she wasn't real. How could anyone except a goddess have such a gorgeous face? Her soft appearance, beautiful blue eyes, refined elegance, and artfully combed golden hair combined with an aura of nobility and gentleness to create a woman whose outstanding beauty could ruin nations.

Adam once heard a story about Helen of Troy, how a woman named Helen was so beautiful that a prince abducted her to force her into marriage. This action was what started the Trojan War. Adam imagined Fayte's beauty was even more outstanding than that woman's.

"Now that we are speaking face to face, please allow me to clear up the misunderstanding between us." Fayte smiled, and the woman before her could say nothing, allowing her to continue. "My companions and I have something very important to discuss and were looking for a private room so we can talk. That is why we wish to rent out a room at your inn. I promise you that nothing 'lewd' will happen while we are here. Won't you please let us rent out a room?"

"Well… um… sure, I guess. So long as nothing of that nature is going to happen…"

"Thank you very much for understanding."

It cost fifty gold coins to rent a room here. Once Fayte handed over the necessary currency, she led their group up the stairs after receiving the key, opened the door to their room, and walked inside with them trailing close behind her.

"Fayte is really impressive, huh?" Aris whispered in Adam's ear.

"She's definitely an amazing woman," he agreed.

"Hee-hee. It sounds like you really like her."

Adam frowned, not sure how to take the comment, but he was not given a chance to say anything as the girl walked into the room with the others and sat down on the bed. There was only one. It also wasn't large enough for all six of them. Aris, Fayte, Susan, and Lilith sat together while Titania fluttered down and took her own spot. Kureha hopped off his head and curled up on Lilith's lap, much to the woman's pleasure.

Aris pouted when she saw this.

"We found a place to speak in private now." Fayte set her hands on her lap. "What did you want to talk about?"

Adam disregarded the distracting thoughts that Aris's words had caused, reached into his item pouch, and pulled out an object.

"I wanted to talk about this."

It was a strange object no bigger than his palm. Shaped like a hexagon, it had a simple appearance with a single set of characters on both sides. Each side had the same characters. Adam could not read it, but the name that appeared on its display screen was [Guild Creation Token].

"This [Guild Creation Token] was something we received after defeating the Elemental Master," Adam said. "I'm sure you all know the significance of this token."

"You can't create a guild without one," Susan said, staring at the object with some fervency. "Not only that, but no other [Guild Creation Token] has appeared yet, according to the online forums, meaning this is the first one to show up."

"Right. This is the first." Adam nodded. "We have a [Guild Creation Token], and I think it is important that we decide on what to do with it."

Adam swept his gaze across the five women and one fox. Titania did not seem to be paying much attention, but she didn't care much for matters like this. On the other hand, Fayte and Susan seemed to understand his meaning and had gone silent. Lilith may or may not understand his words. Busy pampering Kureha, the assassin had never played a video game before now. Aris was the only one who appeared confused.

"Shouldn't we just use it to create a guild?" the innocent woman asked. "I mean, that is what they are for, right?"

"That is correct, but there are a lot of political issues involved with forming the first guild," Fayte said. When Aris just continued to stare at her, the woman smiled and explained. "The creation of the first guild almost always comes with certain benefits and privileges that other guilds do not have. For example, the Pleonexia Alliance created the first guild in the previous game, and not only were other players unable to attack them for one month, but they were given first priority in shops, able to do more business with NPCs, and their reputation climbed higher than any other guild in the game simply because they were the first. It goes without saying that being able to create the first guild comes with huge benefits."

"And because it comes with huge benefits, it also comes with a lot of danger," Adam added. "Even if, like in the previous game, we are given an entire month of protection, once that month wears off, it is very likely our guild will be beset upon by all sides by the other guilds."

Aris finally seemed to understand where they were coming from. Her eyes went wide.

"Now that you understand the problem, I think we should talk about how to resolve it," Adam said.

"I assume you have an idea," Titania finally spoke up, arms crossed and legs kicking back and forth as they dangled off the bed. "You might seem reckless when you fight, but I have noticed that you are very cunning outside of battle. I cannot believe you have not already thought of some method for dealing with this."

Adam smiled behind his own mask. "You are right. I have already thought of a method to resolve this issue, but I would like everyone to tell me what you think of this idea before we do anything."

The women shifted in their seats as they waited for Adam to compose himself. He closed his eyes and briefly thought over his idea before speaking, double and triple-checking his idea from every angle. Adam couldn't find any flaws in his plan, but no plan ever survived first contact with the enemy. Who knew what would happen once they put it into action.

"I was thinking of talking to Solum's Mayor, Bromley Paxton, and asking him to host a tournament for players… with this [Guild Creation Token] as the prize," Adam said.

"Ah?!" Aris and Susan exclaimed at the same time.

"I see." Fayte narrowed her eyes. "Your idea is to have it seem like the mayor is putting this up as a prize to the winner of the tournament, and then you plan to participate and defeat everyone in the tournament as a means of showcasing your power."

Adam couldn't help but be amazed by this woman's intelligence. "That's right. Once everyone learns that a [Guild Creation Token] is being offered as the prize for this tournament, every major guild and power will sign up for it. This will not only give us a great opportunity to observe all the major players, but it will also let us showcase our own powers."

"Our?" Susan asked, suddenly seeming to realize something. "You mean…?"

"I won't be the only one participating," Adam said with a nod. "All of us will be participating. It's important to show everyone how strong we are. If we can display our strength now by defeating every player who participates, they will understand that we aren't a group you can simply mess with just because we lack numbers."

Adam's idea was simple and direct. Have the mayor host a tournament, offer a prize that no one could resist, and then have him and the other members of his party crush every person in the competition. After they won, they could create their own guild. While Adam was sure some people would not be able to resist attacking after their guild was created, showcasing their powers like this would serve as a huge deterrent to smaller guilds who might have otherwise attacked.

"We will still have to worry about the Pleonexia Alliance," Fayte said after thinking things through. "We might have to worry about Daggerfall Dynasty as well. They are the two largest guilds in the American Federation right now. Both have constantly competed against the other, and many people consider their competition to be the only one that matters. If we interfere with that, it might invite trouble."

"This is true, but that just means we need to become powerful enough that we don't have to worry about them," Adam announced.

Fayte went silent. She still seemed uncertain about the idea of forming the first guild, but she also knew that if she wanted to win her bet, then big risks needed to be taken. The higher the risk, the higher the reward.

"If you are worried about being caught up in a fight with the Pleonexia Alliance and Daggerfall Dynasty, then don't worry. I have already thought of a couple solutions to deal with them," Adam said.

"You have?" Fayte looked a little shocked. It hadn't been that long since they had gotten the [Guild Creation Token], after all, but

Adam had already thought of a solution to keep the two largest guilds off their backs? Anyone would be surprised.

"I have." Adam nodded. "It will take a bit of work. I have to contact a few people. However, my idea should serve as an adequate deterrent—at least, in the short term."

Adam grew silent as he waited for Fayte to say something. He took that moment to observe the others. Titania still seemed more or less disinterested in what they were talking about, but she was at least paying attention to him. On the other hand, Susan was staring at him with wide eyes, seemingly enamored by the confidence he projected. Lilith also seemed that way. Her fervent gaze, as she looked at him, was a bit… disturbing, but he knew that was just how she was.

"I think it's a great idea," Aris said at last. "We should do it."

"Should we?" Fayte looked amused as she crossed her arms. The gesture had the effect of pushing her breasts up and causing her robes to stretch taut. Now that he was thinking about it, those robes did not leave much to the imagination—and as he was thinking this, Fayte continued. "Are you agreeing with Adam because he's your lover?"

"That's only half the reason," Aris declared.

"And what is the other half?"

"Hee-hee. I just want to kick some butt and take some names."

"…"

No one, not even Adam, knew what to say to that.

***

Once it was decided they would follow Adam's advice, the others logged off. It was getting late. The only ones who didn't log off just yet were Adam and Lilith.

"Master."

Lilith knelt on the floor the moment everyone vanished. Titania stared at the woman with that odd look of hers. She was most definitely trying to figure out what kind of relationship he shared with this mysterious woman.

"Please stand up. And don't call me that. Don't forget we're still not alone."

Adam glanced at Titania, who noticed his gaze and turned her head to stare right back at him. He had convinced the little fairy not to say anything to the others. However, she did not approve of him keeping his relationship with Lilith a secret.

"Yes, Master."

Struggling to contain his exasperation and guilt, Adam said, "I want you to get in contact with Astaroth and tell him about my plans. He'll know what to do. Can I count on you?"

"Of course you can." Lilith placed a hand against her chest. "You know there is nothing I would not do for you. If you ever have anything you need of me, no matter what it is, just say what you need and this servant will do it without question."

"I've noticed you only ever talk this much when we're discussing matters concerning your loyalty to me." Adam sighed, then waved his hand when Lilith tilted her head like she didn't understand. "Never mind. Please do what I said. Let me know when Astaroth receives the message."

Lilith acknowledged his orders one last time before logging out and leaving a very awkward, very stifling silence behind.

Adam did not want to look at Titania. The woman was drilling holes into his head with her eyes, which were sharp enough to penetrate steel.

"So, what was that about… *master*?" Titania said.

"Please don't say anything," Adam muttered bitterly.

Adam did not want to explain his complicated relationship with Lilith to this woman, and to keep her from asking questions, he traveled out of the inn with Kureha in his arms and began walking to the mayor's mansion. Titania, of course, landed right on his shoulder and began talking anyway.

"Do the other women know that Lilith calls you 'master' yet? I do hope you will tell them eventually. I would also love to know just what sort of brainwashing magic you used to make her call you that."

"What makes you think I did anything?" Adam scowled behind his mask. "I have constantly told her that I am not her master and she has no need to call me that. It was Lilith who made the decision to call me master, and Lilith who refuses to call me anything else."

"Uh-huh. I'm not sure I believe that."

"Are you messing with me?"

"Of course I am."

Adam nearly tripped when Titania admitted she was messing with him. Grumbling about the pint-sized and nosy woman, he continued on his way, spoke with the guards, and was eventually allowed to meet with Bromley Paxton.

The mayor was in his office, sitting behind his desk and signing papers. When Adam entered with Titania and Kureha, the man smiled as if relieved, shoved his work aside, and greeted them.

"If it isn't Adam and his fairy and fox yokai companions. Thank you for coming. You have saved me from a mountain of paperwork—I mean, it seems like you have something important to talk about. How can I help you?"

Adam almost paused when he heard the man speak. That statement about being saved from paperwork left him a little befuddled, but he soon got over it. NPCs in this game were just that realistic. This should not surprise him anymore.

"I wanted to ask you for a favor," Adam said.

He explained what he wanted in the simplest terms possible, how he wanted Bromley Paxton to host a tournament, how he wanted the reward for winning to be the [Guild Creation Token] in his possession, and how he planned to have him and his party participate. Since he needed this man to be on board with the idea, he didn't hold anything back.

"So I see. That is quite the cunning idea you have." Bromley Paxton rubbed his jaw with a thoughtful expression. "When the first guild is formed, they are given a one month period of absolute protection. During that time, no one can harm them. After it, however, they become an open target. You wish to display your strength to act as a deterrent in case someone decides to destroy your guild once that one month is up."

"That is correct," Adam said.

"And you are sure you can win?" asked the mayor.

"Winning will not be a problem."

"Hmmm…"

Adam did not interrupt the man as he thought and instead looked at Titania. She saw his gaze and shook her head, placed a hand on her lips, and gestured for him to look at Bromley Paxton again. This exchange did not go unnoticed by the mayor.

"I can certainly do this for you. However, because of how much paperwork—I mean, because of how difficult it will be to host a tournament right now, I cannot do it for free. Would you be willing to accept a request from me in exchange?" he asked.

Furrowing his brow, Adam did not accept or deny the man right away. "I suppose that would depend. What is the request?"

"This one is not something you have to do right away, nor would I expect you to, but it is something I hope you will do for me at some point in the future." The man coughed into his hand. "As you know, the Fairy Clan disappeared a long time ago. Nobody knows what happened to them or where they are. Now that a fairy has reappeared before me, I have become hopeful that it means the Fairy Clan has not gone extinct from this world. I would like you to discover what happened to the Fairy Clan for me."

Ding!

[You have been offered a new quest: [Discover What Became of the Fairy Clan]! Will you accept? Yes or no?]

Adam glanced at Titania, whose face had turned into a grimace. She didn't seem to like the idea of accepting this quest. He didn't know why since he hadn't asked about her departure from the Fairy

Clan. However, regardless of whether this woman wanted him to accept it or not, they really did not have much of a choice.

"A quest like this might take a while, but I will definitely be sure to fulfill your expectations," Adam said and pressed the "yes" button.

"Good." The mayor smiled. "I knew I could count on you."

Ding!

[You have accepted the quest: [Discover What Became of the Fairy Clan]! This is a long-term quest. Because it is not something you can complete right away, you may also take other quests while fulfilling this one.]

After accepting the quest, Adam and Titania left the mayor's mansion and began traveling back to the inn. Since he was planning to log off, he wanted Titania and Kureha to be somewhere they could relax in peace and private.

"Did you not get along with the other members of your clan?" Adam asked as they walked through the street.

"What makes you say that?" asked Titania, face carefully void of emotion.

"Just a hunch." Adam paused, then spoke in a softer voice. "You know… I will probably find out eventually anyway. Don't you think it would be better to tell me about this now before my opinion can be influenced by outside factors?"

Titania sighed and ran a hand through her hair, pushing her bangs up. "I suppose you bring up a good point. Very well. I will tell you about it. Just… let's wait until after we arrive back to the inn."

Adam accepted this and sped up. He moved around a group of players who had formed a party, passed several children running in the opposite direction swinging around toy sticks, and soon entered the inn. He went up to their room, locked the door, and sat down on the bed. Kureha hopped off and Titania fluttered down to sit on the mattress with her legs crossed.

A moment of silence passed between them. Titania's face was a cross between a grimace and resigned.

"You have probably realized a bit already, but three thousand years ago was a time of great strife. The humans and beastmen declared war on each other, monsters were pouring out from the Forgotten Continent, and races like the Fairy Clan and the dwarves were caught in the middle of these vicious battles. Because of these factors, the Fairy Clan decided to seal themselves off, isolating themselves from the outside world... and I did not agree with their decision."

Adam still did not say anything, waiting for Titania to speak up. She looked at her own hands as if she was pondering something, sighed, and placed her hands behind her. This unconscious act resulted in her chest being thrust out. Adam was admittedly impressed that her breasts could bounce like that, but that was probably because Titania, unlike the other women in his party, did not wear a bra.

"I thought sealing ourselves away was cowardly. I got into a huge argument with the elder council over it and left," Titania finished. "I don't know what happened to them after I left. I assume they created a barrier powerful enough to hide themselves away from the entire world. If the Fairy Clan still exists, they are likely hiding somewhere nobody can find them."

"Including you?" asked Adam.

Titania scrunched up her face. "I am a fairy, so of course I am sensitive to their magic. If we happen upon an area steeped in the magic of the Fairy Clan, I will definitely pick up on it."

"Can I ask why you didn't want to let me know?" asked Adam.

"Let's just say I wanted to put the past behind me."

Adam accepted her words with a nod. "I suppose everyone has skeletons in their closet that they don't wish others to know about. Thank you for telling me this."

Titania smiled wearily but waved off his thanks. "Go on and 'log off.' I am certain your lover and friends are wondering why you haven't returned to your original world by now."

Nodding, Adam opened his status screen and tapped the button to log off.

BIG NEWS

It was late in the evening when Levon received the news. After learning about it, he went to his office within the Pleonexia Family estate, logged onto his computer, and quickly went through several Age of Gods forums. His fingers flew across the keyboard and his eyes were locked firmly onto the screen.

Every single one of them said the same thing.

The Mayor of Solum was hosting a tournament in two weeks. The reward for the winner would be a [Guild Creation Token].

He couldn't believe it.

Ever since the first VRMMO had been created, this name had been synonymous with power. Anyone who got their hands on a [Guild Creation Token] could create a guild. And the most important [Guild Creation Token] of all was the first one that appeared in the game. Whoever got their hands on the first [Guild Creation Token] would hold the prestige of being the first person inside of the game to create a guild, which came with not only substantial in-game benefits, but allowed the reputation of the guild's creator to sore far above those of everyone else.

As the leader of the largest guild in the American Federation, Levon could not let anyone else have this [Guild Creation Token]. The honor of creating the first guild needed to always be him.

He exited the forums, accessed his Skyline app, quickly selected several names, and hit the call button. While waiting for everyone to respond, he leaned back in his seat, crossed his arms, and closed his eyes.

The first one to respond was Connor Sword.

"Levon, I'm guessing this isn't a social call." Connor's face appeared in the center of his screen, the same lazy smile as ever-present. Despite that lackadaisical expression of his, his eyes were sharp like the sword he wielded. "I saw the news in the forums. Is it true?"

"Let's wait for everyone else to arrive before we discuss that," Levon said.

Shortly after Connor accepted the call, the man known as Flame Emperor accepted, and his face appeared on the upper left corner. He was a good-looking man of about twenty-seven. Older than Levon by a few years. He had brown hair and gray eyes like. His masculine jawline and strong features projected an aura of power and arrogance that Fayte lacked.

"Levon," he greeted with a simple nod.

"Congratulations on reaching level 15," Levon said with a good-natured smile.

Flame Emperor's smile looked forced. "I am still behind you."

"I have the added benefit of being in a party with Connor." Levon shrugged. "Between the Sword King and myself, we level up a little quicker than most."

"Still not fast enough to beat Lin, the Spear God, or that Adam player," Connor chimed.

Levon scowled but didn't say anything.

Three more people soon arrived.

The first was a dark-skinned woman with a cold look on her face. She was gorgeous, but it was the kind of untouchable beauty that caused weaker men to look the other way. Her dark eyes were intense, the frown on her face made her look unapproachable, and the straight hair that traveled down her back made her seem more severe somehow. She was the only woman among his Four Elements.

Player Name: Gaia.

The second person looked almost like a slob compared to everyone else. His face was masked by five o'clock shadow. Dirty blond hair surrounded a face that would have been attractive if he took better care of himself. How this man scored so many women was beyond Levon, but perhaps that slightly rugged and devil may care quality the man possessed was what drove women to him. He was a well-known player among his guild. There was even a rumor that he had slept with more than half of the Ploenexia Alliance's female players.

Last among them was a man whose face was even colder than Gaia's. He wore no expression like his face was chiseled from ice. Despite that, or perhaps because of that, his face possessed a chilling beauty. His looks were so feminine it was easy to mistake him for a woman, which further enhanced the aesthetic of a hauntingly beautiful man.

"Hey, Guild Master," the slovenly man greeted with a casual nod as his visage appeared in the bottom right corner. The woman merely gave him a respectful nod. The last among them said nothing.

"I'm sure you already know what's going on, so I won't bore you too much with the details," Levon began. "Just the other day, the Mayor of Solum announced that he was hosting a tournament at the Solum arena. The reward for winning is a [Guild Creation Token]. I'm sure I don't need to tell you what that means."

No one displayed surprise. The news had already spread across the entire globe by this point. The forums were exploding, and it was even being reported in several news stations that paid attention to the virtual world. Since Age of Gods was the biggest game on the market, with more players mere days after its release than any other game available, it was also the one everybody paid the most attention to.

"I'm guessing we're gonna compete?" asked Thor God of Thunder, scratching his beard. "I, uh, hate to be the bearer of bad news, but I don't think I'll be able to help you here."

"Why not?" asked Levon, eyes narrowing.

Thor God of Thunder coughed into his hand as his cheeks turned red. "I, er, I think I might have pissed someone off. The Soul Reapers have been targeting me in Age of Gods ever since I left the Village of Beginnings. They killed me so many times now that I'm back at level 1. I'm… well, I'm trying to regain those lost levels, but it hasn't been easy."

Like with most games, death resulted in a penalty. Some of the more demanding games were so bad that a person who died was forced to start over from the beginning. In this case, death in Age of Gods meant all your experience points and reputation reverted to zero and your character's level was reduced by one.

Levon Pleonexia took a deep breath to contain his anger. The Soul Reapers were a free guild made entirely of players in the Assassin Class who paid homage to no one. Neither his Pleonexia Alliance nor Daggerfall Dynasty was able to bring this guild into their pockets, but it was not for lack of trying. No one wanted to inadvertently push this guild into another's camp. It helped that all of them were skilled at what they did and no one could find any information about their identities in the real world, so pressuring them outside of the virtual world was impossible.

"Fine. I guess it can't be helped." Levon sighed but soon focused on the task at hand. "I want the rest of you to sign up for this tournament if you haven't done so already. I'm sure Daggerfall Dynasty will also have their strongest players sign up as well, including the Spear God."

At the mention of the Spear God, Connor Sword's eyes lit up with a competitive fire. He had once challenged the Spear God during the International Power Ranking Tournament and lost miserably, thus earning him third place on the International Power Rankings. Levon did not doubt that his second in command longed to have a rematch with his rival.

Whether the Spear God felt Connor Sword was worthy of being his rival or not was an entirely different matter.

"Will you also be signing up, Levon?" asked Flame Emperor.

"Of course." Levon smiled. "Nobody will follow a leader if all he does is issue orders from the back."

***

With just two weeks before the tournament was set to begin, Adam decided that the most important thing their party could do was level up. He wanted everyone to gain at least one more level before the tournament. Even if they all had hidden classes, and even if their levels were above everyone else's in the game, he wanted them to shock everyone so much that no one would dare to even think about messing with their guild after it was created.

That was why they had headed back to the valley surrounding the Sunset Mountain Range day after day to level up. This valley was home to monsters that were levels 30 to 40. These monsters earned them the highest amount of experience points they could get so far.

Unfortunately, the current monster they were up against might be a little more than what they had asked for.

It was called a [Twin-Headed Mountain Troll]. It was a 2-Star monster at level 40. Thanks to Titania's [scan] ability, everyone knew what kind of stats it boasted, and all of them were shocked by how powerful this creature was. With over twenty million health points and a Strength stat of six thousand, it was easily one of the strongest 2-Star monsters they had ever fought. It also had five skills, all of which were powerful enough to kill any of them with a single hit. It's five abilities were [Earth Stomp], [Double Layer Smash], [Earth Bullets], [Chomp], and [Fist]. It also had a passive skill called [Gaia's Love]. It was a skill that let it regain health points so long as it was standing on solid ground.

The last ability listed was probably the one it had started with. [Fist] sounded like a pretty generic ability. It also had two AOE skills that were fairly deadly, and one ability that would instantly kill anyone regardless of their level. Combined with its massive amount of health and it was pretty much the most fearsome opponent they had faced since fighting the Elemental Master.

-53,730; -161,190; -483,570; -1,450,710; -4,352,130!

Being the heaviest of their hitters, Adam was fighting the monster up close, pulling in all of its agro so the magic users (Fayte and Kureha) and the Fairy Archer (Susan) wouldn't be targeted. He had immediately activated [Blood Sacrifice] and began [Dance of the Sakura Blossoms] the moment this battle had started. While this monster still had a lot of health, the amount of damage he did was staggering.

Unfortunately, the [Twin-Headed Mountain Troll] was not something that could be defeated just by dealing a lot of damage. The monster roared as it raised one massive leg and stomped on the ground. The earth shook so fiercely that Adam was afraid a landslide would sweep over this mountainside and bury them all.

He leaped in the air and kicked off the monster's other leg to give himself that extra height, then used [double jump] to ascend even higher. With his +6,260 Defense, he would only be dealt -2,740 damage, but he preferred not getting hit at all.

-2,100; -2,100!

While Adam may have been the heaviest hitter who dealt the most damage, two other melee fighters among them could also deal some pretty impressive punishment.

Among those two was Aris, who quickly raced up to the [Twin-Headed Mountain Troll] seconds after its attack ended and began attacking with [Blade Dance]. It was a skill that allowed her to constantly launch attack after attack without the need to pause. The downside was it consumed 5 MP every time she swung her swords. She had +400 MP at present, meaning she could attack 80 times before she needed to retreat and consume an [middle-grade magic potion].

Thanks to Titania's [Song of Vigor], her +700 Physical Attack had tripled. Nearly fifty thousand points of damage were dealt to the [Twin-Headed Mountain Troll] by her in less than five seconds. She wielded her two scimitars as though they were lighter than feathers, swinging them constantly as she danced around the giant monster's legs.

-29,385; -29,385; -29,385; -29,385; -29,385; -29,385; -29,385; -29,385; -29,385!

Lilith was the last among their melee fighters and also someone who had a good amount of Attack Power. The only issue was that, as an assassin, she wasn't really meant for front line combat but stealth attacks. Even with her class changing to the hidden class, Demon Knight Assassin, her skills and most of her stats were all related to her stealth and hidden attack power. Even so, the amount of damage she dealt as she used [slash] was nothing to scoff at.

While Aris was attacking the monster's legs, Lilith leaped onto its body, landed on its hand, and ran up to its shoulders. She swung her dagger while holding it in a reverse grip. Each attack created a line of light along the monster's body and enraged it further. The [Twin-Headed Mountain Troll] beat its fists against its chest and issued what sounded like a roar of challenge.

While Adam, Aris, and Lilith were attacking this monster from close range, Fayte, Kureha, and Susan were lighting it up with magic and arrows from a distance.

-22,620; -56,550; - 22,620!

Because they had yet to find a good weapon for her, Susan dealt the least amount of damage out of their original party. The only person who dealt less damage than her was Aris, who did not have the benefit of +1,000 extra status points. Despite how she didn't do quite the same amount of damage as everyone else, she still fired off a regular [Deadeye], aiming for the weak points on its body before hitting hit with [Fairy Shot], which was like an improved version of [Deadeye]. While [Deadeye] only did x2 critical damage, [Fairy Shot] did x5 critical damage.

-35,640; -27,000; -35,640; -27,000!

While completely unassuming, the little fox standing beside Fayte and Susan shot lightning and fire from its two tails. The respective attacks were called [Thunder Bolt] and [Fireball]. Both attacks had a 10 second cooldown time, but Kureha resolved this issue by using each skill in five-second intervals. In this manner, she could unleash an attack every five seconds.

The heat from her fireballs was scorching as they slammed into the [Twin-Headed Mountain Troll] and exploded. Even when Adam was nowhere near the blast zone, he could feel his body warm up, and the searing wind push against him. The scent of burnt flesh hung heavily in the air. Meanwhile, the lightning bolts sizzled through the air and left black scorch marks on the monster's hard skin. This enraged the creature, but it could not attack their long-range fighters because Adam, Aris, and Lilith were keeping it occupied.

-114,624; -157,608; -95,520!

Ever since she received the Elemental Master hidden class, Fayte could no longer be considered the same person she had been before. Her attack power had increased substantially, she had more magic spells than probably anyone else in the game, and she had gained equipment that suited her class. The damage she now dealt made her their most powerful long-range attacker. The only downside to her new spells was they all had a long cooldown time, but she made up for that by bombarding enemies with [Energy Bolt], which had a 0 second cooldown time, while waiting for the cooldown time on her other spells to end.

"It's using [Double-Layer Smash]! Lilith!" Adam shouted as he jumped back.

Lilith leaped in front of Adam just as the [Twin-Headed Mountain Troll] swung its clasped hands down. The attack was so fierce it created a burst of air that slammed into Adam and blew his hair out of his face. Facing this intense attack was Lilith, who only narrowed her eyes and timed the attack so she could unleash a stunning [Counter].

-95,950!

The [Twin-Headed Mountain Troll] roared in surprise and stumbled back when its own attack was turned against it. A large number sign floated above its head, though compared to the amount of health this creature had, -95,950 damage was not very high.

They had already dealt around ten million points worth of damage, give or take two or three million, but this monster had twenty million health, so they still had a ways to go. They were fortunate it was so slow and dull-witted, unlike Alexandra Mystique. Its attack patterns were predictable and because it was so slow, it was easy to tell what skill it was going to use several seconds in advance. The only real issue they had was that it automatically regenerated health.

"Hee-hee. Looks like it's my turn again!"

With a tinkling, bell-like laugh, Aris rushed forward and unleashed her special skill [Dancing Swords]. It was a technique similar to Adam's [Dance of the Sakura Blossoms]. Aris used her two swords to continuously attack in quick succession. Each successful attack consumed 50 MP, but they also did x2 damage with every attack, and the damage stacked so the amount increased with each attack.

-2,100; -4,200; -8,400; -16,800!

There were a few downsides to her skill. The biggest one was that it couldn't be interrupted. If Aris was interrupted while executing her skill, she would receive twice the damage she normally did and would be stunned for 10 seconds. Since they were fighting a monster with a Strength of six thousand and Aris only had 2,240 HP, a single attack from this monster would kill her.

As she was executing her attack, she ended up pulling all of the [Twin-Headed Mountain Troll's] agro. It raised its leg to stomp on her with [Earth Stomp].

"Lilith!" Adam shouted.

As if she could read his mind, Lilith once more stepped in front of the attack, timing her own attack to counter this monster's. Her timing was impeccable. Just as the [Twin-Headed Mountain Troll] brought its foot down, she swung her dagger up and flawlessly countered the attack.

-95,950!

-17,910; -53,730; -161,190; -483,570; -1,450,710!

Immediately after Lilith used [Counter] to block the monster's attack, Adam rushed in and used activated [Dance of the Sakura Blossoms]. His Attack Power was lower than when he used this the first time because [Blood Sacrifice] had entered its cooldown period, but he still removed a large chunk from the monster's health.

Their attacks continued, with Adam issuing commands to everyone on the field, directing the flow of battle, and while there were several close calls, it did not take more than maybe one hour before the [Twin-Headed Mountain Troll] lost all of its health. When its health reached zero, the monster stumbled back and released an unwilling but pitiful roar as it fell to the ground. Aris screamed as she nearly fell when the earth shook, but Adam held onto her and bent his knees to keep himself steady. Lilith was much the same.

Fayte, Kureha, and Susan were far enough away to not be affected by the titanic crash and Titania had wings, thus she was unaffected.

Ding!

[Congratulations! You have defeated the 2-Star [Twin-Headed Mountain Troll]! The [Twin-Headed Mountain Troll] has dropped the items [Mountain Troll's Club], [Ring of Earthly Protection], [Crystal Mountain Boots], and 300,000 gold coins! +50,000 experience points! +50,000 ability points! +25,000 Reputation!]

Ding!

[Congratulations! Changing_Fayte has leveled up! She is now at level 17! +1,600 HP! +7,960 MP! +5 SP!]

Ding!

[Congratulations! Lilith has leveled up! She is now at level 17! +600 HP! +200 MP! +5 SP!]

Ding!

[Congratulations! Little_Su has leveled up! She is now at level 17! +500 HP! +200 MP! +5 SP!]

Adam could only stare stupidly at the windows popping up in his field of view. Three of their party had just leveled up in quick succession. It wasn't that he was shocked they had leveled up. All of them had been on the cusp of doing so, but the utterly ridiculous rise in each of their health and MP was what shocked him.

When Adam and the others defeated the dean of the magic academy, they had earned a reward of +1,000 status points. Status points were normally something players only got after leveling up, and they only received +5 status points per level. Giving them +1,000 status points meant they could increase the amount of health and magic they had by an astounding degree. Their attack power and magic attack power could soar, their abilities becoming so broken no other player in the game could stand up to them.

Adam had put most of his status points into his Strength stat, raising his Attack Power to 6,140. He also put some status points into Speed, Dexterity, Constitution, and Intelligence to even them out a little. He figured with this many status points, he didn't have to put all of them into a single stat like he normally did.

The others seemed to have allocated their status points more evenly than him.

And with the death of the [Twin-headed Mountain Troll], Adam now had the ability points needed to upgrade [Dance of the Sakura Blossoms], which he did without hesitation. His other skills were mostly maxed out. The only two that weren't was [Energy Sweep] and [Energy Thrust], but he was more interested in [Dance of the Sakura Blossoms] for sentimental reasons.

After upgrading his skill, Adam looked at the items the [Twin-Headed Mountain Troll] had dropped.

Item Name: Mountain Troll's Club
Item Type: Weapon
Grade: 1-Star
Use requirements: Can be used by Warriors, Swordsman, and Swordmasters level 15 and above.
Description: A club used by a mountain troll. It was made out of rock instead of a tree.
Abilities: Physical Attack+200; Speed-50

Item Name: Ring of Earthly Protection

Item Type: Accessory
Grade: 2-Star
Use requirements: Can be used by any class of any level.
**Description: This ring was born from the earth and offers
incredible protection against physical attacks plus a passive
regeneration ability.**
Abilities: Defense+500; Recovers +1 HP every 1 second

Item Name: Crystal Mountain Boots
Item Type: Footwear
Grade: 3-Star
**Use requirements: Can only be used by melee classes level 20
and above.**
**Description: These boots were carved from crystals buried deep
beneath the earth. They are very sturdy.**
Abilities: Defense+300; Magic Defense+300

None of the items were bad, but the only thing Adam felt was useful was the [Ring of Earthly Protection]. Rather than keep that for himself, he turned to Susan and handed it over.

"Su, I think you should equip this. Out of all the people here, you are the only one who still has basic equipment."

"Ah?" Susan looked startled, but then her cheeks lit up as she reached out and gently took the ring from him. "Th-thank you."

Adam always felt a little bad that she was the only one who didn't have amazing equipment. Fayte, Lilith, and even Aris had received incredible equipment to go along with their hidden classes, but Susan had not. He thought it was because she had received her class from the scroll he found inside of Bromely Paxton's vault. Meanwhile, the others had earned their hidden classes by braving dungeons and facing trials.

"It looks like we've succeeded in reaching the next level," Fayte said. "And with just two days to spare too."

Adam nodded. "The tournament will begin two days from now. That should be enough time to reach Solum if we don't battle any monsters. Is everyone ready?"

"I am!" Aris pumped a fist into the air. "I am so ready for this!"

While no one could see past his mask, he was certain everyone could tell he was smiling as he looked at Aris.

"I-I am a little nervous," Susan admitted. "But I will definitely do my betch—ack!"

Adam winced when Susan bit her tongue. It had been a long time since she'd bitten her tongue like that. Perhaps the upcoming tournament was making her nervous.

"Lilith?" Adam questioned.

Lilith had been kneeling on the ground to pick up Kureha, but she paused when Adam questioned her. After a brief moment of hesitation, she resumed picking up the little fox yokai, stood to her feet, and turned to him as she stroked Kureha's soft fur.

"I am ready," she said with quiet confidence.

Since there was no point in remaining on this mountainside, Adam, Aris, Fayte, Lilith, and Susan began walking down. Titania settled on Adam's shoulder like usual. Kureha would have taken his head, but she was still nestled in Lilith's arms, and the silent woman was not letting her go any time soon.

Aris stared at Titania. "I wish I could sit on Adam's shoulder like that."

"No, you don't," Adam said immediately.

"Hmph. It is not that I enjoy sitting on his shoulder," Titania blustered, her cheeks dusted with a light shade of pink. "Flying for so long tires my wings."

"Then why don't you come sit on my shoulder?" Aris asked.

"… Adam's is more comfortable."

"What is that supposed to mean?"

"I-it means nothing."

"Hee-hee."

"I've been constantly monitoring the levels of all the players," Fayte said as they finished descending from the mountainside. "The highest level outside of our own is still Lin Akamine. She reached level 17 two days ago. After her is the Spear God. He's also had level 17, but he reached that level just yesterday. Everyone else, including the leaders of Daggerfall Dynasty, Levon Pleonexia, Connor Sword, and the Pleonexia Alliance's Four Elements are at level 15. Oddly enough, Thor God of Thunder is only at level 10. I don't think he will be participating in the tournament."

"It sounds like everyone has been grinding hard," Adam said.

"Yes."

Adam didn't think Fayte had intended it, but when she mentioned Connor Sword, she had looked at Susan. There was something meaningful in that look. He wondered what sort of relationship Connor Sword had with Susan.

"Who is Connor Sword?" asked Adam.

"He is the Vice-Commander of the Pleonexia Alliance," Fayte answered. "Not only is he Levon's right-hand man, but he is a skilled swordsman in real life. He has won numerous championships both nationally and internationally. The only person he ever lost to was Lin Akamine, who defeated him during an international swordsman competition held in Japan, and then beat him again during the International Power Ranking Tournament alongside the Spear God. He is fiercely competitive as well. I heard he has challenged both Lin Akamine and the Spear God several times since his loss, though they rebuffed him each time. Because of his skills with a sword, he was nicknamed the Sword King."

"I'm surprised that wasn't Lin Akamine's nickname," Adam said.

Fayte shook her head, veil swaying. "Her nickname is God of Flash because all you see when she attacks you is a flash of light and then it's over." She paused, head tilting. "At least, this is what I've read in the online forums."

Adam nodded as they reached their horses and untied them from around the trees. Titania flew into the air, but she settled back down once Adam mounted the horse. Kureha also escaped from Lilith when she mounted her horse and made his head her perch once again. While this caused Lilith to look at the fox like she'd been betrayed, Aris, Fayte, and even Susan quietly giggled as they each climbed onto their horses.

It took two days to reach Solum. They had to log off several times to eat, sleep, and Adam was still helping Aris with her rehabilitation. Susan also had her home-schooling. Once they reached the city, they all traveled to an inn together and logged off. Tomorrow was the beginning of the tournament, and they wanted to be well-rested.

THE TOP TWO GUILDS

Solum was packed with players. It was no surprise since today was the day of the tournament, which the reward for winning was a [Guild Creation Token]. Even the people who didn't plan on participating were present so they could watch. This was why players lined every inch of the streets, jam-packed like sardines in a can, as they all walked toward the arena.

Adam was walking hand in hand with Aris and the others, who had decided holding hands was a great way to avoid being separated. Kureha and Titania were the only ones who didn't have this problem. They were sitting on Adam's shoulder and head respectively.

The arena was a massive multi-story structure that looked similar to a Gothic cathedral, except it was a lot gaudier. There was a massive construct at the very top that looked like a giant sword piercing the building. Stone statues were located near the entrance, featuring muscular men and women dressed in armor and holding weapons aloft as though proclaiming their victory. Columns lined the streets surrounding the building and there were even more along the walkway leading up to the building. Each one was like a gateway with an arch traveling between them.

Lights flashed all around the arena. They flittered between people and traveled above their heads. Adam didn't know what they were at first, until Titania informed him.

"These are sprites," she said when she noticed him curiously gazing at a light ball floating past him. "They could be classified as a form of low-level fairy, but they more closely resemble monsters in that they lack intelligence. They tend to gather where magic is strong. However, they avoid places that are thick with negative emotions, which is why we didn't see them at the magic academy or the Deadlands."

Adam nodded as he and his companions entered the arena.

The inside was every bit as massive as he imagined. It reminded him of the extravagant entrance to a five-star resort, with marble flooring, an expansive ceiling decorated with paintings depicting various battles, and columns rising from the floor to the ceiling. On top of being gigantic, this vast interior was also filled to the brim with people.

Adam was shocked to notice some of the people present were not players but NPCs, which he recognized because they had floating signs over their heads that gave him their names and other basic information.

"Since we have already signed up, I believe we can just head down to the waiting rooms," Fayte said.

The waiting room for players participating in the tournament was located down a flight of stairs that led to the basement floor. Because of how this building was designed, the basement level was where all the fights took place. Meanwhile, the seating was located on the first, second, third, and fourth floors. The fourth-floor seating was dedicated to the VIP booths.

When Adam and the others entered, it was to discover that several hundred people were already present. Some of the players waiting inside stood alone, but most of them appeared to be part of a guild. The best way to tell who belonged to a guild and who didn't was the generally matching clothing.

"That group over there belongs to the Thirteen Holy Swords," Fayte said as she pointed to a group of men and women. Their outfits were similar with some minor variations, but each one possessed a sword. "They are another branch guild of the Pleonexia Alliance. I'm told their name is derived from an old religion that was popular back in the early 2000s. Their leader is a man named Travis Baker, but his in-game name is One Thousand Blades Gabriel."

"Kind of an extravagant name," Adam muttered.

"No more extravagant than Sword King, Spear God, or Flame Emperor." Fayte shrugged. "Just wait until people begin giving you nicknames like Emperor of the Spear or the Indomitable Thousand Thrust Spearman."

"Those sound awful."

Adam conceded her point with a nod. There were indeed many extravagant names among players.

"I wonder what kind of nickname I might be given?" Aris asked before giggling. "Adam, what sort of nickname do you think people will give me?"

"Hmmm…" Adam looked at Aris as she stood there in her belly dancing bikini armor outfit and veil. He wished she wouldn't wear clothes like that because he hated other men looking at her, but the Speed stat on these clothes was just too good to pass up. "I think… maybe Dancing Beauty?"

While he could not see her face behind that veil, he could tell from experience that she was giving him an amused smile.

"You never were good at creating nicknames," she teased.

Adam was glad he wore a mask so no one could see him blush.

Because it was so crowded, only a few people had paid attention to their group, though more than a few men were gazing at Aris in her skimpy outfit. He wished he could light those people on fire. Was it too late to change classes? Or maybe he should ask Fayte if she could do it for him? The idea had merit.

While they did attract some attention, it only lasted for a moment before the gazes of everyone present shifted to the entrance again. Five people were walking down the stairs. They emerged from the staircase, their bodies relaxed, projecting a confident aura that forced everyone present to back off.

Adam clenched his fists when he saw the familiar face leading them.

He was a handsome man with a refined bearing and a polite smile on his face. The metal breastplate he wore looked freshly polished. A dragon was engraved on the left breast. His gauntlets were plainer by comparison, showing that his breastplate was probably something he found in a dungeon—or more like something one of his subordinates found that he purloined for his personal use. The greaves he wore were similarly adorned with a dragon motif.

The weapon he carried was impressive. It was long, at least two meters in length, and the blade jutting from a dragon's mouth at one side was not shaped like a leaf but a curved single-edged blade with a single hook on the back. A glaive. Adam could not help but frown when he noticed the man was not using a traditional spear.

"That's Levon Pleonexia," Fayte informed him. "The person on his right is Connor Sword, and the three behind him are Gaia, Ymir, and… the Flame Emperor."

Adam's attention shifted away from Levon to focus on the one called the Flame Emperor. He had brown hair, gray eyes, and a straight nose. Just like any aristocrat, he was a handsome man who could have seduced any woman he wanted. His features, masculine and sturdy, lent him an air that made him seem indomitable and cold. His face looked like it had been chiseled from stone.

He wore bright red and gold mage robes, and the staff in his hand was made from a kind of red wood and possessed an equally red gem at the top. It was an extravagant outfit, but Adam wondered how practical such clothing was. It looked to him like this outfit was something he had paid to have specifically tailored, but he didn't believe it contained any major stat boosting properties.

"So that is your brother," Adam said with a murmur.

Beside him, Fayte remained silent for a moment before nodding. "Yes."

"You two don't really look like brother and sister," Adam mused. "I'm guessing you take after your mother, while he takes after your father?"

"Something like that."

While Adam could not see her face, the pain in her voice was so prominent that it silenced him from saying anything else.

He turned away from the Flame Emperor to focus on the man next to Levon, the one called Connor Sword. His height was average, but he had an impressive countenance. Sharp eyebrows, a refined jawline, and a powerful body hidden beneath his armor. There was a lazy smile on his handsome face that gave him an air of arrogance.

His outfit consisted of a leather breastplate, greaves, pauldrons, and gauntlets. Adam had seen that kind of armor at the blacksmith. It was the most expensive light armor that could be bought in Solum, and while it didn't compare to the equipment Adam and his party were wearing, it offered some of the best defensive stats currently available.

As he looked at the man nicknamed the Sword King, he noticed something else, but it had nothing to do with the man himself. It was Susan. She was shaking. When he looked at her, he discovered that her eyes were locked onto Connor Sword as her entire body shook, from her head to her boots. Her face had also become pale as a sheet of paper.

Concerned, Adam leaned down and whispered. "Are you okay?"

Susan squeaked as if startled. She looked at him, her eyes wide, then took several deep breaths and tried to calm herself down.

"Y-yes, I am fine," she said with an unconvincing smile.

Adam wanted to say she was not fine. She was clearly frightened, or perhaps nervous, and he knew it had something to do with that man. He once more found himself tempted to ask her about it, but he knew it was not his place. Everyone had their troubles. If Susan wanted to tell him, he would of course hear her out, but if she didn't say anything, he would assume she didn't want him to know.

That didn't mean he couldn't help her.

"Get behind me, please."

"Huh? Ah."

Susan released a startled noise as Adam placed a hand on her shoulder and shifted her until she was standing behind him, hidden from Connor Sword.

"T-thank you very much," Susan whispered into his back.

Adam turned his head just slightly and whispered, "You are welcome."

Once he was certain Connor Sword could not see Susan and visa versa, Adam realized Aris, Fayte, Lilith, and even Titania were looking at him. He couldn't see the expressions of anyone but Titania (everyone else was covering their faces, after all). However, just their eyes was enough to make him feel uncomfortable.

"What is it?" he asked.

"It is nothing," Fayte said. He thought she might be smiling beneath that veil.

"I've said it before, but you are very good at looking after people," Titania muttered.

"Hee-hee. I always knew you were a kind person," Aris said with a giggle. She reached over and hugged his arm, which sent a jolt through his brain because she was wearing very skimpy clothing and he could feel her skin and body heat.

"I'm not that kind," Adam muttered.

"I beg to differ." The one who said that was Lilith, which startled everyone and made them look at the normally taciturn woman. Lilith, however, only had eyes for Adam. "You have always been very kind to others."

Adam wanted to deny her words, but he couldn't find it in himself to speak, so he instead observed the remaining two people in Levon's group.

The woman whom he guessed was Gaia had dark skin, straight black hair, and wore a sort of earthy-looking robe. It was made of greens and browns to resemble the earth. Her staff had a similar color scheme. It was, in many ways, just like Flame Emperor's clothing, but it was designed to represent this woman's element.

It was interesting. Gaia was the name of the Greek primordial goddess of the Earth, which he assumed was the inspiration for her name. He wondered how she found it. Greek mythology had fallen out of the limelight in the early 2100s.

Last among them was the man known as Ymir. He had a feminine face and a cold demeanor. Because his features more closely resembled a woman's, it gave him a slightly off vibe, but Adam did not let that fool him. This man radiated a chilling intent as though his very body was made of ice. Adam wondered if the man was an esper. Like his counterparts, he wore Mage robes, but these were ice blue with darker blue lining the hem.

"Titania," Adam whispered. "Can you cast [scan] on those people?"

"Leave it to me," Titania said.

Before long, Adam saw several screens appear in front of him to display the stats of the Pleonexia Alliance's leadership.

Name: Levon_Ploenexia
Class: Warrior
Lvl: 16
SP: 0
AP: 500
Experience: 225/4,915,200
Reputation: 179,000
Strength: +30
Constitution: +45
Dexterity: +5
Intelligence: +5
Speed: +5
Physical Attack: +300
Health: 580/580
Hit-Rate: 35%
MP: 200/200
Movement: +50
Physical Defense: +500
Magical Defense: +120
Dodge-Rate: 35%
Magic Attack: +5

Skills:
Skill Name: Slash
Description: A basic skill where the player swings his or her sword and attacks the enemy!
Current lvl: 5 MAXED
Ability: Causes 150% damage to enemy if it hits
MP Cost: 1
Cooldown Time: 0 seconds

Skill Name: Thrust
Description: A basic skill where the player thrusts his or her sword at the enemy!
Current Lvl: 5 MAXED
Ability: Causes 160% damage with a 5% chance at getting a critical hit
MP Cost: 5
Cooldown Time: 0 seconds

Skill Name: Sweep
Description: A skill meant for spear users. Can be learned at a training hall. By swinging your spear around your body, you can attack multiple targets within range and knock them off their feet.
Current Lvl: 5 MAXED
Ability: Does 150% damage to all enemies within range of the spear
Has a 25% chance of knocking enemies off their feet
MP Cost: 10
Cooldown Time: 30 seconds

Skill Name: Cascading Pierce
Description: A skill meant for spearmen. The spearman leaps into the air and descends toward the target, piercing them with a swift and lethal thrust.

Current lvl: 1
AP needed to reach lvl 2: 10,000
Ability: Does x2 critical damage if it hits
MP Cost: 50
Cooldown Time: 30 seconds

Name: Sword King
Class: Warrior
Lvl: 16
SP: 0
AP: 1,000
Experience: 1,050/4,195,200
Strength: +50
Constitution: +35
Dexterity: +5
Intelligence: +5
Speed: +5
Physical Attack: +420
Health: 460/460
Hit-Rate: 5%
MP: 200/200
Movement: +15
Physical Defense: +400
Magical Defense: +30
Dodge-Rate: 5%
Magic Attack: +5

Skills:
Skill Name: Slash
Description: A basic skill where the player swings his or her
sword and attacks the enemy!
Current lvl: 5 MAXED
Ability: Causes 150% damage to enemy if it hits
MP Cost: 1
Cooldown Time: 0 seconds

Skill Name: Thrust
Description: A basic skill where the player thrusts his or her sword at the enemy!
Current Lvl: 5 MAXED
Ability: Causes 160% damage with a 5% chance at getting a critical hit
MP Cost: 5
Cooldown Time: 0 seconds

Skill Name: Blade Storm
Description: The user of this skill launches several slashing attacks at lightning speed to deliver maximum damage. Can be learned at a training hall.
Current lvl: 5 MAXED
Ability: Does 400% damage, but only has a 50% chance of hitting
Chances go down if the enemy's Dodge-rate is higher than the user's Hit-Rate
MP Cost: 20
Cooldown Time: 30 seconds

Skill Name: Disarm
Description: A skill that skilled swordsmen can use to disarm their opponent. Can be learned at a training hall.
Current lvl: 1
AP needed to reach lvl 2: 5,000
Ability: By perfectly timing your strike with your enemies, you can disarm them of their weapon
20% of disarming opponents
MP Cost: 20
Cooldown Time: 30 seconds

Name: Gaia
Class: Mage

Lvl: 15
SP: 0
AP: 100
Experience: 1,322,365/2,457,600
Strength: +5
Constitution: +35
Dexterity: +5
Intelligence: +45
Speed: +5
Physical Attack: +5
Health: 440/440
Hit-Rate: 5%
MP: 860/860
Movement: +5
Physical Defense: +50
Magical Defense: +300
Dodge-Rate: 5%
Magic Attack: +295

Skills:
Skill Name: Energy Bolt:
Description: A mage aims their staff and calls the name [Energy Bolt] to release a bolt of magical energy at enemies.
Current lvl: 5 MAXED
Ability: Deals 200% non-elemental damage to enemies
MP Cost: 10
Cooldown Time: 0 seconds

Skill Name: Energy Blast
Description: An area of effect attack that targets multiple enemies and fires a beam that sweeps across the battlefield.
Current lvl: 5 MAXED
Ability: Causes 150% non-elemental damage to multiple targets
MP Cost: 25
Cooldown Time: 5 seconds

Skill Name: Mud Bullet
Description: The caster uses MP to create bullets that shoot from the ground and slams into opponents.
Current lvl: 5 MAXED
Ability: Fires a maximum of five bullets
Each bullet does 100% damage
MP Cost: 100
Cooldown Time: 10 seconds

Skill Name: Earth Dragon
Description: A mage casts a spell on the ground, creating a dragon that attacks the mage's enemy.
Current lvl: 5 MAXED
Ability: Creates a 5-meter tall dragon
Any attacks done by the dragon do double the amount of the Mage's Magic Attack stat
The dragon has x2 the health as the one who created it.
MP Cost: 120
Cooldown Time: 120 seconds

Name: Ymir
Class: Mage
Lvl: 15
SP: 0
AP: 450
Experience: 500,100/2,457,600
Strength: +5
Constitution: +30
Dexterity: +50
Speed: +5
Physical Attack: +10
Health: 400/400
Hit-Rate: 5%
MP: 960/960

Movement: +5
Physical Defense: +40
Magical Defense: +320

Skills:
Skill Name: Energy Bolt
Description: A mage aims their staff and calls the name [Energy Bolt] to release a bolt of magical energy at enemies.
Current lvl: 5 MAXED
Ability: Deals 200% non-elemental damage to enemies
MP Cost: 10
Cooldown Time: 0 seconds

Skill Name: Energy Blast
Description: An area of effect attack that targets multiple enemies and fires a beam that sweeps across the battlefield.
Current lvl: 5 MAXED
Ability: Deals 200% non-elemental damage to enemies
MP Cost: 10
Cooldown Time: 0 seconds

Skill Name: Freeze
Description: The mage casts a spell on multiple targets to freeze them in place.
Current lvl: 5 MAXED
Ability: Freezes all enemies within 20 feet of the targeted area for 5 seconds
MP Cost: 50
Cooldown Time: 30 seconds

Skill Name: Blizzard
Description: Creates a storm of icy cold winds that damages multiple opponents.
Current lvl: 4
AP needed to reach lvl 5: 30,000

Ability: Damages multiple enemies. Range is ten yards from targeted enemy

Has 40% chance of freezing opponents

MP Cost: 150

Cooldown Time: 60 seconds

Name: Flame_Emperor

Class: Mage

Lvl: 16

SP: 0

AP: 300

Experience: 60/4,195,200

Strength: +5

Constitution: +30

Dexterity: +5

Intelligence: +50

Speed: +5

Physical Attack: +1

Health: 360/360

Hit-Rate: 5%

MP: 650/650

Movement: +5

Physical Defense: +40

Magical Defense: +120

Dodge-Rate: 5%

Magic Attack: +200

Skills:

Skill Name: Energy Bolt

Description: A mage aims their staff and calls the name [Energy Bolt] to release a bolt of magical energy at enemies.

Current lvl: 5 MAXED

Ability: Deals 200% non-elemental damage to enemies

MP Cost: 10

Cooldown Time: 0 seconds

Skill Name: Energy Blast
Description: An area of effect attack that targets multiple enemies and fires a beam that sweeps across the battlefield.
Current lvl: 5 MAXED
Ability: Deals 200% non-elemental damage to enemies
MP Cost: 10
Cooldown Time: 0 seconds

Skill Name: Scorching Blaze
Description: The mage casts a spell on a single target, creating a fire tornado to surround and damage the enemy.
Current lvl: 5 MAXED
Ability: Creates a fire tornado that lasts for 30 seconds and does 150% damage every second
MP Cost: 200
Cooldown Time: 60 seconds

Skill Name: Fire Spear
Description: Launches a spear of fire at the enemy.
Current lvl: 5 MAXED
Ability: Does 200% damage and has a 50% chance of causing the burn status effect
MP Cost: 250
Cooldown Time: 60 seconds

Skill Name: Firestorm
Description: User creates a powerful storm of fire that sweeps over enemies within a fifteen-yard radius.
Current lvl: 4
AP needed to reach lvl 5: 30,000
Ability: Does 140% damage to enemies
Has a 20% chance of burning enemies
MP Cost 100
Cooldown Time: 30 seconds

"Levon, Connor, and the Flame Emperor appear to have leveled up since you last checked the forums. It looks like they also learned some extra skills," Adam said.

Titania nodded. "Learning a new skill is rather easy. You can learn them from scrolls, though a scroll is rare. You can also learn them from someone willing to teach you. I believe the guard at the front gate mentioned the training hall when we first arrived here."

"He did. I guess they paid the trainers to teach them those skills. I'm a little surprised they didn't change class, but I guess they want to wait for a better class to come along," Adam muttered as he studied their stats. "Their skills don't look as powerful as the ones we have, but I guess that's because they are normal skills that anyone can learn if they have enough money. Hmm. Their levels aren't bad, though. They were probably grinding hard to reach their current level before the tournament began."

"That seems likely," Fayte said with a nod. "This tournament is important to everyone. Well, I say it is important to everyone, but most of these people belong to subsidiary branches for one of the two major guilds."

By two major guilds, Fayte was, of course, referring to the Pleonexia Alliance and Daggerfall Dynasty. They were the largest guilds in the American Federation. Adam had learned a little about them both from Fayte. According to her, the Pleonexia Alliance was larger with around 50.3 million members. Daggerfall Dynasty had approximately 49.5 million.

Of course, that only added up to around 100 million people, and the American Federation contained around 750 million players. The rest of the players were either part of a smaller guild or worked independently from the guilds.

Aris also studied their stats. She didn't say anything at first, but then a giggle escaped her lips.

"These stats suck," she said bluntly.

Fayte turned just her head to look at the girl. In a voice that seeped with amusement, she said, "Adam said the same thing when he first saw our stats before we gained a hidden class."

While Aris was giggling at how she and Adam had the same thought process, Levon and his group walked further into the room. Just as Levon was looking around, his eyes stopped on their group. His eyes first locked onto Fayte. Then, as if pulled by some magical force, his gaze traveled to Adam. At that moment, as their eyes locked, the man's complexion grew dark and stormy. It only lasted for a single instant. However, that instant was long enough for Adam to see what Levon hid underneath that polite exterior of his.

"Looks like he hasn't changed at all," Adam muttered.

"What was that?" asked Fayte.

"I said it looks like he's angry," Adam said with a small head shake.

Levon could obviously not hear what they were saying, but he seemed to recognize that Adam and Fayte were talking to each other. With his lips drawn into a tight smile, he began wading toward them.

"Bwa ha ha ha ha! Look at all these people! I never thought there'd be so many players who thought they could snatch the [Guild Creation Token] from my hands!"

Before Levon could make his way over, a loud and rambunctious voice resounded throughout the waiting room. Everyone, Levon included, looked toward the stairs as five more people emerged.

Four of those people were men. They all looked relatively similar, with strong jaws and a masculine appearance. Their skin was dark like obsidian, their eyes equally black. Each possessed a powerful bearing that all but demanded attention. It was easy for anyone to see they were brothers.

The person leading the group looked like the oldest, at several heads taller than the other three. He wore a golden chestplate that gleamed in the light. However, the rest of his armor was made of steel. A simple-looking sword was strapped to his waist.

Perhaps because he was the oldest and the most charismatic, the other three people merely stood behind him like decorations. This man had an overbearing presence that made him the center of attention.

Or it would have if not for the person beside him.

While the dark-skinned man was loud and raucous, the person at his side did not say a single word, but that hardly mattered. Their very presence drew Adam's gaze to them.

Adam couldn't see what this person looked like. His entire body was covered in a white cloak with a hood that hid their face.

He could see nothing beyond the hood either because their face was covered by a plain white mask.

There was nothing about this person that stood out to him; he was around the same height as the average adult male, and because his entire body was covered from head to toe, it was impossible to make out any defining features. Held within this person's right hand was a spear.

Unlike Levon's glaive, the spear this person wielded was a traditional weapon. The shaft was about two yards in length, its entire body made from gleaming silver. Near the spear's blade was the head of a roaring lion surrounded by a thick mane. The blade itself, meanwhile, had several hook-like blades sticking out near the base, but then it turned into a more traditional leaf shape further out. Adam estimated the blade's overall length to be about one foot long.

"Those are the leaders of Daggerfall Dynasty," Fayte explained. "The man in front is called Daren Daggerfall. The three behind him are his brothers: Skyrim, Morrowind, and Oblivion."

"Pffft! Did they name themselves after old video games? Who does that?" asked Aris with a giggle.

Fayte shrugged as if to say, *"I wasn't the one who came up with those names."*

"I'm guessing the person next to Daren is the Spear God?" asked Adam.

"That's right," Fayte said with a subtle nod. "In every game he has ever played, the Spear God has the same outfit and never changes it. No one has ever seen what he looks like either. Some people have tried to discover his identity by tracking him when he first begins playing, but no one has succeeded."

Adam nodded as he turned to his fairy companion. "Titania?"

Because she knew exactly what he wanted, Titania did not hesitate to cast [scan], but this time she only cast scan on the Spear God.

Name: Spear_God
Class: Spear Dancer
Lvl: 17
SP: 0
AP: 5,000
Experience: 100,050/9,830,400
Strength: +150
Constitution: +100
Dexterity: +5
Intelligence: +5
Speed: +5
Physical Attack: +2,350
Hit-Rate: ???
MP: 440/440
Movement: +15
Physical Defense: +860
Magical Defense: +400
Dodge-Rate: 50%
Magic Attack: +5

Skills:
Skill Name: Slash
Description: A basic skill where the player swings his or her sword and attacks the enemy!
Current lvl: 5 MAXED
Ability: Causes 150% damage to enemy if it hits

MP Cost: 1
Cooldown Time: 0 seconds

Skill Name: Thrust
Description: A basic skill where the player thrusts his or her sword at the enemy!
Current Lvl: 5 MAXED
Ability: Causes 160% damage with a 5% chance at getting a critical hit
MP Cost: 5
Cooldown Time: 0 seconds

Skill Name: First Form
Description: Much like a spider weaves its webs, the user of this skill will create numerous flashes of light with their spear intent to weave an impenetrable offense that entraps opponents, making it impossible for them to escape.
Current lvl: 4
AP needed to reach lvl 5: 60,000
Ability: Enemies who fall into this barrier receive 300% damage for every spear light they hit
MP Cost: 100
Cooldown Time: 30

Skill Name: Second Form
Description: This dance is one that requires the spearman to lunge forward with quick and powerful movements just like a striking serpent. The attack happens so fast that most people cannot even see the spearman move.
Current lvl: 4
AP needed to reach lvl 5: 80,000
Ability: Lunges forward six times to do x6 damage
MP Cost: 100
Cooldown Time: 30 seconds

Skill Name: Martyr
Description: A kamikaze skill that sacrifices oneself to damage their enemy.
Current lvl: 4
AP needed to reach lvl 5: 100,000
Ability: Sacrifices 80% HP to do 80% damage to selected enemy
MP Cost: 400
Cooldown Time: 120 seconds

Skill Name: Cherry Blossom Dance
Description: A dance that allows the user five consecutive attacks as they dance around their opponent. When all the attacks are completed, an outline will form on the ground in the shape of a cherry blossom.
Current lvl: 10 MAXED
Ability: Release a constant stream of attacks, does x3 damage increase for every hit, and resets when attack misses
Hit-Rate: 100%
MP Cost: 50
Cooldown Time: 30 seconds

While the Spear God's stats were more impressive than anyone else's he had seen outside of his own party's, it was not his stats that caused Adam to feel like his brain had shut down; it was the three skills this person had.

[First Form].

[Second Form].

[Cherry Blossom Dance].

Anyone not familiar with the Pleonexia Family's school of spearmanship would never be able to recognize the first two skills, but it was impossible for Adam to not know of them. The first two skills bore similar names as the first two stances within the

Pleonexia Family's combat style. Known as the Seven Spear Dances, the Pleonexia Family's school of spearmanship had seven powerful stances that were used in conjunction with the spear. Each stance relied on a different pattern of attack and rhythm to throw their enemies off balance. While it was not the best of spear techniques, it was most comprehensive and intricate.

Each stance was called a form, and there were seven forms titled Form I through VII. The difference between the naming scheme was quite subtle. Adam was honestly a little surprised Levon didn't seem to have recognized the skills, or perhaps he had and chose not to say anything? There were a lot of combat schools, after all. Maybe he just thought the similarity between the two naming schemes was a mere coincidence?

Of course, it was [Cherry Blossom Dance] that made Adam's heart stop beating. While the name was slightly different from his [Dance of the Sakura Blossoms], how could he not realize that those differences were minuscule? Cherry blossoms and sakura blossoms were the same things. The difference was that one was a Japanese word and the other was English.

Seeing those three skills in this person's skill set made Adam's entire body shake and his pupils contract.

CLASH

"Lexi?" Adam whispered, his voice so soft only Aris could hear it. She was right next to him, hugging his arm as she helped block Susan from Connor Sword's view.

"Adam, is everything okay?" she asked in a worried voice.

Adam shuddered as he tore his gaze away from the cloaked figure. This person couldn't be Lexi. It simply couldn't be possible. That was what he told himself, repeating it over and over again in his mind until he was forced to believe his own words.

"Everything is fine," Adam said as he directed a smile toward Aris. "I was just a little startled by something."

"Hmm… that's fine then." Aris smiled at him, but there was something about her smile that made Adam understand he wasn't fooling her. The words she spoke next confirmed this feeling. "But if you ever feel troubled, please come to me. I want you to share your burdens with me."

"Thank you," he whispered.

A strong feeling of warmth surged through his heart as he looked at the eyes hidden behind that veil. He didn't need anyone but this girl. Adam had already promised himself to her, so there was no need to think about whether the Spear God was Lexi or not. This person was obviously different anyway. They didn't walk with the refined grace and elegance he remembered Lexi possessing. Their bearing and demeanor was rough and inelegant, sharp like a sword drawn from its sheath.

The tension in the room had grown stifling ever since the arrival of Daggerfall Dynasty's four leaders and their famous bodyguard. Levon, who had originally been traveling toward Fayte, was now forced to stop and turn to Daren Daggerfall. He wore a polite and refined smile. If Adam had not seen the blatant anger and darkness brimming within Levon's eyes seconds before, he would have believed the man wasn't capable of feeling such vile emotions.

"Daren, I knew you and I would meet again once the tournament was announced," Levon said. "It seems we will once again be battling for a [Guild Creation Token]."

"Bwa ha ha ha! It certainly seems that way, doesn't it?" Daggerfall grinned as he squared his shoulders. His body produced an intimidating aura that caused the weaker people in the room to feel faint. "The last time the first [Guild Creation Token] appeared, it was auctioned off. You won because you had more money available than us, but this time, it will be a contest of skill." The man glanced at his cloaked bodyguard and his smile widened. "I do not believe you will be able to beat us this time."

The words were blunt, a clear challenge directed at Levon and the Pleonexia Alliance. While Gaia bristled and glared at Daggerfall like she wanted to stab his eyes out with icicles, Levon retained his calm and polite demeanor. He nodded at the Spear God, but most of his attention was still on Daren, his own refined elegance allowing him to stand on par with the larger man's imposing pressure and overbearing confidence.

"I wouldn't be so sure about that," Levon said faintly. "It is true that the Spear God is indeed ranked second on the International Power Rankings, beating out my friend here, but Connor has been practicing diligently every day in the hopes of winning back his honor in a rematch. I do not believe he will lose this time."

As he spoke, Connor Sword stepped forward and stood in front of the Spear God. A faint aura seemed to rise from the man. Even Adam, who was standing several yards away and hidden behind numerous people, could feel the sharp aura emanating from him.

"Sword intent, huh?" Adam muttered.

"Excuse me, but what is 'sword intent'?" asked Aris.

As someone who didn't have much contact with these kinds of people, Aris was woefully unknowledgeable about the subject, and Adam had never enlightened her because he didn't want to taint her innocence. This had become even more true after she contracted Mortems Disease. But now that she had seen someone with sword intent, there was no need to hide it.

Adam would have answered, but Fayte beat him to it. "Sword intent is the physical manifestation of a swordsman's sharp intentions. You could call it their fighting spirit if you wanted.

Powerful swordsmen with esper abilities can manifest sword intent to create an aura like the one coming from Connor Sword. There are even some powerful swordsmen who are so skilled, they can launch their sword intent at opponents, attacking them from a distance."

"Connor Sword also practices a powerful form of swordsmanship called Eight-Headed Serpent Style," Susan said in a voice so soft everyone else almost missed it. When they glanced at the girl hiding behind Adam, she flushed bright red but continued talking. "The Eight-Headed Serpent Style is a Japanese sword style said to invoke the powers of the famous Yamata no Orochi. It has eight stances and each stance maximizes a different physical attribute. There's the Speed Stance, Strength Stance, Dexterity Stance, Reflex Stance, Endurance Stance, Formless Stance, Counter Stance, and Serpent Stance."

Adam was shocked that Susan knew so much about the Eight-Headed Serpent Style of swordsmanship, but it also solidified his belief that she had some kind of history with Connor Sword. Why else would she know so much about his sword style?

While they were receiving a slight lesson regarding the sword style Connor Sword used, the conversation between Daren Daggerfall and Levon Pleonexia continued unabated.

"Bwa ha ha! Well, I suppose you can believe whatever you want, just like I choose to believe there is no way your vice commander or anyone else here can win against my bodyguard."

Levon wore a faint smile as his gaze flickered from the Spear God and back to Daren too rapidly for most people to catch. "I guess we shall see in the tournament."

It looked like the conversation was winding down, so Adam suggested to Fayte they all change locations. Levon had seen them already. Adam was sure Fayte wished to avoid this man, and he also didn't want to be in this man's presence. He did not believe he would be able to withstand his desire to kill Levon if the man got too close. Adam was already suppressing his killing intent to the greatest extent possible.

Several minutes after the confrontation ended, a large screen suddenly appeared in the air above their heads. Adam looked up with everyone else. The screen showed a large stage made of white tiles with four pillars at each corner. In the center of this stage was a beautiful girl with blonde hair and a bright smile, wearing a skimpy outfit that was obviously meant to draw attention from the crowd.

"Is that a television?!" Fayte asked in shock.

"I do not know what a te-lee-vishion is, but this is just a magic screen," Titania told her. "Like those magic screens that appear when those announcements are made. If you look at the ceiling, you will see a small crystal embedded in the center. That is a magic crystal, which has all kinds of uses. One of its many uses is being able to project images into thin air. There should be a corresponding crystal outside that is connected to this one."

"Oh. So that's how it works," Fayte murmured with a nod.

"Hello, everyone!" the girl shouted into something that vaguely resembled a microphone. "I would like to welcome everyone here to the Solum arena's first-ever otherworld tournament! My name is Sandra Rowland! I will be your host during this tournament! I hope everyone here is as excited as I am for this!"

The girl's bubbly personality, attractive appearance, and skimpy clothes made the men in the stands go wild. Even Adam could hear the loud roar of approval coming from outside. The men inside the waiting room also seemed to like this girl. Adam heard several comments that he did not think were at all appropriate to say out loud. From the dark pressure emanating from Aris, Fayte, Titania, and even Lilith, they did not either.

On that note, Adam believed the only reason Susan was not expressing displeasure like them was that she was too timid.

"Before we begin, I have some regrettable news for everyone," Sandra continued. "Don't worry. Don't worry. The tournament will continue as usual. However, because we received over three hundred applicants, it won't be possible to host such a large-scale event. We need to whittle down the number of people participating before we can get to the main event. That is why we have decided that the first battle will be a large-scale all or nothing elimination round."

Her words caused the many players participating in the tournament to mutter. A large-scale elimination round was pretty unheard of in the real world, but Adam understood the reason she was doing this. Bromley Paxton probably hadn't understood how enticing a [Guild Creation Token] was to players and didn't realize so many would enter. If he didn't do this, the tournament would last for at least a week if not longer as they slowly whittled away the number of players through a normal tournament.

"Here is how the preliminary round is going to work," Sandra began her explanation. "Everyone who is participating will come on this stage, and when I give the signal, you will all fight. Don't worry.

There is a magic barrier around this stage that will prevent people from dying. Once your health reaches +1, you will automatically be teleported off the platform. The fight will continue until just twenty people are left standing. Now! Will everyone participating please exit through the doors and climb onto the platform?"

A large set of double doors opened on the opposite side of the entrance. The players who'd been anxiously waiting surged forward, streaming outside. Adam, Aris, Fayte, Susan, and Lilith were forced to follow the crowd. Titania and Kureha had no such issues, but Titania was forced to grab his shirt when she was almost knocked off his shoulder after someone bumped into him.

"Watch where you're going!" Titania snapped, though the man who hit them was already traveling away and paid no attention to her words. She huffed indignantly and muttered something harsh and threatening under her breath.

The platform was a lot larger than Adam expected; it was so large that he couldn't accurately judge how big it was. It was at least two times bigger than a football field, shaped like a square, and elevated about three feet above ground level. Even with over three hundred players participating, this platform was more than capable of accommodating them all and then some.

Unlike the Roman Colosseum, which Adam had originally assumed this structure would be based on, the arena was enclosed with a large ceiling above their heads. The ribbed ceiling had several lights hanging from it. They looked a little high-tech to him, but after Titania's explanation about the magic projection, he knew these modern conveniences would be explained away with magic.

"Let's move to one of the corners," Adam suggested.

"Why one of the corners?" asked Fayte. "Isn't that a bad position to be in? We could be knocked out of the ring."

Adam gave the woman an amused smile that she couldn't see behind his mask. However, he didn't doubt she could hear the emotion in his voice as he asked, "Do you honestly believe there is anyone capable of knocking us out of the ring?"

"Oh. I guess you have a point."

Under Adam's advice, the group moved to one of the four corners, which meant they wouldn't have to worry about attacks from behind. Several other people seemed to have the same idea. At each of the four corners was at least one group of people. Levon, Connor Sword, and his Four—Three—Elements had chosen the corner diametrically opposite of theirs. He felt this was a good thing since Adam wanted to defeat them in single combat.

Adam did not recognize the other two groups. He had believed Daggerfall Dynasty would choose a corner as well, but he soon discovered they had decided to remain in the middle. The group of five was already standing back to back.

"Kureha, Titania, you two will have to get off the stage since you can't participate," Adam said.

The tournament was player-only, meaning Adam's two NPC companions were not allowed to take part. While Titania crossed her arms and huffed, she still fluttered off his shoulder. Kureha didn't mind as much. She yipped once as she jumped off his head, landed on the platform, and leaped off the stage. The two took up a position just a few yards from the platform. Adam was amused to note that Titania had decided to use Kureha's head as a chair.

Sandra was no longer on the platform but standing on a smaller platform hovering in midair. He wondered what sort of magic governed that object. However, he didn't think there was anyone present who could explain it to him, and it looked like the tournament was about to start.

"Since it looks like everyone is here, allow me to explain the rules!" Sandra continued. "The rules go like this. Losers are determined by ring out, surrender, or when their health reaches +1. You are not allowed to use potions, but you can use buffs and healing magic. You can choose to fight alone or in a group. However, you should be aware that once the tournament officially starts, all battles will be one on one. Do you all understand? In that case, let this battle begin!"

The moment Sandra announced the start of the battle was the moment chaos reigned on the platform. Everyone began fighting. Swords clashed. Arrows flew through space and impaled people with lightning quickness. Spells flashed out. Fire. Ice. Water. Lightning. Energy. A myriad of magical projectiles flew through the air as people began bombarding each other with spells.

Several people charged toward their group. Adam had noticed it before, but they had garnered a lot of attention, either because all but one of them were concealing their faces or because he was the only man in the party. A group of ten people had come to attack them. There wasn't a single woman in this group.

"I'd like everyone to keep their skills hidden so we can surprise our opponents in the actual tournament, so please leave this to me," Adam said as he took a step forward.

"We will let you take care of this then," Fayte said.

"Kick their butts good, Adam!" Aris cheered.

While Susan and Lilith didn't say anything, Adam thought he sensed a similar sentiment coming from them.

When the ten men saw Adam stepping up to fight them alone, they stopped walking and instead stared at him, incredulity seeping from their eyes. This group seemed to be a mixed one. They didn't have any uniform that identified them as a guild. Adam wondered if this was because they hadn't been able to buy custom clothes yet, or if it was because they were independent players who belonged to no guild and just decided to gang up on his party.

He supposed it didn't matter.

"Get a load of this asshat," one of the men standing at the front said. He wore an arrogant grin as he placed his sword on his shoulder. "This loser thinks he can take us on by himself! Isn't that hilarious?!"

"Hmph. Does he think he's invincible or something?"

"Ha! The jerkwad is just trying to show off in front of those women! Let's show these bitches what real men are like!"

"Don't worry, ladies. After we take care of this fucktard, we'll be sure to show you a good time. We'll treat you real good."

Immediately after the first man spoke, the others also began speaking. Adam thought they would have been better off keeping their mouths shut. He didn't even have to look behind him to know the girls were not happy. Their killing intent was so potent even he shivered, though perhaps owing to their stupidity, none of the players confronting him could feel it.

Since Adam had no real desire to prolong this fight and wanted to make an example out of these people, he began walking toward them. He walked slowly as if he was just out for a stroll. Placing the tip of his spear against the ground, he created loud scraping noises that grated on the ears of his enemies.

"If you people are going to attack, then hurry it up. I don't have all day," Adam said.

"Fucking bastard!"

"Go die!"

"Let's teach this son of a bitch a lesson he'll never forget!"

The men took offense to his calm and disdaining demeanor. With a loud roar, they charged at him. Adam felt a smile tug at his lips. He waited, and waited, and waited, until all ten of them were within range of his spear.

Then he used [Energy Sweep].

[Energy Sweep] was an AOE skill with a limited range of five yards. He slammed his left foot against the ground, flexed the muscles in his calf, and swung the spear in his hands with all his might. By channeling his spear intent into his weapon and swinging it around in a long arc, he could release a powerful blade of energy that swept over his opponents.

-10,298; -10,208; -10,468; -10,398; -10,358; -10,403; -10,468; -10,398; -10,468; -10,438!

Ten massive numbers appeared over the head of every man who attacked him. This number was more than ten times higher than the amount of health most of these players had. Ten thousand points of damage. That was a number only boss level monsters could deal, and yet, here was a player who had simply swung his spear and instantly killed ten other players in the blink of an eye with a single attack.

The moment his attack hit the players, all of them were instantly teleported to just outside of the platform. Most of them landed on their butts and were staring wide-eyed at nothing. The one who seemed like their leader looked incredibly confused, like he couldn't figure out how he'd suddenly ended up outside of the platform.

Adam's grand attack caused many of the players participating to stop what they were doing and stare at him. He gazed at everyone through his mask. Several of the people who locked eyes with him shuddered and looked away, not daring to maintain eye contact for fear that he would attack them as well.

With a snort, Adam walked back to his party, turned to face the crowd, and slammed the butt of his spear against the ground as if daring the other players to attack him.

No one did.

***

Among the many players who had seen Adam's instant kill AOE attack was Daren Daggerfall and his three brothers. He had sucked in a deep breath upon seeing that magnificent skill. The man had swung his spear in a powerful arc that created a fan-shaped wave of energy, which swept over the ten attacking players and would have killed them if not for the effects of the magic barrier that Sandra spoke of.

The first to speak was Skyrim, the third oldest among the siblings. "Brother… did you see that attack just now…? That person, do you think he's…?"

"That man is definitely the Adam we've been hearing so much about," Daggerfall answered the question that never fully formed. "I suspected he would be taking part in this tournament ever since it was announced. I had been hoping to see his skills in action, but this is far beyond what even I could have imagined. Bwa ha ha! He certainly doesn't disappoint."

Ten thousand points of damage. That was an insane number that should not be possible for a player to produce at this stage of the game. Even if Adam was at level 50 and had the best weapon available, it would have been hard for Daren to believe he could deal that kind of damage. The man hadn't even used a single buff!

"Come to think of it, wasn't there someone named Adam who shocked the gaming world three years ago?" asked Oblivion. He was the youngest of the four siblings at only twenty-two years old.

"There was. I remember watching him defeat Lin Akamine in one of the international tournaments," Daggerfall said, reminiscing. "He would have been ranked number one on the International Power Rankings, but he disappeared after demolishing the strongest players at the time."

"Think this could be him?" asked Skyrim.

"I think there is a very real possibility."

Because of their position as the second-largest guild in the American Federation, nobody dared come near them. This meant Daren was free to look at the cloaked figure standing beside him.

"Do you think you can beat him?" he asked in a low voice.

The Spear God did not say anything, but Daren did not feel insulted by the silence. This person had never spoken a single word since coming into his family's service. All he cared about was the skill this figure displayed and the trust they had earned.

Finally, the Spear God made a single motion, nodding their head once.

Daren gave a relieved sigh. Then he smiled.

"It doesn't matter how powerful Adam is. He might have defeated Lin Akamine, but he won't defeat the Spear God, especially when they use the same type of weapon."

With his confidence bolstered, Daren went back to observing the battles happening around them. He completely missed the gaze the Spear God sent Adam as the other man stood in front of the members of his party like an immovable object.

* * *

Like the members of Daggerfall Dynasty, the Pleonexia Alliance's five members were free of fighting. No one wanted to come over and attack them. Even if they believed they could defeat this group, nobody wanted to risk offending the Pleonexia Alliance, which could result in untold suffering both in the game and in real life. This meant they also had a perfect view of Adam's astonishing performance.

"Levon, that attack just now…" Connor Sword began.

"I know!" Levon snapped through gritted teeth.

Levon had spent untold amounts of money to discover Adam's identity in the real world, but not only had all of his searches come to naught, he'd eventually learned that Adam had teamed up with none other than Fayte Dairing.

He remembered the International Announcement three weeks ago. Adam, Fayte, Lilith, and Susan had defeated a 4-Star enemy and earned one thousand status points. That was a ridiculous reward no matter who you were. However, more than the status points, what really made Levon feel like someone had placed his heart in an oven was learning that this man was a member of Fayte's party. It was a combination of intense jealousy and hatred that he felt. Jealousy that this man was working with the woman he planned to marry, and hatred because it was clear that Adam was working against him to help Fayte.

"Do not pay them any attention right now," Levon ordered. "Being able to deal such incredible damage means nothing if you can't hit your opponent. No matter what happens, we have to win this tournament." He looked at Connor. "You may need to rely on your secret weapon if you face him during the tournament."

"Don't worry," Connor Sword said with a sharp smile. "That man is also partying alongside my fiance, so I understand how you feel perfectly. If we fight in the tournament, I will use my strongest ability right from the start."

Levon nodded, feeling reassured, and turned his head to gaze at Adam. The man in the mask was not doing anything. He was just standing there with the butt of his spear resting against the platform. Levon narrowed his eyes as darkness flashed within his pupils.

"Enjoy your small moment of fame while you can. I will be sure to crush that fame before the tournament ends."

***

The preliminary match ended several minutes after it began. Just as Adam expected, aside from his party, the ones who survived with their parties intact were Daggerfall Dynasty and the Pleonexia Alliance. Nobody had bothered to attack them. Adam was almost willing to believe anyone who fought against them in the tournament would surrender just to avoid offending these two great powers.

Among the remaining five people who survived the preliminary round, there was the leader of the Holy Sword Sect, American Samurai, Daniel Frost of the Rising Phoenix Alliance, Kevin Swift, leader of an independent guild called American Kitsune, and two people who did not belong to any guild but were still ranked sixth and seventh on the International Power Rankings. Cherry Summers and Mist.

Cherry Summers was an archer with a bow and quiver of arrows attached to his back. He wore a leather jerkin, brown pants, and brown boots. His outfit didn't look that sturdy, but Adam knew better than to assume. Even weak-looking equipment could have impressive stats like Aris's Blade Dancer outfit. He wasn't what Adam would call a handsome man, but Cherry Summers did have a somewhat roguish aura about him. His cheerful smile also made him seem very amiable.

On the other hand, Mist seemed disinterested in everything. His somewhat feminine appearance gave him the androgynous charm all pretty boys possessed, and his cool demeanor lent him an aura of mystery. His hair was long and jet black, glossy, and tied into a ponytail behind his head. He wore the white robes of a Priest. Gripped firmly in his hand was a praying staff with a cross at the very top.

"Now that the preliminaries have come to an end, it is time to begin the main event!" Sandra said from her place on high. She seemed extra cheerful after having watched all the players beat the crap out of each other. "I want everyone to pay attention to the magic projection above your heads."

As she spoke, a large screen appeared in the air above the platform, projected from a magic stone in the ceiling. It currently displayed two empty boxes with the letters "VS" between them.

"Participants will be selected to fight via random drawing. When your face appears in one of those two boxes, it will be your turn to fight. Because the fights are determined by random selection, there are no brackets, so you could fight two or more times in a row. Consequently, you could also only fight once in the entire tournament. The same rules from the elimination round apply here.

You are not allowed to use potions, though you can use buffs. Participants will lose when their health reaches +1, they surrender, or they are knocked out of the ring. Does everyone understand? Does anyone have any questions? No? That's great! In that case, let's begin the true tournament now!"

Loud roars of approval echoed from the crowd in the stands. Adam looked up at the stands to see a sea of bobbing heads and flailing limbs.

The screen above flashed and the faces of those participating appeared in the boxes, flashing by in the blink of an eye as if the boxes were scrolling through the participants at light speed. The faces being scrolled through slowed down until two faces appeared, signifying who would get to fight in the first battle of the tournament.

THE TOURNAMENT BEGINS

Spear God versus Cherry Summers.

"Awwww, man! Why the hell do I have to fight the second most powerful player in the entire freaking world?! What did I do to deserve this?!" Cherry Summers immediately screamed when he saw his face appear on the screen. He grabbed his hair as if wishing he could tear it out. "This sucks! This blows! I'd rather face anyone but him? Hey, Mist! Wanna take my place? You do, right? Right?!"

Mist gave the man beside him a cold look. "Shut up and fight, idiot."

With that, Mist walked away from the man who could only wail in despair and beg him not to leave.

Adam found the strange interaction between the two unusual, but he didn't say anything as he stepped off the platform with everyone else. Sandra directed the players to stand off to the side instead of return to the waiting room. This meant they had front row seats to the competition. He wondered if she was doing this so everyone would be able to study their opponents, but he dismissed the thought as irrelevant.

"Titania, can you [scan] Cherry Summers?" Adam asked the fairy as she floated back onto his shoulder.

"Give me a moment," Titania said as she cast [scan].

Name: Cherry_Summers
Class: Archer
Lvl: 16
SP: 0
AP: 215
Experience: 115/4,915,200
Reputation: 20,000
Strength: +205
Constitution: +60
Dexterity: +50
Intelligence: +25
Speed: +50
Physical Attack: +650
Health: 620/620
Hit-Rate: 300%
MP: 230/230
Movement: +100
Luck: +2

Physical Defense: +125
Magic Defense: +60
Dodge-Rate: 200%
Magic Attack: +25

Skills:
Skill Name: Deadeye
Description: Archers can increase their hit-rate and critical hit-rate by increasing their perceptions through the Deadeye skill.
Current lvl: 5 MAXED
Ability: Increases Hit-rate to 110%. 30% chance of dealing x2 critical damage
MP Cost: 5
Cooldown Time: 0 seconds

Skill Name: Rain of Arrows
Description: Archers who learn this skill can fire a hailstorm of arrows that deals damage to multiple enemies.
Current lvl: 5 MAXED
Ability: Causes 150% damage to all enemies within 15 yards of targeted enemy
MP Cost: 5
Cooldown Time: 0 seconds

Skill Name: Triple Fire
Description: Archer fires three arrows at the same time.
Current lvl: 4
AP needed to reach lvl 5: 50,000\
Ability: Fires three arrows
Each arrow has a 50% of causing critical damage
X3 damage if critical hit is struck
MP Cost: 20
Cooldown Time: 30 seconds

Skill Name: Curve Shot

Description: Archer fires an arrow that curves mid-flight and strikes enemy from their blind spot.
Current lvl: 4
AP needed to reach lvl 5: 40,000
Ability: The arrow curves and strikes the enemy in their blind spot
It cannot be dodged
100% hit-rate
MP Cost: 20
Cooldown Time: 15

"His stats are surprisingly high. I didn't realize there was someone outside of the big guilds who reached level 16. He also has some decent equipment," Adam muttered as he studied the man's stats and skill set.

Titania, also examining his stats, nodded. "That bow of his is definitely something that was forged by the dwarves. You can tell because of its exceptional craftsmanship. He probably found it in a dungeon."

Adam glanced at the bow in Cherry Summers's hand. It was indeed an exceptional weapon. It was a compound bow, a weapon that was mechanically operated using cams, pulleys, and cables to help archers hold onto heavy draw weights at full draw. They were known mostly for their lightweight and incredible speed.

He didn't know what this bow was made from, but since it was a fantasy setting, he assumed it was created from something other than fiberglass. The bow itself was beautifully crafted and had rune-like designs drawn onto the surface. Adam didn't know if they were for decoration or had a practical use.

"Are both fighters ready?" asked Sandra.

"No!" Cherry Summers shouted. "Can I get a redraw? I don't want to fight this guy!"

"You can surrender if you want," Sandra said with a shrug.

"Fuck that!"

"Then fight! The competition starts now!"

"Damn it!!!"

The moment Sandra said the competition was beginning, the Spear God launched himself forward like a bullet fired from a sniper rifle. He moved so fast even Adam was shocked. The girls standing by his side made surprised exclamations. Only Aris didn't say anything, narrowing her eyes as she followed the Spear God's movement.

Cherry Summers proved that he was not as dimwitted as he acted. The man leaped backward and quickly used [Triple Fire], shooting three arrows at the same time. All of them flew in different directions but curved around to attack the Spear God. It looked like each one would hit, but then the Spear God spun his spear around and created an impenetrable barrier that the arrows bounced off of.

"What the fuck?! That wasn't even a skill! I call foul!" Cherry Summers accused, but then he screamed like a little girl upon realizing the Spear God hadn't lost any speed. He fired several more arrows, unleashing [Deadeye] and [Rain of Arrows] in quick succession. His first attack was swatted away. Then the Spear God showed off his incredible reflexes when he moved through the arrows raining down on him. Seeing this caused Cherry Summers to scream. "Don't blame me for this! It's your own fault for being too damn strong!"

His last attack was [Curve Shot], which was the attack that couldn't be dodged. The arrow flew from his bow and curved around. If the attack hit, it would penetrate the Spear God's flank, right where he couldn't see it.

If it hit.

The Spear God did not dodge this attack. Just like when Cherry Summers used [Triple Fire], he spun the spear around in his grip and created what appeared to be an impenetrable shield. It was at this moment that Adam realized what that shield was.

"Form Five," he whispered.

"Adam?" Aris looked at him.

"That's the form the Spear God is using," Adam said. "It's… a little different from what I remember, but he is definitely using the Pleonexia Family's fifth form. Known as Form Five, it is a stance that combines their spear intent with an intense spinning motion that allows the spearman to create an impenetrable shield that can block even bullets."

Aris looked at Adam curiously, but she didn't express any suspicions over how he knew about the Pleonexia Family's spear technique. Fayte, on the other hand, was staring at him with a look so hard he could feel her eyes drilling into his skull.

"How do you know so much about the Pleonexia Family's spear techniques?" she asked.

He sighed and replied evasively. "Let's just say I have as much reason to hate the Ploenexia Family as you and leave it at that."

Fayte didn't look like she was satisfied, at least from what Adam could see of her eyes, but she didn't say anything and turned her head.

The battle between the Spear God and Cherry Summers was already winding to close. The Spear God shifted from the defensive Form Five to the poisonous [First Form], which was an actual skill for the game. His movements became choppy and erratic. It looked almost like he was moving on eight legs instead of two as he closed the distance between him and Cherry Summers in an instant.

Cherry Summers did try to get away, but what made [First Form] so deadly was how it trapped opponents within a web of attacks. Even if someone could dodge one or two of them, it was impossible to dodge all of them, and these attacks could not be blocked. Cherry Summers was struck by several webs formed from spear intent and his health was decimated.

-7,050!

Cherry Summers was "killed," but he was revived using whatever magic was woven into this platform and reappeared next to the combatants, leaving Spear God alone on the platform.

"And Spear God wins!" Sandra screamed. "What an incredible match! Cherry Summers did his best to take down this incredible spearman, but he just wasn't good enough!"

The crowd was going crazy over Spear God's victory, shouting and clapping and screaming his name over and over. The thunderous roar mixed with the stomping of feet to create an intense vibration that made Kureha cover her ears and whimper. Daren looked so proud, as if he'd been the one who earned that victory himself. On the opposite end of the spectrum, Connor Sword and Levon Pleonexia looked like they had swallowed something sour.

"Fuck you!" Cherry Summers shouted obstinately. "I would have beaten anyone else! It's your fault for pitting me against that monster!"

Mist sighed. "Don't be stupid. You would have lost against most of these players."

"Wha—don't say that, man! You know how talented I am! Hey! Say something! Come on! Don't go silent on me like that!"

Despite Cherry Summers screaming at Mist, the man remained silent, stoically looking at the screen as several faces flashed by until two faces appeared.

Adam versus Kevin Swift.

"Looks like I'm up," Adam said.

"Good luck!" Aris, Fayte, and Susan said. Lilith only nodded at him.

Adam waved at them as Titania fluttered off his shoulder and moved to sit on Aris's shoulder. He walked up the platform at the same time as Kevin Swift, an attractive blond man with blue eyes and a boyish smile. He looked younger than Adam by a few years. He carried a basic sword at his side. Down below, three women were cheering him on.

"Go get him, Beloved!"

"Hey, Stud! If you kick his ass, I will plow your ass tonight when we're in bed!"

"Don't be so lewd, you damn fox! K-Kevin! Don't lose to this guy! I won't forgive you if you do!"

"Your harem?" asked Adam, raising an eyebrow.

"Ah ha ha ha… kinda. It's… complicated." Kevin rubbed the back of his head.

"Are both fighters ready?" asked Sandra as the two stood several yards apart and faced each other.

"I am," Kevin said.

"Me too," said Adam.

"Then let the match… begin!"

The moment Sanda said "begin," Kevin was throwing himself forward into an all-out sprint. Adam didn't know what this boy's stats were, but he must have thrown most of his status points into his Speed. He was sure that Kevin believed anyone else would have been shocked by how fast he could move.

However, Adam had already seen Aris's Speed.

Aris, who had a Speed of +6,400 and a Movement of +51,200.

There was no contest.

-9,080!

The moment Kevin reached Adam's range of attack, Adam swung his spear, activating the [slash] skill and demolishing the poor kid with a single hit. It didn't matter if Adam didn't know what his health looked like. Nobody in the game had enough health to withstand this attack. Kevin's health dropped to zero, then revived to +1, and then he found himself standing outside the platform with a befuddled expression on his face.

"W-what… just happened?" he asked himself.

"You lost," the redhead said.

"You lost badly," the raven-haired vixen added.

The littlest among Kevin's harem scowled. "You had your ass beat even faster than that loser, Cherry Summers."

"I heard that!" Cherry Summers screamed.

"Oh…"

"Don't worry, Beloved. I'm sure the only reason you lost is because we're just cameos," the redhead tried to reassure her boyfriend.

Kevin still didn't look like he understood how he'd lost, but he wasn't the only one. No one in the audience spoke up. The entire crowd was quiet. They couldn't understand what had just happened either. Adam could see after enhancing his eyesight with energy that everyone was whispering to each other. He could read lips, so he knew they were trying to figure out how he could deal so much damage in a single attack. A few of those people were looking pale.

They must have used [scan] on him.

"Good job," Fayte said as he walked down the platform and stood next to his party members.

"Thank you," Adam said with a courteous nod.

The other players were staring at him again, all of them wary. Levon, in particular, wore a dark expression as he stared at Adam. However, it was the Spear God's stare that caught his attention the most. Even though the man was wearing a hood and covering his face with a mask, Adam could tell the man was staring at him. He turned his head and stared right back through the other man's mask.

"All right! Adam defeated Kevin Swift. Not sure how, but he did. Anyway, it is time to select who will fight next!" Sandra declared.

The battle after Adam's was between Levon Pleonexia and Skyrim. Levon had the Warrior Class, while Skyrim was a Mage class with several additional skills aside from the beginner skills. His two additional skills were [Water Dragon Roar] and [Wind Wall].

Adam noticed the moment the fight started that Levon's skill with a spear had improved greatly from when they were kids, but he did not have the Spear God's heaven shattering talent. He was also not as good with his spear as Lexi had been.

Being familiar with the Pleonexia Family's style of spearmanship, he did not fail to notice that the Spear God's style varied a little from the standard Seven Forms that Levon used. The Spear God's style was highly modified for someone with a lower center of gravity. The Seven Phoenix Forms Style was originally designed for someone with a center of gravity near their chest, but the Spear God had modified it to fit someone who had a center of gravity near their hips.

The battle between Levon Pleonexia and Skyrim lasted a lot longer than his or the Spear God's battles, but it eventually ended in Levon's victory after Skyrim ran out of MP.

"Thank you for letting me win," Levon said with a polite smile as he bowed toward Skyrim. It was a very respectful attitude that did not contain a hint of arrogance—at least, no arrogance that any normal person could see.

"Haaa… It looks like you've improved," Skyrim said politely. "It's unfortunate I'm a Mage in this game. Perhaps I could have given you a better fight if I chose the Warrior Class."

Levon did not say anything and only kept his polite facade in place as the two left the stage.

"Levon Pleonexia has won! That was a good match! Now let's see who will fight next!" Sandra shouted as the screen once more shifted through the faces of every competitor at neck-breaking speed.

The following two battles were Connor Sword versus Oblivion, and Ymir versus Gaia. Connor Sword defeated Oblivion. Meanwhile, Gaia beat Ymir. After those two battles came one that caused Adam to pause.

Flame Emperor versus Fayte.

Adam glanced at Fayte when her veiled visage appeared next to her brother's on the screen. Her eyes were calm, composed, and tranquil, but her left hand was clenched into a fist and shaking. No matter how determined she might be, how much stronger than her brother she became, it was still hard for someone as kind and compassionate as her to fight against her family.

"Fayte." Adam placed his hands on her shoulder, startling the woman. Veil and mask met. She stared into his eyes as he said, "You've got this."

Fayte took a deep breath, her eyes softened almost imperceptibly, and it looked like she was smiling behind her veil.

"I know," she said. "I'll be sure to bring back victory."

Adam nodded and removed his hands. As Fayte walked onto the platform, he noticed Levon glaring daggers at him, which made him very glad he wore a mask. No one could see his smile.

"Hey, Adam?" Aris suddenly looked at him curiously.

"Yes?" Adam looked at her.

"Do you love Fayte?" she asked.

While Kureha did not respond to the question, Lilith, Susan, and Titania all focused on Adam, making him feel like several lasers were being pointed at him. He worked his mouth to say something, but he didn't know what to say. He knew he should say no. However, the words "Of course I don't love her" never left his lips, like they were stuck in the back of his throat.

"Why… do you ask?" asked Adam after several seconds of silence.

"Hee-hee. No reason."

Even though she was wearing a mask, Adam could tell through long-term exposure to Aris's personality that she was giving him one of her more mischievous smiles.

He decided to focus on the battle instead of the girl hugging his arm.

On the stage, Fayte was staring at her older brother's cold visage with uncertainty. The staff she now held in both hands shook only slightly. She took several deep breaths as though hardening her resolve. As she did, her gaze became deeper, calmer, and more placid, like the bottom of an ancient well.

"Elder brother," she said in a soft voice.

Flame Emperor snorted and tapped his staff against the ground. "A little girl who ran away from her responsibilities has no right to call me brother. I was hoping Levon would be the one to battle you, to show you the error of your ways, but since he is not the one standing before you now, that means it is up to me to beat some sense into you."

Nobody could tell what sort of expression Fayte was making underneath her veil, but those who knew her could probably imagine. Susan was tearing up. She looked like she wanted to say something. Adam was also biting his lip behind his mask. While Lilith's expression was as cold as always, Aris looked at the two of them before she cupped her hands and shouted.

"Fayte! Kick your older brother's butt! Show him you're not some weak little girl who needs to be shown 'the error of her ways.' Don't let that loser get the better of you!"

Flame Emperor cast a glare at Aris. If looks could kill, she would have been dead, but all Aris did was make a hand gesture like she was blowing him a raspberry. She couldn't do that since she was wearing a mask, but the intent was clear.

Fayte saw this and smiled before casting a hard gaze at Flame Emperor. "I hope you're ready, Elder Brother... no, forgive me. I hope you are ready, Flame Emperor. I won't hold back."

"Hmph. That should be my line."

"Huh? What is this?! Are these two related?! Is this a sibling rivalry here?!" Sandra asked uncertainly. "It seems both fighters are more than ready for this. So let the battle begin... now!"

Flame Emperor had a magic class like Fayte, but his class was simply Mage while hers was Elemental Master. He had all the basics skills of a Mage like [Energy Bolt] and [Energy Blast], but he also had the [Scorching Blaze], [Fire Spear], and [Firestorm] skills. Each skill was impressive, to be sure. Anyone else would have been stunned by how powerful his skills were.

Unfortunately, he was fighting Fayte.

Perhaps it was because he was upset, but Flame Emperor used [Scorching Blaze] right from the beginning. The ground beneath Fayte's feet turned bright red before a tornado shot up around her. Even though Adam was standing below the platform, he could still feel the incredible heat from the skill.

+300; +300!

Adam was not sure what impressed him more. The quietness of the crowd that had been roaring for blood seconds before, or the way Flame Emperor's jaw dropped when he saw his own attack healing Fayte.

"Hee-hee. I bet Fayte's idiot older brother didn't expect that," Aris said in a self-satisfied voice. She looked quite smug with her hands on her hips, chest thrust out.

"He most certainly didn't," Susan added with a small smile of her own. Despite her generally timid nature, it was clear from the look in her eyes that she was happy to see the scene unfolding before her.

"W-what is happening?!" Flame Emperor asked in shock, though the question seemed rhetorical. "This is impossible! This shouldn't be impossible!"

"It is not impossible," Fayte said after the 30 second period for [Scorching Blaze] ended. Her veil fluttered a little as the intense winds died down. "You don't know because you probably haven't looked at the most recent Class Ranking Chart, but I had a class change recently. I'm an Elemental Master now, and I have several pieces of equipment that lets me replenish my health when I'm hit by elemental attacks."

"W-wha—but how?! How could you get such a class?!" screamed Flame Emperor.

"How?" Fayte tilted her head, then looked back at Adam. A softness appeared within her eyes as they locked gazes, though it was only for a moment before she turned back to her brother. "I have great friends who helped me."

That was all Fayte said before she unleashed her own attack. She cast [Firestorm]. She could have used [Fireball], but it was clear to the members of her party that she was trying to make a point.

A great wave of flames erupted from her staff and swept over the platform like a tidal wave sweeping over a small village. Flame Emperor tried to dodge, but that was no simple matter. It would have been easier to avoid a hailstorm of bullets fired from a fully automated assault rifle at point-blank range. The wave of flames swept over Flame Emperor.

-16,716!

It looked like Flame Emperor's equipment negated a portion of the fire damage, but it didn't really matter in the end. Whether Fayte's attack did the full -23,880 or only -16,000, Flame Emperor did not have the health to survive. His HP dropped to zero. Then he was revived and transported off the platform. He appeared next to a dead faced Levon, whose lips were drawn into a very tight line.

"Well... that... was... impressive," Sandra said into her magic microphone. Even she sounded like she didn't know what to make of that battle. "It seems there are quite a few strong people here. In either event, it is time for the next battle to begin!"

The next battle ended up being Gaia versus Mist. Adam originally did not pay much attention to the battle because neither opponent interested him, but as the fight wore on, he began focusing more and more on Mist. What he saw left him stunned.

Mist was of the Priest Class, which meant he had no offensive abilities to speak of. All he had were the spells [Healing], [Physical Boost], and [Mana Up]. Those were the spells every Priest Class player started with, and he didn't use any others, so Adam assumed he didn't have them.

-10; -10; -10!

The first thing Mist had done was cast [Physical Boost] on himself. [Physical Boost] was a simple buff spell that increased a person's Strength. It was clear from how little damage he did that his Strength and Physical Attack stats were pathetic because he only did -10 damage even with [Physical Boost] active, but that was what made the man all the more astonishing.

-10; -10; -10!

"Hold still, you little bastard!" Gaia shrieked in a chilling voice—not that it did much good.

Mist was an incredible staff wielder. He spun the prayer staff in his hand as though it was a battoujutsu staff instead of something used for healing. Each time he lashed out against Gaia, his staff would smack the woman across her face, breasts, or butt, and all of them did exactly ten points of damage. Gaia tried to attack with [Energy Bolt], but Mist was too close and able to constantly evade her attacks. Bolts of magical energy flew from her staff, none of them hitting Mist, who was like his namesake. His style of combat made him almost seem like mist.

-10; -10; -10!

"Why is he attacking her butt and breasts?" asked Titania with a curled upper lip. "Is he sexist?"

"That's not it." Adam shook his head. "His attacks are as much psychological ones as they are physical ones."

"What do you mean?" asked Aris.

"How many women do you know who enjoy getting hit on the breasts and butt by some random person they don't even know?" Adam saw the confused looks on their faces, but he didn't give them time to answer his rhetorical question. "None, of course. No woman wants a man she doesn't know smacking ass and breasts. Most don't even like men they are intimate with doing that. He's doing this to enrage Gaia. It's hard to make tactically sound decisions when you're so angry you can't even think straight."

While Titania still didn't look convinced, Aris and Lilith both nodded. Lilith used this tactic many times herself—on men. Aris probably didn't understand like Lilith did, but she was Adam's biggest supporter and would take anything he said at face value.

"That... is actually a very viable method of combat," Fayte said after several seconds of silence. "I can't say I approve of fighting like that, but I can't deny it's a brilliant strategy. He's robbing the woman of her ability to think, which leaves her prone to making mistakes."

"Exactly," Adam said.

Titania huffed but said nothing further.

The crowd was not silent as the battle progressed. Men were laughing and jeering, which further antagonized the thoroughly humiliated Gaia. With a rage-filled scream, she cast [Earth Dragon], which consumed more than half her remaining MP. The [Earth Dragon] was a massive creature created from stone, stood on four legs, and had a long tail that swept out behind it. It locked onto Mist and roared before trying to hit him.

Mist ignored it. Completely.

Gaia probably never expected that Mist would ignore her greatest attack spell in favor of attacking her. He moved around Gaia, interposing her between him and the dragon, then continued attacking until her HP was reduced to zero. Once she was "killed," the [Earth Dragon] spell was disrupted and broke apart.

It was a flawless victory.

"That was impressive," Fayte admitted. "A little vulgar, but I can respect Mist's tenacity and ingenuity, if not his methods."

"It was repulsive," Titania said.

"His method of fighting was perfectly viable," the quietest among their group said. Everyone looked at Lilith, who shrugged. "I have used this method to fight men before. I target their groin and their pride. Men hate it when you chip away at their pride."

No one could deny those words.

The faces on the screen flashed again, and two faces suddenly appeared. Fayte gasped in shock while Susan went completely pale.

The next battle was Susan versus Connor Sword.

RAGE

Susan's entire body was shaking as she stared at her image on the screen next to Connor's. The blood had drained from her already pale face, making it look almost translucent. Even someone who didn't know her would be able to sense the terror in her gaze.

If Adam needed any more proof that Susan and Connor had some kind of history or relationship, this was it.

Connor was grinning as he walked onto the platform. He sent a look Susan's way, which caused the girl to shake even more. She was like a frightened dog who knew it was about to be abused by its owner.

"Su…" Fayte murmured. Her eyes displayed clear worry and her voice was laced with concern.

Aris placed a hand on Adam's back and pushed him forward. "Adam, say something."

"I'm not sure anything I say will help," Adam whispered to Aris, frowning.

"That isn't true." Aris shook her head and gave him an odd smile that he couldn't quite place. It was half-loving and half-mischievous. "Everyone here looks up to you. You're the only one who can help her right now, so stop thinking about it and just help her."

Aris pushed him from behind again, and Adam didn't resist as he walked forward, until he was standing right in front of Susan. The youngest among them tilted her head to look up at him. Her body was still shivering, her eyes held traces of tears, and her lips trembled fiercely. She looked seconds away from having a nervous breakdown.

"Susan?"

"Uh… yes?"

Adam placed his hands on Susan's shoulder and looked into the girl's eyes, locking her in place. His presence washed over her. She couldn't have moved even if she wanted to.

"Don't be afraid," he said.

"Uh… huh?"

"Maybe in the real world, you are the kind of person who is meek, who can't tell others no, and who is afraid of conflict… but that's the real world. It isn't this one." Adam was choosing each word carefully. He needed to give her strength, but he also understood that true strength couldn't be acquired in a single day or from simple words. "In this world, you are one of the strongest players in existence. Your level is higher than Connor's, your stats are better than his, and your class is better than his. In this world, you are a strong and courageous woman who has braved numerous dangers with me and the others. He cannot beat you."

Adam had always possessed a natural charisma. It was this charisma that made Lilith give herself to him, which made the other assassins follow him when he rebelled against Lucifer. He normally didn't use his charisma like this anymore because it was dangerous, but he used it now, pushing his presence onto this girl.

Susan suddenly stood straighter, eyes widening as color returned to her face. She blinked at him several times like this was her first time really looking at him. Then she sucked in a deep breath, held it, and closed her eyes. When she released that breath in a single gust, she opened her eyes and gave him a thankful smile.

"Thank you," she said softly.

"Are you going to beat him?"

"Y-yes!" Susan nodded once.

Adam smiled even as he resisted the urge to gently kiss her forehead. While his charisma might be considered dangerous, especially to members of the opposite sex, Susan's shy demeanor and meek personality were also dangerous to someone like him.

Instead of kissing her on the head, he squeezed her shoulders once before letting go and stepping back.

Susan looked a lot more confident now. Her back was straight, and while her eyes still shook, she walked onto the platform without hesitation.

Connor was staring at her with a frown, eyes flickering to Adam, the frown deepening further.

"Thank you for helping her," Fayte said to Adam.

Adam shook his head. "I didn't do much."

"I don't know why you can't accept a compliment." Fayte sighed bitterly. "You might not think what you did was much, but I have been trying without success to help Susan gain some confidence for a long time now. You just did what I couldn't do after five years of knowing her, and you did it with just a few words. That isn't what I would call 'not much doing much.'"

Adam had never been the greatest at accepting compliments, perhaps because only one person had ever complimented him before. He closed his eyes and thought of Lexi. It had been more than nine years since he had seen her, but her very existence was still etched firmly into his heart even now.

Fayte perhaps sensed his reluctance to speak further about this and grew quiet. Aris hugged his arm as if she too could sense his conflicted emotions.

Titania looked at Kureha, now resting on top of Adam's head. "I do not understand human relationships."

The fox yokai just looked at her and yipped.

On the stage, Susan and Connor were standing about one dozen yards apart. Susan's shaking had stopped. She still didn't look good, face still pale, but she at least no longer looked terrified.

"I'm surprised you found the courage to get on stage, my bride," Connor said with a lazy grin. His words had been loud enough that everyone could hear them. Adam furrowed his brow as he glanced at Fayte, but the blonde woman was not looking at him. Her eyes were focused on Susan.

Susan didn't say anything, but the way she pursed her lips was telling.

"Well, whatever." Connor swung the sword in his hand. "It doesn't matter where you found your courage. It won't make a single difference."

"It seems these two have some kind of history together," Sandra said. "Is this a battle between husband and wife?! A marriage showdown?! Either way, let's start this battle now!"

While the battle had started, neither side moved at first. Connor merely stared at Susan with that same lazy grin. It was mocking and arrogant, and it seemed to put pressure on Susan.

"You should just give up," Connor said. "Forfeit right now. A bride should not go against her future husband."

"… No," Susan said in a soft voice.

"What was that?"

Susan took a deep breath. Then she suddenly straightened her back, raised her bow, and aimed it at Connor.

"I said no. I'm not… going to forfeit."

Connor's face went flat, his eyes growing cold. It only lasted for a second before the lazy grin returned.

"Is that so? You won't give up, huh? Well, do your best then. I'm not going to hold back just because we're getting married."

Susan didn't say anything to his provocative words. She knocked an arrow back and took aim. Connor clicked his tongue as he held the sword in a standard two-handed grip, shifted his feet against the ground, and adopted the Speed Form of his family's sword style.

A moment of silence passed, the tension rising as the two stared at each other. It didn't last long. Connor blasted off the ground with his dominant foot propelling him forward. He was fast, but it was nowhere near as fast as the people in Susan's party.

Susan unleashed a [Fairy Shot] from her bow. The arrow traveled in a straight line toward Connor, but he stopped running and shifted his stance into the Defense Form. This form was wider and more grounded, which meant he couldn't move much, but his swings would also contain more power. Adam narrowed his eyes when the man swung his sword and struck the arrow head-on, knocking it away.

"You know, I've always wondered how combat works in this game," Adam said.

"Excuse me?" Titania asked with narrowed eyes.

Adam didn't know why she seemed so angry, but he continued talking as he watched the fight. "I've noticed this before, but even though stats determine how fights progress to some degree, they don't determine everything. This battle is a good example. Susan's stats are clearly way higher than Connor's, but he was able to deflect her arrow as if it was nothing."

"I noticed that as well." Fayte nodded once. "There seems to be an odd level of realism added into the game's combat system. Your fights are all good examples of this. It should not be possible for you to dodge an AOE attack at point-blank range, but I have seen you do so on any number of occasions."

"I do not know what you people are talking about, but stats do not determine everything," Titania said, sounding bitter.

"What do you mean?" asked Aris.

"I mean stats only determine your base power," Titania explained. "They don't determine how well you can fight. The reason Adam and Lilith can do what most people would consider impossible is because they have previous combat experience—and a lot of it at that."

"So you're saying that knowing how to fight is more important than your stats?" asked Fayte.

Titania shrugged. "Stats determine how much damage you do, how much damage you take, whether or not an attack will hit, and other such matters, but they do not determine how good you are at fighting."

"In other words, real combat experience is just as important in this game as your stats," Adam concluded.

Once again, Titania looked at him like she was displeased by something, but he couldn't for the life of him figure out what had upset her.

On the platform, Connor closed the distance between him and Susan. He swung his sword to activate the [slash] skill, but Susan leaped away from him and avoided it. She was fast. Much faster than Connor. Within a split second, she had already cleared several yards of distance. Taking aim once again, she shot her arrow, but this time she shot it high into the air.

[Rain of Arrows] was the Archer Class' only AOE skill. When Susan fired her arrow into the sky, it turned into hundreds of arrows that rained down from above. While AOE skills against a single opponent might sound silly, against an opponent who could knock her arrows away with a swing of his sword, it was a good strategy.

But Connor once again changed forms and began moving in an erratic pattern as if he could see where the arrows would land before they struck the ground. Adam thought he could sense some energy being infused into the man's eyes and wondered if Connor was using an esper power. He somehow managed to dodge each arrow, though it wasn't easy. His face was drawn tight and sweat formed on his brow.

Susan aimed her arrow at Connor while he was dodging, waited for several seconds, and released the bowstring when he was forced to stop. Her arrow this time flew true. It struck him in the chest, but it didn't cause any damage. The man screamed when vines sprouted from the arrow, entangling him where he stood. It wasn't long before all of his limbs and most of his body was covered in vines. Only his face remained visible.

"Don't do this, Susan! Think about our positions! Think about our marriage!" Connor suddenly shouted as he tried to struggle free. It wouldn't work. He'd remain stuck like that for 120 seconds. "I am your husband!"

"Y-you aren't my husband yet, and I... I don't want to marry you anyway," Susan said as she knocked back an arrow. She didn't say anything else before releasing the arrow. The skill she used was [Deadeye], another Archer Class skill used by beginners. It might not have hit Connor under normal circumstances, but with his body entangled in vines, he could do nothing as the arrow impaled him through the forehead.

-7,540!

Connor only had four hundred HP, so Susan's attack instantly killed him. His body vanished and reappeared next to Levon and the Four Elements, his health reduced to just one. When he realized what happened, his face morphed into an expression of outrage.

"It looks like Little_Su has won!" Sandra exclaimed.

Shouts and cheers suddenly erupted from the audience. Everyone seemed shocked but ecstatic by the surprising upset. An unknown girl had just defeated the player ranked third on the International Power Rankings. What's more, Connor had called this girl his bride, meaning they were engaged. This was the kind of drama average people lived for, and it was happening right in front of them. How could they not be excited?

As Susan walked down the platform, the enraged Connor marched over to her, but Adam and Fayte ran interference. Fayte raced forward and engulfed Susan in a hug. Adam, on the other hand, gave Kureha to Lilith, had Titania sit on Aris's shoulder, and stepped in front of Connor.

"Out of my way," Connor said, his voice an enraged growl.

"If you want me to move, you'll need to make me." Adam tapped the butt of his spear against the ground. "Go on, feel free to attack me. See where it gets you."

Connor's face became truly twisted and dark as he stared at Adam. They both knew he couldn't do anything. Not only was he not stronger than Adam, but fighting in the arena when it wasn't his turn would result in him being sent outside. It would also further ruin his reputation. Tens of thousands of people had already seen what happened here, and more would find out when the videos of this tournament spread through online forums.

"Come back, Connor," Levon said.

After several seconds of silence, Connor clicked his tongue and stormed back over to Levon. The Pleonexia Alliance leader did not seem too upset by what happened. He gave Adam a polite nod as if to apologize on behalf of his subordinate. It was a truly wonderful performance.

Adam did not pay attention to Connor anymore. He turned around and looked at Fayte and Susan as they hugged. Fayte was stroking the young girl's hair.

"I'm so proud of you, Su," she said.

"Th-thank you," Susan muttered. She removed herself from Fayte's embrace a moment later and walked over to Adam. There was a faint but proud smile on her face. "I… I did it. I won."

"You did." Adam smiled back even though he knew she couldn't see it. "You did a great job."

"Eh heh heh…"

Susan rubbed the back of her head and looked down and gave a happy but embarrassed smile. Behind her, Fayte watched the interaction with a gentle look in her eyes.

The battle after Susan's was between Daniel Frost and Aris, and it was probably the least suspenseful battle Adam had ever seen. Daniel Frost tried to launch a spell at Aris, but his lover had merely used her incredible speed to close the distance between them and launch a single attack, which reduced all of his health to zero. It happened so fast that even Adam felt like he missed something.

"That girl's speed is something else," said Titania, arms crossed.

"She's definitely the fastest player in the game," Adam agreed.

After the battle between Aris and Daniel Frost was the battle between Mist and American Samurai, which was a lot more intense and ended with American Samurai barely pulling out a victory against the insanely skilled Priest.

The faces that appeared on the screen after that battle was, shockingly, Adam's and Lilith's. Adam and Lilith shared a look before stepping onto the stage. In the sky above them, Sandra began talking into her microphone.

"The last battle was filled with a lot of action, and it looks like this one might be as well! The fight this time is between the incredibly strong Adam and the mysterious Lilith! Without further ado, let the match begin!"

Adam lowered himself into a standard spearman stance. He was not using a stance derived from the Seven Phoenix Forms Style since he was certain Levon would recognize it. He placed his left foot in front of him, right foot behind him, and held his spear at a forty-five-degree angle.

Several yards away was Lilith, who had not even moved into a combat stance. She stared at Adam with the same fervent expression she always did. No one else would be able to see it, but Adam was not so blind that he failed to recognize the emotions hidden behind her cold eyes.

"I forfeit," Lilith announced in a quiet voice that nevertheless spread through the stadium.

"H-huh?!" Sandra shouted in shock.

"Lilith…" Adam began.

But Lilith shook his head. "After we survived in Eden together, after you helped us regain our freedom and lives, I swore to myself that I would never raise my blade against you… not even in practice, not even an illusion of you. There is no way I can bring myself to fight you."

Adam wished Lilith was not wearing a mask so he could see what expression she was making. He watched the woman as she turned around and walked off the stage, his emotions in conflict.

The crowd did not approve of someone forfeiting, and they made their displeasure known by booing Lilith, but she ignored everyone as she walked back to their group. She took Kureha from Aris's arms and began petting the fox yokai's soft fur.

"W-well… that was unexpected. Um… let's see who the next matchup is," said Sandra, sounding like she was at a loss about how to proceed. This was the first time someone had forfeit in this tournament so far.

The faces again began randomly flashing across the screen before it ended on two people, both wearing masks.

Adam versus Spear God.

Fayte and Susan looked shocked that he would be facing such a strong opponent. They looked worried, anxious. He ignored the concerned expressions they sent him as he gazed at the masked and cloaked Spear God, who walked unhurriedly onto the platform.

Adam kept his own thoughts carefully masked as he followed the Spear God with his eyes. As they stood on the platform, the

Spear God shifted his stance into that heavily modified version of the Seven Phoenix Forms Style. That cloak of theirs kept their entire body covered to the point where it was impossible to see whether this person was a man or a woman. After a moment, Adam finally shifted into a stance.

It was the mirror image of the Spear God's.

"The last battle was disappointing, but let's hope this one will make up for it!" Sandra said. "This time it is Adam versus Spear God! Let the match begin!"

Before Adam could move, the Spear God propelled himself forward, his spear forming many spear shadows as he thrust it too fast for the human eye to track.

However, Adam had seen this attack before.

"Form Two," he muttered, evading each attack as if he knew how this person would attack before they did.

The Spear God suddenly shifted, their attacks no longer swift and deadly like a snake lunging forward, but instead powerful and decisive. A strange roar seemed to echo from the spear. If Adam didn't know any better, he would have said the spear had become a dragon.

"Form Seven," he whispered.

He did not dodge these attacks. Adam met each of the Spear God's strikes head-on, using the same technique this person was using. They activated [slash] with every swing to deal their damage, but since they kept counteracting each other's attacks, neither of them received any hits. Spears clashed. Sparks flew. Adam gritted his teeth as he withstood the Spear God's powerful blows and launched his own.

When the Spear God saw what was happening, he jumped back. It wasn't for long. Without pause, he shifted from powerful movements to deceptive ones. Each swing of his spear seemed to form a web that trapped Adam. If he made even a slight move to avoid one web, he would find himself being struck by another.

"Form One."

Adam dropped to the ground and swept his spear at the Spear God's legs. Just like he expected, the Spear God did not jump over it, choosing instead to slam the butt of his spear into the ground to block the attack. Adam grimaced when he felt a jolt travel up his arm, but he knew the Spear God would not be in any better shape than him.

The Spear God used the force of Adam's attack to twirl the spear in his hands above his head, shifted his feet along the ground, and bent his knees, adopting a wider stance as he pointed the tip at Adam.

"Form Four."

The Spear God took two quick steps forward and thrust out their spear. The [thrust] skill activated. It was just a single thrust, but it seemed to contain the power of a rampaging rhinoceros. There was so much strength in that attack that Adam was certain it could have pierced through two feet thick steel.

Adam did not meet this attack head-on, stepping back before spinning his weapon around. This time, he used a stance this person had not yet shown in their battle. Form Five was a form that had been made purely with defense in mind. He spun the spear in his hands, then knocked aside the spear set to impale him. His attack would have normally thrown his opponent off-balance, but the Spear God proved to be well-versed in this style by not only not falling, but shifting back into the Form Two stance, relying on the quick and agile lunging movements to attack despite being in a disadvantageous position.

As the battle progressed, with the Spear God showing more familiarity with the Seven Phoenix Forms Style than anyone outside the family had a right to know, Adam found himself feeling more and more uncertain. His emotions were in flux. His confusion was reaching a peak.

How did this person know the Pleonexia Family's spearmanship so thoroughly? This style was never taught to outsiders. Adam only knew it because Lexi had violated her family's rules to teach him. However, they had always done so in secret.

Who was this person? Why did they know the Seven Phoenix Forms Style?

The Spear God leaped forward and attacked with a lunge so fast Adam could only block because he was expecting it. The Spear God jumped back, but it was only for a moment before he leaped forward and attacked from a different angle. Adam blocked it again. However, the Spear God increased the speed of his attacks, until his spear had once more formed several afterimage spear shadows.

"Form Three."

A cry like the sounds of a songbird echoed around Adam as the Spear God began twirling the spear in a deadly dance that was full of vigor and tenacity. Each attack came in at a different angle. Flames erupted from the spear, but it was not normal flames brought about by magic. This fire was created from the friction of the Spear God's weapon slicing through the air. It was an attack filled with the fires of life.

"Form Six."

All seven forms of the Seven Phoenix Forms Style style of the Pleonexia Family had been used during this battle, but not a single one of them could land a blow on Adam. They wouldn't have hit even if Adam hadn't known about this style. However, Adam's familiarity with it made it even easier for him to avoid the attacks.

His only concern was how good the Spear God was at changing forms. He could shift from one form to another without any warning, which gave him an infinite number of methods of attacking. Adam was forced to rely on his adaptability and reflexes to avoid being punched full of holes.

When it became obvious that Adam would not be defeated like this, the Spear God did something that shook him right down to his core.

He thrust his spear forward and moved around in a dance that, had Adam been able to see it from a bird's eye view, he knew it would have looked just like the petals of a sakura blossom. The blossom of a cherry tree. The Spear God moved left and thrust out their spear, then danced along the ground to create a petal-like shape. Then he thrust out the spear again after creating another petal, then another, and another. Adam blocked each attack as they came, but while the attacks didn't hit him, they still sent him reeling.

It couldn't be…

It couldn't be!

His face shifted into a snarl as he thrust out his spear to disrupt the attack. Each thrust of his spear was perfectly timed and impeccably aimed to counter the Spear God's attacks. It was more than knowing where each attack would be ahead of time. It was like the Spear God was attacking a mirror image of himself. The two of them danced around each other, their movements creating the shape of sakura blossoms as they launched the same attack.

"Where did you learn that dance?!" Adam barely recognized his own voice as he screamed at the Spear God. "Who taught it to you?!"

The Spear God said nothing. They fought in grim silence, which only served to further piss Adam off. Up to this point, all he had been doing was silently observing this person so he could try and discover more about them. He wanted to know who this person was. However, everyone had a breaking point, and seeing the dance that he and Lexi created together being used by someone else was Adam's.

With a roar, Adam took one hand off his spear and dodged to the side. As the Spear God's thrust spear moved past him, he gripped the weapon and, with raw strength, yanked it out of the Spear God's grip. He tossed the spear away, dropped to the floor, and performed a perfect leg sweep that knocked the Spear God's feet out from underneath him. Before the Spear God could scramble back to his feet, Adam was holding the tip of his spear against his opponent's throat.

"Who taught you that technique?! Tell me now!" Adam could feel tears stinging his eyes, though he refused to let them fall. His rage increased when the Spear God remained silent. "Only two people in the entire world know that dance. Myself and one other, and she died several years ago. You will tell me who taught you that technique or so help me, I will find where you live in the real world, rip out your entrails, and hang you by them! I will make you regret ever being born! NOW TELL ME!!!"

CHAMPION

The entire arena had become silent. Not a single soul spoke as Adam pointed his spear at the Spear God, who sat on the ground and gazed up at him in defeat. The Spear God's own weapon lay discarded several yards away. Even if he wanted to grab it, he could not.

Adam could see nothing past his opponent's mask, not even their eyes. The hood remained tied over their head as well. The cloak was so baggy that he could see nothing beyond it, but perhaps due to Adam's own out of control emotions, he thought maybe the person hidden behind all that fabric was not a man at all.

The Spear God's arms began shaking. Adam only had a moment to widen his eyes before his spear was smacked away. After that, the Spear God scrambled to his feet, raced over to grab his discarded spear, and darted away from the platform after grabbing his weapon. Not a single word was spoken as the Spear God, the second most powerful player in the entire world, fled the arena.

Biting his lip as he stared at the disappearing figure, Adam wondered what he should do. Chase after them? Matters were taken out of his hand when Sandra coughed into her hand and spoke into her microphone.

"W-well, that was certainly quite the battle. This might be the most heart-pumping battle yet! And it looks like Adam has won! N-now, why don't we move onto the next battle?"

Adam felt numb as he climbed off the platform, ignoring the screen as it began scrolling through the players. He walked over to Aris, Fayte, Lilith, Susan, Titania, and Kureha in silence. He could feel their eyes on him, but he didn't look at any of them.

While no one spoke at first, Aris eventually took a deep breath and walked over to him, peering into his eyes through his mask.

"Are you okay?" she asked in a soft, worried voice.

"I'm fine," he muttered, though even he couldn't stop from wincing at the lack of emotion he heard in his own voice.

"You don't need to lie to me." Adam could feel Aris's stern gaze through her mask. "I don't know what just happened, but I know you, and I can tell your emotions are all over the place." She stepped into his personal space, wrapped her arms around his waist, and pressed her veiled face against his chest. "I won't ask you about what just happened. You can tell me if you want, but I can wait until you're ready. Until then, I hope you'll rely on me for support."

Adam's emotions slowly settled as Aris's warmth suffused his body, spreading from his chest to the rest of him. He wrapped her up in his arms, holding her tight as he buried his masked face in her hair, the familiar scent easing his troubled heart. It didn't matter to him that everyone could see what was happening. The entire world had disappeared to him and only this woman remained.

"Thank you, Aris."

"Hee-hee. You're welcome."

Once his feelings had settled down, Adam released Aris from his hug, though he ended up grabbing her hand, and turned his attention toward the platform.

The battle immediately after his had already ended. Daren Daggerfall defeated American Samurai. Adam had completely missed the battle, but he really didn't care. It didn't matter what kind of fighting style Daggerfall had because even if the man faced him or anyone else in his party, he would still lose.

After the battle between Daggerfall and American Samurai was a fight between Levon and Morrowind, which ended in Levon's victory. The man had once again proven that he wasn't a weakling. His spear technique was nowhere near as refined as the Spear God's, but he was still well-versed in the Seven Phoenix Forms Style. Now the only remaining competitors were Adam, Aris, Fayte, Susan, Levon, and Daggerfall.

Aris versus Daggerfall was the next match.

Adam stared at the screen that proclaimed his lover would fight against the leader of Daggerfall Dynasty. Aris was also looking up. She didn't seem all that worried.

"Hee-hee. Looks like I'm going to fight one of the big guild bosses."

"Think you're up for it?"

"Of course."

Aris squeezed Adam's hand before walking onto the platform alongside Daren, who was staring at the veiled girl with a contemplative expression. Adam was pleased to see no lust in this man's eyes. It was a testament to the man's mental fortitude, but it also meant Adam wouldn't have to send Astaroth and the rest of the Soul Reapers after him.

"I noticed how fast you were in your last battle," Daren said as they stood several yards apart. He had already unsheathed his sword and was holding it in a two-handed grip, feet spread shoulder-width apart, knees bent. "But don't think speed alone will be enough to beat me."

"You can only say that because you don't understand how fast I am." Aris unsheathed the two swords she was carrying and twirled them in her hands. "You'll understand once I beat you."

"Bwa ha ha ha! I like your confidence, girl! All right. Let's see who will win this match!"

"Can anyone else feel their blood pumping from this pre-battle banter?! I know I can!" Sandra said into her microphone. The rest of the crowd cheered. "Is everybody ready?! In that case, let the battle commence!"

The moment Sandra started the match, Aris disappeared from where she stood. Even Adam could not see her move. It was the kind of speed that a human could never hope to match in real life.

Daren had obviously been expecting this because he didn't bother dodging and instead slammed his foot into the platform. The platform shook fiercely. Aris suddenly appeared as if out of thin air and stumbled several times trying to catch herself. While she was off-balance, Daren swung his sword in a powerful arc that caught her in the chest.

-230!

Adam clenched his hands into fists when he saw Aris get hit. He knew it was just a game, knew she would only feel a bit of pain, but he loathed seeing the woman he loved being hurt. It took everything he had not to run onto the platform and kill Daren on the spot.

While he was upset, Aris merely flipped through the air, landed on her feet, and launched herself at Daren again. She was fast. Her entire body had become invisible as if the light particles could not keep up with her.

However, Daren seemed to have discovered the weakness to her speed. Namely, she could only move this quickly in a linear motion. She could not maintain that speed while turning. Once he realized how she would attack, predicting where her next attack would land was easy.

After blocking Aris's first attack, Daren began swinging his sword at her, forcing her back. Aris might have the advantage in speed. She might also have the advantage of wielding two weapons. But those were the only advantages, and the last one might even be a disadvantage since it was clear to Adam that Aris didn't actually know how to use her swords.

"Titania, [scan] Daren for me please," Adam said.

"All right."

Name: Daren_Daggerfall

Class: Warrior
Lvl: 16
SP: 0
AP: 4,000,000
Experience: 22,000/9,830,400
Fame: 65,000
Strength: +120
Constitution: +55
Dexterity: +5
MP: +5
Speed: +5
Physical Attack: +550
Health: 710/710
Hit-Rate: 50%
MP: 120/120
Movement: +10
Physical Attack: +550
Physical Defense: +500
Magical Defense: +350
Dodge-Rate: 50%
Magic Attack: +25

Skills:
Skill Name: Slash
Description: A basic skill where the player swings his or her sword and attacks the enemy!
Current lvl: 5 MAXED
Ability: Causes 150% damage to enemy if it hits
MP Cost: 1
Cooldown Time: 0 seconds

Skill Name: Thrust
Description: A basic skill where the player thrusts his or her sword at the enemy!
Current Lvl: 5 MAXED

**Ability: Causes 160% damage with a 5% chance at getting a
critical hit
MP Cost: 5
Cooldown Time: 0 seconds**

**Skill Name: Quake
Description: The player stomps on the ground and releases a
powerful earthquake. This skill is only usable by
Daren_Daggerfall, who completed the [Earth Dragon's Dungeon]
quest.
Current Lvl: 5
AP needed to reach lvl 6: 100,000
Ability: Has a 100% chance of stopping opponents in their
tracks
Has a 50% chance of stunning opponents
MP Cost: 15
Cooldown Time: 10 seconds**

His stats weren't that amazing. They were decent, but they weren't incredible. The only thing that caught Adam's attention was his skill [Quake]. The description said it was only usable by Daren, meaning it was a unique skill like his [Dance of the Sakura Blossoms] or the Spear God's [Cherry Blossom Dance].

-230; -230; -230!

Daren had completely locked Aris down now and was systematically whittling away at her health. Aris only managed to attack once, but because Daren had a Physical Defense of +500, her attack only did two hundred points of damage. To make matters worse, he was not giving her time to activate her blade dance skills like [Double Slash] or [Dancing Swords]. He forced her to remain on the defensive by constantly attacking with [slash] and [thrust] in a never-ending stream.

Daren obviously had real-life combat experience.

Despite how clear it was that she was on the losing side, Aris did not give up. She moved backward, dancing on the platform like her class's namesake. Her elegant movements entranced Adam and made him stare at her in awe.

Just when it looked like Aris might be beaten, she suddenly surprised everyone by spinning around in a full circle and swinging her swords. [Spirited Twirl] was one of her Blade Dancer specific skills. It was an AOE skill, but it could be used to attack a single player just as well. The benefit of this skill was that she only needed to spin in a circle to activate it, which she could do while moving backward.

-200!

While the damage was decent, it was not enough to defeat Daren, who still possessed +310 HP. Her attacks also didn't do as much damage as they did when she was fighting monsters.

That was the difference between fighting monsters and players. Just like you, a player had a defense stat. If the other person's defensive stats were higher than your attack stats, the amount of damage you did was negated. If Daren's Physical Defense was higher than Aris's Physical Attack, she would have done no damage at all.

-230; -230; -230; -230!

Thanks to Daren constantly attacking her, Aris only had +800 health now. Her health had dropped by nearly a third. Daren still had

+310. It might seem like he had less health, but when Adam considered how much health Aris possessed in total, it became obvious who was in the lead.

Still not willing to give up, Aris finally found a chance to turn the situation around. She locked one of her blades with Daren, leaped backward, then came in swinging both swords. This was [Double Slash]. It was a skill that attacked with both swords at the same time, dealing twice the damage.

Daren seemed to already have grasped this. He knew he couldn't completely negate the damage, so he chose to block one attack and take the other.

-175!

Now Daggerfall's health was at +135, but all that meant was he and Aris were about equal in terms of how much damage they had taken, and he was still more skilled at fighting than she was.

-230!

Seeing these two combatants fighting so hard set the other players' hearts ablaze. The sound of their cheering had increased in volume. Two chants came from the crowd. The vast majority of people were screaming "Aris! Aris! Aris!" over and over in a repeated mantra, but there were also people screaming Daren's name as well. As Adam observed the crowd, he saw that everyone was standing up as they cheered, waving their hands and making spastic motions that caused him to shake his head.

-230; -230!

Aris was now finding herself hard-pressed to fight back as Daren overwhelmed her with attacks. He was dealing her constant damage and it looked like she might never take back the offensive, but then Aris surprised Daggerfall by leaping backward. It was just a single jump. However, it took her nearly six yards back. That was a distance he could not clear simply by running. That said, it was something Aris would have no trouble clearing.

"You're a lot stronger than I gave you credit for," Aris grumbled.

"And you're a lot better than I thought you'd be. Bwa ha ha ha! I assumed you were just a little girl who got lucky, but it seems you actually have some skill!"

"Hmph. I'll show you my true skills right now, so be sure to stand still and watch!"

Aris once more disappeared, but this time she also activated her most powerful skill: [Dancing Swords]. She appeared before Daren, blades already singing a song of death as she swung them. If this attack hit, everything would be over. The entire crowd seemed to be holding its breath, wondering if Daren would lose to his unknown girl who came onto the gaming scene like a storm.

Unfortunately, Aris forgot something when she was attacking.

Daren had a unique skill as well.

When [Quake] was activated, it came as a complete surprise to Aris, whose eyes went wide. Not only did the attack make her stumble, but it added the [stun] effect. Now unable to move, she was completely open to Daren, who swung his sword without ceasing until her health was reduced to zero.

Aris reappeared right next to Adam after being defeated. While he could not see her expression, the way she slumped her shoulders in obvious dejection told him about her mental state.

"Take this." Adam pressed a [middle-grade health potion] into her hands.

Aris looked at the [middle-grade health potion] before, with a sigh, she lifted her veil a little and downed the potion in a single gulp. She wiped her mouth and lowered her veil after finishing.

"I can't believe I lost," she muttered.

"Daren is trained in swordsmanship in real life." Adam wrapped an arm around her shoulder and pulled her close. Titania huffed as she was forced to fly off his shoulder and land on the opposite shoulder. "He's not as talented as Connor Sword, but he *is* one of the top swordsmen in the American Federation and has won numerous national championships. The fact that you managed to nearly beat him is already incredible." He could not kiss her head, but he pressed as his masked face against her as if he was. "I'm very proud of you."

"Hee-hee. Well, I guess I can accept this loss then, but I won't lose next time," Aris said with a large smile.

"You did a great job," Fayte added from Adam's other side. "I know it might not mean as much as a compliment from your lover, but I was very impressed."

"M-me too!" Susan said. "I thought you did a great jotch—ack! My tongue!"

Fayte rubbed Susan's head as the girl pressed a hand to her mouth, tears leaking from her eyes.

"There are many talented combatants among you otherworlders," Titania muttered. "Even though your levels are pathetic, you can fight very well."

"Gee, thanks," Adam said with a roll of his eyes.

"You say that our levels are pathetic, but isn't your level just as low?" asked Aris.

Titania turned red. "That is only because my level reset when my class changed to Guardian of the Spear! If I was at my level before my class change, all of you would have been bowing in awe of me!"

The screen continued to flash as Titania ranted before landing on two faces. When Adam saw his face appearing next to Levon's, he could not help but smile grimly.

Adam felt many emotions burning inside of him as he stood across from Levon Pleonexia, the man who was directly responsible for what happened to him all those years ago, for tearing him and Lexi apart. He had long ago dreamed of getting revenge on this man. Even now, the hatred he had for Levon burned inside of his gut like a small, black flame.

Both he and Levon were standing on opposite ends of the platform. Adam was trying hard to contain his hatred. His emotions were already quite raw from his fight against the Spear God, so confronting this man was doing a number on his psyche.

"I hope you don't mind answering a question for me," Levon said with a slight smile.

Adam paused in his thoughts. "What is your question?"

"You are working for Fayte, right? How much is she paying you? I don't know how aware you are of the circumstances between us, but that woman is bound to be wed with me. I'm sure you know about the bet she made with me, yes? It is not possible for her to win that bet. Once three years have passed, she will become mine. Nothing you can do will change that, so I would appreciate it if you could quietly leave her side."

While the smile on his face was polite, there was an undercurrent of resentment that Adam could feel from him. It seemed Levon really wanted Fayte. He wanted her badly enough that he was willing to tell Adam off despite being in a public setting with hundreds of thousands of viewers. Even with his public mask still in place, how could all these people not see the intense dislike Levon had for Adam?

And in learning this, Adam found the perfect path to revenge.

"You want me to stop supporting Fayte?" he asked.

"That's right." Levon nodded, a polite smile still up. "Of course, I do not expect you to do this for free. I've noticed it already, but you are incredibly skilled. If you agree to stop supporting Fayte, I would be more than happy to hire you and make you into a vice-commander alongside Connor. With your skills, you could easily become one of the greatest men in my force."

"That is a tempting offer..." Adam began slowly, causing Levon's smile to widen. "But I'm gonna have to pass."

The smile Levon wore left. His face became blank.

"May I ask why?"

Adam almost wished he could remove his mask so Levon could see his smile. "Because what Fayte has given me is something you never could."

He glanced at Levon's groin.

While Adam didn't outright say it, the meaning behind his words was clear, and Levon understood the meaning. His face grew even more unsightly as he looked from Adam to Fayte. His stare was sharp enough to cut through diamonds. He looked back at Adam seconds later. Then he smiled.

It was a very cold smile.

"Good. Very good. You… certainly know how to upset a man." Levon's voice was dark and grating, filled with hatred. Adam felt like he'd been blessed by the four goddesses of this game. "With those words, you and I have become irreconcilable enemies. It is a pity. Really. If you hadn't touched something that didn't belong to you, perhaps we could have been friends."

"Friends?" Adam snorted. "Even if I had never met Fayte, you and I could never be friends. We were enemies long before I met her."

Levon furrowed his brow.

"Well, well, ladies and gentlemen! It looks like there is more on the line in this match than any of the previous matches! Is this a battle for a woman's hand in marriage?! A battle for love?! Let us all find out! Let the battle begin!" Sandra shouted.

From the frown on his face, Levon clearly didn't know what Adam was talking about, but it didn't matter to him. The moment Sandra said, "Let the battle begin," Adam had closed the distance between the two of them in the blink of an eye. He swung his spear in a powerful arc that sliced through the air. It was blocked, but the attack was so strong that it sent Levon stumbling backward.

Adam did not give Levon a chance to attack. He moved the spear gripped firmly in his hand into a relentless streak of swings that constantly forced Levon back. He didn't use a single skill. Adam wanted this battle to last, so he avoided using skills and instead only dealt Levon one point of damage with every attack. Without pause, without mercy, Adam whittled away Levon's health one point at a time.

-1; -1; -1; -1; -1; -1; -1; -1; -1; -1; -1; -1; -1; -1; -1; -1; -1; -1; -1; -1; -1; -1; -1; -1; -1; -1; -1; -1; -1; -1; -1; -1; -1; -1; -1; -1; -1; -1; -1; -1; -1; -1; -1; -1; -1; -1; -1; -1; -1; -1; -1; -1; -1; -1; -1; -1; -1; -1; -1; -1; -1; -1; -1; -1; -1; -1; -1!

Levin did try to block him, but Adam already knew the Seven Phoenix Forms Style even better than Levon did. Lexi had taught him everything she knew. What's more, even back then, her skill had far exceeded Levon's current abilities. That had always been one of the reasons Levon was jealous of her. He lacked the aptitude to use the Seven Phoenix Forms Style to its full potential.

-1; -1; -1; -1; -1; -1; -1; -1; -1; -1; -1; -1; -1; -1; -1; -1; -1; -1; -1; -1; -1; -1; -1; -1; -1; -1; -1; -1; -1; -1; -1; -1; -1; -1; -1; -1; -1; -1; -1; -1; -1; -1; -1; -1; -1; -1; -1; -1; -1; -1; -1; -1; -1; -1; -1; -1; -1; -1; -1; -1; -1; -1; -1; -1; -1; -1; -1!

It wasn't until Adam had dealt Levon 250 points of damage that the man seemed to realize how outclassed he was. With a ferocious howl, he began attacking with [slash], [thrust], and [sweep]. Adam moved back when the man slashed at him, stepped aside when Levon attacked with a thrust, and jumped over the sweeping motion. None of Levon's attacks could even touch him. It was as if Adam was simply wading through the storm of spear strikes.

-1; -1; -1; -1; -1; -1; -1; -1; -1; -1; -1; -1; -1; -1; -1; -1; -1; -1; -1; -1; -1; -1; -1; -1; -1; -1; -1; -1; -1; -1; -1; -1; -1; -1; -1; -1; -1; -1; -1; -1; -1; -1; -1; -1; -1; -1; -1; -1; -1; -1; -1; -1; -1; -1; -1; -1; -1; -1; -1; -1; -1; -1; -1; -1; -1; -1; -1!

Another one hundred points were taken off Levon's health. The entire crowd was silent as they watched the systematic destruction of the Pleonexia Alliance's leader. Adam wondered what these now silent viewers were thinking. Were they shocked by his audacity? Did they admire how he wasn't showing mercy even to the leader of the American Federation's strongest guild leader? Or perhaps they were frightened? After all, a man who so thoroughly humiliated a person of Levon's stature must either be extremely powerful or completely insane.

Well, it didn't matter to him.

-1; -1; -1; -1; -1; -1; -1; -1; -1; -1; -1; -1; -1; -1; -1; -1; -1; -1; -1; -1; -1; -1; -1; -1; -1; -1; -1; -1; -1; -1; -1; -1; -1; -1; -1; -1; -1; -1; -1; -1; -1; -1; -1; -1; -1; -1; -1; -1; -1; -1; -1; -1; -1; -1; -1; -1; -1; -1; -1; -1; -1; -1; -1; -1; -1; -1; -1!

"Will you stop that?!" Levon screamed as Adam continued attacking without using a single skill. "If you're going to defeat me, then hurry up and do it!"

"I don't think so." Adam's cold laughter filled the arena. "You deserve to have so much worse done to you, but I'll settle for humiliating and crushing you for now! Have fun picking up the pieces if your tattered reputation and pride!"

Levon's face was something Adam would cherish in his memory forever. The way it twisted with hatred and shame, the sense of humiliation that was written all over it. At the same time, he didn't feel like this was nearly enough. This man had ruined his life. This man was indirectly responsible for Lexi's death. Adam could forgive the first offense, but he could never forgive the second.

-1; -1; -1; -1; -1; -1; -1; -1; -1; -1; -1; -1; -1; -1; -1; -1; -1; -1; -1; -1; -1; -1; -1; -1; -1; -1; -1; -1; -1; -1; -1; -1; -1; -1; -1; -1; -1; -1; -1; -1; -1; -1; -1; -1; -1; -1; -1; -1; -1; -1; -1; -1; -1; -1; -1; -1; -1; -1; -1; -1; -1; -1; -1; -1; -1; -1; -1!

It was not long before Levon's health was reduced to just one. Levon released a howl of insanity and charged at Adam, but that was the moment Adam finally decided to activate his two most powerful skills.

[Blood Sacrifice].

[Dance of the Sakura Blossoms].

-17,920; -53,760; -161,280; -483,840; -1,451,520!

The numbers that appeared over Levon's head stunned the crowd. If they had not been silent already, this would have shut them up completely.

At this stage in the game, the average player could only deal maybe five hundred points of damage at the most, and that was in extreme cases. The damage Aris, Fayte, the Spear God, and Susan dealt was shocking enough. Fayte's twenty-three thousand points of damage was astonishing enough, but even that was nothing compared to this. Each of Adam's attack dealt three times the damage it did previously, generating somewhere around -two million points of damage total. Forget the amount of damage they did, most of the currently known dungeon bosses did not even possess that much health.

Levon was felled in an instant. His hideous visage appeared next to Connor and the Four—Three—Elements, none of whom looked like they knew what to say. Adam glanced over at them, snorted, and marched off the platform to stand beside Aris, Fayte, Susan, and Lilith. As he did, Titania floated onto his shoulder.

"That was quite brutal," she said.

"That was just the start," Adam informed her. "I don't intend to let that man off so easily after everything he has done to me."

"Then you have a personal grudge against this man?"

"I most certainly do."

While Adam and Titania were talking, Aris skipped over to him and hugged his arm. Susan looked like she wanted to say something, but she was holding back from coming over. Adam wondered if it was out of fear and felt just a little uncomfortable. Lilith stared in his direction. Kureha was in her arms, but for once, she was not paying attention to the fox as her dark eyes blazed with passionate intensity.

"Adam." Fayte stepped up to him. "Are you sure that was a wise idea? Humiliating Levon like that?"

"It probably wasn't," Adam admitted. "But you don't have to worry. I will never let him lay a single hand on you."

"Adam… you should worry more about yourself," Fayte admonished. "That man is more vindictive than anyone I know. I'm worried he might do something to you."

"Don't worry." Adam laughed. "I won't let him lay a hand on me either, though he's free to try. In fact, I almost hope he does."

Fayte shook her head, but Adam thought he detected a smile behind her exasperation. In either event, the battle was over and only he, Fayte, Susan, and Daren were still left.

"W-well..." Sandra began, her face paler than a corpse. "It looks like... Adam won. That was, um, quite the victory. B-but anyway! Let's see who will be battling next!"

Daren_Daggerfall versus Adam.

Once his face appeared next to Daren's on the board, the crowd began to stir once again. Adam walked back onto the platform amidst the excited whisperings of the crowd. Everyone looked like they were anticipating this match.

However, before the battle could begin, Daren shocked the crowd.

"I forfeit." The man raised his hand and surrendered. "Having seen you defeat the Spear God, I already know I'm no match for you. Rather than let myself be humiliated like Levon, I will instead surrender. Bwa ha ha ha! You are really skilled! I never imagined anyone but Lin Akamine would be able to defeat the Spear God!"

Adam shrugged. "Since you've surrendered, I'll thank you for giving me this victory. You are a very shrewd man, aren't you?"

"Not at all! I just know when to back off!"

"W-well... that was... unexpected," Sandra said. "But I guess I can't fault Daren_Daggerfall for surrendering after seeing the way Adam fights. Anyway, let's get onto the next round!"

The next battle was between him and Fayte. The veiled woman walked onto the platform, stood several yards away from him, and waited for Sandra to start the battle. Adam likewise did not stray from where he stood as he watched Fayte with crystal clear eyes.

"The last battle ended in surrender, and the previous one shocked us all! I wonder what surprises wait in store for this battle! Let the semi-finals begin!"

Once the battle began, Adam walked over to Fayte, who watched him curiously. They had not decided on what to do if they faced each other. Maybe she was thinking of forfeiting, but Adam would not give her the chance.

He knelt before Fayte like a knight kneeling before a princess.

"I forfeit," he announced in a loud voice. "I have already sworn to support Fayte with everything I have. There's no way I could ever harm a single hair on her head."

His words sent the stage into an uproar, but it was not the boos and hisses like when Lilith forfeit to Adam. Everyone was going crazy over his words. Even Sandra was stuttering into her microphone.

"I-I-I don't believe it! Is this a declaration of love?! This is, isn't it?! Unbelievable! Adam has declared his love for Fayte in front of all these people!"

Adam did not care what Sandra said or what the others thought. He stared at Fayte, still kneeling, and waited for her to say something.

"You don't need to go this far," Fayte said in a soft voice.

"It is not a matter of whether I need to or not." Adam shook his head. "This is something I decided on my own. It no longer has anything to do with how you helped me. I want to support you."

Fayte took a shuddering breath. Adam could even hear the sharp intake of air.

"In that case, I will gratefully accept your support now and in the future. Please rise," Fayte said.

Adam stood to his feet, bowed to Fayte, and then walked off the stage. Fayte remained on the stage because she was going on to the last match, which was between her and Susan. However, Susan ended up forfeiting, and thus Fayte won the final round by default.

VICTORY
BUFFET

Levon roared as he threw his phone against the wall, shattering it. He had just logged off Age of Gods and his rage had not abated at all. If anything, the anger he felt bubbling beneath the surface had grown even more powerful, even more overwhelming. A red haze had been cast over his vision. He'd never felt such a violent desire to kill someone as he did now.

"Damn him!!!!"

Unable to quell his hatred with just that, Levon proceeded to smash his computer to pieces. He used his bare fists to do it. The pain he felt as his fists slammed into the computer, shattering the keyboard, busting apart the monitor, and denting the plastic casing felt good. It was a delicious pain that helped settle his mind.

It was just as he withdrew his bloody hands that the door opened and Connor stepped in. The man paused in the doorway.

"Whoa. Anger issues much?" he asked.

"Fuck off," Levon snapped.

"Don't think you're the only one who's angry," Connor said, his voice no longer light, no longer arrogant. There was a coldness to it that even Levon had never heard before. "Did you forget about what happened to me? That fucker was also with my fiance. I don't know what happened to Susan, but she's never been defiant like during any of our marriage meetings. I'm sure Adam did or said something to make her this way."

"Fuck. I didn't realize Adam would be so much fucking trouble." Levon gripped bloody hands so tightly blood oozed between his fingers. "If I had known he was working with Fayte, I would have done everything I could to eliminate him."

"Speaking of eliminating, I just received a response from the Soul Reapers," Connor said.

Levon took several deep breaths, sat down behind his desk, and looked at Connor. "What did they say?"

"They said they discovered who Adam is, but they can't tell us."

The response almost made his anger flare up again, but he shook and shuddered until the rage was grounded and, through gritted teeth, asked, "Did they say why?"

"They did." Connor nodded. "Adam is apparently on their 'Do Not Touch' list."

Levon sucked in a breath. The Soul Reapers were a group of assassins who eliminate any player in the game so long as you could afford their price, and they did not discriminate against targets. Levon had used their services many times and was never dissatisfied with their results.

There were only a few people they would not act against, and every single one of them was so powerful that acting against them was impossible. Even the Pleonexia Family was not on this list. That went to show just how powerful these individuals were. If Adam was on their "Do Not Touch" list, then it meant his background was even greater than Levon's.

"Only three other people are on their 'Do Not Touch' list," Connor continued. "Lin Akamine, Spear God, and Euphemia Chrysos. For Adam to be on the list means he has power comparable to them."

"Why is there nothing on this guy?!" asked Levon. "Someone like that can't just spring up from out of nowhere! He must have a history! A background! Something!"

"About that… I think I might know who he is," Connor said.

Levon straightened in his chair. "You do? Who?"

Connor ran a hand through his hair, lowered his arm, and said, "Do you remember the player three years ago who shocked the virtual world? He played in several tournaments and virtual games, beat every record, defeated every top-ranked player, and earned over one hundred million dollars in less than three months before disappearing. His in-game name was Adam."

"Adam…" Levon murmured. "You think this is the same Adam?"

Connor shrugged. "Who else could it be? How many players do you know who can do what he did?"

Sighing, Levon realized that this "Adam" was a lot more mysterious and complex of a person than he expected. Moving against him was not going to be easy.

"Since the Soul Reapers refuse to work with us, we'll have to rely on ourselves," Levon said at last. "I want you to send out your men and have them track Susan's movements. Susan is friends with Fayte, and Fayte knows Adam. They are even… intimate together. I'm sure we'll be able to find something if we use Susan to track Fayte."

Connor nodded and, knowing that Levon was still angry, decided to leave and do as ordered. Once Levon was alone in his office, he leaned back in his chair and closed his eyes. His face was as twisted and dark as the storm raging inside of him.

"Just you wait. I don't care how powerful you are. I will find you, and then I will take everything from you. I will make you suffer before slowly killing you."

***

To celebrate Fayte's victory in the tournament, Adam decided to make a feast for dinner. He was standing in the kitchen with an apron tied around his waist. He was currently in the process of making dessert—strawberry vanilla cupcakes with lime icing. The main course was currently cooking in the oven.

Fayte and Aris were sitting on the couch in the living room. They were playing Street King VII, and it looked like Fayte was winning. He could hear Aris whining in complaint as her character got the crap kicked out of him, which caused him to smile as he remembered when she did the same thing to him every time she lost. From his position, he could only see the two in profile, but Fayte was wearing an amused smile as she teased Aris.

"I'm afraid you won't be able to beat me. I might not be a match for Adam, but I have a lot of experience when it comes to playing Street King."

"Hmph! I don't care how experienced you are. I won't lose to you. Just watch. I'll beat you in the next round."

Even though she said that, Aris still ended up losing the next round, which only made her more "upset." Her anger would have been more convincing if her eyes weren't sparkling with joy. Playing games like this was something she had not been able to do since getting Mortems Disease.

The entree Adam created was sitting on the coffee table. Aris and Fayte would periodically grab a chip from the bowl, dip it into his entree, and chow down. The crunching sound as they chewed their food echoed through the room. He hoped they wouldn't stuff themselves on his 7-layer taco dip since the last thing he wanted was for them to be too full for dinner and dessert.

A soft ding echoed from the oven, causing him to turn his attention away from watching the two women as they played video games. He opened the oven, put on some mitts, and pulled the main course from the stove. It was a special recipe of his: chicken chimichangas with poblano cream sauce. Since dinner was done cooking, Adam placed the cupcakes into the oven and set a timer for 28 minutes.

Adam placed a serving of chimichangas on three plates and brought them into the living room. They were presented on white plates. The chimichangas were quite a colorful mix of poblano cream sauce, cheese, radish, corn, and cilantro decorating the top. The inside was stuffed with black beans, shredded chicken, rice, and cheese. This version was a little healthier than the normally fried chimichangas because they didn't have a deep-frier and he'd been forced to get creative, baking them with olive oil instead. They still had a nice and crispy golden-brown texture. He was sure they tasted fine.

"Dinner's ready," he announced as he set all three plates down.

"Oh, wow. That smells incredible," Fayte complimented.

"Are those chimichangas?!" Aris squealed. "It's been so long since we've had those!"

Adam shrugged as a small smile appeared on his face. "You couldn't eat them when you had Mortems Disease because they're so unhealthy. Since you're cured now, I thought it would be okay."

"Hee-hee. Knowing I get to eat your chimichangas makes me even happier that I'm cured."

Because these chimichangas were covered in sauce, they had to be eaten with a fork. He also made them watermelon lemonade coolers because they were refreshing and went well with foods that had a nice kick.

Dinner was filled with conversation and laughter, but most of it was between Aris and Fayte. It did Adam's heart good to see the two getting along so well. Once she had gotten better, Aris had taken quite the shine to Fayte. He didn't know if he would say they acted just like sisters, because he didn't know how sisters treated each other, but he thought it was great that they were friends. Aris needed more people in her life than just him.

However, while dinner was a lively event, Adam could not help but think about his battle with the Spear God. Those movements, those spear skills, and that attack his opponent used had all been so familiar to him. It had brought to mind the past. Lexi had moved in almost the same way as the Spear God. More refined and elegant, but far less deadly. Even so, he could almost see Lexi in the Spear God's movements.

Seeing those skills being used had plunged Adam's emotions into turmoil, causing him to lash out and viciously attack the Spear God, but now that he'd had the chance to clear his head, he was beginning to wonder if maybe the Spear God was Lexi.

He thought that person might be Lexi for various reasons, but the first was the Spear God's clothing. This person wore a large cloak to hide their body. It was impossible to tell whether the Spear God was a man or woman, which meant it was perfectly viable for them to be a woman, and the Spear God's stance was adapted for someone whose center of gravity was near their pelvis—in other words, it was designed for a woman. There was also their obvious mastery of the Seven Phoenix Forms Style and their ability to use

Dance of the Sakura Blossoms. The Spear God's attack had some variations from Adam's, but it had still been almost identical.

"Adam, are you okay?"

"Huh?"

Aris's sudden question made Adam snap out of his daze. He blinked several times before turning his head to find Aris and Fayte staring at him in concern. Seeing them look at him with such worry caused him to force a smile onto his face.

"I'm fine. Just thinking about something."

The two women looked at each other, clearly not believing him, but they didn't pursue the subject either, which he was grateful for.

"I know now might not be the best time, but I think we should talk about what happened between you and Levon during the tournament," Fayte said, clearing her throat. "Adam, I won't lie and tell you I'm not happy about what you did to him, because I am. I'm very happy. But I also don't think humiliating Levon like that was a good idea. I hope you have a plan to deal with him."

Adam knew this conversation was coming up eventually. He'd already pondered how to answer Fayte and come up with what he believed was a suitable solution.

"I don't think we need to worry too much about Levon right now. However, he will probably try to find out our real identities. That was the reason why I had Aris and myself hide our faces. Aris and Adam are fairly common names, so he won't be able to find us just from our names alone, and that's assuming he thinks our in-game names are the same as our real names."

"But he could still stumble upon your identity, couldn't he?" pressed Fayte. "Especially if he looks up a list of people named Adam who are living with a woman named Aris. You're right. Those names are popular these days. But how many Adams do you know who live with an Aris?"

Adam nodded. "You do bring up a good point, but that's why I'm planning on having that information blocked. I actually wanted to talk to Susan about using her hacking skills to make the information impossible to acquire."

"You want Susan's help?"

"Is that a problem?" asked Adam when he saw Fayte furrow her brow.

"I wouldn't say it's a problem… I guess I just don't like the idea of using Susan for matters like this. You know how she is about telling people 'no,' and what you are asking her to do is illegal."

"Isn't tracking someone using their driver's license also illegal?" asked Adam, causing Fayte to blush. "Don't worry. I don't plan on getting her anymore involved in our issues than this. I just want her help so I can guarantee Aris's safety."

Aris remained the single most important person in his life, and he would spare no expense and effort to keep her safe.

"I understand." Fayte sighed as a resigned smile appeared on her face. "You can ask her to help you when we log on tomorrow. We'll have our work cut out for us since we'll be registering our guild, but you can talk to her about it once we have a place to stay."

Adam accepted that offer. He wasn't in a hurry yet. There was still time before Levon could get any information on him, but they would need to do something within the week. The sooner the better.

Fayte offered to clean the dishes after dinner since Adam had prepared the food. Aris stood up and offered to help her. After more than two weeks of being awake, Aris was now capable of walking without aid, but she still lacked the stamina to walk for long. Adam planned on taking her outside soon.

Since Aris and Fayte were cleaning the dishes, Adam took a quick shower and went into his bedroom. He saw his phone sitting on the wireless charger and noticed he had a message. It was from Astaroth. The message was simple and only told him that the Soul Reapers had sent Levon a refund with a claim that they couldn't give him any information about Adam because he was on their "do not touch" list, which was a list of powerful people who even the Soul Reapers would not act against no matter how much money was involved. This was a good way to throw Levon off the trail. He'd now assume Adam was someone with a background so extensive not even the most famous guild of assassins would touch him.

Just as he was putting his phone away, the door opened and Aris stepped in. Adam turned to her and opened his mouth in greeting. He closed it seconds later and found himself staring wide-eyed at the sight before him.

Aris was covered in nothing but a towel. Her wet hair looked glossy and droplets of water trailed over her shoulders and collarbone. The pale smoothness of her skin contained a slightly rosy hue, increasing her allure. His lips became dry as he stared at her. When she noticed his state, Aris giggled and walked into the room, shutting the door behind her.

"Adam…"

"Aris…" Adam restarted his brain and frowned a little. "You took a shower on your own?"

"Was that a bad idea?" asked Aris as she sat down beside him.

"No. I guess not. Sorry. I suppose I'm still a little worried about you. Your body has recovered well, but you're still not at full strength. It would be disastrous if you slipped and fell."

He knew he was being overprotective, but just thinking about Aris getting hurt sent chills down his spine.

"I'll be careful," Aris said with a smile as she leaned into him. The scent of her freshly washed hair and skin pervaded his nose and made it hard to think about anything other than how good she smelled. "Hey, Adam? Can you tell me about what happened between you and the Spear God now? I've never seen you get so angry before… it was a little scary."

"Ah. That. I'm sorry." Adam's left shoulder was taken by Aris, so he raised his right hand and rubbed the back of his neck.

"It's okay. You don't have to apologize. But could you tell me why you acted like that?" Aris peered at him with concern shining in her beautiful eyes. "I know it's brazen to ask something so personal, but I want to know more about you. I'm only just beginning to realize you have an entire history that I know almost nothing about."

Adam only felt a moment of conflict before relenting. While he didn't want anyone knowing about his past, the person asking him was Aris, the one person he could never lie to or deny.

Placing his hands behind his back, Adam looked up at the ceiling as he began his tale.

"I used to be an orphan. Ever since I was a child, I lived on the streets, scrounging through the trash for food, huddling inside cardboard boxes to keep warm, and using whatever I found for clothes. It was a miserable existence, but I didn't know anything else."

Adam paused to make sure Aris was listening. When he saw her looking at him with those eyes he loved so much, he continued.

"Around when I was five or six, I was being bullied by a couple of rich kids. I'm not sure what they wanted. Maybe they just liked flaunting their superiority to someone less fortunate than themselves, but either way, it was getting pretty bad." Adam felt a soft smile tug on his lips as he remembered what happened. "But on that day, a young girl around the same age as me appeared. She beat up those bullies and scared them off. She said her name was Lexi. She told me she had run away from her guards and was looking to explore when she came across me. I'm not sure what her intentions were, but she asked me if I wanted to play with her. I didn't trust her, so I said no and told her to leave me alone, but she came back the next day and every day after that, until I eventually relented."

Images flashed through Adam's mind as he went back to those times. He felt his eyes sting a little, but he couldn't bring himself to cry. Even if he wanted to, his tears had long since dried up.

"Once I accepted her offer, Lexi would show up at least once a week to play with me, but soon it became twice or even three times a week. I grew used to her presence and even began to enjoy playing with her. It wasn't long before she became my best and only friend. Lexi wasn't just strong and kind. She was also smart. When Lexi realized I wasn't being schooled, she began teaching me everything I needed to know. She taught me math, English, history… she even taught me how to wield a spear. You know that technique I use in the game called Dance of the Sakura Blossoms? That was a technique Lexi and I made together after she taught me the Seven Phoenix Forms Style."

"It sounds like you two were really close," Aris murmured, biting her lower lip. "Did you love her?"

"I think I did," Adam admitted in a whisper. "I was young at the time, so I didn't recognize my own feelings. It wasn't until we were forced apart that I began to understand how much she meant to me."

"How were you forced apart?"

Adam took a deep breath. This was getting into the territory he didn't want to tell anyone, but he pressed on anyway. Aris not only deserved to know more about him, but he also wanted her to know his origins. He wanted her to understand him. More than that, he didn't want to have any secrets between them.

"I later learned that Lexi's full name was Alexis Pleonexia. She was Levon's younger sister and the heiress to the Pleonexia Family. According to what I know, she had already been pledged to someone else from the moment she was born, but she told me once that she'd never marry someone she didn't know or love. Anyway, her family one day discovered our friendship and forbade Lexi from seeing me. I remember not seeing her for nearly a month before she appeared again and told me about what happened. At that time, she asked me if I would run away with her."

"What did you say?"

Aris looked captivated by Adam's story. Her eyes were wide as she stared at him without blinking. The sparkle was gone from her eyes, however, and now only worry remained.

"I said 'yes.'" Adam scratched his chin, feeling the smoothness. He couldn't grow facial hair, so he didn't have any stubble. "We didn't get far though. The Pleonexia Family noticed Lexi had snuck out, tracked her down, and chased after us. We tried our best to run, but they quickly caught up to us. I still remember… Lexi's tear-filled face as her parents were dragging her away and Levon ordered several men to beat me. I can't remember much after that. I'm pretty sure I lost consciousness at some point, but I do remember waking up trapped inside of a bag. Some people grabbed the bag I was in and then my world became engulfed in coldness." Adam gave Aris a mirthless smile. "They threw me into a river, in case you were wondering."

Aris gasped as tears sprang to her eyes. With a sudden lunge, she pressed her face into his chest, her shoulders shaking as she silently cried for him.

Adam felt his heart settle as he witnessed Aris's tears. He caressed her hair. Perhaps it was because he now had someone in his life who would cry for his sake, but he didn't feel as bad about what happened.

"What happened after that?" asked Aris, voice choked with emotion.

Adam hummed. "After that, I somehow managed to survive despite nearly drowning and was picked up by a man who called himself Lucifer. He was a madman who dreamed of creating a god, and I was his experiment. Lucifer kidnapped hundreds of children across the world and experimented on them in his efforts to create a god, but all of them died except for me. I was his only successful creation."

Adam did not tell Aris about his time in Eden, not because he didn't think she deserved to know, but because it was the darkest time of his life. Death had been his daily companion. He had learned the art of assassination and slaughter. By the time Adam escaped from Lucifer's control and left the island with Lilith, Astaroth, and the others, he had killed so many people that he could have created a mountain with their corpses. He did not want Aris tainted with that knowledge.

"I eventually escaped from Lucifer's clutches and went back to New York. I wanted to see Lexi again. Back then, my desire to see her was the only thing that kept me going. However, when I arrived in New York and searched for her, I heard a rumor that she'd run away from home and disappeared. I remember sneaking into the Pleonexia Family estate to find out if the rumor was true or not. I was actually caught, but I did learn that Lexi had run away sometime after I was taken by Lucifer. I searched for her for almost a year before giving up. I realized there was no way Lexi could be alive after all this time. She was only a year older than me, and I was only fourteen years old at the time."

Lexi had gone missing several years before Adam escaped from Hell, which meant she couldn't have been older than ten or eleven at the most. Even if she was skilled with a spear, she was still a child. He didn't believe such a young child could survive in this world alone. Even Adam had only survived because of Lilith and the training he'd received.

"Anyway, the reason I got so worked up when I was fighting the Spear God is because of the combat style they use. The Pleonexia Family style is called the Seven Phoenix Forms, and it's something I am intimately familiar with because Lexi taught it to me. What's more, the Spear God can use Dance of the Cherry Blossoms, which is identical to my Dance of the Sakura Blossoms. The only people who knew that dance was myself and Lexi."

As Adam finished his story, Aris bit her lower lip and looked at him, her eyes rimmed with red. He reached out and cupped her face. Aris blinked as he rubbed the tears away with his thumb.

"Do you think the Spear God is Lexi?" asked Aris.

"I don't know," Adam admitted.

"Then you should find out!"

"Huh?"

"You should find out," Aris repeated. "This is important. Lexi was important to you—no, she's still important to you or you wouldn't feel so strongly about her! You need to find out if the Spear God is her!"

"What would it matter now?" Adam asked, shaking his head. "Even if the Spear God is Lexi, we've been apart for so long that I'm sure she's forgotten all about me, and besides, I have you now."

"No!" Aris shouted, adamant as she shook her head. "You can't do that! Adam, you might think you can fool everyone, but you can't fool me. I know you want to know if the Spear God is Lexi. I know you want to see her again. You have to find out if they're the same person."

Adam sighed. "And so what if she is? Even if she is the Spear God, what will come of it?"

"You can start over," Aris said. "You can ask her to come live with us and start your relationship over again."

"You realize I can't do that," Adam said. "Don't forget, I already have you."

"Why can't you have Lexi too?"

Aris's question brought him up short. He closed his mouth and stared at the girl, blinking several times.

"What… are you suggesting?" he asked.

"I'm saying you can be with her and me. You can be with both of us."

"That's not how relationships work, Aris."

"And why not? Who said you can't be with both of us?" Once again, Adam was brought up short. Even if he wanted to say something, Aris wasn't going to let him. "I know why you think this isn't okay. I'm not dumb, Adam. I know polygamy is illegal, but that's only officially. So long as we don't get legally married, you can have as many wives as you want." She grabbed his arm, her grip surprisingly strong. "Lexi is important to you. She's so important that it was thoughts of her that kept you alive when you were experiencing your darkest moments. You can't give up on her. If you do… if you just give up and accept this… I'll never forgive you."

Aris stared at him with tears in her eyes, her expression set into a fierce pout.

Adam was stunned speechless, not just by her words, but because of how stubborn she was being. He already knew about how obstinate Aris could be. He remembered how adamant she had been about letting him live with her family, how she had fought tooth and nail to convince her parents. It was only thanks to her that he found a family, though her parents had been taken from him barely three years later.

He thought about what he should do here. What should he say? But, of course, there was only one thing he could do. Adam knew when to fold.

"A-all right," Adam said. "I'll confront the Spear God and ask them if they're really Lexi. If the Spear God is Lexi, I'll ask her if she'd be willing to start over again."

"You'll ask her to come live with us, you mean," Aris corrected.

"Yes."

"Hee-hee, you had better," Aris said with a bright smile. "Like I said, I won't forgive you if you don't do this."

"What am I going to do with you?" Adam asked, shaking his head as a wry smile appeared on his face.

"Love me forever?"

"That goes without saying."

Adam and Aris shared a smile. Despite how difficult and painful this subject was, he did feel much better.

"Hey, Adam. Do you remember your promise to me?"

Aris was staring at him with a different look from before. Her eyes contained a quiet intensity that he didn't recognize, but it caused his body to jolt as if he'd been shocked. That look in her eyes made him feel like an electric current had passed through his body.

"Which promise was that?" he asked.

"The one where you said you would take my virginity after I got better," Aris said.

"Ah… yeah, I remember."

"Adam, I'm better now."

"S-so you are."

Now that this had been brought up, Adam found himself inexplicably nervous. He wasn't a virgin, but it wasn't like he was experienced either. The only person he'd slept with was Lilith. Even then, he had simply been relieving his lust and pent up emotions. It had been akin to abuse no matter how many times Lilith denied that he had abused her.

Aris was staring at him. She didn't say anything. He wondered why at first, but then he realized the reason. She was waiting for him to make the first move.

Knowing he couldn't disappoint her, Adam leaned down and kissed her. It started soft, but as the kiss continued, it became deeper and more passionate. His tongue slipped into her mouth, and Aris moaned as she tried to keep up.

Adam pushed Aris onto the bed as he continued to kiss her. She was already naked except for the towel, so all he needed to do was pull the towel away to reveal her splendid figure. He leaned back after kissing her so thoroughly he thought their lips might bruise.

Aris lay naked before him, bare as the day she'd been born, flawless and perfect. She didn't have large breasts or wide hips, but her figure contained a purity that he'd never seen from someone else. Her beauty was akin to a goddess's. In his eyes, no one was more beautiful.

He admired her flushed face and budding breasts capped with pink nipples. She had tiny areolas, which he thought were cute. Her stomach was flat but soft, a result of his constant massages and channeling energy into her body to help stimulate her nerves and cells. Further down was her hairless crotch. She had nothing there, just a pair of small lips. They looked soft and squishy. He licked his dry lips as he imagined kneeling between her thighs and kissing her to an orgasm.

"Adam… you're going to make me embarrassed if you continue to stare at me like that," Aris said.

"Mmm. Sorry. I just can't help but think about how beautiful you are. I really am lucky to have such a wonderful lover in my life."

"Hee-hee. You most certainly are. But it's not like you're the only one. I'm grateful you entered my life too. You're the person I love the most in this world."

Adam smiled as he stood up from the bed, removed his shirt, pants, and boxers. He reached out to grab Aris's hips and pulled her closer to the edge. He leaned down and placed a kiss between her breasts, then traveled further down to press his mouth against her stomach before, finally, he reached her lips.

Aris bucked her hips against his mouth as if she'd been shocked, but he wrapped his arms around her legs and kept a firm grip on them as he began licking her, tracing her outer labia with his tongue before uncovering the small pearl from its hood and suckling on it. Tiny spasms made Aris jolt like she'd been shocked. Loud breathing, throaty moans, and the soft slurping as Adam licked and kissed her nether regions were the only sounds in the room.

"Adam… Adam! I! I feel it! I'm—I'm gonna cum!"

Adam didn't answer Aris with words but applied more pressure with his tongue. Her tiny clit was already hard and easy to stimulate. She was getting wet and her insides were growing warm. Not only did he lick her, but Adam placed a hand against her lips, slowly inserting a single finger. It was a tight fit, but he pumped his finger in and out, and even curled it a little to rub the inside of her fleshy walls.

Aris released a loud cry, her body tightening, thighs clenching, and back arching as she came in his mouth. A second passed before she slumped back onto the bed. Adam stood up and wiped his mouth as he admired the young woman.

Aris had never looked more enchanting to him than she did just then, with her hair in disarray, her skin flushed and covered in glistening droplets, and her eyes glazed over as she blinked several times like she wasn't all there. It was his first time really paying attention to a woman after she orgasmed. He'd never done this to

Lilith when they had sex. After satisfying himself, he had basically ignored her. He couldn't even remember if she orgasmed…

Gritting his teeth, Adam shoved aside his guilt. He would not allow his guilty conscience to ruin this moment for Aris.

Lifting Aris into his arms, Adam set her against the pillows. This was the moment Aris came to. She surprised him, grabbing the back of his head and pulling him into a deep, intense, and passionate kiss. She pushed her tongue into his mouth with enthusiasm but also inexperience. They'd never shared kisses this intense before.

Adam didn't try to fight her or push himself on her. He merely kept their lips locked as he shifted between her legs and guided himself to her entrance. Of course, he didn't push himself inside of her yet. There was something he needed to do first.

"I'm putting it in, okay?" he asked after Aris stopped kissing him so she could breathe.

"Yes. Do it. Please." Aris gasped. "I can't wait any longer."

Adam nodded as he guided himself to her wet entrance. He took a deep breath when his tip spread her lips apart. The warmth that engulfed him forced him to pause. He wanted to thrust himself inside of her in one go, but he knew that would hurt. Placing a hand on her stomach, Adam channeled just a little of his energy into her body before, ever so slowly, pushing his way inside of her. The invisible tendrils of energy invaded her lower stomach and disappeared.

"Hnnnn!"

Aris clenched her eyes shut as he intruded inside of her, spreading her open. She took several deep breaths. Her cheeks, already red, became an even deeper shade of scarlet. A breathy moan escaped her parted lips. Adam bit his lower lip as he finally bottomed out. Aris was so tight. It was a hard fit. Her insides wrapped around him, warm, tight, soft. He was very glad he'd gotten her warmed up or going in would have been painful for them both.

"You okay?" he asked.

"I'm… fine," Aris gasped, then smiled. "That didn't hurt as much as I thought it would."

"Of course. I'd never forgive myself if I hurt you."

There was no way Aris could understand what he meant, and Adam didn't explain things to her as he began moving. Aris moaned as she wrapped her arms and legs around him. He felt her nails scratch against his back as he thrust himself inside of her, moving his hips slowly at first but picking up the pace as time went on.

Sweat formed on their skin and created a slick coat as they made love. The only sounds were their moans, gasps, and groans. Adam's vigorous thrusts caused Aris to produce sounds he'd never heard before but hoped he'd get to hear a lot more of in the future. As their lovemaking continued, Adam leaned down and began kissing her despite being breathless. He also placed one hand on her chest, rubbing her breast until her nipple became hard. Aris moaned into his mouth as he lightly pinched her nipple.

Adam had no idea how much time passed, but it couldn't have been that long before Aris came a second time. He still hadn't orgasmed, so he kept going. By this point, Aris no longer had the strength to keep her legs locked around his waist, so they hung limply on either side of his body, small feet shaking every time he thrust his hips. She did not stop kissing him, however. It was the one thing she refused to relent on. Her hungry mouth hampered his, and her tongue filled him, stirring up the saliva between them.

"Aris," he grunted. "I'm. About. To cum."

"Hm. Do it. Ahn. Cum inside me. Haaaah. Haaaah. It's okay. I can't… get pregnant."

Adam nodded as he leaned forward again and claimed her mouth once more. He increased the speed of his thrusts before, with a grunt muffled by her mouth, released several spurts of his seed directly inside of her.

After cumming, Adam rolled onto his back and pulled Aris with him. She shifted so she could rest her head on his chest, eyes closed as they cuddled. Her warmth against him was comforting.

"You don't know how long I've been waiting for this," she murmured.

"Probably about as long as I have," he said.

Aris shook her head. "I wanted to have sex with you ever since we first met."

"Weren't you twelve?"

"Hee-hee. So?"

Adam shook his head but didn't say anything. He couldn't say he wanted to sleep with her at that age, but he had certainly fallen for her at first sight. Even now, he remembered their first meeting as vividly as if it had happened yesterday. Aris had been his salvation from the moment they met.

Closing his eyes, Adam listened to Aris's breathing as it grew softer and deeper. Once he confirmed that she was asleep, he allowed himself to drift off as well.

Neither of them knew someone had been listening to their conversation.

✳✳✳

Fayte fell face first onto her bed, not bothering to wipe away her tears, which soaked into the mattress. It wasn't like there was anyone around to shame her for them.

She had heard the entire conversation between Aris and Adam, along with the lovemaking session immediately afterward. Listening to Adam tell Aris about his past caused her no end of turmoil. Of course, she felt awful for spying on them, but she felt even worse for Adam. She'd had no idea he had that kind of past. However…

"His hatred for Levon makes sense now," she whispered. "How could they… how could those people do something like that to a child?"

It was a rhetorical question. She already knew the answer. The Pleonexia Family acted humble and kind on the outside, but they were despicable on the inside, monsters every one of them.

"Is there anything I can do… to help him?" Fayte wondered as she rolled onto her back. She stared up at the ceiling and smiled sadly. "I guess there isn't. After all, he has Aris."

Yes, Adam had Aris. Aris was a great girl and didn't come with any baggage. She was good for Adam. She healed him. Compared to

Aris, what could Fayte possibly offer aside from excess baggage and a ridiculous number of skeletons in her closet?

With a sigh, Fayte buried herself under the blanket and tried to get some sleep. Yet no matter how hard she tried, sleep would not come. It was a long night.

To Be Continued...

AFTERWORD

Here we are at the end of Man Made God 003. It's your favorite chuunibyo—no, wait. It's your favorite filthy weeaboo author, Brandon Varnell. I'd like to take this first paragraph to say that I hope everyone enjoyed this series. Please remember to write a review if you did. It might not seem like much, but they help indie books like mine a lot.

We have reached the third volume and Adam and Aris have finally consummated their relationship. I know a lot of people were probably waiting for this moment. I wonder if anyone else heard the millions of fanboys crying out "FINALLY" in the Force. Just kidding. In either event, I do hope this scene made the wait all worth it.

One thing I want to mention about this series is that Man Made God is not really a sexy harem series. It will have a harem, and there will be sex, but the plot and character development will play a much stronger role. This means that some volumes may have multiple sex scenes while other volumes might have none. It really depends on how the story goes and whether or not a sex scene is warranted.

For the curious, volume 4 will probably have several, but I haven't written it yet, so we will see.

Now that Adam has royally pissed off Levon, the series is going to be taking several serious and potentially violent turns. I don't want to spoil anything, but I just want to say everyone will find out in the next few volumes why I made Adam and his harem so overpowered in Age of Gods.

Before I leave you all, I would like to give some last minute thank yous.

I first want to thank my editor and proofreaders for helping me a lot with my syntax, homonyms, and all those silly spelling mistakes that make it through my self-edits. I really do appreciate the help.

I also want to thank Lonwa_A. He's my artist for this series and he's doing awesome. I actually hired him a really long time ago for all 3 volumes, so I need to contact him again to do volume 4. It's been awhile since we talked, so I hope he still remembers me.

And finally, I would like to thank you guys. Yes, you. Thank you for reading this series. If you wrote a review on Amazon, thank you so much for that too. It really means a lot that you would continue to support me like this. I hope I can keep living up to your expectations. I also hope you'll join me in Man Made God 004!

~Brandon Varnell

BRANDON VARNELL IS WRITING STORIES AND CRE-ATING COMICS ON PATREON!

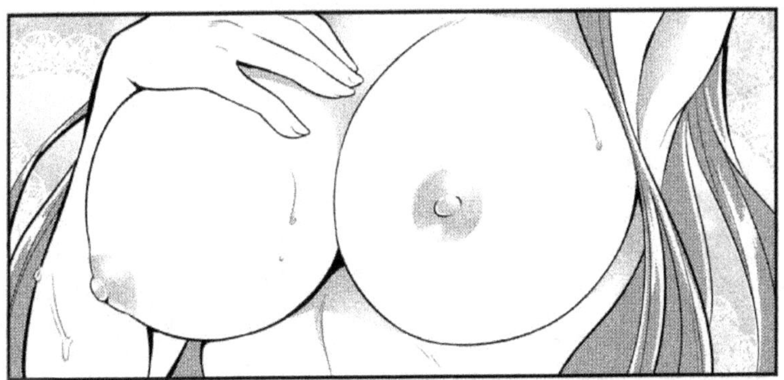

HAVE YOU EVER EXPERIENCED ONE OF THOSE LIFE-CHANGING INSTANCES? AN EVENT SO MOMENTOUS THAT, YEARS LATER, YOU'RE STILL MARVELING AT HOW IT CHANGED YOUR LIFE?

I HAD ONE OF THOSE. IT HAPPENED A WHILE AGO

EVEN TO THIS DAY, THROUGH ALL THE CHANGES THAT HAVE HAPPENED, THROUGH ALL THE EXPERIENCES THAT I'VE BEEN THROUGH, I STILL CAN'T BELIEVE HOW THIS ONE MOMENT CHANGED MY LIFE FOREVER.

NO MATTER WHAT CAME AFTER, OUR FIRST MEETING IS SOMETHING THAT I'LL ALWAYS REMEMBER.

ESPECIALLY SINCE, AT THE BEGINNING OF THIS TALE, I THOUGHT SHE WAS NOTHING BUT AN ORDINARY FOX WITH, UNORDINARILY ENOUGH, TWO BUSHY RED TAILS.

LIFE

.

.

.

.

.

.

.

.

IT HITS YOU WHEN YOU LEAST EXPECT IT TO.

American Kitsune

Hey, did you know?
Brandon Varnell has started a Patreon
You can get all kinds of awesome exclusives
Like:

1. The chance to read his stories before anyone else!
2. Free ebooks!
3. exclusive SFW and NSFW artwork!
4. Signed paperback copies!
Er... maybe we don't want that last one, but the rest is pretty cool, right?

To get this awesome exlusive conent go to:
https://www.patreon.com/BrandonVarnell
and sigh up today!

AMERICAN KITSUNE

volumes 1-12
are available now!

catgirl doctor
NOW AVAILABLE ON PAPERBACK, KINDLE, AND KINDLE UNLIMITED!

INCUBUS
VERTICAL
NOW AVAILABLE ON PAPERBACK,
KINDLE, AND KINDLE UNLIMITED!

MMG:001
NOW AVAILABLE ON
PAPERBACK, KINDLE, AND
KINDLE UNLIMITED!
MAN
MADE
GOD

Available in paperback, kindle, and Kindle Unlimited!
A Most Unlikely Hero

Arcadia's
IgnobleKnight
Volumes 1-7
are available now!

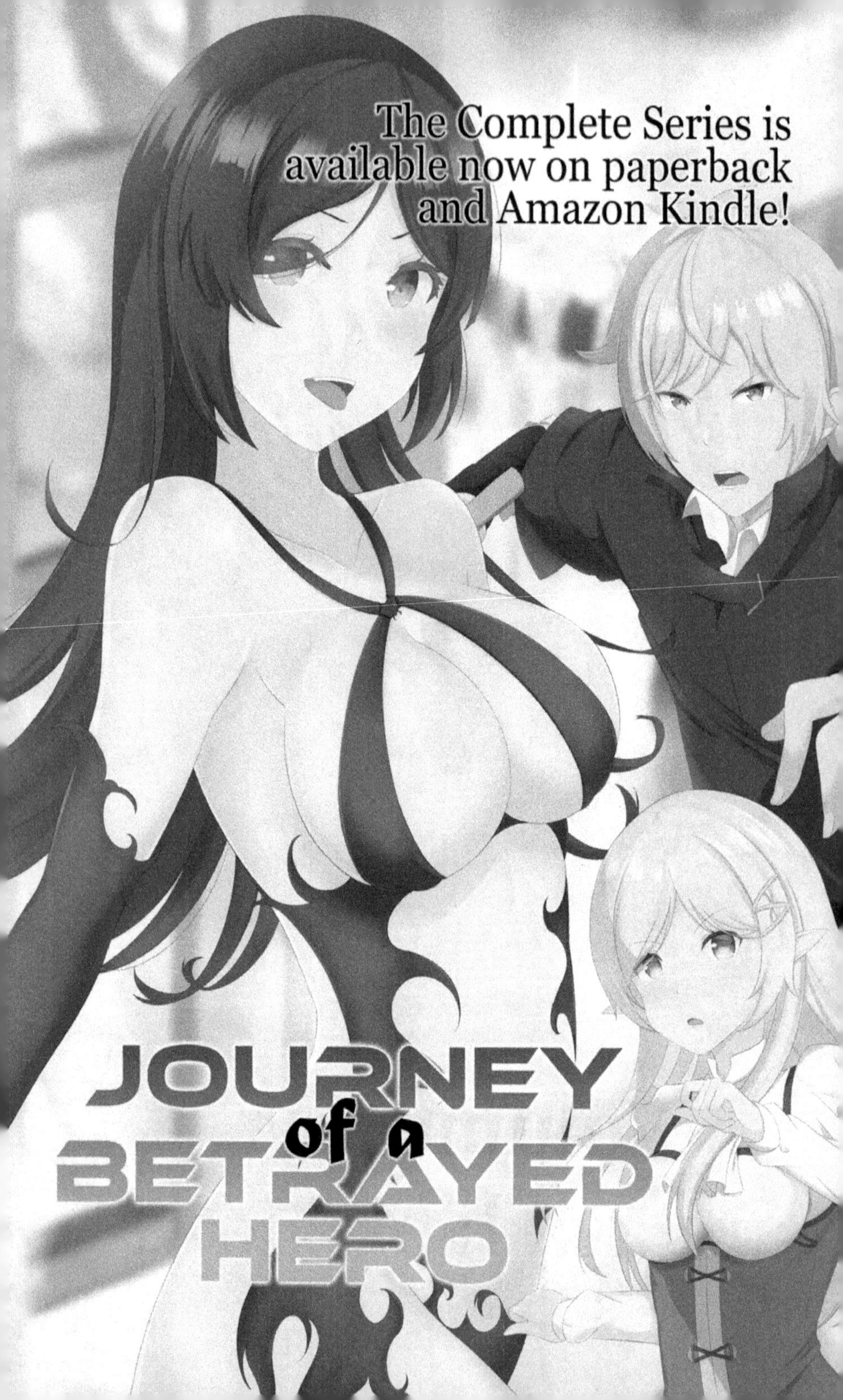

The Complete Series is available now on paperback and Amazon Kindle!
JOURNEY of a BETRAYED HERO

Volumes 1 & 2 are available on
paperback,
Amazon,
and Kindle Unlimited
Swordsman
Of the
Rift 2

The Executioner Series
The complete series
is available now!